STELLARLUNE

Also by Shannon Messenger

The KEEPER OF THE LOST CITIES Series
Keeper of the Lost Cities
Exile
Everblaze
Neverseen
Lodestar
Nightfall
Flashback
Legacy
Unlocked Book 8.5

The SKY FALL Series
Let the Sky Fall
Let the Storm Break
Let the Wind Rise

KEEPER
OF THE LOST CITIES
STELLARLUNE

SHANNON MESSENGER

Aladdin
New York   London   Toronto   Sydney   New Delhi

ALADDIN

An imprint of Simon & Schuster Children's Publishing Division
1230 Avenue of the Americas, New York, NY 10020
First Aladdin paperback edition October 2023
Text copyright © 2022 by Shannon Messenger
Cover illustration copyright © 2022 by Jason Chan
Also available in an Aladdin hardcover edition.
All rights reserved, including the right of reproduction in whole or in part in any form.
ALADDIN and related logo are registered trademarks of Simon & Schuster, Inc.
For information about special discounts for bulk purchases, please contact
Simon & Schuster Special Sales at 1-866-506-1949 or business@simonandschuster.com.
The Simon & Schuster Speakers Bureau can bring authors to your live event.
For more information or to book an event contact the Simon & Schuster Speakers Bureau
at 1-866-248-3049 or visit our website at www.simonspeakers.com.
Cover designed by Karin Paprocki
Interior designed by Mike Rosamilia
The text of this book was set in Scala.
Manufactured in the United States of America 0923 OFF
2 4 6 8 10 9 7 5 3 1
Library of Congress Control Number 2022936648
ISBN 9781534438521 (hc)
ISBN 9781534438545 (pbk)
ISBN 9781534438538 (ebook)

For my son.

Who made writing this book
exponentially more challenging.
And makes my life infinitely better.

PREFACE

THERE'S NOTHING HERE."

Sophie wasn't sure who'd said it—but all her friends had to be thinking the same thing as they trudged through the long moonlit grass, which seemed to stretch endlessly into the darkness.

She squinted at the sky, checking the stars again.

"There has to be *something*," she murmured.

Every clue they'd solved.

Every truth they'd pieced together.

All of it had led to this place.

This moment.

This rare chance to finally get ahead of their enemies.

Sophie turned in a slow circle, searching for the clue she had to be missing.

An edge to an illusion.

A sliver of hope.

There was always another trick.

Another lie.

And this time, she wouldn't let herself be fooled.

She was taking control of stellarlune.

Seizing its power.

Otherwise . . .

She glanced at the sky again, watching the new star fade with the light of early dawn.

Time was almost up.

Which left only one option.

A desperate risk.

A last resort.

The path everyone else was against.

Sophie was ready to take it—no matter what it cost.

She *had* to.

For Keefe.

For her world.

For the future.

ONE

ARE YOU OKAY?"

Grady had asked the question three times, and Sophie still didn't have an answer. All she could do was stare at the crumpled note she'd found waiting for her in her bedroom, hoping she'd somehow misread it.

Keefe couldn't . . .

Wouldn't . . .

A sound bubbled up her throat, something between a laugh, a cry, and a groan.

This was Keefe.

He definitely would.

"How long ago did Keefe leave?" she asked, glancing between

Grady and the tiny gnome standing near her canopied bed.

Grady shrugged.

Flori shook her head, making her plaited hair rustle like windblown leaves. "I didn't see him—but I was out in the pastures, waiting for the new patrols to arrive."

Sophie sighed.

Sandor was in the process of frantically amping up Havenfield's security because she'd burned down one of the Neverseen's storehouses a few hours earlier, and everyone seemed to think that meant she'd officially started the war they'd been teetering on the brink of for years—but she couldn't worry about that at the moment.

"Is Sandor still outside?" she asked, hoping he'd gotten a report about Keefe from one of the other guards.

Grady blocked her. "Listen, kiddo. I know what you're thinking—"

"I doubt that." Even *she* wasn't sure if she wanted to clobber Keefe, lock him up somewhere, or wrap him in a huge strangle-hug and tell him everything was going to be okay—though the last option seemed the least likely.

"Keefe will be fine," Grady promised, carefully steering her away from her doorway. "He's very resourceful."

She locked her knees. "If you knew what he's planning, you wouldn't be saying that."

Silence followed, and Grady wouldn't meet her eyes.

"You talked to him while he was here, didn't you?" Sophie

guessed, tapping her temples when he stayed quiet. "You know I can find out what you're hiding."

"Not without violating the rules of telepathy," Grady reminded her. "But to answer your question . . . yes, I did talk to him—and he didn't say much. He was obviously still afraid to use his voice."

Something sour coated Sophie's tongue, and she tried not to think about the fear she'd seen in Keefe's eyes after he'd accidentally given his first *command*. Or how empty and hopeless she'd felt when the command turned everyone numb.

"That's why he's running away," she murmured.

Part of the reason, at least.

Keefe's letter had also implied that he'd manifested other scarier abilities—but he didn't tell her what they were. All he'd said was that it was too dangerous for him to be in the Lost Cities and he was planning to hide among humans—which was why Sophie had to find him.

"How long ago did he leave?" she asked in a tone that hopefully made it clear she wouldn't let Grady shrug away the question again.

He glanced out her windows, where the clouds were slowly turning pink with the sunset. "At least an hour ago, so it's too late to stop him—but it'll be okay. I think he actually has a solid plan this time."

"Oh really? So you think he'll be able to survive on his own in the Forbidden Cities?"

She'd hoped Grady's mouth would fall open when he heard Keefe's destination.

Instead, his lips set into a grim line.

"Wow," she mumbled. "You really did know what he was up to, and you still let him go. I know Keefe's never been your favorite, but—"

"I never said that," Grady interrupted.

"You didn't have to. You call him 'That Boy' and glare at him all the time."

"Not *all* the time."

His smile was probably supposed to soften her mood.

It didn't.

"Okay, fine. Sometimes your friendship with Keefe . . . makes me a little nervous," Grady admitted, dragging the toe of his boot through the flowers woven into her carpet. "He has a gift for getting in trouble—and you do that more than enough on your own. But he wasn't his usual overconfident self today. He looked tired. And terrified—"

"And that didn't seem like a sign that maybe you should stop him?" Sophie cut in.

"Hey, we both know there's no *stopping* Keefe Sencen once he makes up his mind."

"Um, last time I checked, you're still a Mesmer," Sophie felt the need to point out, even though she wouldn't have wanted Grady to use his ability that way.

It was easier having someone to blame.

Then she wouldn't have to wonder if she could've talked Keefe into staying if she'd been home when he came by, instead of spending so long at Solreef answering Mr. Forkle's questions about her unexpected inferno.

Or if she'd checked on Keefe more often after he woke up from his trance-coma thing, instead of letting him push her away.

Or if she'd fought a little harder in Loamnore and stopped his mom before she triggered Keefe's unnerving new abilities.

Or if she'd at least been able to learn more about Keefe's "legacy," so they had some idea of what they were dealing with.

Grady stepped closer, tucking a strand of Sophie's hair behind her ear. "I know this is hard. And for what it's worth, I actually did try to talk Keefe out of leaving. But I've never seen him so determined. Best I could do was . . ."

"Was?" Sophie prompted when he didn't finish.

Grady closed his eyes, and his lips formed a few different words before he asked, "You trust me, don't you?"

"Why do I need to?"

"Because . . . I promised Keefe something. And I'd like to keep that promise. But it's hard to do that if you keep asking questions."

Sophie studied him, wishing she were an Empath and could tell what he was feeling. But the Black Swan had left her without that particular talent.

"Fine," she decided. "I'll stop asking questions—if you stop trying to talk me out of going after him."

Grady blew out a breath. "I think you're forgetting that now's really not a smart time for you to leave Havenfield. We have no idea how the Neverseen are going to respond when they discover what you've done to their storehouse. And you have your own army here—"

"And the Neverseen know exactly where to find me," Sophie argued. "Besides, I'm not going to sit around, waiting for some attack that may never happen. I'm not afraid of them!"

"You should be." Grady lowered himself onto the edge of her bed and rested his head in his hands—which made it hard to hear him when he said, "I am."

Sophie wished she could sink down next to him—lean on each other as they tried to prepare for whatever came next. But she forced herself to stay standing. "I'm done making decisions based on fear. It gives the Neverseen more power."

"Isn't fear the reason you're so desperate to track Keefe down?" Grady countered.

Sophie glanced at Keefe's note again. "Yeah, but . . . *this* is something I can fix."

"Can you?"

And there it was.

The question Sophie had been trying so hard not to let herself ask.

Could she fix Keefe?

Could anyone?

"Only one way to find out," she said, mostly to herself.

Grady grabbed her hand as she turned for the door, and as his fingers pressed against her skin, she realized she wasn't wearing her gloves.

She technically didn't need them anymore, now that she'd learned how to switch off her enhancing. But she still tended to wear them as backup.

Maybe it was time to start believing that abilities truly could be controlled.

"I can help him," she told Grady, pulling her hand free and continuing forward without going back for her gloves.

"I hope you're right. But finding him is going to be harder than you think. I watched him spin to a random facet on his pathfinder and leap wherever it led."

"Was it a blue crystal?" Sophie asked, feeling her stomach go *thud* when Grady confirmed it.

Keefe really was in a human city.

And the city could be *anywhere*.

Grady gently pulled her closer. "I know you hate letting your friends take risks. But Keefe can handle himself—"

"No, he can't! Keefe doesn't know how the human world works. He doesn't have any money, or any kind of ID, and he doesn't speak their languages."

Well . . . he was a Polyglot now, so he might be okay with the last one—but that wouldn't get him very far.

"Humans have tons of laws about loitering and trespassing," she added, "so you can't just show up and expect to find shelter—or food and water. They have a million other rules too, like when you're allowed to cross the street, and how late you're allowed to be out at night. A lot of times it can be hard just finding a bathroom! And every country is different, so if he moves around, that's only going to make it worse— especially since Keefe's terrible at keeping a low profile. Even if he tries to keep his head down, people are going to notice how good-looking he is—by human standards," she quickly clarified, feeling her cheeks burn. "I lived with humans for twelve years, and I doubt I'd be able to hide there without ending up with Child Protective Services or something. He could get himself arrested. Or hit by a bus. Or—"

"I'm not saying you're wrong," Grady jumped in. "But . . . I think you're also forgetting that Keefe's not exactly safe around here."

He wasn't.

But neither was she, as everyone loved to keep reminding her.

And they never would be, until they stopped the Neverseen— which they'd have a much better chance of doing if they worked together. Yes, Keefe's new abilities were probably scary—and his mom was absolutely going to try to exploit them. But there had to be a way to use his powers against her.

"I have to *try*," she said, stepping away from Grady. "If I can't find him . . ."

She didn't know how to finish that sentence.

Hopefully she wouldn't have to.

Grady dragged a hand down his face. "Just . . . promise me you'll stay in the Lost Cities."

"She will," a high, squeaky voice announced from the hallway. "I'll make sure of it."

Sophie fought the urge to roll her eyes.

She'd had enough experience with her overprotective goblin bodyguard to know that Sandor *would* be coming with her. She'd honestly been surprised he was willing to let her out of his sight after he brought her home from Solreef. And she was grateful to have his protection. She needed it now more than ever.

But she was also done being cautious—and Sandor was going to have to get used to that.

If Keefe was in the Forbidden Cities, she *would* be going after him.

Still, she'd learned to fight Sandor one battle at a time—and at the moment, she needed more information before she could figure out the smartest plan. So all she told him was "Let's go" as she headed upstairs to the Leapmaster.

"Go where?" Sandor, Flori, and Grady asked as they trailed behind her.

Sophie studied the giant orb made up of small, glittering crystals dangling from the roof of Havenfield's cupola. "Ro wasn't with Keefe, right?"

"He was alone," Grady confirmed.

Sophie had no idea what lengths Keefe must've gone to in order to sneak away from his ogre bodyguard. But she was sure Ro would do everything in her power to find him—mostly so she could torture Keefe with humiliating punishments.

"Splendor Plains," Sophie called, turning to Flori as the Leapmaster shifted into motion. "Are you coming with us?"

"I'd prefer to have Flori stay here and continue organizing the new security," Sandor cut in.

"As you wish." Flori closed her eyes, swaying like a tree in a storm. "I hope our moonlark doesn't worry too much. I hear songs of change in the air. But they're not unhappy melodies. They sing of freedom. And new opportunities."

Sophie wished she could hear the same tunes.

The only sound in her ears was her heartbeat, hammering like a war drum as she took Sandor's hand and stepped into the light, letting the rushing warmth carry them away.

TWO

"JUST AS I FEARED," SANDOR MUTTERED AS he marched through the main entrance of Elwin's colorful home.

Sophie peeked around his huge gray body. "Really? You were afraid we were going to find *this*?"

The downstairs level of Splendor Plains was framed by glass walls with panes in every tint and tone of the spectrum—a giant, empty space, save for a single armchair and table in the center, which were both toppled over. Elwin and Ro were crouched beside them, in the middle of some sort of bizarre showdown. The ogre princess held several stuffed animals with her sword pressed against their throats, while Elwin seemed to be using telekinesis to make a dozen shimmering vials hover around Ro's head.

"Hey, Dr. Sparkles could've spared his snuggle buddies if he'd taken me to find Funkyhair!" Ro shouted, angling her blade to target the stuffed boobrie. "Instead, he chose to be stubborn. So now his little birdie needs to pay!"

"Harm one thread on Boo Boo," Elwin warned, "and I'll have glitter pouring out of your body for the next three days!"

Ro gritted her pointed teeth. "I told you, I'm not afraid of your elf-y potions! *But* it looks like I won't need your help anymore." She nudged her chin toward the letter still clutched in Sophie's hand. "Let me guess. Captain Mopeypants told you he's running away forever, and you've dragged Gigantor here on a quest to save our reckless boy from his terrible life choices."

"Pretty much," Sophie agreed. "Any idea where he went?"

"Not at the moment." Ro sheathed her sword with a little more force than necessary. "I'd been planning to catch him at your place, since I knew he'd never disappear without some sort of mushy goodbye—but *someone* refused to take me."

"*Refused?*" Sophie stumbled back when Elwin nodded.

"It's not how it sounds," he promised. "I found Ro crawling around upstairs with two dead legs, and—"

"Dead legs?" Sandor interrupted.

"Hunkyhair commanded me to *sleep* so I couldn't stop him from leaving," Ro admitted. "And his command to wake me up only worked halfway. I was strong enough to sit up and shred his ridiculous bedsheet bonds. But even after I freed my legs, they still dragged for a little while."

"It was more than *a little while*," Elwin argued as the floating medicine vials drifted into the satchel slung across his shoulders. "Took me nearly an hour to get her circulation back to normal. And by then, it would've been too late to catch up with Keefe."

"You didn't know that! I'm sure he went home to Daddy Dearest's to pack the rest of his stuff before he went over to Blondie's—and I'm sure he spent a while at Blondie's feeling all weepy and conflicted about abandoning her. We should've checked!"

"You should have!" Sophie agreed, shooting a death glare at Elwin.

He'd saved her life so many times, she never would've expected him to let Keefe down like this.

Elwin scrubbed his fingers through his dark, messy hair. "Pretty sure I can guess what you're thinking, Sophie. But . . . I've seen how terrified Keefe is to use his voice right now—and how hard he's fought to stop himself from giving any commands. So if he was willing to tell Ro to *sleep* and didn't even stick around long enough to make sure she fully woke up, something big must've scared him away. And maybe we should trust that he knows what he's doing."

"Except—spoiler alert—Funkyhair *never* knows what he's doing," Ro argued, tossing Boo Boo at Elwin's head.

Elwin caught the fluffy boobrie with his mind. "I think he actually did this time."

"Ugh, you sound like Grady," Sophie grumbled, still not sure she'd forgiven her adoptive father for letting Keefe go. "I had to remind him how little Keefe knows about humans and how easily he could end up in jail—or worse."

Elwin winced.

Ro muttered a string of inappropriate Ogreish words. "I'm assuming that means our boy's planning to hide with the only creatures that are even more annoying than goblins?" She flung the rest of the stuffed animals at Elwin. "See what you've done?"

Elwin scrambled to catch his fluffy friends. "Hey, we all know that even if we'd dragged Keefe back, he just would've run away again—maybe after using commands that caused serious problems."

"Not if I'd gagged him and chained him up in my father's dungeon!" Ro snapped back.

"Or if I'd talked to him!" Sophie added—even though some of her recent conversations with Keefe hadn't exactly gone well.

Elwin hugged his snuggle buddies. "I know this is hard to accept. I've been struggling with it too. But . . . Keefe *needs* to take control of his new abilities—and I think he might have to do that on his own. I'd been hoping that Kesler and I could create elixirs to help, or that Dex could build some sort of gadget. But so far we're getting nowhere—and until we do, Keefe's going to make himself sick worrying about hurting someone or getting manipulated by his mother or—"

"That's why the dungeon would be perfect!" Ro interrupted. "I also know a lovely bog that looks and smells like all the vomit in the world went there to die. A few days floating in that sludge and our boy will be *begging* to head back to Sparkle Town. Except now we have to find him first—and apparently he could be anywhere on the planet, because of *course* he decided to hide with the species you elves gave *way* too much land to, but we can discuss your Council's absurd ruling choices another time. First . . . let's think." She twisted one of her bright red pigtails around her clawed finger. "You lived with humans for a while, right, Blondie? Is there anywhere that'd be a particularly good spot for sitting around, feeling sorry for yourself?"

"You're *not* going to the Forbidden Cities!" Sandor reminded Sophie.

"Try and stop us!" Ro countered.

"The problem," Sophie cut in before Sandor could draw his sword, "is that Keefe spun to a random facet on his pathfinder when he leaped away. Logic isn't going to help us find him."

Ro heaved a dramatic sigh. "Then I don't suppose there's some fancy mind trick you can use to track him down, is there, Little Miss Moonlark?"

"Not from this far away. I can't hear his thoughts if he ignores me. And I can't track his mind if I don't know where I'm supposed to *feel*."

"Ugh. Yet another reason I'll never understand why you elves care so much about your elf-y abilities."

Sandor's snort sounded like agreement—and Sophie didn't necessarily blame either of them. The Black Swan had modified her genetics and given her more abilities than any elf had ever had before. And still, more often than not, she was outmatched and underprepared.

"Can't *you* track your charge?" Sandor asked Ro. "Surely you keep him covered in one of those enzymes you ogres love so much."

Sophie's heart did a backflip. "That's right—I forgot about aromark!"

But Ro shook her head. "My boy made me promise I wouldn't expose him to anything that would require melting off his skin if we needed to remove it. And after what his mommy's put him through, I figured . . . fair enough."

Sophie couldn't fault Ro for that—but Sandor apparently could.

"A bodyguard's job is to keep track of their charge, not cater to their wishes!" he snapped.

"No, our job is to *protect* our charge, which I can do just fine with these." Ro waved her hands in front of the rows of daggers strapped to her muscled thighs.

"How are those protecting him right now?" Sandor countered.

"I'll admit, I wasn't fully prepared for my boy to learn how to knock everyone out with a single word." She shuddered. "But you would've been just as dead-legged as I was—and if you think those silly disks you like to sew into Blondie's clothes would've changed anything, you're delusional. He would've ripped those out in two seconds."

"Only if he could find them." Sandor's smile was so smug, it made Sophie want to tear through everything she was wearing.

But it didn't matter. "Fighting isn't going to help us find Keefe," Sophie reminded them.

"It isn't," Ro agreed. "But for the record, *if* I have been giving my boy a little more breathing room, it's only because I could tell he was on the verge of a meltdown. Plus, I was waiting for him to realize that he's looking at these new powers all wrong. Sure, accidentally numbing his friends is less-than-awesome—but he also doesn't have to fear Mommy Dearest anymore! Next time she shows up, he can just command her to sleep. Or better yet, tell her to jump off a sparkly building—problem solved!"

Sophie wished it would be that easy. "I'm sure Lady Gisela has a way to protect herself."

The Neverseen were always five steps ahead.

Sometimes ten.

Or fifty.

Then again, she'd managed to find their secret storehouse and burn it to the ground. That's why the inferno had felt like Sophie's first *real* victory—and why she had to be ready to make lots more terrifying decisions.

"May I?" Ro asked, pointing to Keefe's letter.

"There's nothing useful in there," Sophie warned. But she still handed over the paper as she turned to pace. "Did Keefe say anything before he left?"

"Not that I know of," Elwin told her. "But I was down here with earplugs in while he tested the Imparter with Dex."

"They wanted to see if Hunkyhair could talk with a gadget and not feel the urge to give any commands," Ro explained. "Which totally worked, by the way."

Sophie halted midstep. "Something happened during that conversation, didn't it?"

"I'm assuming so, since Keefe left right after," Elwin said. "But I wasn't listening."

"Hang on! How are we not talking about *this*?" Ro pointed to a sentence near the end of Keefe's letter.

Sophie realized what it said the same second Ro shifted to a fairly convincing impersonation of Keefe's voice.

"'*You mean a lot to me, Foster. More than you'll ever know.*'"

Sophie lunged for the paper.

"Nope! No destroying the evidence—and don't even *think* about telling me you don't know what he meant by that, Blondie! Your cheeks are way too red!"

Sophie tugged her hair forward.

She'd been so thrown by the rest of Keefe's message that she'd forgotten that part was in there—and her brain honestly had no idea what to do with it.

It almost felt like Keefe was trying to tell her . . .

But he couldn't mean that.

. . . Could he?

"Whoa. I think the Great Foster Oblivion might actually be over!" Ro pumped her fist. "Now I'm even more excited to drag Hunkyhair home! You two can have *the talk* and—"

"Are you serious right now?" Sophie lunged for the letter again, managing to snatch it back this time—though part of the paper tore in the process. "Two minutes ago you were threatening to behead a bunch of stuffed animals because Elwin wouldn't help you find Keefe. And now you're wasting time teasing me about some throwaway line—"

"That line is *not* a throwaway! You know it. I know it. Dr. Sparkles knows it. Shoot, even Gigantor knows it—look how intently he's studying his feet right now. *But* . . . I suppose you might have a point about priorities. Sorry. I'm just so excited! Do you have any idea how long I've been waiting for this? It's going to be so adorable when you two finally . . ."

She made a disgustingly loud smooching sound—and Sophie hated her brain for imagining it.

Hated how sweaty her palms felt even more.

She stuffed the letter into her pocket and crossed her arms, trying to dry her hands on her sleeves. "Can we focus, please? I need to know what happened when Keefe talked to Dex."

Ro's smile faded. "You should probably ask your techy friend about that."

"That'll waste more time."

"Not really. I only understood some of the stuff they were freaking out about, and if you're going to have to cross-check everything, you might as well start at the source, right?"

Sophie *really* hated that Ro had made a good point—and she was still tempted to whip her Imparter at Ro's head like a goblin throwing star. But she fought the urge, digging out the small, flat gadget and telling it, "Show me Dex Dizznee."

The Imparter stayed blank.

Sophie tapped the screen harder. "Dex Dizznee!"

More seconds crawled by.

"Is that thing working?" Ro asked. "Or is he ignoring you?"

"I have no idea." Sophie held the Imparter closer to her mouth and repeated Dex's name.

Still nothing.

She rubbed her temples and turned back to Ro. "Okay, why don't you tell me everything you remember, and if I need clarification, I'll—"

"Sophie?" Dex's face flashed across the screen. "Sorry . . . I was, um . . . Is everything okay?"

"I was about to ask you the same question." His periwinkle eyes looked red and puffy, and his pale skin was super blotchy. "What's wrong? And don't say 'nothing,' because it's pretty obvious that you've been crying."

"No, I haven't!" He swiped at his nose and cheeks. "I'm fine."

It might've been the worst lie in the history of lying.

Sophie sighed. "We don't have time to argue, okay? I need to know what happened between you and Keefe."

All the color drained from Dex's face. "Why? What did he tell you?"

"Nothing. But . . . he ran away."

Dex closed his eyes and somehow managed to turn even paler. "You're sure?"

"Unfortunately, yeah." She stopped herself from mentioning Keefe's letter—no need to relive *that* humiliation. "I'm still figuring out how to find him, but—"

"Are you sure that's a good idea?" Dex interrupted. "I mean . . . maybe he needs to be alone for a while, you know? Might be safer."

"Seriously?" Sophie asked.

What was wrong with everybody?

"Keefe needs *help*!" she snapped. "And to know that people still care about him and believe in him no matter what. It's also way safer here than with the humans—"

Dex's eyes popped open. "Wait—he's in the Forbidden Cities?"

"Yep. And he doesn't know how to survive there. He also doesn't have any money—and he can't accidentally rob an ATM like *some* people."

Sophie had hoped the tiny tease might lighten the mood—but Dex just looked away, chewing his lip so hard, his teeth left dents in his skin.

"Maybe if you tell me why Keefe left, I'll understand what you're so afraid of," Sophie suggested. "Don't you trust me?"

"It's not about trust."

"It's *always* about trust—and Keefe's life is on the line, Dex. I know that sounds dramatic, but it's true. Every minute we waste is a minute when he could be hurt, or arrested—or things I don't even want to think about."

An eternity passed before Dex said, "I might be able to track him down."

He disappeared from the screen and reappeared holding a small copper cube with twisted wires sticking out of it. "If he's still wearing his registry pendant, I can find the signal. Just give me a minute."

Sophie counted every second.

By four hundred nineteen, Dex had rearranged the wires a zillion different ways—and Sophie had tugged out two itchy eyelashes.

"I'm assuming he removed his pendant?" she guessed.

Dex set the gadget aside. "Sorry."

"Ugh, the one time we needed our boy to be clueless!" Ro unsheathed one of her daggers and stabbed the air. "Got any other techy tricks?"

Dex shook his head. "Keefe doesn't wear a nexus anymore—"

"What about his panic switch?" Sophie held up her slightly lopsided ring, wishing she'd thought of it earlier. "You put trackers in them, didn't you?"

"I did. But . . . I never gave one to Keefe. I made yours first, remember? And then I made all the others while Keefe was off with the Neverseen—and I kept meaning to make him one after he got back, but there were always other projects I had to work on, you know?"

Sophie *did* know. But she couldn't quite keep the disappointment out of her voice when she said, "That's okay."

"I'm sorry," Dex mumbled. "I wish I could help."

"You *can*. Tell me what happened when you tested the Imparter. If it's easier to talk in person, I could come there—"

"NO!"

Dex disappeared from the screen, followed by a series of thuds that sounded like he was barricading his door.

"What do you think I'm going to do?" Sophie called after him. "Leap there and drag the secrets out of your mind?"

Honestly, she was tempted to do exactly that when Dex called back, "Just promise you won't come here, okay?"

"Why not?"

"Because"—more thuds—"it's . . . um . . . chaos right now!"

"It's always chaos there! I've met the triplets, remember?"

"I know. But . . . Lex and Bex manifested, so it's extra insane. Lex is covering everything in ice, and Bex is trying to walk through every wall."

"Then why don't you come here? Or we can meet at Havenfield. Or—"

"I can't."

"Can't? Or *won't*?"

"To save time," Ro jumped in, "it might help if I mention that I heard your whole conversation with Hunkyhair. I told Blondie to ask you about it because I don't understand all your elf-y weirdnesses—but if you'd rather be a pain, I can tell her about—"

"STOP!" Dex rushed back into view, and for a second Sophie wondered if he was going to hang up on them. Instead he took a long, shaky breath and said, "The thing is . . . it's not really my secret to share."

"Whose is it?" Sophie asked.

"I can't tell you that, either."

"Well then, it's a good thing I can!" Ro draped her arm around Sophie's shoulders. "I'll give him ten seconds to start talking, or I'm taking over. Ten . . . nine . . . eight . . ."

"*Please* stop." The crack in Dex's voice made Sophie's heart feel twenty pounds heavier.

"I don't want to hurt you, Dex. Or force you to share something you're not comfortable with. But Keefe's out there right now, lost in some human city with no food, no ID, no place to go, and no one to help him. I have no idea how I'm going to find him—but I have to try. And if I *do* manage to track him down, I need to be able to convince him to come back. He thinks he's too dangerous to be in the Lost Cities—and I won't be able to prove him wrong if I don't know why he believes that. So please, tell me what you know—I promise I won't tell *anyone*."

Dex buried his face in his hands.

It felt like a year passed before he mumbled, "*No one* else can hear this. In fact . . ."

He disappeared from the screen again, and a loud click echoed in the background, followed by a steady crackling hum, like static.

"That's my silencer," he explained as he stepped back in front of the Imparter. "It guarantees that no one can eavesdrop—over here at least."

"I guess that's my cue," Elwin said, making Sophie jump. "Forgot I was here, did ya? Don't worry, I won't mention anything I've already heard—not that it's made a whole lot of sense." He turned to head for the stairs, shoving earplugs in as he walked. "I'll be in my room."

"What about Sandor?" Dex asked.

Sandor leaned closer to the screen. "I go where Sophie goes. And I stay where she stays."

"Aw, come on, Gigantor!" Ro whined. "We're finally getting somewhere! I can protect Blondie—"

"That's debatable," Sandor interrupted. "But I'm far more concerned about the two of you running off to the Forbidden Cities."

"I won't go anywhere without you," Sophie promised.

"Besides, I thought you had trackers sewn into her clothes," Ro reminded him with a smirk. "Surely Mr. Perfect Bodyguard would be able to catch us if we tried to—"

"We're not going to try anything!" Sophie cut in. "I swear on Ella—and Wynn and Luna!"

Sandor cracked his knuckles. "I'll be *right* outside, watching you through the windows."

Ro snorted. "Because *that* doesn't sound creepy!"

Sandor slammed the door so hard, the glass walls rattled.

"Okay, start talking," Sophie told Dex.

He turned a vomit-y shade of green. "I . . . don't know how to say this."

"Then blurt it out—it doesn't have to be a big, fancy speech."

"The shorter, the better!" Ro added.

Dex swallowed hard and closed his eyes. "Okay . . . so . . . Keefe manifested another ability. We're not a hundred percent sure how it works, but . . . it seems like he can sense if someone is going to manifest and tell what ability they'll get."

Sophie let the words tumble around her head.

"Why is that such a bad thing?" she had to ask.

"THANK YOU!" Ro shouted. "Glad I'm not the only one who thinks Tech-Boy and Hunkyhair are being *way* overdramatic!"

"You seriously don't see how scary that is?" Dex asked.

Sophie shrugged. "I can see how Keefe might have a ton of people asking him what their ability is going to be. Kind of like what happened to Councillor Terik with his descrying. But Terik just stopped doing readings."

"Yeah, well, descrying only measures someone's potential," Dex reminded her. "Abilities define us for the rest of our lives."

"For the record, that's where you elves lose me," Ro noted.

"Me too," Sophie said quietly. "And that still doesn't sound *that* bad, Dex, so I'm assuming there's more you haven't told me."

Dex glanced over his shoulder again, then leaned closer to the Imparter and whispered, "We're pretty sure Keefe can *make* someone manifest."

"How would you know . . . ?" Sophie's voice trailed off as she answered her own question. "You think Keefe *made* Rex and Bex manifest?"

"*Lex* and Bex," Dex corrected, choking strangely on the names. He had to clear his throat twice before he could add, "Keefe was around them yesterday, and he said Lex's hand felt super cold, and Bex's hand felt weirdly squishy—and no one else could feel that. Then today Lex manifested as a Froster, and Bex manifested as a Phaser. No way that's a coincidence."

Sophie had to agree. But she also wasn't ready to make *as* huge of a leap. "Couldn't Keefe have just been sensing what was about to happen?"

"He could—but given how young they are, it seems more likely that he caused it. And if he did . . ."

Sophie tried to find an end to that sentence with the right amount of *dun dun dunnnnnnn*.

"I still don't get why Keefe ran away," she admitted. "Even if he *can* trigger abilities, he's just speeding up something that's going to happen anyway, right? And Mr. Forkle has triggered abilities—"

"That's different," Dex cut in. "There was no guarantee that what Mr. Forkle did would work—well, except with you, but you're . . . you know . . ."

"Weird?" Sophie finished for him.

"I was going to say *unique*," Dex corrected.

"Suuuuuuure you were."

Her smile faded when Dex didn't return it.

He looked so serious.

So sad.

So . . . *scared*.

"What aren't you telling me?" she mumbled.

She tried replaying the conversation, looking for any clue she might've missed.

The only thing that stood out was Dex saying that Keefe's ability was different from what Mr. Forkle did to trigger her abilities.

"So . . . Mr. Forkle *can't* guarantee that someone will manifest," she said slowly. "Does that mean Keefe . . . can?"

Dex's eyes welled with tears. "No."

She was about to ask how he could be so sure when she remembered something he'd told her earlier.

It's not really my secret to share.

She'd assumed he'd meant Keefe. But now all she could think about was the fact that only two of the triplets had manifested.

A lump lodged in her throat, making it hard to choke out

her next question. But she cleared it away and whispered, "Was Rex there when Keefe touched Bex's and Lex's hands?"

Dex's tears spilled over—which pretty much answered her question. But he still said, "Keefe said Rex's hand felt empty somehow. And . . . he felt the same thing from my dad."

"Oh."

The tiny word seemed to pulse, growing louder with every beat until the sound filled the enormous room.

So did the word none of them said.

Talentless.

More tears dripped down Dex's cheeks, and Sophie felt her own eyes turn watery.

She wanted to insist it was a mistake. After all, Keefe was barely beginning to understand his power.

But truth always felt different.

It carried a heavier weight.

"Promise me you won't tell Rex," Dex whispered, drying his face with his sleeve.

"He doesn't know?"

Dex shook his head. "He's already been sobbing most of the day because he's worried it *might* happen. Can you imagine how he'd feel if he knew for sure? He still has years before he gets to the point where everyone will give up on him—unless the Council finds out what Keefe can do and makes him start testing everyone in ability detecting at Foxfire."

Sophie sucked in a breath. "Do you think they'd do that?"

"I wouldn't put it past them. It'd make it way easier to decide who belongs at Foxfire and who doesn't. And who knows? They might even start testing everyone at birth. I'm sure they'd claim it's better for everyone to know as early as possible. But all it would do is make the Talentless be judged their entire lives."

Chills rippled down Sophie's spine. "Keefe would never go along with that."

"He might not have a choice. All they'd have to do is restrain him and have a Telepath read his mind while people touched his hands."

Sophie wasn't sure if she could picture the Councillors ordering something so cruel.

But she *could* imagine his mom doing it.

"Why would Lady Gisela want that?" she said, mostly to herself. "Why endure all the painful experiments on herself and her husband—and everything she put Keefe through—just so Keefe could tell if someone is or isn't going to manifest?"

"He might also be able to trigger abilities," Dex reminded her. "Plus, he's now a Polyglot and can give commands that do all kinds of scary things. And maybe there's other stuff we haven't discovered yet."

"There probably is," Sophie hated to admit. "But . . . I still don't see a connection. She's trying to rule the world—how does this help with that?"

"I don't know," Dex said. "But I don't want to find out."

Neither did Sophie.

Keefe clearly didn't either—which finally explained why he'd fled the Lost Cities.

And this was going to make it pretty impossible to convince him to come back.

"Do you think he'll ever be able to control this ability?" she asked, staring at her gloveless hands.

She'd found a way to master her enhancing. . . .

But it had taken her months.

And several special gadgets.

And a strange mental exercise.

And help.

Lots of help.

"I'm working on some prototypes," Dex said, as if he knew what she was thinking. "And I'll talk to Tinker—though it's going to be hard to get her to understand what I need without telling her why. But . . . there has to be something we can do."

"I'll tell Keefe that," she promised. "Well . . . if I find him."

"Oh, we're finding him!" Ro said with way more confidence than Sophie was capable of mustering. "I don't care if we have to tear through every human city."

"Where will you start?" Dex asked.

"Somewhere random, I guess," Sophie said quietly. "Grady said Keefe spun the blue crystal on his pathfinder and leaped wherever it stopped."

"Where did he get a blue crystal?"

"Probably from Daddy Dearest," Ro grumbled. "Hunkyhair was always bragging about how he used to steal it."

"Do you think Lord Cassius knows which cities his pathfinder can access?" Sophie asked.

"He'd have to," Dex agreed. "Otherwise he wouldn't be able to use it."

A spark of hope flared to life. "Looks like we need to stop by the Shores of Solace."

Ro sheathed her dagger—then stretched her arms and cracked her knuckles. "I *really* hope Lord Bossypants decides to be difficult. I'm in the mood to punch something."

Sophie wouldn't mind an excuse either.

"If there's anything I can do, let me know," Dex told them. "And keep me updated, okay?"

"I will. And . . . thank you for telling me. I know it wasn't easy."

"Nothing's easy anymore," Dex mumbled.

"It isn't," Sophie agreed, wishing she could reach through the tiny screen and hug him.

She couldn't.

Just like she couldn't promise him that everything would be okay.

All she could do was keep going.

Keep trying.

Keep fighting with everything she had.

And always hope for the best.

THREE

WHERE IS MY SON?"

Of *course* Lord Cassius greeted them with the question that Sophie had been hoping to avoid.

She'd realized as they were teleporting to the Shores of Solace that Keefe's father had no idea his son was missing—and it'd probably be better to keep it that way. But Lord Cassius would never answer questions about his pathfinder without knowing why she was asking. And lying to Empaths was annoyingly challenging.

So she cut straight to the brutal truth: "Keefe ran away."

Normal parents would've cried—panicked—pummeled Sophie with questions.

Lord Cassius simply smoothed his already perfect blond hair and stepped aside to let Sophie, Ro, and Sandor into his fancy beach house.

He led them to the farthest corner of the property, to a bougainvillea-lined patio facing the ocean, and settled onto the only chair—a chaise covered in worn turquoise pillows.

"I assumed this would happen," he said as he flicked a speck of lint off his pristine gray cape. "If Keefe had come home with me—"

"He would've run off even faster," Ro finished for him. "Probably left a Keefe-shaped hole in one of the walls."

Lord Cassius's lips curled into a smile—but it was a dark, twisted thing. "Such bravado coming from the one whose job was to prevent something like this from happening."

"Yeah, well, wasn't it *your* job to make sure no one did creepy experiments on your son, instead of signing him up for them before he was born?" Ro snapped back. "And while we're discussing failed responsibilities, shall we acknowledge the fact that it's *also* a father's job to make sure their child feels happy and secure and loved?"

"Is that what your scar displays?" Lord Cassius said, referencing the jagged mark that ran the length of Ro's spine. "Your father's *love*?"

Ro reached behind her, trailing her fingers gently along the rough, raised skin. "You're right. My father *did* make this mark. He's done the same thing to all his most trusted warriors. And when he cut it, I felt his pride, and respect—and yes, I actually *did* feel his love. Can Keefe say the same about *anything* you've done for him?" She waited for Lord Cassius's smile to fade before she added, "You elves like to talk about ogres as if we're these cold, brutal creatures. But I've never seen anything as cold and brutal as the way you treat your son."

Sophie wanted to hoist Ro on her shoulders and parade her around the room—but that would probably get them kicked out of the Shores of Solace.

Still, she hoped Lord Cassius could feel her disgust slashing through the air.

He looked away, staring at the darkening horizon. "How long has Keefe been gone?"

"A few hours," Sophie told him. "And we're pretty sure he used your pathfinder when he left, so I need a list of all the places that pathfinder goes."

"That will be a very long list."

"How long?" Sandor asked.

"*Long.* The Council granted me their highest level of clearance. I was one of their top Emissaries—"

"I don't care if it's a long list," Sophie interrupted before he could launch into a speech about the wonder that was him.

"You should. It's over a hundred cities. And I suspect my son plans to visit each and every one." He folded his hands neatly in his lap. "Keefe has likely realized by now that his mother surely borrowed my pathfinder over the years without my knowledge, and is hoping he'll find one of her secret hide-outs. He hasn't accepted the futility of such endeavors. Just as you won't accept the futility of leaping all over the planet, trying to hunt down a boy who obviously doesn't want to be found."

"A scared boy with no idea how to survive in the Forbidden Cities," Sophie argued. "I can't believe you don't—"

She cut her sentence short.

Lord Cassius's lack of concern *wasn't* a surprise.

"So much judgment," he murmured, trailing his fingers through the air, testing her emotions. "It's as if you've forgotten what you found in my mind."

Sophie rolled her eyes.

She *had* unearthed memories that proved he actually did love his son—but they didn't count. He'd buried the feelings too deep, claiming that love convoluted things.

Lord Cassius sighed. "Affection comes in many forms. Even surrender. Which is why I'm willing to admit that I never have been and never will be able to control my son. No one can. Not even you—though I'm certain you'll continue to try. You're even more stubborn than he is. The good news, though, is that my wife might be the most stubborn out of all of you—and she foolishly made Keefe integral to her plan. I suspect it will be her downfall—which would be rather poetic, wouldn't it?"

It would.

But Sophie wasn't in the mood to agree with him.

"Do you need me to get you some paper?" she asked. "Or should I just pull the list of cities from your mind?"

She'd meant the second option as a threat. But Lord Cassius flashed another twisted smile and said, "Pulling it from my mind will be much more convenient."

Sophie glanced at Ro and Sandor.

"Hey, if Lord Creepypants wants to let you dig through his head, I say go for it," Ro told her. "You can dredge up all his embarrassing secrets!"

"Or it could be a trick," Sandor warned.

Lord Cassius clicked his tongue. "Need I remind you that we're on the same side?" He reached under his tunic and showed them the swan-neck monocle he'd received after swearing fealty to the Black Swan. "Your Collective trusts me. Surely you can do the—"

"What assignment did they give you?" Sophie interrupted.

The last time she'd seen Lord Cassius, he'd mentioned an assignment for the Black Swan. But he hadn't told her what it was.

"If you want me to trust you," she added, "you should tell me what you're working on."

He flicked away more invisible lint. "My assignment is classi-fied."

"But if you're inviting Blondie into your head, her super-brain can find out anything she wants," Ro reminded him. "So there's no point keeping it secret."

"Perhaps not from *her*. But she's not the only one here, is she?" He bent his knees and slid his feet back toward himself, then motioned to the now-empty portion of his chaise. "You prefer to sit when using your telepathy, don't you, Miss Foster?"

Sophie stared at the lumpy cushions.

"If you want answers," he snapped, "and that list—you have permission to enter my mind. Otherwise, you may see yourself out."

He raised one eyebrow in challenge, and the expression made him look much more like his son—if Keefe was also harsh and cold and . . .

Sad.

"Fine," she said, lowering herself onto the farthest edge of the chaise. "But you're not going to like this."

"Oh, I'm quite certain of that. And yet, here we are." He waved one hand in a sweeping, circular gesture, inviting her into his mind.

Sophie closed her eyes and let her consciousness harden into steel—into armor—with just enough edge to slice through his flimsy mental barriers in one quick shove.

Let's make this quick, she transmitted. *I need . . .*

Her words trailed off as she took in the disarray.

Lord Cassius's mind used to be meticulous—everything carefully sorted and rigidly arranged, as if his head were a stuffy library where no one was allowed to touch any of the books.

Now it looked like an earthquake had crashed through, knocking all the memories to the floor and leaving a sea of jumbled piles, flashing and blaring in full color and volume, like mounds of broken televisions.

You'll get used to the noise, Lord Cassius thought as she reached up to rub her temples.

Sophie doubted that.

And if it'd been anyone else, she would've checked to make sure he was okay.

Instead, she transmitted, *What are you working on for the Black Swan?*

Nothing that caused the mental disruption you're seeing, if that's what you're wondering. Nor is it anything that merits the level of frustration I felt when I told you the assignment was classified. You truly despise secrets, don't you?

I do, Sophie agreed.

And yet, you're keeping more of them than anyone, aren't you? Our fearless moonlark, with her impenetrable mind. The leader of Team Valiant, doing the Council's bidding—

You didn't answer my question, Sophie reminded him.

A low rumble shook the mounds of memories as he struggled to keep his temper. *I wasn't lying when I said the assignment is classified. But before you throw a tantrum—*

I don't throw tantrums!

Yes, and you aren't gripping one of my pillows right now, tempted to hurl it at my face.

Sophie relaxed her grip on the cushion. *So this is where Keefe gets his obnoxious side from.*

I suppose that's possible. His mind brightened slightly with the thought. *But as I was trying to say before your unnecessary interruption, I'm sure you can guess enough to satisfy your curiosity if I tell you that my assignment involves stalled treaty negotiations.*

Sophie needed several seconds to piece together a theory. *Do you mean the negotiations with the trolls?*

I can't think of any other negotiations in progress, can you?

She couldn't. But she also hadn't realized that things with the trolls weren't already settled—though she probably should have, since Tarina still hadn't returned to her post as one of Sophie's bodyguards.

Why are the negotiations stalled? she asked.

Why do you think? You and your friends uncovered an illegal hive hidden within our borders, filled with bloodthirsty, genetically manipulated newborns that were clearly part of an ongoing experiment.

Flashbacks of shredding claws and bloody teeth tore through Sophie's brain, so it took her a second to catch the key word in that sentence.

Ongoing? Does that mean there are more hives?

That's what the Council would like to find out. Particularly since

Empress Pernille has now closed the borders to Marintrylla and requested a treaty similar to what King Dimitar demanded after the destruction at Ravagog. She wants to sever ties with the Lost Cities and keep the trolls isolated from everyone.

And just like that, Sophie was back in Mr. Forkle's strange egg-shaped office, staring at a 3-D map of the world and listening to him explain how he believed that the Neverseen were trying to keep the other intelligent species fragmented and distracted, so they'd be too weak or busy to cause trouble when the Neverseen overthrew the Council.

She couldn't decide if this proved their plan was working—or if they were creating an even bigger mess.

Probably both.

Do you think the Council will agree to the terms of Empress Pernille's treaty? she asked.

Possibly. If she proves she's not amassing a mutant newborn army.

Sophie shuddered. *So THAT'S why you said we should talk telepathically. You didn't want Ro and Sandor to know about this.*

Actually, I'm sure their leaders are monitoring the situation just as closely as we are—if not more so. I suggested a mental conversation, because . . . there's something else I need to share with you—and it will be far easier to show you than to try to explain it out loud. Particularly given your annoying propensity to interrupt.

Sophie wanted to argue with his insult, but she was too focused on what his offer meant.

You remembered something.

I did. In fact, I'm surprised you haven't already asked me about it, since you were the one to trigger the memory. The last time we spoke, when you mentioned "merged abilities."

Goose bumps erupted across Sophie's skin—mostly from irritation. *You told me those words DIDN'T trigger any memories.*

No, I said I wished they had—and that I needed time to process. Both of which were true. I knew something felt uncomfortably familiar, but I couldn't connect it to anything—until this morning, when I woke up from a nightmare and realized it was actually a moment I'd lived.

His mind rumbled again—louder and longer this time—and the piles of memories shifted, clearing a narrow, winding path.

Sophie couldn't tell where it led—only that it disappeared into the shadowy depths of his consciousness.

Nervous? he asked as Sophie studied the sludgy black. *Or curious? Funny how those two emotions feel similar, isn't it?*

Actually, I'm mostly wondering why you're suddenly so eager to share your secrets with me.

"EAGER" is the wrong word. But I'm WILLING to, because— as I keep assuring you—we're on the same side. I want to protect my son any way I can. And I want to stop my wife every bit as much as you do—maybe more so, now that I know how far she's willing to go.

How far is that?

See for yourself.

The path widened with the invitation—but his mind also sharpened.

With impatience, maybe?

Or something more ominous?

There was no way to tell—and Sophie was sure that if Keefe were there, he'd beg her not to follow his dad's eerie path into the deep mental gloom.

But Keefe *wasn't* there.

And Sophie needed answers. She didn't get to choose who gave them to her.

So she took a long, steadying breath and gathered as much mental energy as she could muster.

Then she let her consciousness sink into the darkness.

FOUR

"YOU OKAY THERE, BLONDIE?" RO called from somewhere far, far away. "You keep getting that little worry crease between your eyebrows—and it's making Gigantor twitchy!"

Sophie couldn't respond.

She could barely think.

Her mind was spinning, spinning, spinning as Lord Cassius's mental path swooped and swerved and swayed through the shadows.

Her stomach wobbled and her brain throbbed, and she had to remind herself to keep breathing as she focused on a halo of gray in the distance.

Bit by bit—turn by turn—the light grew closer.

And brighter.

And so much *colder.*

She shivered—teeth chattering—as a mental blizzard roared to life, the ice scraping and stinging and whiting out the world.

Sorry, Lord Cassius told her, his voice like a ghost whispering on the wind. *I don't know how to lower these defenses. I didn't even know I had them until this morning. But I'm assuming you can manage.*

I can, Sophie assured him, charging deeper into the storm—shoving and thrashing and scratching until she crashed through some sort of frigid barrier.

Then she was falling, falling, falling.

Faster, faster, faster.

Through mist.

And shadow.

Into . . . warmth.

She sank into the blissful heat, studying the dim space she'd landed in.

It felt small.

And quiet.

And familiar.

A mental nook—almost exactly like the one she'd found in Alden's mind.

My wife went to great lengths to ensure that I'd never recall the conversation you're about to witness, Lord Cassius explained as a jagged shard of memory emerged from the fog. *I honestly have no idea how I managed to preserve it.*

Sophie wasn't sure either.

She'd thought only specially trained Telepaths knew how to reach that particular mental nook and preserve something inside.

Obviously not.

The images looked dim and blurry—but some of that might've been because Lord Cassius didn't have a photographic memory. And the soundtrack was a little faded and scratchy in places. Still Sophie could easily tell that she was watching Lord Cassius and Lady Gisela in some sort of glittering office with curved walls and a large, dark desk. And she could make out every word when he said, "Why are you asking so many questions about Keefe's empathy?"

"Why are you surprised?" Lady Gisela countered. "Our son is a reflection of *us*. I want to make sure he's *impressive*. Don't you?"

"Of course." Lord Cassius stepped closer, reaching for her hand. The gesture looked reassuring and tender—until their skin made contact. Then his eyes narrowed. "There's something you're not telling me. I feel a strange tension radiating from you. Some sort of . . . expectation."

"Yes, I *expect* our son to be a powerful Empath, like his father."

"Then why did I feel the same tension when you had him tested to see if he would be a Conjurer? We don't have any Conjurers in our genetic line—unless there's something you haven't told me."

Lady Gisela tossed her head back and laughed. "Oh please, you're not still wondering if I have a second ability, are you? I thought we'd settled that."

"Did we?" He tightened his grip on her hand. "It doesn't feel like we have."

Lady Gisela sighed. "You know as well as I do that not all Polyglots manifest an additional talent—and thank you so much for making me feel inadequate."

"That's not actually an answer," Lord Cassius noted.

"Because it's an absurd question!"

"Then why do you feel so tense?"

IS she a Conjurer? Sophie asked, remembering a hastily scratched note that Keefe had stuck to the wall of his room in Alluveterre, back when he was trying to search his mind for any clues his mother might've accidentally given away.

WHY DID SHE MAKE THEM TEST ME TWICE TO SEE IF I'D MANIFESTED AS A CONJURER?

Keep watching, Lord Cassius told Sophie.

In the memory, he reached for his wife's other hand. "I can tell you're hiding something, Gisela. You can't lie to an Empath."

Her laugh turned colder. "Believe me, Cassius. I can. But I didn't realize you were paying such close attention. I'll have to be more careful."

"What does *that* mean?"

"Nothing to concern yourself with." A quick twist of her

wrists had her slipping free from his grasp, and she turned to pace. "I suppose . . . since this conversation is clearly a wash already, I might as well make the most of it. So how about this? You answer a few more of my questions—and I'll answer all of yours."

"*All* of them?" Lord Cassius verified.

She nodded. "Do we have a deal?"

He tilted his head to study her. "We do."

"Excellent. Then let's get back to our son. Is there anything about Keefe's empathy that feels different from yours?"

"Yes. It's far less disciplined—and I fear with his attitude, it always will be."

"No, I meant . . . the intensity of it."

Lord Cassius frowned. "He's powerful, if that's what you're wondering."

"More powerful than you?"

"That'll depend on how much he practices."

"Then we'll have to make sure he practices." She paced the room twice before she said, "I guess what I'm really trying to figure out is . . . can he do anything new? Anything . . . special?"

"Like what?"

"I don't know." She paused in front of her desk, tracing her finger along the edge. "Do you think he'll be able to influence someone's emotions?"

Lord Cassius stalked closer. "No Empath can do that."

"They can't *yet*," she corrected. "That doesn't mean our son won't be the first."

"Actually, it does. Abilities have limits—and those limits don't change."

"Under normal circumstances, yes. But Keefe is different."

"How?"

She shook her head. "We agreed you'd answer my questions first, remember?"

"But your questions are ridiculous!"

"Oh, you'll see their value someday. Assuming my research is correct."

"What research?"

She *tsk*ed her tongue and sidestepped around him to resume her pacing. "It's still my turn. Though . . . I suppose a bit more information might help us determine if Keefe's progressing properly. So let's just say that I've been studying our world's natural forces. Star and planetary alignments. Moon cycles. The Prime Sources. Shadowflux and quintessence. They all have so much more power than anyone truly understands. And I'm working to harness all of it."

Lord Cassius stared at his wife like she'd grown a second head. "To what end?"

"Many, many things. But . . . a large part is making sure our son reaches his full potential—in a way that you and I will never be able to. I've developed a very specific process. I just need to know if it's having any effect. The first step already happened—though you don't remember that part. The second will take me a few more years to arrange. And the third . . . well . . . there's one piece that's still a bit vague at the moment—but I'm working on it."

There's a THIRD step to stellarlune? Sophie asked, wanting to scream into one of the cushions and then rip it to shreds.

So it would seem. I'm assuming the first step involved those miserable elixirs she made me drink. The second must be what she did to Keefe in Loamnore. And the third is anyone's guess.

Distantly Sophie could feel Ro shaking her shoulders. "Still good, Blondie? You're looking pretty pale."

Of course she was pale!

The second step had nearly killed Keefe—and there was still one more to go?

Are you honestly surprised? Lord Cassius asked. *Given everything you've seen. Everything you know my wife is capable of. Is this really so shocking?*

Sadly, it wasn't.

But that didn't stop the terrifying theories from forming.

You can sit there picturing my son enduring all manner of horror, Lord Cassius told her. *Or you can focus on the rest of the memory. There's still more to learn.*

Like what?

He didn't answer. But in the memory, he told Gisela, "You're not making any sense."

"I don't need to." She tucked a loose tendril of her blond

hair back into her intricate bun. "At least not to you. Your role is already done."

"And what role was that?"

"Providing your DNA. I needed a powerful Empath to merge with my abilities."

"Merge?" he repeated.

"That's how I like to think of it—though I'll admit, I don't fully know how the merged abilities will function. My research has proven that special abilities aren't nearly as finite as we believe them to be. Given the right conditions, they can shift and recombine—and I'm hoping I can create something new. Something *better*."

What exactly can Keefe do? Lord Cassius asked Sophie. *I know about the commands—but I'm assuming there's more to it than that.*

Sophie wanted to tell him it was none of his business. But . . . he *was* being much more cooperative than usual.

There IS more, she admitted. *But it's better if no one knows any specifics. At least not until Keefe learns how to control his new abilities.*

Abilities, Lord Cassius noted. *So there's more than one.*

Wait—didn't Lady Gisela just make the same slip? Sophie realized. She replayed the last part of the conversation. *She said she needed a powerful Empath to merge with her abilities.*

Very good. You caught that faster than I did—though you'll see I put the pieces together right . . . now.

On cue the memory of him grabbed Lady Gisela's wrist. "Did you just say 'abili*ties*'?"

Her smile faded.

Then she shrugged. "Oh fine—it's not like this is going to matter."

She pulled her wrist free and snapped her fingers.

A small silver box appeared in her hand.

Lord Cassius gasped.

So did Sophie.

Gisela laughed. "I'm actually impressed you started to suspect I'm a Conjurer. I've been so careful."

He took a step back, shaking his head. "Why would you hide it? You'd be far more respected if—"

"Because sometimes it's better to be underestimated," Lady Gisela interrupted. "I realized long ago that I see our world differently than others do. I've never been fooled by the Council's grandstanding and self-congratulating. And I knew if I wanted to change anything, I'd have to be careful. Avoid scrutiny as much as possible. Work in secret. Until the optimal moment."

"And that moment is now?"

"I wish."

She tapped her finger along the top of her silver box, and Sophie noticed a symbol etched into the metal: two crescents, forming a loose circle around a glowing star.

Gisela had stamped the same symbol onto a letter she'd

made Keefe deliver—to a human man she'd murdered soon after, along with his daughter.

"We're getting close," Gisela murmured. "And we'll be even closer once I recruit a Flasher and a Shade. Then I just need to solve the final riddle. . . ."

Lord Cassius dragged a hand down his face. "Do you realize how insane you sound?"

"Do you realize how ignorant *you* sound?" She snapped her fingers, making the silver box disappear. "I'm not the one who started any of this! The Council did that *ages* ago when they took away a tremendous source of power and then tried to bury any proof of its existence. We've been stifled for millennia! All I'm trying to do is expose them—and take back what we've been denied. Give our son—and our world—the future we should've had all along. And you agreed with me! That's why you took those serums—"

"What serums?" he interrupted. "I don't remember taking anything."

"Of course you don't. Just like you won't remember any of this."

Lord Cassius's eyes widened. *"You've been erasing my memories?"*

"*I* haven't. My Washer has—and don't look so betrayed. It's better this way! The hardest part of this process is living the lie. Measuring every word—every thought—every mood. I've spared you those headaches. A few hours from now you'll be back to blissful ignorance, and I'll—"

"If you think I'm going to let you—"

"You don't *let* me do anything, Cassius. But if it makes you feel better to think that, go right ahead." She tucked another loose strand of hair back into her bun—and this time Sophie noticed a soft blue glint.

It was hard to tell from the blurry image, but Sophie was pretty sure it was the starstone hairpin that Lady Gisela used to access her Nightfall facility.

"The truth is," Gisela continued, "I'm so far ahead of you, you'll never be able to keep up. But you don't need to. I'm taking care of everything."

He snorted a bitter laugh. "You expect me to trust you after you've admitted to experimenting on our son, scheming against the Council, erasing my memories, *and* hiding an ability?"

"Well done! I've been wondering how much of this conversation you actually understood. I believe that means it's time to wrap it up. Usually I use tea, but I think we'll need something stronger this time." She snapped her fingers, making a folded blue handkerchief appear in her hand. "Actually, before I do this, I should probably make sure you haven't learned something useful during any of your assignments from the Council. So here's one final question for you. Have you ever heard of Elysian?"

Lord Cassius frowned. "Is that a star?"

"So that's a no, then. I figured as much—but it couldn't hurt to double-check."

"Stay back," he warned as she moved toward him.

"Oh, Cassius, it's so much easier when you don't resist." She lunged, ducking neatly under his flailing arms and spinning around behind him, pressing the handkerchief over his mouth and nose as she pinned him with her free hand.

Sophie's stomach twisted and her eyes burned as the sweet smell of sedatives turned the memory dimmer and blurrier until everything was a swirl of inky black.

The soundtrack faded to a low ringing tone. But Sophie could still make out Lady Gisela's final whisper.

"Don't fight it. This will all be over soon enough."

FIVE

Wow.

It was the only word Sophie could come up with.

What else was she supposed to say after watching a memory like that?

I don't need your pity, Lord Cassius told her.

It's not pity, she promised.

She doubted she could ever feel sorry for Lord Cassius.

But she was surprisingly . . . impressed.

You really have no idea how you stopped the Washer from erasing everything? she asked as her consciousness drifted back to the main cavern of Lord Cassius's mind—which seemed even messier and louder than it'd been earlier.

Not really. My best guess is that Gisela's candor about how she was planning to erase everything switched on some sort of defense mechanism and made my subconscious protect whatever it could.

Sophie had never heard of something like that. But it sounded plausible. *I'll have to ask Mr. Forkle—*

I'd prefer that you didn't. In fact, I'd prefer you keep this memory to yourself as much as possible. I'm sure there are certain revelations you'll feel the need to share—but that can be done without replaying a moment that's very . . . personal.

Sophie was pretty sure he meant *painful.* And she couldn't blame him for wanting a little privacy.

I'll stick with the essentials, she assured him.

Thank you. The noise in his head faded, and the flickering memories started sorting back into piles, as if he was slowly recovering a bit of mental order. *And whatever you do, please don't share any of this with my son.*

Normally Sophie had the same instinct when it came to protecting Keefe from his mom's awfulness. But . . .

Some of the things Lady Gisela said might help him understand his new abilities, she reminded him. *Plus, he needs to know there's a third step to stellarlune so he can prepare.*

Prepare. The thought sounded like a snort. *Do you honestly think he can prepare for whatever my wife is planning?*

What's he supposed to do? Give up? Stand outside Candleshade with a sign that says "I'm here, Mommy—come and get me"?

You know, for a smart girl, you can be incredibly foolish.

Particularly when it comes to my son. You get so caught up in your worries that you lose sight of what will truly benefit him.

And what's that?

At the moment? It's staying hidden, so the rest of us can focus on finding my wife without any distractions.

Distractions, Sophie repeated, wishing she could pick up the word and smack his brain with it. *Keefe is NOT a distraction.*

Of course he is! Think of the things you could be doing instead of leaping around the planet trying to find him.

"I gotta say, this whole mental talky-talky thing is getting pretty boring," Ro announced. "How about you switch to out-loud voices so the rest of us can hear what's making Blondie all rage-y!"

"Let me know if you need help," Sandor added.

"I don't," Sophie told him, twisting to stretch her back. Crouching on the edge of his chaise was *not* comfortable. "We're almost done."

Are we? Lord Cassius asked. *And here I thought you still had so much to learn.*

"Oooh, I don't know what he just said," Ro told her, "but I see those clenched fists, Blondie. If you want me to punch him for you, just say the word!"

Lord Cassius sighed. *I'm simply trying to do what's best for my son. Being a parent isn't easy. It involves making impossible choices all the time—and yes, I can feel that you're ready to point out my mistakes. I won't deny that I've made many. But that doesn't mean there aren't also times when I'm right—times when my objective approach to situations—*

You mean your heartless approach, Sophie cut in.

No, my OBJECTIVE approach—which allows me to see things that others, closer to the situation, miss. If you don't believe me, ask yourself why I volunteered to show you this memory.

Sophie had actually been wondering about that. Best theory she could come up with was *You wanted to see if I'd tell you anything about Elysian.*

I suppose that might've been a small motivation—and I definitely noticed the way you reacted to the term. Clearly you've heard it before.

Maybe I have—maybe I haven't.

Oh, you absolutely have.

He was right, of course, but Sophie wasn't about to admit it—and not just because she wanted to annoy him. Any confirmation would probably be treason, since she'd learned the word from a Forgotten Secret stored in Councillor Oralie's cache.

Relax. I never expected you to share—though I can also feel enough confusion to tell that you know little beyond the name. So no, Elysian wasn't my reason for revealing this memory. I decided to share because it raises an important possibility. One you need to consider—even though I know you'll resist.

And what's that?

Well . . . I'm assuming that Keefe's new abilities are somewhat unstable—correct? The commands certainly sounded as if they were. And the others must be even worse to make Keefe run off.

What's your point?

Only this: If his abilities are as volatile as I'm assuming, there's a good chance that's because my wife's plan is still incomplete. Perhaps after her third step—

ARE YOU KIDDING ME? Sophie cut in. *Are you seriously going to suggest that we let her FINISH?*

We may have no choice. It might be the only way that Keefe will ever be able to function properly.

Or it'll kill him!

Did it kill you when you allowed the Black Swan to reset your abilities?

It ALMOST did—and that was different.

How? Project Moonlark was an experiment. So is stellarlune—regardless of what Gisela may like to claim. And just as your creators were the only ones who knew how to help you when things went awry, Gisela may very well be the only one who can help Keefe.

"You're getting pale again," Ro told Sophie. "Seriously, just let me punch him a few times. It'll make everyone feel better!"

"I'm fine," Sophie said, even though she totally wasn't.

Lord Cassius couldn't be right . . .

. . .

. . .

. . . could he?

We won't know until we find my wife—or we learn more about this third step she's planning. Don't you think focusing on those would be a better use of your time than some foolish attempt to drag Keefe somewhere he doesn't want to be?

And how do you propose we find Gisela? Sophie countered. *I don't hear an actual plan for that—or for how we're supposed to learn more about stellarlune.*

Well, we probably could've learned quite a bit from that hideout you just destroyed, he noted. *Yes, I've heard about that. The Collective contacted me, so I'll be prepared for any possible retaliation. They're warning all the members of our order.*

Sophie's insides shriveled.

She'd used Lady Gisela's Archetype as kindling without even reading it!

What if it'd mentioned something about stellarlune?

I'm not condemning you for the fire, if that's what you're assuming. Honestly, if I'd been in your position, I would've made the same choice.

Somehow that didn't make her feel any better.

"I don't like how long this is taking," Sandor decided, placing a heavy hand on Sophie's shoulder. "You should have your list of cities by now."

She should. But she'd forgotten all about it.

You can have the list if you want, Lord Cassius offered. *It's right here.*

The piles of memories rustled, and a single piece toppled toward her—different from the others. No color. No flashing movement. Just a gray, static image—a schematic of a path-finder, with each facet labeled in tiny black writing.

I can't read some of this, Sophie noted as she studied the detailed drawing.

Yes, well, we can't all have photographic memories, can we? And no, I don't have a copy of that diagram. The Council doesn't allow the path maps for blue crystals to leave their possession.

Then how did you use the pathfinder?

My assignments were all to places I was able to remember.

What about Lady Gisela? How would she have known where she was going?

She wouldn't have. I'd wager she used the pathfinder much like Keefe is doing now, selecting random facets and making notes of the places she visited. You can do the same, of course. Lose days or weeks—and likely still not find him. Or you can choose the smarter play.

Her skin bristled at his smugness—and her stubborn side wanted to grab Ro and Sandor and teleport to the first place on the list.

But the more she stared at the schematic, the more the tiny writing seemed to blur.

There were so many cities.

So.

Many.

Cities.

And even if they picked the right one, there was no guarantee they'd be able to find Keefe among the millions of humans.

So you CAN see reason, Lord Cassius thought. *And before you go changing your mind just to spite me—*

I haven't made up my mind! Sophie argued.

Yes, you have. I can feel your resignation. And your heartache.

There's no heartache!

Interesting that you would choose that emotion to deny . . .

"If you won't let me punch him, will *you* at least knock him around a little?" Ro asked. "I can tell you're dying to."

Sophie cracked her knuckles.

But she kept her fists at her sides.

You know I'm right, Miss Foster. Don't let your doubt stop you from making the wise choice. Let Keefe take care of himself. It's what he wants.

Right. He WANTS to be all alone in a world he doesn't understand.

Of course he does. Do you really think the Lost Cities are a happy place for him after everything he's been through? I'm sure he's glad to finally escape.

Sophie's stomach twisted.

Is that what Keefe was doing?

Escaping?

He *had* wrapped up his letter by telling her, *It'll be better for everyone.*

She hadn't considered that he might've been including himself when he said that.

Let him go, Lord Cassius told her. *He's better off where he is. And he can handle himself.*

How can you be so sure?

He sighed, and his mind rumbled again—shaking and shaking and shaking, until several dim memories rose up from the shadows.

Sophie's chest tightened as she watched the scenes from Keefe's childhood.

So many tears.

So many lectures.

So little warmth or support or love.

I'll only say this once, he told her, *and I'll deny it if you ever bring it up again. But . . . if there's one thing I know about my son, it's that he's a survivor. And if he could endure more than a decade at Candleshade with his mother and me, he can handle anything the humans throw at him. Let him take care of himself. He's been doing it his whole life.*

SIX

"LET ME GET THIS STRAIGHT," RO SAID as she followed Sophie down the moonlit path that wove through Havenfield's creature-filled pastures. "Five minutes in Lord Creepypants's head and suddenly we're *not* going after Hunkyhair?"

"It was far more than five minutes," Sandor grumbled. "But I'm glad you've come to your senses."

Sophie ignored him. "I still have the list of cities if we need it," she told Ro. "But . . . we're never going to find him that way."

"Not with *that* attitude!" Ro jumped in front of her. "Where's that Foster ferocity I adore? Come on, if you're powerful enough to do that crazy-fast running thing you keep doing, dragging

Sandor and me along with you like we weigh less than my tiniest daggers as you launch us in and out of that dark void, you are powerful enough to track down Sir Sulks-a-Lot!"

Sophie sighed. "It doesn't work that way. Trust me, I hate this as much as you do. But . . . I've also realized that Keefe will probably be safer if he stays hidden."

"*Probably*? You're giving me *probably*?"

Sophie stared up at the night sky, focusing on the twinkling stars. "Probably is all we really have anymore."

"Oh, how powerful. How poetic." Ro made a bunch of gagging noises. "Come on, Blondie! Let's call this what it is! You're giving up on our boy!"

"No, I'm not!" Sophie scooted around Ro, needing to keep moving. "I just realized there are definitely reasons why Keefe's better off being far away from here right now. And there are other things we can focus on that will do a lot more to help him."

Ro leaped in front of her again. "Like *what*? And if you say 'finding the Neverseen,' you can expect a great big *THAT'S NEVER GONNA HAPPEN!* And if you say 'research,' I swear, I'm going to—"

"I'm not saying anything—yet!"

"Greeeeeeeeeeeaaaaaaaaaaat. So you don't actually have a plan, but you'd still rather do nothing than—"

"I'm not doing *nothing*!" Sophie tried to shove past Ro, but Ro knocked her back with her extra-long ogre arms.

"Do not touch my charge!" Sandor warned, unsheathing his sword as he dragged Sophie behind him.

"Bring it on, Gigantor!" Ro drew two of her daggers. "She pushed me first."

"STOP!" Sophie begged, wrenching free from Sandor so she could stand between them.

"Not until you give me some actual answers! I don't get it— you were the one with the big panicky speech about how our boy will never survive on his own in Humanland. And now you're going to abandon him?"

"I'm not *abandoning* him. I'm just . . . admitting I might have overreacted a bit. The Forbidden Cities are complicated and confusing, but Keefe's a quick thinker. And he's a survivor. He also begged me not to come after him—"

"Yeah, well, since when do we listen to that weirdo?"

Sophie closed her eyes, needing a moment to clear her head.

She was getting a little too tempted to blast Ro with one of her red-lightning Inflictor beams.

"Close your eyes all you want—I'll still be standing right here, judging you!" Ro informed her.

"I'm sure you will."

Sophie took a long, slow breath.

Then another.

And another.

"Now I'm judging you *and* deciding which bacteria to slip into your next beverage," Ro felt the need to tell her. "The one that causes fire farts? Or the one that causes burps of doom?"

"Not on my watch!" Sandor snarled.

"Eh, you'll be too busy drooling foam," Ro countered.

Sophie rubbed her temples. "You know what? If you want to search for Keefe, no one's stopping you! I'll even give you the list Lord Cassius gave me."

"Oh, *there's* a brilliant plan. I'm sure it won't cause any problems, having an ogre pop out of the ground around tons of humans. Definitely wouldn't violate any treaties! Besides, I travel slower than you do."

"Then I guess you're going to have to trust me."

"Maybe I would if you'd give me a reason to!"

"I'm working on that, okay?"

Sophie stomped past Ro, heading toward her favorite place to think. Sitting under the wispy branches of Calla's Panakes tree always gave her a special kind of clarity—and the twin baby alicorns snoozing in the soft, flower-dusted grass were a definite bonus.

"Sparkly horse snuggle time?" Ro grumbled when she noticed where Sophie was going. "*That's* your plan?"

It wasn't—but it did give Sophie an idea. "Actually, I need to talk to Silveny."

The mama alicorn was busy grazing in a nearby pasture, but she raised her shimmering head when she heard her name.

FRIEND! SOPHIE! FLY!

I wish, Sophie transmitted, imagining the look on Ro's face if she jumped on Silveny's back and soared far, far away. *Right now, I need your help.*

Silveny trotted closer. *FRIEND! SOPHIE! HELP!*

She nuzzled her velvet-soft nose into Sophie's neck, and Sophie leaned against her, trailing her hands through the silky strands of her mane. *I need you to try transmitting to Keefe.*

She paused, knowing Silveny would interrupt with a brain-rattling *KEEFE! KEEFE! KEEFE!*

Yes! she said when Silveny finished. *Call for him just like that—but transmit as far as you can, okay? Like you do when you need to reach me and don't know where I am. His mind is different than mine since he's not a Telepath. But he should be able to pick up a transmission if it's loud enough—and no one is louder than you.*

Silveny stepped back and angled her head, studying Sophie with her gold-flecked brown eyes. *KEEFE GONE?*

Sophie nodded. *He ran off this afternoon.*

Silveny let out a screechy whinny. *KEEFE SAFE?*

I don't know. I hope so, but . . .

She tried to shut down her brain—tried to stop it from flashing through nightmare images of Keefe passed out in a ditch or locked behind bars. But Silveny saw them anyway and flapped her wings like she wanted to start scouring the planet.

You can't, Sophie told her. *He's hiding with humans.*

HELP! KEEFE! FRIEND! Silveny argued, flapping harder.

But then she glanced at her tiny twin babies, and her mind

filled with memories of all the times she'd had to flee for her life to avoid human hunters or trappers.

She hung her head and tucked her wings.

I know, Sophie said, gently stroking Silveny's fur. *I'm worried about him too. That's why I need you to transmit to him. He'll ignore me because he doesn't want me coming after him—but I'm hoping he won't ignore you.*

Keefe would probably worry something was seriously wrong if he suddenly heard Silveny calling for him. Plus, Sophie wasn't sure it was possible for anyone to ignore the exuberant alicorn when she really set her mind on getting their attention.

Silveny studied Sophie again, and Sophie's head filled with images of Keefe flashing his trademark smirk and tossing his artfully mussed hair and calling Silveny Glitter Butt—but a grayish sort of sadness tinted each of the memories.

I miss him too, Sophie said, resting her head against Silveny's cheek.

Silveny snuffled. *SOPHIE OKAY?*

I'm trying to be. But I'll feel a lot better if you can make contact with him, so I can make sure he's safe.

SAFE! SAFE! SAFE! Silveny agreed. *KEEFE! KEEFE! KEEFE!*

The last chant was so loud, Sophie could feel the words vibrating all the way to her bones.

Perfect! she told Silveny, stepping back to get a little space. *Keep doing that as much as you can. Hopefully it'll make him reach out to me to find out what's going on. Or who knows? He may even let you into his mind, and you'll be able to ask where he is.*

HOPE! HOPE! HOPE! Silveny cheered. *FIND! KEEFE! SAFE!*

She followed that with another round of *KEEFE! KEEFE! KEEFE!*

Then another.

And another.

Wynn and Luna soon joined in, galloping circles around Sophie as they transmitted. Their baby calls weren't nearly as loud as their mom's, but they were the most adorable *Keefe-Keefe-Keefes* ever.

"Okay," Sophie said, fighting the urge to tug on her eyelashes as she spun around to face Ro, "I'm having the alicorns try transmitting to Keefe since they'll have a way better chance of getting his attention. Hopefully they'll figure out how to make contact soon and either find out where Keefe is or at least pass on some messages from us."

Ro re-sheathed her daggers. "Well . . . I suppose that's a *start*—but that better not be your whole plan!"

"It isn't."

A salty ocean breeze whipped through the pastures, and Sophie rubbed her arms, partially for warmth and partially so she'd have something to do with her angsty energy.

She hated that Lord Cassius had made some valid points— and she really hated the idea of leaving Keefe on his own. And she really really *really* hated the way Ro kept staring at her.

So much judgment. And anticipation. And *pressure*.

It wasn't fair!

She didn't hear Ro coming up with any brilliant ideas or solutions.

Besides . . . Keefe did *beg* her not to come after him.

He'd even told her . . .

"Wait," Sophie said, pulling Keefe's note out of her pocket—and keeping a very tight grip on the paper as she reread the part she'd just remembered. She checked it three more times before she whispered, "I . . . might actually know where he went."

She shoved the letter back into her pocket and took off running, ignoring Ro's and Sandor's demands for an explanation—and Grady's and Edaline's startled greetings—as she raced into Havenfield's mansion and bolted upstairs.

She stumbled into her room, heading straight to her desk and yanking open one of the drawers.

"Okay, Blondie—spill it," Ro demanded as she burst into the bedroom, huffing to catch her breath. "What's going on?"

"And know that I'm blocking your path to the Leapmaster!" Sandor called from the hall.

"I don't need it!" Sophie called back as her fingers closed around the small silver gadget she'd been searching for. "I have this!"

She spun around to face Ro and held out her hand with a flourish.

"Oh good, another talky-square thing," Ro muttered.

"A *special* talky-square thing!" Sophie corrected. "I'm only allowed to use it in an emergency—but I think this counts, don't you?"

She hugged the Imparter to her chest and made her way over to her bed, collapsing onto the pile of pillows.

Ro flopped down beside her. "Soooooooooo . . . care to explain why you're suddenly all confident and smiley? Otherwise I'm going to assume it's because you just reread my favorite line in Hunkyhair's letter."

Sophie rolled her eyes. "No, I reread a *different* line. The one that says, 'I want to make sure you understand who you'd be putting in danger.' Right after that he wrote, 'I'm going to be hiding the same way the Black Swan hid you,' so I thought that was his way of making it clear he'd be hiding with humans. But now I'm wondering if the 'who' meant a very specific person."

"*Who?*" Ro demanded.

Sophie hugged the special Imparter a little tighter. "My sister."

SEVEN

"AMY FOSTER," SOPHIE WHISPERED, hoping she was using the right name.

Her sister had become Natalie Freeman after Sophie was brought to live in the Lost Cities. And she'd been given another new name after the Neverseen took her parents hostage and their lives had to be erased and relocated *again*—but that identity had been kept completely secret.

Thankfully the Imparter must've been programmed to work with any of Amy's aliases, because despite a long pause, Amy's familiar face flashed across the screen.

Her curly brown hair looked extra wild, and her green eyes had a tiny stress crinkle between them—but it was *her*.

The only person from Sophie's human life who remembered her, thanks to a very special arrangement with the Council.

"Sophie?" Amy asked. "Sorry, I was with Mom, so it took me a second to get somewhere I could talk."

Mom.

Sophie had such a complicated relationship with that word.

Sometimes she used it for Edaline—but not very often. Probably because she'd used it for her human mother for twelve years before having her existence permanently erased.

Or maybe it was because of the genetic mother she was trying *super* hard not to think about.

"How's . . . your mom doing?" Sophie asked, stumbling a little as she added the "your" to the question. For some reason it felt like she should start making that distinction.

If Amy noticed the change, she didn't acknowledge it. "She's good—though she made me go shopping with her today, and I swear, if she comes at me with one more frumpy dress and tells me how pretty I'll look in it, I'm going to barricade myself in this fitting room forever! Don't worry, there's no one else in here. Pretty sure no one actually shops in this store. I mean, look at these things!"

She turned her Imparter toward a wall hung with at least a dozen much-too-colorful, much-too-flowery dresses—which made Sophie incredibly grateful for her tunics and leggings.

"Why are you dress shopping?" she asked.

Ro cleared her throat. "Can we save the sister bonding session for another time?"

"Who's that?" Amy craned her neck, trying to see behind Sophie. "Whoa—what is that thing?"

"Um, did you just call me a *thing*?" Ro snapped.

Amy covered her mouth. "Sorry! Human mistake! I've just never seen . . . uh . . ."

"An ogre princess," Ro finished for her, tracing one of her bloodred claws along the tattoos on her forehead. "Also the deadliest warrior you'll ever meet."

Somewhere down the hallway, Sandor snorted.

"Ro is Keefe's bodyguard," Sophie explained—which reminded her why they were having this conversation. "Is he there? We really need to talk to him."

"Keefe?" Amy repeated, her lips curling into a grin. "He's the supercute blond guy you picked up cookies for, right? The one who kept staring at you all intense when I met him, like you were the only person that mattered to him in the entire universe?"

Someone coughed near the doorway.

It was probably Grady, maybe Edaline too, but Sophie decided she'd rather not know who was eavesdropping.

"He *doesn't* stare at me like that," she said, hoping her cheeks weren't blushing too badly.

It didn't help that Ro kept cackling beside her.

Sophie cleared her throat. *"Anyway* . . . yeah, that's Keefe. I need to know if he's there—even if he told you not to tell me."

Amy shook her head. "Sorry. I haven't seen him."

"You're *sure*?"

"Yep! The only guys at this mall are, like, a hundred years old—or the biggest nerds ever—which is super depressing, by the way. I swear, you have no idea how lucky you are, getting to be around so many gorgeous boys all the time. I don't know how you haven't dated any of them—or *have* you?"

"She tried with Fitzy," Ro answered for her. "But then she realized he was too boring, so they broke up."

"That's *not* what happened!" Sophie argued—over lots more coughing from the doorway. "We didn't really date. We just sort of . . . liked each other . . . openly. But then it got super complicated, so we decided to focus on being friends."

She didn't bother explaining that not having her genetic parents in her registry file made her unmatchable—or that Fitz had tried not to let that bother him, but it clearly did.

"Why are we talking about this?" Sophie asked, fighting the urge to rub her chest, where her heart felt like it was scraping and stabbing her lungs. She kept trying to "get over" what happened. Sometimes she even thought she had. But her heart still turned sharp and heavy every time she thought about it.

"Because it's fun watching you get all red and fidgety!" Amy told her.

"Plus, there's a chance our boy is somewhere nearby, listening to this conversation," Ro added before she raised her voice to a shout. *"Hear that, Hunkyhair? Get your overdramatic butt back here! Your girl is single—and the Great Foster Oblivion is over! This is what you've been waiting for!"*

"Hunkyhair?" Amy asked, raising one eyebrow as Sophie contemplated smothering herself with her blankets. "Great Foster Oblivion?"

"Never mind," Sophie mumbled, sinking deeper into her pillows. "Just . . . if Keefe shows up, I need you to hail me immediately, okay? In fact, he may be hiding back at your house. When you get home, will you check?"

"Sure," Amy said slowly. "Um . . . should I be worried about this?"

"About Keefe?" Sophie asked, realizing how the whole "hiding" thing probably sounded. "Not at all. He's just . . . going through something right now, and he ran away thinking it'd be safer—"

"But he's *wrong*," Ro jumped in, elbowing Sophie. "We can agree on that again, can't we, Blondie?"

"I don't really know," Sophie admitted. "That's why I need to talk to him."

"I'll definitely keep an eye out," Amy promised as Ro heaved an enormous sigh. "What makes you think he's coming here?"

"He said something in his letter that kinda sounded like he might be—though now that I'm thinking about it, I don't know how he'd get there. The nearest city he could leap to is still a few hours away, and it's not like he has any money to get a ride. Plus, I don't think he even knows where you live."

And now that she'd pieced that together, her hope went *poof!*

"You okay?" Amy asked as Sophie pulled a few pillows over her face.

She wallowed in the dark for a few seconds before she forced herself to sit back up. "I'm fine. I'm just worried about him. There's . . . a lot going on."

"I bet." The crinkle between Amy's eyebrows got a whole lot deeper. "The last time I saw you—well, not the time you stole my E.L. Fudges, the time *before* that—things sounded pretty intense."

Sophie nodded, trying not to relive too much of the day Mr. Forkle returned her and Amy's missing memories. That was the day she'd learned that she'd once accidentally inflicted on her sister—and that her inflicting was malfunctioning. She'd also been given the *wonderful* news that she had to let Mr. Forkle almost kill her again if she wanted her abilities to work properly.

He'd been right, of course. She now had way more power and control—which dredged up the awful, terrifying, impossible-to-answer question.

Was Lord Cassius right about Keefe needing the third step to stellarlune?

She tried to imagine explaining the possibility to Keefe.

Would he shout?

Cry?

Throw things?

She wouldn't blame him if he did. There were so many horrible unknowns.

How would it change him?

Would he survive?

How could they even make it happen without giving Lady Gisela everything she wanted?

"You don't have to tell me what's going on," Amy said quietly. "I'm sure it has to do with a bunch of evil elves trying to prove they're smarter than everyone by doing terrible stuff."

"I like this girl," Ro decided. "Just don't call me a 'thing' again." ·

"I won't," Amy promised. "But . . . I am a little curious about something—and I get it if you can't tell me, Sophie. I just thought I'd ask, because I've been wondering about it ever since it happened. Is any of what's going on connected to the missing islands?"

"What missing islands?" Sophie, Ro, Sandor, Grady, and Edaline all asked in unison.

Amy blinked. "So that wasn't the elves?"

"I have no idea what you're talking about." Sophie glanced at Grady as he made his way closer. "Do you?"

"Not at all," he admitted.

"Huh. I guess it really is a fluky nature thing like everyone keeps saying," Amy mumbled. "It just sounded a lot like the story you told me, about how elves sank Atlantis. So I figured elves had to be behind this, too."

Sophie and Grady shared another look.

"What exactly happened?" Grady asked.

"Well . . . there were these three huge tsunamis that hit out of nowhere, and once the ocean calmed back down, three islands were gone."

"*Gone?*" Sophie repeated. "Were people hurt?"

Amy shook her head. "That's the good part. The islands were all small and uninhabited, so I guess it's not *that* huge of a deal. The news story just caught my attention because it sounded like something elves might be involved with, and I'm always keeping an eye out for stuff like that. I want to be able to prepare if something big is going down."

"Smart," Sophie said as her stomach churned and churned. "We should check with the Council—and the Black Swan."

"I will," Grady promised. "But I feel like I would've heard something about this if it was connected to anything."

"Unless it was the Neverseen," Sophie argued, "and no one was paying attention because it happened to human lands, and no one cares about those."

"I wouldn't say *no one* cares," Grady countered. "The Black Swan certainly keeps a close eye on everything—though of course it's possible that something escaped their notice. How long ago did this happen, Amy?"

"I know it's been a couple of weeks. If you need me to look up the exact date, I can."

Grady shook his head. "Shouldn't be necessary. And that

seems like a long enough stretch that I would've heard *something* if there was any significance to it."

"But you'll still check?" Sophie pressed.

"Of course."

"Were the islands near each other?" Edaline asked, moving to stand with Sophie and Grady.

"Not really—though scientists keep saying they were all above some sort of oceanic fault-line thing, and that's what caused the tsunamis. Maybe they're right. I just wasn't sure if it was more than that. Will you let me know if it does turn out to be something?"

Sophie nodded, trying to figure out how to rank this new worry.

There were so many problems—and so many people she cared about—she needed some sort of prioritizing system to tell her which to focus on.

"Sorry if it's a waste of time," Amy mumbled. "I may be totally wrong. I just—" She cut herself off and shouted over her shoulder, "No, Mom, I'm not going to show you what I'm trying on! And no, I don't need you to bring me any more dresses!"

She turned back, giving Sophie one of those *Isn't Mom ridiculous?* head shakes—and Sophie tried to return the smile. But it must have looked as empty as it felt.

Edaline squeezed her shoulder.

"I should go," Amy whispered. "Mom's wondering what's

taking me so long. And, ugh, I'm probably going to have to get one of these ugly things." She fished out a dress that at least had some pretty colors. "I'll still check the house when I get home and let you know if I see your boy. If he's there, I'll hide him in my room and feed him some Rice Krispies or something. I'm sure he'll love it if I show him Snap, Crackle, and Pop."

Sophie wished Keefe really could be with her sister, munching on cereal and laughing at the elves on the box, instead of wherever he was.

"Talk soon?" Amy asked.

"I hope so," Sophie whispered. "And . . . hail me if you notice anything else weird, okay? Even if you're not sure."

Amy nodded and slung the ugly dress over her shoulder. "Bye, sis. Flirt with all the cute boys for me!"

"Yep, definitely a fan of that girl," Ro said as the screen went blank. "Aaaaaaaaaaaaaand . . . now what?"

"Now I'll go check in with the Council and the Black Swan." Grady reached for Sophie's hand. "Yes, I'll tell you anything they tell me. And does this mean you're home for the night?"

"She *is*," Sandor answered for her, positioning his massive body in her doorway. "It's late. You have no plan. It's time to rest."

Sophie braced for another epic Ro argument—but Ro just burrowed under Sophie's blankets and said, "Fine. I guess a little sleep won't hurt. We'll call it 'regrouping.'"

"Wait—are you staying *here*?" Sophie asked as Ro tucked several daggers under her pillow.

"Of course! I'm not letting you out of my sight, Blondie. And thank goodness your bed is comfy, because there's no way I'm sleeping on that flowery floor! It's bad enough that I have to stare up at a bunch of dangling crystal stars. You elves and your sparkles."

Sophie glanced at Grady and Edaline, hoping one of them would have a solution for how to get the giant ogre out of her bed.

Sadly, they were too busy trying not to laugh.

"Where am I supposed to sleep?" she asked.

"Um, this bed is big enough to fit half a squadron," Ro reminded her.

It was.

But it looked a whole lot smaller at the moment.

Ro rolled her eyes. "Don't worry, I don't move in my sleep, so I'm not going to kick you—unless you annoy me. And I don't snore. Do you?"

"I . . ."

Sophie had no words.

"I could set you up outside under the Panakes," Edaline offered.

Sophie had been sleeping out there a lot, needing the fresh air and alicorn snuggles to help her relax. But she didn't want to be chased out of her room.

She also had a feeling Ro would follow her, so she said, "No, this is fine," and stalked into her bathroom to wash her face and brush her teeth and change into pajamas.

She took an extra-long time and wasn't surprised that Grady and Edaline were gone when she finally finished. But she'd been hoping Ro would be asleep.

No such luck.

"What happened to this poor creature?" Ro asked, pointing to the tiny imp snuggled into her palm. "These colors are ridiculous!"

Iggy was currently several shades of blue, green, and purple, with black tiger stripes cutting through.

"I have no idea," Sophie admitted. "I think Keefe gave him some elixirs when he dropped off his letter."

"Ah, so this is Funkyhair's 'something to remember me by.'" Ro scratched Iggy's cheeks, triggering his squeaky purr. "I think we can do better than this, don't you, little guy?"

Iggy responded with a room-rattling burp.

Ro coughed. "Woof, that is some potent breath you have, little dude. Remind me to scrape your tongue later so I can save some of the bacteria."

"Gross," Sophie mumbled, realizing she was going to have to stop staring at her bed and actually climb into it.

Ro grinned and held out Ella—the bright blue elephant that everyone knew Sophie couldn't sleep without. "Figured you were going to need something to snuggle—unless you want a real hug."

She stretched out her other arm, looking anything but cuddly in her metal corset and spike-rimmed metal diaper.

Sophie reached for Ella. "This is fine. I'm . . . fine."

"No, you're not."

She wasn't. But she was getting pretty used to that.

"Well, if you change your mind, let me know." Ro flopped back onto her pillow.

"You're really going to sleep in your armor?" Sophie had to ask.

"Better than sparkly alicorn pajamas—don't think I didn't notice those."

"I wasn't trying to hide them," Sophie said, clapping her hands to lower shades over all the windows. Which left her with nothing else to do except crawl into bed.

"Relax, I'm not going to stab you in your sleep or anything," Ro told her. "But I'm game for staying up all night gossiping about boys! You could tell me what really went down between you and the Fitzster—and then we can read Hunkyhair's letter over and over."

"Hard pass," Sophie grumbled.

"Boo—you're no fun!" Ro rolled to her side, and her metal corset creaked in ways that couldn't be comfortable—but she didn't seem to notice. "Wake me up if you change your mind."

"Not gonna happen." Sophie slid under the blankets and squeezed Ella tight as Iggy fluttered over to her pillow. "Um . . . good night."

Ro yawned. "Night, Blondie. Have fun dreaming about the Keefster."

Sophie hoped Ro was wrong, since those dreams would probably be nightmares.

And even though she knew he'd ignore her, she couldn't resist closing her eyes and sending him one transmission.

Please be safe, Keefe. Please be smart. And please come back as soon as you can.

The only answer was silence.

EIGHT

CHECK IT OUT, BLONDIE!"

Sophie squinted, trying to focus on the fuzzy purple-gray shapes in front of her—but her eyes were still much too sleepy.

"Clearly you're a grumpy riser," Ro noted. "Another thing you and Funkyhair have in common—but tough! Wake up! Wake up! Wake up!"

Ro yanked back Sophie's covers and dragged Sophie's pillow out from under her head.

Sophie grabbed another pillow and smacked her in the chest as Ro said, "There's that Foster feistiness I've been waiting for! And much as I'd enjoy pummeling you in an epic pillow war, we're wasting time! We have a plan to put together, some elf-y mysteries to solve, and a sulky boy to find! Plus, I'm starving. So get your scrawny butt up, throw on some clothes—maybe fix that hair because it's *not* cute at the moment—and let's do this! Oh, and what do you think of our new look?"

"Our?" Sophie asked, combing her fingers through some of her tangles as her eyes finally shifted into focus.

"Ta-da!" Ro held up Iggy with one hand and tossed one of her choppy pigtails with the other.

"You . . . match" was the only response Sophie could come up with.

Iggy's fur and Ro's hair were now deep shades of purple, blue, and gray, with each color fading into the next in an ombré effect. It reminded Sophie of the night sky, right before the stars appear—and it was definitely an improvement from the weird mermaid-tiger thing Iggy had going on before. But . . .

Keefe's final gift was gone.

Just like him.

"I thought about coloring your hair too," Ro said as Sophie focused on her tangles, hoping Ro wouldn't notice how watery her eyes were. "But then I wouldn't be able to call you Blondie anymore." .

"Where did you get the dye?" Sophie asked.

Ro patted her armored corset. "Secret pockets. I never go anywhere without pouches of microbes and packets of hair color. You know—the necessities."

"Uh-huh," Sophie said as Iggy flapped his batlike wings and flitted over to her shoulder.

He'd been so many colors at that point, she wasn't sure if anyone remembered what his natural fur even looked like. But he was always happy about each change—and he *really* seemed to love this one. He kept spinning in circles, trying to admire himself from every angle.

Sophie scratched his fuzzy ears and asked Ro, "How long have you been awake?"

"Long enough to thoroughly search this place for all your embarrassing secrets. But you disappoint me, Blondie! No juicy diaries! No love letters from Fitzy! Best I could find was *this.*"

She held up a charm bracelet covered in little dangling hearts, as well as the note that had come with it. "Who's Valin—and why have I never met this mysterious member of the Foster Fan Club?"

Sophie blinked.

She'd completely forgotten about Valin—and his awkward midterms gift.

"He goes to Foxfire," she mumbled. "Or he used to. I don't actually know where he is anymore. I haven't seen him since I was a Level Two."

"Is that because you broke his heart?" Ro asked, pointing to the *Love, Valin* signature on the card.

"*No!* If anything, he probably got freaked out by my kidnapping and started avoiding me."

She'd also been banished for a while—and almost died a bunch of times. So keeping up with the other kids at Foxfire had been kind of a challenge.

"*Or* Hunkyhair, Fitzy, and the Dexinator scared him off," Ro suggested. "I mean, that *is* some pretty steep competition."

Sophie tried to decide if she wanted to lunge for the bracelet or smack Ro with a pillow again. "Is this seriously why you woke me up at the crack of dawn?"

"Uh, hate to break it to you, but it's *way* past the crack of dawn." She tossed the bracelet into Sophie's lap and clapped her hands to raise the shades, letting in a flood of early-afternoon sunlight. "I let you sleep late because I also got an update from Gigantor this morning, and he told me about your little fire attack yesterday—high five for that, by the way. I thought you deserved a nice long rest after all that awesome butt-kicking. But you started making these pathetic little whimpery sounds, so I figured it was time for you to get up and *do* something instead of just having stress dreams. That's also why I made sure that Iggy and I look extra fierce—to show you we're not going to sit around moping about boys, or worrying about how those black-cloaked losers might be planning to retaliate. We're going to start making some actual progress—on *what*, I don't know yet. But we'll figure that out! So hop to it, Blondie. We've wasted enough daylight. Plus, like I said—I'm hungry!"

"Glad to hear it," Edaline called from the doorway. "I heard you were finally up, so I came to see if you two wanted any sweetberry swirls. I baked them fresh this morning."

She snapped her fingers, and a tray of huge, buttery pastries appeared on Sophie's bed. They looked like cinnamon rolls filled with some sort of reddish berries, and the tops were drizzled with cream and sprinkled with sugar.

"Delicious food mysteriously appearing from nowhere— now *that* is an elf-y talent I can get behind," Ro said, shoving an entire sweetberry swirl into her mouth. She sprayed crumbs everywhere as she warned Sophie, "Better dive in quick, or I'm eating all these myself."

Sophie couldn't even think about food.

She stumbled to her feet, needing to move as she told Edaline, "Lady Gisela is a Conjurer."

Edaline froze midsnap. "You're sure?"

Sophie nodded. "Lord Cassius showed me one of his memories yesterday—one she'd tried super hard to erase—and I watched her conjure something and admit she's been hiding the ability. I meant to tell you last night, but I got sidetracked."

"Why?" Ro asked with her mouth full of another sweetberry swirl.

"Um, because you threw a huge fit after I brought us to Havenfield instead of to a Forbidden City to search for Keefe," Sophie reminded her.

"No, I threw a fit because you abandoned our plan without discussing it with me, *and* without having another plan ready to go—but that's not what I meant. I meant why would Lady Evilskirts want to hide the ability? Seems like she'd want to show it off so everyone would know how fancy and powerful she is—assuming conjuring is useful for more than food delivery."

"It is," Edaline assured her. "Though it's also one of the more limited abilities. I can only work with physical things, and it doesn't give me any deeper knowledge or insights."

"Seems pretty useful to me," Sophie told her, thinking of the hundreds and hundreds of times she'd seen Edaline snap her fingers. "And Lady Gisela told Lord Cassius that she's hiding the ability because she wants to be underestimated."

Ro snorted more crumbs. "That's the most ridiculous thing I've ever heard! If you're *actually* strong and powerful, you don't need to be underestimated. That would be like me hiding my awesome muscles and acting like, 'Leave me alone, I'm so weak.' Forget that! I want everyone to *know* that if they mess with me, they're going to get a good pounding. Then the scrawny ones won't waste my time—and the strong ones will still get whooped because I'm amazing!"

"Yeah, well, this is Lady Gisela," Sophie reminded her. "Everything she does is sneaky."

"I think you mean wimpy," Ro muttered, stuffing her mouth with another sweetberry swirl.

"That too." Sophie turned back to Edaline. "How exactly does conjuring work again?"

Edaline snapped her fingers, making a bottle of Youth

appear in her hands. "Everything is connected by invisible energy strings, and Conjurers are able to feel those ties and tug on them with our minds, dragging what we want back and forth through the void—but we have to be able to visualize exactly where something is or we won't be able to move it."

She snapped her fingers again, and two bottles of lushberry juice appeared on the tray next to the sweetberry swirls.

Ro grabbed one and took a long swig. "I can see how that could give Gisela certain tactical advantages."

"Like what?" Sophie asked.

"Well, for one thing, she could conjure up weapons anytime—anywhere. Or better yet—conjure up some explosives. Think about it! One snap"—Ro snapped her fingers—"and anything she wants goes *boom*!"

Sophie really, really, *really* didn't want to think about that—but now she couldn't stop her mind from imagining the glittering elvin cities collapsing into piles of rubble. And then she realized something *much* scarier.

The same thing could happen at Havenfield—even with the goblin patrols everywhere.

One second everything could be bright and sunny. Animals grazing. Waves crashing.

Then some sort of explosive could appear out of nowhere and . . .

"Does conjuring work through force fields?" Sophie asked, wondering if Maruca was strong enough to form one around the entire estate. Probably not, since she hadn't manifested that long ago—but Sophie wasn't friends with any other Psionipaths.

Maybe the Council could ask one. . . .

"It depends on the force field—and the Conjurer." Edaline stepped closer, taking Sophie's hand before she could reach for her eyelashes. "I'm pretty sure I know what you're worrying about, Sophie. And I don't think you need to. None of the Neverseen's attacks have ever involved explosives."

"Yet," Ro countered. "That doesn't mean they aren't saving them for their grand finale. I know you elves are used to solving all your problems with your weird little talents or endless boring conversations, but that's not how you take over the world—and Gisela knows that. There's no way this ends without some death and destruction—you get that, don't you?"

Sophie sank down onto her bed, curling her knees into her chest.

It was a little easier to think about these kinds of horrors in a Sophie-ball.

Edaline sat beside her, wrapping an arm around her shoulders.

"Gisela went to great lengths to make sure no one knows she's a Conjurer," Sophie mumbled. "She has to be planning something huge—something *only* a Conjurer can do. And it must need to happen at a specific moment. Otherwise she would've revealed the ability by now. Think of how many times it could've changed the way everything went! She could've conjured up another net to stop us from escaping the first time she tried to steal Silveny, or—"

"Uh, couldn't she have just conjured up *Silveny*?" Ro interrupted.

Edaline shook her head. "Conjuring only works on inanimate objects—nothing living."

"Huh, I guess that's good news—though it would've been nice if you could've snapped your fingers and brought home the Keefster."

Edaline hugged Sophie a little tighter. "That *would* be nice."

"Except then Lady Gisela could snap her fingers and grab him too," Sophie felt the need to point out, even though it didn't really matter. "But . . . she *could* have conjured up a weapon on Mount Everest instead of having to jump off the mountain and retreat. Or she could've conjured up something to defend herself from Brant and Fintan, instead of getting all those shamkniv scars on her face. Or she could've conjured up the key to her cell and escaped the ogre prison way sooner—"

"Uh, the locks are the first of *many* defenses," Ro cut in. "I still don't understand how she got out—even with help from traitors. But whatever. Speaking of keys, I'm actually surprised she didn't conjure up those annoying metal puzzle pieces that Keefe spent hours and hours playing with. Didn't they turn out to be the key to that Archetype thing she wanted you all to get for her from Nightfall? And come to think of it, couldn't she have just conjured up the Archetype and saved everyone a lot of trouble?"

"Not if she couldn't picture exactly where those items were," Edaline reminded them. "Especially if she doesn't have a lot of practice using her ability. It took me years to learn what cues I needed to focus on so I'd be able to reach the things I need."

"Plus, I don't think she actually cared about her Archetype," Sophie added, mostly to herself. That was why she'd felt okay letting it burn with the rest of the storehouse.

Hopefully that wouldn't turn out to be a huge mistake.

"But she could've conjured up something to stop Linh from saving Atlantis," Sophie added. "Or something to restrain Tam in Loamnore after Glimmer set him free from his ethertine bonds. I could keep going, but I think you get my point—if she'd been using that ability, she would've had much bigger victories."

"Not necessarily," Edaline insisted. "For one thing, conjuring can drain tremendous amounts of energy if you don't do it right. But let's also not forget that if she's not in the habit of using the ability, it likely wouldn't occur to her to rely on it. How many times have you looked back at a situation and realized it could've gone differently if you'd used your abilities—or skills, for that matter—but didn't, because you spent so much of your life having to hide them?"

"Maybe," Sophie conceded. "But . . . Lady Gisela is way too calculating for her to not have a *good* reason for hiding the ability for this long. I mean . . . she probably manifested when she was a teenager. That's a *long* time to wait."

"I'm with Blondie on this one," Ro agreed, devouring the final sweetberry swirl and swiping the crumbs off her lips. "I'm sure she's holding out for some big, dramatic moment, when revealing the power will let her do something awful that no one will be expecting."

"Any idea what that could be?" Sophie asked, turning to face Edaline. "Can you think of any situations where being a Conjurer would give you a huge advantage? Especially if no one knows you are one?"

"It's hard to say. I would never use my ability for something like that." She snapped her fingers and made a second plate of sweetberry swirls appear. "But . . . I'll think about it."

"You'll need to *really* think like an evil, murdering psychopath," Ro warned. "Otherwise you'll never get anywhere. You have to get in her head—figure out what makes Gisela *Gisela*. In fact, let's see if we can get you to embody her a little better. Close those big blue eyes."

Edaline sighed but did as Ro asked.

"Good. Now tilt your chin up the same snotty way she does," Ro told her. "Set your jaw, and pull your hair back so tight, it looks like it's stretching your face. And remember: You used to be elf-y pretty, but now your skin is super wonky because of all the surgeries you had to cover up your scars."

Edaline nodded and twisted her amber hair into a

painful-looking bun as she sat up straighter, angling her nose toward the ceiling while turning her face slightly away from everyone.

The changes were subtle, but somehow she didn't look like the Edaline Sophie knew anymore.

She looked cold. And rigid. And angry.

"Perfect," Ro said. "Now try to imagine yourself insisting that everyone call you *Lady*—and correcting them if they don't. Imagine seething deep inside because everyone is less than you, but you can't show them your full greatness—yet. You have to wait for the right moment, knowing it will take years of planning and sacrifice. Imagine choosing to marry someone like Lord Cassius—"

"She chose him for his DNA," Sophie interrupted. "She wanted a powerful Empath."

"Yeah, but there have to be other powerful Empaths that are better than *that* guy. And she picked him *knowing* she'd have to kiss him."

Sophie groaned. "Ugh, can we please not talk about Lord Cassius and kissing?"

"Fine—let's talk about a more important piece to the Gisela puzzle. Imagine treating your son like an experiment. Planning and strategizing and manipulating everything about him—even before he was born—mostly so he can make *you* look better. Imagine watching him grow up, knowing what you're going to put him through. Lying to his face over and over. Erasing his memories if you slip. Then finally strapping him to a dwarven throne, slamming a crown on his head, and forcing a Flasher and a Shade to blast him with shadows and light until he's almost dead—all so he can fulfill his mysterious legacy."

"She only forced Tam," Sophie had to remind her—even though she'd kinda sorta started trusting Glimmer.

She also almost blurted out that Keefe might have one more step to endure in his mother's experiment. But it didn't feel right to share that news until she'd broken it to Keefe and let him decide what he wanted to do.

"That doesn't matter," Ro told her, leaning closer to Edaline. "Think about how patient you'd have to be. How cruel. How calculating. Then remember that everything you've done so far is part of a bigger plan—your chance to finally take control in some sort of epic climax. And ask yourself, how would conjuring help make your ultimate dream come true? What would you—and *only* you—be able to do?"

Edaline squeezed her eyes tight, and Sophie counted the passing seconds—but after only a hundred nineteen, Edaline shook her head and slumped into a slouch.

"I'll keep trying," she promised, untwisting her hair and letting it fall loose around her shoulders. "But it's not an easy question."

"It isn't," Ro agreed. "If it were, we'd have already figured it out and Lady Gisela would be dead."

Dead.

The word shouldn't have hit Sophie so hard.

She knew that was how this had to end.

But it sounded so . . . brutal.

"Don't worry, Blondie. When the time comes, I'll *happily* be the one to make sure she never breathes again," Ro promised. "You just need to find her for me and get me a clear shot—preferably before she does too much more damage."

"I'll try," Sophie and Edaline said together.

"You're gonna have to do more than *try*. We need an actual plan—not just the goal of making one. And believe me, I know how hard it is to do that, so let's take it one small step at a time. Maybe it'll help if we think of it more like a to-do list. What's one thing we can do right now that would actually be an accomplishment?"

Sophie sat on her hands so she wouldn't tug on her eyelashes. "Well . . . I guess I can check in with Silveny. See if she's made contact with Keefe yet."

"Works for me!" Ro said. "I also wouldn't mind chatting with some of your patrols, to make sure they actually know how to protect the borders of this place, in case the Neverseen are planning some revenge."

"My soldiers are *well* prepared for anything!" Sandor snapped from the doorway. "Even the things you were just discussing, in regards to this new ability. There's nothing capable of completely surprising me."

Ro grinned. "We'll see."

They argued about tactics the whole way down the stairs, and Sophie did her best to tune them out. Somehow it sounded like too much and not enough all at the same time. But as she stepped outside to find Silveny, she realized that Sandor's security patrols did at least need to improve their communicating. Because there were all her friends, standing among the pastures, waiting for her.

And they did *not* look happy.

NINE

WHAT'S GOING ON?" SOPHIE
asked, sprinting over to the group,
which had formed a large circle near
the stegosaurus enclosure.

She probably should've been embarrassed that all her
friends had perfectly styled hair and were wearing actual
clothes while she was a tangled mess in sparkly alicorn
pajamas—and it wasn't even morning. But she didn't care.
Because if Fitz, Biana, Dex, Marella, Wylie, Maruca, Tam,
Linh, *and* Stina were all there, something big must've happened.

And they seemed to be fighting about it.

Only their bodyguards noticed her approach, stepping back

to give the group more space as Sophie tried to make sense of what her friends were saying. Everyone was talking on top of each other, turning their words into garbled mush.

"Seriously, what happened?" she said, waving her hands, trying to get someone's attention.

When that still didn't work, Ro slipped her claws between her lips and made a screechy whistle that had everyone flailing to cover their ears—and sent the stegosauruses stampeding around their pasture.

"You're welcome," she told Sophie—or that's what Sophie assumed she said.

The loud ringing in her head and the pounding stegosaurus feet made it pretty hard to tell.

When Sophie could hear again, she waved the dust and dinosaur feathers away from her face and turned to Dex. "Is this about Keefe? Did you find him?"

Dex shook his head.

Biana peered behind Ro, like she expected Keefe to be hiding back there. "Why would he need to find him?"

"I'll take this one, Blondie!" Ro shoved her way into the center of the group circle. "Otherwise this is going to turn into an endless question-and-answer session—and no one has time for that. So here's what you need to know, okay? Hunkyhair ran away to some random human city to hide from his horrible mommy. We don't have a way to find him yet—but we're working on it."

She rested her hands on her hips and nodded, as if that ended the conversation.

Dozens and *dozens* of questions later, Ro had been forced to share every possible additional detail—though she thankfully avoided any mention of Rex being Talentless, or Keefe's ability to sense when people manifest.

She also didn't bring up Keefe's letter—or her favorite line in it—which felt like a small miracle. But it probably meant she was saving that bombshell for a particularly humiliating moment.

And the group took the Keefe-ran-away-again news better than Sophie would've expected.

Fitz said, "I've told Keefe a bunch of stories about the times I visited the Forbidden Cities when I was searching for Sophie—and Alvar also used to talk about his trips. So he knows a lot of tricks for how to survive over there."

Then Wylie added, "He can always light leap away if he gets in any trouble."

And that seemed to satisfy everyone that Keefe would be okay.

They still wanted him home, of course. But there was no pan-icked arguing about how to find him. No angsty fretting about what might happen. Most even seemed to think the freedom was exactly what Keefe needed at the moment.

A chance to find himself, after so many traumas and changes.

Sophie hoped they were right.

She had definitely come on board the Keefe-should-stay-hidden-for-now train—but that didn't mean that part of her wasn't still doubting the decision. She'd just choked back her lingering worries, letting them stew in the pit of her stomach with the rest of the anxieties she wasn't focusing on at the moment.

Which left one very important question.

"If you're *not* here about Keefe," she said, "will someone please tell me what's going on?"

Fitz cleared his throat, and his teal eyes shifted toward his boots. "Well . . . Biana and I reached out to Dex and Wylie and Linh and Marella and Maruca to warn them that the Neverseen might retaliate because you burned down their storehouse yesterday."

"Yeah, thanks for forgetting to warn *me*," Stina cut in, crossing her arms against her chest. "Fortunately, my *friends*"—she pointed her chin toward Linh, Marella, and Maruca—"made sure I knew what was happening, though my dad had already gotten a warning from the Black Swan. And nice job, Foster. Brilliant plan! Provoke the enemy for no reason!"

"*No reason?*" Sophie repeated, not even sure where to begin.

She pointed to the scars streaking across Biana's shoulders and arms, then to Fitz's leg, which still sometimes caused him to limp a little if he pushed himself too hard. Then she held up her right hand, which had been shattered in the same attack, and pointed to Tam's wrists, which were slightly discolored from the ethertine bonds that Lady Gisela had forced him to wear while he was her captive. "How many of us have to almost die—or be held hostage—before we can agree that the Neverseen deserve *anything* we can throw at them?"

"And how many of us are going to suffer *now*?" Stina countered. "Do you think they're just going to let this go?"

"Actually, I do," Ro cut in. "I mean, it's always smart to be prepared—but it's already been a day, and they haven't made a move yet, have they?"

"They're probably still figuring out the best target," Stina argued.

"Eh. I doubt it. Don't get me wrong—I'm sure they threw a tantrum when they first heard the news." Ro's eyes turned dreamy. "Oh, how I wish I could've been there! *But* . . . I'm betting that's the end of it—for now, at least. The Neverseen are all about their precious timelines and careful planning. And they're smart enough to know that if they retaliate, *we'll* retaliate, and they'll get stuck having to focus on defense instead of offense. So I think they'll sulk in their little hideouts for a few days—maybe even make a few threats trying to scare us. And then they'll get right back to work on their big, final strategy for world domination."

No one found that as comforting as Ro did.

It also didn't help that Sandor, Grizel, Woltzer, and Lovise had formed a goblin huddle, whispering much too loudly to each other about whether everyone in the group now needed their own personal bodyguard.

Sophie definitely understood everyone's fear. But she was a little surprised that so many of her friends looked . . . angry.

At *her*.

"You really think I shouldn't have burned down the storehouse?" she had to ask.

No one would meet her eyes.

"Wow," she mumbled.

"We know you *meant* well," Biana said carefully. "We're just . . . not sure it was the smartest decision. After all, we're not hidden like the Neverseen. They know who we are. Where we live. Who we care about."

"Basically, they know exactly how to hurt us, and now you've given them a perfect reason to lash out," Fitz added.

"You think they need one?" Sophie asked. "Did they have a reason to send ogres to my house and almost kill Grady and Edaline? Or to show up while you and I were training and shatter our bones? Or to drag Wylie from his bedroom in the Silver Tower and torture him?"

Wylie's dark skin turned slightly ashen with the reminder, and Maruca reached for her cousin's hand.

"This was different," Fitz insisted. "This was you basically telling them we're ready to fight."

"Aren't we?" Sophie asked, glancing from her friends to

their bodyguards and back again. "Don't we have to be—or this is never going to end?"

"I don't know," Biana admitted—though her crisp Vacker accent still gave the words a slight air of haughtiness. "But I *do* know that you also destroyed a mountain of evidence and intelligence, which probably would've told us everything we needed to take down the Neverseen."

"And I'm sure you're going to say, 'We don't know that!'" Marella added. "And that's true. We don't know if any of it was super valuable. *But* . . . that's kinda the point, isn't it? You torched it, so now we'll never know what we lost, or how it could've helped us."

"I didn't destroy *everything*," Sophie argued, glancing at Tam, wondering why he was standing there, hiding behind his long, silver-tipped bangs.

He'd been with her in the storehouse.

He'd heard all the reasons she'd started that fire.

"Tam and I grabbed as much as we could carry," she said, hoping it would draw him into the conversation.

It didn't.

But it did make Stina demand to know, "And what was that?"

Sophie had to think for a second. "Lots of scrolls. And a bunch of vials and elixirs."

No one looked impressed.

Tough crowd.

"I think you're also forgetting that destroying everything in the storehouse was a huge blow for the Neverseen!" Sophie reminded them. "I took out twenty big barrels—which had to be their entire supply of soporidine. And I burned all kinds of other stuff they were obviously storing for a reason. I even used their spare cloaks for kindling! So, yeah, I'm sure I destroyed some stuff that might've been useful—but that's the thing. Now *they* can't use it. Isn't that more important?"

Silence followed.

If it was a movie, the soundtrack would make that *womp, womp, wooooomp* sound.

Sophie crossed her arms and held everyone's gaze. "If you'd been there, you'd understand."

"But we *weren't* there," Fitz said quietly. "You wouldn't let us go with you."

"Is *that* what this is about?" she asked. "You're mad that I made you stay behind?"

"Don't make it sound like we're pouting because we didn't get to go on some cool adventure!" Fitz told her. "We're a *team*. We all share the same risk—so we should also get to share in the decision-making. But you took over, decided who was coming with you, and told the rest of us that we were only allowed to worry if you were gone longer than fifteen minutes. And then you showed up after twelve minutes, smelling like smoke and holding a few scrolls and vials—which you immediately gave to Tiergan without even looking at."

"He has better places to hide them—and he promised to

share *everything* he learns," Sophie reminded him—then made a mental addition to her new to-do list.

Follow up with the Black Swan about the Neverseen stuff.

"Maybe he does," Fitz conceded, "and maybe Tiergan will keep us updated—but that doesn't change the fact that we're all in extra danger now, and what do we have to show for it?"

It would've been the perfect moment to pull out Kenric's and Fintan's caches—the reason she'd gone to the storehouse in the first place—and let all the Forgotten Secrets they'd now be able to access glint in the sunlight. But Sophie had left the tiny, marble-size gadgets in the pocket of yesterday's dirty tunic, balled up on the floor of her bathroom.

Not her smartest move.

Put the caches somewhere safe, she added to her to-do list before she mumbled, "It really was the right decision."

"I sure hope so," Biana told her. "But it still would've been nice if you'd at least discussed it with us before you set a giant fire."

"When was I supposed to do that? There wasn't time! We'd planned that mission all wrong—"

"Don't you mean *you'd* planned it wrong?" Stina corrected.

"I wasn't the only one who weighed in! And I guarantee, no one would've suggested the things we needed to do. We always think too small and too safe. If Glimmer hadn't—"

"And there it is!" Stina interrupted, pointing a very accusing finger in Sophie's face. "Now it all makes sense. Little Miss Neverseen told you to set that fire."

"Actually, she didn't," Tam said, apparently finding his voice. And he was right. Glimmer had seemed pretty shocked when Sophie sparked the flames.

But she'd also thought it was the right call.

Because it *was*.

"Glimmer helped me realize how shortsighted it would be to grab the caches and flee," Sophie clarified. "We should've gone there with an army and seized the storehouse—but we didn't think of that. And we didn't bring enough people to clear it out either. So the only good option left was to destroy everything to make sure it couldn't be used against us. Yes, it was scary. Yes, it may have consequences. And yes, it definitely wasn't a perfect decision. But guess what? It's also the first real victory we've had against the Neverseen. And if we want to keep winning, we're going to have to be ready to make a lot of imperfect decisions."

"Let me guess," Stina grumbled. "Glimmer told you that, too?"

Tam rolled his silver-blue eyes. "We get it! You don't trust Glimmer!"

"None of us should! That's why *we*"—Stina pointed to herself, Linh, Marella, and Maruca—"asked everyone to meet us here—though I still don't get why we had to go to Foster's house. This isn't Team Valiant—she's not in charge of this group, no matter how many moonlarks she scratches into the ground."

"That's not why I did that!" Sophie snapped, surprised Stina had even heard about the symbol she'd left behind at the store-house. "I just . . . wanted to send a message."

"Was the message 'I've decided I'm smarter than everyone else'?" Stina asked, proving why she and Sophie were never going to be friends.

"*No*. I wanted to show them I wasn't afraid of them any-more! That I'm not the same scared girl they've tried to kill over and over. I'm ready to fight back—and willing to do what-ever it takes to stop them."

Stina glanced at Linh, Marella, and Maruca. "Did anyone count how many times she just said 'I'? Had to be at least four—which seems like a lot for ten seconds, doesn't it? But I guess if you're 'the moonlark,' it's normal to think you're the queen of everything."

"If you want me to smack her for you," Ro leaned in and whispered—loud enough for everyone to hear, "I'd be happy to."

Sophie flashed Stina her coldest smile. "That won't be nec-essary."

She didn't care if Stina hated her.

But she didn't like how many of her friends were still avoid-ing eye contact.

Even Sandor and the other bodyguards looked uncomfortable.

"I'm not trying to be the leader," she assured everyone. "I even told Mr. Forkle that when we talked yesterday. I *would've* checked in if there'd been time. But there wasn't. And I'd like to hope that if any of you ever ended up in a situation like that, you'd step up and do what needed to be done—not because you're trying to take over. But because it's the only way we're going to win."

"And Glimmer *is* on our side," Tam added. "You all need to accept that."

"No, *you* need to start seeing your little Neverseen besty for who she really is!" Marella snapped back. She nudged Linh forward. "Go on. Tell him what we learned."

Linh closed her silver-blue eyes and took a long, slow breath as she angled her face toward the sky.

"Here we go," Tam muttered.

Linh stalked closer to her twin. "Yes, Tam—we're finally having this conversation!"

Tam was taller than her, but Linh didn't cower. In fact, Sophie had never seen her look so fierce. Her soft pink cheeks had sharpened with her scowl, and the hair around her face seemed to have extra silver highlights, which shimmered as the wind tossed the silky strands around.

"I'm tired of hiding at Choralmere, waiting for you to come to your senses," Linh told him. "I know you've been through a lot—and I can see how that situation might make it easy to form strange bonds with someone and mistake it for friendship. But Glimmer is *not* your friend."

Everything darkened.

Sophie thought it must be Tam's shadows, but then she noticed the gray storm clouds gathering over their heads.

"Um, can you maybe try telling him the rest *without* soaking us?" Maruca asked. "I don't think I can make a force field to keep out the water."

"Yeah, I know Sophie could use a shower to wash away her bedhead," Marella added, "but I don't think my hair can take another drench-and-dry session without turning into a big ball of frizz." She adjusted the tiny braids scattered throughout her blond hair—which did look poofier than normal.

"Same," Maruca said, coiling her dreadlocks into a bun just in case. One fell loose and hung against her cheek—the one she'd dyed a bright shade of blue.

Linh took a deep breath, and the dark clouds slowly evaporated. But her gaze remained stormy. "I—"

"I get it," Tam cut in. "Glimmer's hard to like. And yes, she *was* a member of the Neverseen—"

"She still *is*," Stina interrupted. "She's still wearing their cloak and hiding behind a stupid title."

"That's because she doesn't trust us!" Tam argued. "And this is why, in case you're wondering. And I know what you're going to say—"

"No, you don't," Linh assured him. "I'm not that scared little girl who caused too many floods and needed her brother to protect her after the Council sent her away! Now you're the one who needs help—and I may not be able to read people's shadowvapor, but I know how to spot the enemy."

Tam gritted his teeth. "Glimmer is *not* the enemy."

Linh reached for his hand, taking a small step closer as she twined their fingers together. "Yes, she is, Tam. I can prove it."

Tam pulled his hand free and crossed his arms. "Fine. Prove it, then."

If he'd thought Linh was bluffing, he was wrong.

She didn't even blink before she told him, "Glimmer's the one who helped Lady Gisela escape from Loamnore."

The words crashed over their group like a tidal wave.

Fitz was the first to come up for air. "How do you know?"

"I talked to my dwarven bodyguards. Urre and Timur were in Loamnore after the battle, and they trailed Lady Gisela's scent to the tunnel she escaped from." She turned back to Tam, making sure he was listening when she added, "They found footprints and handprints that *only* could've been made if Lady Gisela was free of the shadow bonds you put on her. And you know there's no way she could've removed those on her own."

"There was only one person in Loamnore who could've removed them," Marella added. "Well . . . aside from you—but we're pretty sure you wouldn't do that."

Tam's shadow stretched toward the horizon, as if that part of him wanted to run far, far away.

But he stayed right where he was and reached for his sister. "You're sure?"

Linh nodded. "You can ask Urre and Timur if you want. I'm sure they're listening right now and would be happy to surface and repeat their story."

"That won't be necessary." His shadow crept back, settling into the lines and dips of his features. Making him look as dark and cold as his voice when he told everyone, "Sounds like I need to talk to Glimmer."

TEN

"THIS SHOULD BE FUN." GLIMMER'S voice oozed sarcasm as Sophie and her friends all crammed into a bedroom at Solreef, which was even smaller than the sitting room where they'd met with her the last time.

Sophie hadn't bothered suggesting that some of their group should wait outside. She knew how well *that* would go over. But she was grateful that Sandor and Ro had sent the rest of the bodyguards to discuss security with Bo and Tiergan—especially once they were barricaded inside and the room turned hot and stuffy. They had to stand so close together, no one could move without bumping into each other.

Glimmer watched their struggles from her narrow bed, still

wearing her wrinkled black cloak. She pulled her hood lower, making sure no one could see even the tiniest sliver of her face as she said, "Let me guess—you're here to throw me a welcome-to-the-good-side party! Do I get presents?"

Tam sighed. "Not a smart time to be a brat, Glimmer."

"See, and here I thought it was always a good time for that," Glimmer countered, crossing her legs.

Ro snorted. "She's got a good mouth on her—I'll give her that. But let's see if she can talk her way out of this one."

"Talk my way out of *what*?" Glimmer angled her head toward Sophie. "They better not be blaming *me* for *your* little fire show—even if it was the only decent move you had left."

"We're not here about that," Sophie said, glancing at Tam and hoping he'd change the subject *quickly*. They'd decided before they left Havenfield that he deserved to be the one to confront Glimmer about everything—and after Stina's grumblings, Sophie was more than happy to have someone else take the lead.

She was also glad she didn't have to be there in her pajamas with bed hair. Stina had tried to convince everyone to leave her behind if she stopped by her room to change, since it was her fault for "sleeping later than a sasquatch." But Ro told them she'd only share what Sophie had learned from Lord Cassius if they "stopped being jerks and gave Blondie a chance to look less like a sparkly bed-monster." Then she'd caught everyone up about Keefe's mom being a Conjurer while Sophie threw on a fresh tunic and leggings, pulled her hair into a ponytail, and grabbed the caches.

By the time she met them under the Leapmaster, Ro was picking everyone's brains about what Lady Gisela might be planning to do with her secret power. It sounded like no one had any useful suggestions—but they sure looked shaken, so Ro must've mentioned "conjuring up explosives" again.

I want to see that memory, Fitz had transmitted as everyone locked hands to light leap to Solreef together.

Sophie pretended not to hear him.

It wasn't the most mature way of handling the situation— she knew that. But she couldn't believe that Fitz hadn't backed her up about burning down the storehouse—or when Stina tried to rush everyone so she wouldn't have time to change. She also wasn't a fan of the fact that he didn't *ask* to see the memory—he'd basically demanded it.

She'd thought things were finally starting to return to normal between Fitz and her, but clearly the whole almost-dating-but-then-having-it-not-work-out thing was still making everything extra complicated—which was probably why her mind kept repeating the now infamous line from Keefe's letter.

Would he regret writing that when he came back to the Lost Cities? Did he only say it because he thought he'd never see her again? Did it even mean what she thought it meant? Did she WANT it to?

She shook her head, ordering her brain to focus on things

that were actually important as Tam shoved his way closer to Glimmer and pointed to the small, sparkly cat statue sitting on the table next to her bed.

"Looks like Tiergan gave you back the stuff you took from the Neverseen's storehouse," he said.

"You mean *my* stuff," Glimmer corrected. "And yep! Surprise, surprise, it turns out I can be trusted—though I'm assuming you're all here because I'm going to have to prove myself yet again. You realize how old this is getting, right?"

"It *is* getting old," Tam agreed. "So how about you try telling me the truth this time?"

"I *have*."

Stina coughed the word "liar" under her breath.

"Oh no—not a coughed insult!" Glimmer flailed her arms dramatically. "How will I ever survive something so mundane? So uninspired? Especially from a Heks?"

"What's your problem with my family?" Stina demanded.

"You're a bunch of rude, judgmental hypocrites," Glimmer told her without the slightest hesitation.

Sophie stole a glance at Dex, noting that he was fighting a smile just as hard as she was.

"Hey," Maruca said, grabbing Stina's arm as Stina tried to push closer to the bed. "We agreed that Tam gets to confront her."

"Confront me about what?" Glimmer sat up taller and crossed her arms. "Let me guess—you're all bothered that I still haven't taken my hood down or told you my name or let your little Telepaths into my head!"

"That's definitely a problem," Tam agreed. "But right now, we're mostly upset because we know you freed Lady Gisela from the shadow bonds I put on her wrists and helped her escape from Loamnore."

Sophie held her breath, waiting for Glimmer to deny it. But Glimmer was either fearless, or smart enough to know that she was cornered, because she shrugged and said, "I owed her. You can't judge me for that."

"Uh, yes, we can!" Maruca said—then covered her mouth. "Sorry, Tam."

Tam didn't respond.

He was too busy tilting his head and frowning at Glimmer.

"Reading my shadowvapor again?" she asked, pointing to the way his shadow was stretching across her. "It still says you can trust me, doesn't it? That must be so frustrating for you! What's a moody Shade to do when his power says 'yes' but his head says, 'No, I'm too jaded and scared!'"

Ro choked back her laugh. "Gotta admit, I'm really hoping you can get yourself out of this mess because we could use more of that snark around here."

"Yeah, well, I wouldn't count on it," Glimmer told her. "In my experience, people are better at staying closed-minded and judgy."

"Elves definitely are," Ro agreed. "But you're not helping

yourself by hiding behind that ugly cloak—which is also start-ing to smell." She plugged her nose and fanned the air away from her face. *"Wheeeeeeeeeeeew!"*

Glimmer pulled her hood even lower. "Ugh, I'm getting *so* sick of everyone whining about this!"

"The stench?" Ro asked. "Or the wimpy disguise? Either way, it's a simple fix." She mimed flipping back a hood. "Look, I get it. It's easier to hide than it is to put yourself out there. But you seem like someone who likes to be unapologetically *you*. So *be you*—unless you're all attitude and no actual courage to back it up."

Glimmer grabbed the pillow next to her and screamed into it. "I don't owe any of you anything!"

"You do if you don't want us to turn you in to the Council!" Marella argued. "Sorry, Tam, I know I'm not supposed to talk."

"What did you all do? Rehearse?" Glimmer tossed the pil-low back onto the bed. "And I'm glad you said that. Anyone else planning to make threats if I don't tell you what you want to hear?"

Linh, Stina, Marella, Maruca, Wylie, Fitz, Biana, Dex, and Sandor all raised their hands.

"Well, at least three of you know an ally when you see one," Glimmer said, pointing to Tam, Sophie, and Ro.

"I'm still deciding," Sophie admitted.

"So am I," Tam said quietly.

Ro shrugged. "Pretty sure I'm Team Glimmer. But we'll see how it goes."

"Still *deciding*?" Linh said, mostly to her brother—though she shot a quick glare at Sophie. "Glimmer already admitted she let a killer escape! She should be locked up in Exile—and I'm sure the Council would agree if they knew. Haven't they been holding off on her Tribunal, waiting for more information? We need to tell them about this!"

"Oh, so *that's* how it is," Glimmer said. "You're trying to get me exiled."

"No, we're not," Tam promised.

"Actually, I am," Linh corrected. "It's where traitors belong."

"Not always," Wylie argued, taking a step away from Linh.

Sophie couldn't tell if Linh had forgotten that Wylie's father had spent the majority of Wylie's life withering away in one of those cells even though his only crime was being a member of the Black Swan—or if she was just too angry to care.

Tam reached for his sister's arm, waiting for her to look at him. "We agreed that *I* would be the one to do the talking here, remember?"

Linh's nostrils flared, and she looked like she wanted to scream at him like a banshee. But all she did was jerk her arm free. "Fine. If you need more convincing . . . go ahead. Ask more questions. But nothing's going to change what she's done."

"Maybe not. But I'd like to know *why*." Tam turned back to

Glimmer. "Lady Gisela is a *murderer*—you get that, right? And she's not going to stop. So every person she hurts or kills from now on is partially *your* fault."

"You think I don't know that?" Glimmer reached for the cat statue Tam had commented on earlier and hugged it to her chest. "I didn't *want* to let her go. But . . . I owed her. And a debt is a debt."

No one looked satisfied by that answer.

Especially Tam.

"We're going to need the rest of that story," he told her. "Otherwise I can't help you."

Glimmer snorted. "Isn't it funny how *help* rarely comes for free? That's how I got into this mess in the first place."

She hugged the sparkly cat tighter as the room dimmed—then flared so bright, everyone flailed to shield their eyes.

"Fine," she said as the light faded back to normal. "You can have the sob story—but you're not going to like it. It won't fit the evil narrative you're all so busy imagining."

"Pretty sure it'll be worse," Linh muttered under her breath.

"Big talk coming from the Girl of Many Floods," Glimmer snapped. "You know what's funny? We're not that different, you and I. But *I* didn't have a brother who stuck by me and took care of me. And it wasn't Sophie Foster and her little Black Swan buddies who showed up and brought me into a group that promised I'd be able to help them fix all our world's problems. Crazy how that goes, right? A few simple twists, and

I could be the one with the silver highlights in my hair—and you could be the one in the cloak."

"I would *never* join the Neverseen!" Linh insisted.

"You *say* that," Glimmer told her. "But they're not wrong about everything. In fact, I'm pretty sure they agree with you on most of the big issues. They just have different solutions."

"Like destroying cities, and infecting the gnomes with a deadly plague, and murdering people or holding them hostage and torturing them," Sophie couldn't help reminding her.

The light dimmed again. "I . . . didn't know about a lot of that stuff. And I wasn't involved with most of it."

"You shouldn't have been involved with *any* of it!" Maruca argued.

Wylie draped his arm around his cousin's shoulders. "We're supposed to be letting Tam handle this."

"And I'm waiting for Glimmer to share her story." Tam lowered himself onto the edge of Glimmer's bed. "Or did you wimp out because you realized you'd have to tell us who you are?"

"I never wimp out." Glimmer set her cat statue back on the table and snapped her fingers, surrounding herself in a halo of sunlight.

She looked almost angelic as she reached up and swept back her hood—so fast, Sophie's brain could only process what she was seeing in bits and pieces.

Long black hair.

Arched eyebrows.

Bronze skin.

Pale blue eyes framed by thick lashes.

Full lips pressed into a determined line.

Glimmer was stunning—which made sense, since she was an elf. But Sophie had started to wonder if she had some other reason for wanting to keep her face hidden.

"Happy now?" Glimmer asked, the attitude in her voice matching the angry rise of her eyebrows.

No one knew what to say.

They just kept staring at the striking stranger in front of them—except Wylie.

He stepped closer, squinting at Glimmer's face. "I know you . . . don't I?"

The light framing Glimmer faded. "You may *recognize* me. But I guarantee you don't *know* me. No one did."

"Maybe not," Wylie conceded. "But you were a Level behind me at Foxfire, weren't you? I think I even faced off against you in the Ultimate Splotching Championship one time."

"You did. And I won." Glimmer's fingers shook as she tucked her hair behind her ear—the only hint that she might be nervous. "I'll give you my cat statue if you can remember my name."

Wylie frowned at the sparkly feline. "It starts with an *R*, doesn't it? Roshani. No—Rati!"

Glimmer looked away, still fussing with her hair. "You're

actually closer than I thought you'd be. But still wrong. So I get to keep my cat statue. And the rest of you can call me . . ." She cleared her throat—then cleared it again before she squeaked out, "Rayni."

"Rayni," they all repeated.

The name felt weird on Sophie's tongue.

Too soft and pretty and namelike after using a vague title for so long.

She had a feeling it was going to take a little while to remember to use it.

"Wait!" Marella said, narrowing her eyes. "Are you . . . Rayni Aria?"

Glimmer—Rayni—sighed. "I figured at least one of you would've heard the gossip."

No one was surprised it was Marella.

"I haven't heard much," she admitted. "Just that there was a Tribunal for your dad a few years ago—or maybe it was for your mom. Actually, I think it was for both of them. Otherwise why would I know both of their names? Behnam and Esha Aria, right?"

Glimmer—Rayni—cringed as she nodded. "Did you hear what they were on trial for?"

Marella shook her head. "Sophie showed up a couple of days later, and then all I heard about was the mysterious human girl."

"Oh, trust me, there were still people talking about my

family," Glimmer—Rayni—assured her. "But . . . Sophie was a pretty convenient distraction. I should probably thank you for that."

"Um . . . you're welcome?" Sophie said as her mind filled with an image of a glittering building made of emeralds with a blue banner flying from the top. "Was their Tribunal the one I saw in progress when you first brought me to Eternalia?" she asked Fitz.

He shrugged. "Probably. Tribunals are pretty rare."

"And yet Sophie's had how many now?" Stina asked.

Everyone ignored her.

"I guess that proves *you* weren't at the Tribunal," Glimmer—Rayni—told Fitz. "But I'm sure your family was. Pretty much all the nobility turned up to see the verdict. It was quite the spectacle! After all, my dad was a longtime matchmaker accused of altering his results to pair himself with my mom. And my mom was accused of knowingly going along with it. The scandal!" She covered her mouth and mimed a gasp. "They were both found guilty, of course—which wasn't a surprise since they both confessed. But they'd hoped that if they came clean, the Council would show them a little mercy—or better yet, realize their system was flawed and needed to be done away with. The Council should've been thanking my dad for pointing out the problems with the matchmaking process so it wouldn't hurt anyone else. But nope! They banished both of them instead—even though nothing's ever happened to *your* parents"—she pointed to Stina—"and everyone knows they did pretty much the same thing."

All eyes focused on Stina.

She crossed her arms. "I don't know what you're talking about."

"Yes, you do," Glimmer—Rayni—assured her. "Ask anyone about the Heks family, and they'll tell you two things: You breed unicorns, and Vika and Timkin should've been a bad match but mysteriously weren't."

She was right. Sophie had heard plenty of rumors about the Hekses' questionable match status, since Vika was an Empath and Timkin was Talentless.

And yet, Stina still turned up her nose and insisted, "That's just a lie people say because they're jealous of us."

"Of *course* it is!" Glimmer—Rayni—gave her an exaggerated wink. "Go right on believing that if it helps you sleep at night. I'm sure that's what your parents told you. Mine did the same thing to me when the rumors first started flying. *It's a lie! It's a mistake! Don't listen to anything anyone tells you!* That's the only way this kind of thing works. They had to deny, deny, deny to protect me—and themselves. Honestly, I have no idea how they got caught. But I guess all it takes is one person figuring it out—and *wham!* It all came crashing down. Maybe someday it'll happen to you. Though I doubt it. Your mom is too important. As long as she keeps the unicorn population safe from extinction—and no blatant evidence comes out in the open—the Council will hopefully keep looking the other way. Must be nice."

For once, Stina didn't seem to know what to say.

Ro cleared her throat. "Much as I love seeing Miss Snobbyhair looking all awkward and speechless, I gotta admit, this matchmaking thing you elves insist on doing is seriously the worst."

"Said the princess currently married to someone she can't stand because her father arranged it," Fitz reminded her.

Ro tossed one of her pigtails. "I suppose that's a valid point—even though it's a totally different situation. I only agreed to marry Bo because—"

"Doesn't matter," Tam cut in, dragging a hand down his face. "We're talking to Glim—uh—Rayni right now."

Sophie was glad she wasn't the only one struggling to remember to use Glimmer's real name.

"So . . . your parents were banished," Tam added. "What happened to you?"

Rayni's smile turned bitter. "*I* was a 'problem' no one knew what to do with. The Council couldn't punish me, since I didn't know anything. And my parents wouldn't let me go with them. They disappeared without leaving me any way of finding where they went. I didn't even get to say goodbye. I just found a note saying they loved me too much to let me throw my life away because of them—thanks, Mom and Dad! Way to pretend my life wasn't already trashed. None of my relatives wanted anything to do with the girl with the banished parents who was technically the daughter of a bad match. Neither did any of my friends. So there was no happy adoption story for me! Not like *some* people—even though your group has plenty of scandals in your pasts."

She nudged her chin toward Sophie and Wylie. And sadly, she was right. Sophie was a genetically manipulated experiment who grew up with humans, and Wylie's father was an exiled accused-traitor. His mother also died in a suspicious leaping accident, which turned out to be murder. And yet both Sophie and Wylie still ended up with loving adoptive families.

"Funny how that goes, isn't it?" Rayni asked. "And you even got to take the elite levels," she reminded Wylie. "Meanwhile my acceptance was redacted. The Council just wanted me to go away. So I did. I didn't even bother finishing Level Six. I knew it wouldn't matter—and I was right. The only jobs that would consider me were those for the Talentless. I ended up hiding in Mysterium, in a tiny room for rent, hoping if I kept my head down, everyone would forget about me. And everyone pretty much did. But Lady Gisela found me. Said she'd been trying to track me down since she'd heard the verdict."

"And let me guess," Marella jumped in. "She promised she'd lift the banishment on your parents and make your life perfect again if you joined her evil organization?"

"Actually, she didn't—and I wouldn't have cared if she had. My parents abandoned me without even saying goodbye. They can stay banished, for all I care."

"So she promised you revenge," Tam guessed.

Rayni snorted. "You think this is about *revenge*?"

"I don't know—you sound pretty angry," Maruca noted.

"Of course I'm angry! My life got destroyed because some arbitrary rules labeled my parents a bad match!"

"Okay . . . I get that," Dex told her. "*But* . . . if your dad was a top matchmaker, that means he had no problem applying those rules to tons of other couples. I bet some of them complained about their lists, and he didn't care—until it affected *him*. And even then, it wasn't like he started protesting the system. He just made a few secret tweaks to help himself and went right back to matching other people—for how many more years?"

"About forty," Rayni reluctantly admitted.

Dex whistled. "Who knows? Maybe he even doomed my parents—or Brant and Jolie. Pretty sure the timelines sync up. And even if he didn't, I'm sure he knew what was going on. But he didn't say a thing—until he got caught. *Then* he was Mr. Matchmaking Is Wrong!"

"Isn't that how it always goes?" Rayni countered. "We're all willing to believe that everything is perfect and shiny and wonderful here in the Lost Cities—until something happens that forces us to admit it's absolutely not. And even then, it feels scary and hopeless to actually speak up."

"I guess," Dex mumbled. "But don't act like your parents couldn't have taken the bad match label instead of trying to cheat their way around it. That's what my parents did."

Sophie had been thinking the same thing.

Though . . . Dex's family had to deal with tons of scorn and problems because of it.

"Why do you think my parents' punishment was so extreme?" Rayni asked him. "The Council needed to make them an example! Otherwise people might wonder what it meant if one of the matchmakers had started questioning the system. The match could crumble! Especially if people found out how little my dad had to change in order to alter his result. He tweaked *one* answer in his questionnaire. *One!* That's it. And suddenly they went from a bad match to a good match. The Council knew that, of course—but instead of thinking, 'Wow, if *one* answer makes that big of a difference, maybe this system is fundamentally flawed,' they thought, 'We must make sure no one ever finds out so they don't lose faith in our methods.' That's how the Council works. Secrets and lies and endless cover-ups. Anything to keep the status quo."

"So you decided to take them down," Tam said quietly.

"No, I decided I wanted to help get rid of a broken, unfair system we've all been stuck with for way too long because *some* people benefit from it and the rest are too afraid to speak out! After the verdict was handed down, I got *lots* of pats on the back telling me everything would be okay even though we all knew it wouldn't be. But the worst were the sad stares and sympathetic head bobs from all the people who clearly thought my family had been wronged but didn't have the courage to admit it. Lady Gisela was the first person I met who was willing to say—out loud—that matchmaking was a problem. Do you have any idea how much that meant to me? I'm not sure I'd still be here if she hadn't proven that I wasn't the only one truly bothered by the injustice of it all. And then she pointed out all the other messed-up methods of the Council and told me I could help her build something so much better. I realize now that I should've asked more questions about her plans. But . . . I didn't, because I knew change wouldn't come easy. I knew there would have to be a little bad to bring on true good—and before any of you judge me for that, think about the things your Black Swan order has done. Can you honestly say that none of it has caused any harm to anyone? And do you really think they've told you about all their plans and schemes? But you still play along, because you know it's necessary. And . . . for what it's worth, Gisela promised me that she'd never ask me to do anything that would hurt someone."

Linh laughed at that, and the air in the room turned thick and humid, making Rayni's shiny hair stick to her cheeks. "You have a funny definition of 'hurt' if you thought it was okay to turn my brother into her little Shade puppet."

Rayni hugged herself again, and her finger traced the lines of the Neverseen symbol sewn to her sleeve. "Actually . . . that was the first order she gave me that felt *wrong*."

"And yet you did it anyway," Linh noted.

"I did. But . . . she said it was the only way to help her son.

She told me he was special, and that he was going to help her prove that the Council had been hiding incredibly important things. But she needed a Flasher and a Shade to make it all possible—and Umber was dead, and there wasn't time for her to properly recruit someone else. She said she just needed Tam to cooperate for a little while, and then he'd be free. She *promised*."

"And I told you she'd break that promise," Tam reminded her as he snatched her cat statue off the table.

Rayni didn't try to stop him. Even when he started twisting the tail like he wanted to break it off.

"I know," she mumbled. "That's why I set you free."

"Just like you set Lady Gisela free," Linh said as the moisture in the air thickened into beads of mist, peppering their skin. "We haven't forgotten that, right? I haven't heard anything in this story that justifies setting a murderer free. Have you, Tam?"

"I never said I could *justify* it," Rayni argued. "I said a debt is a debt. I owed her."

"For *what*?" Linh, Stina, Maruca, and Marella all demanded in unison.

"There wasn't a specific *thing*. That was just . . . how it worked." Her fingers tightened around her Neverseen patch. "She didn't make anyone swear fealty when they joined—or vow their undying loyalty to her or her cause—"

"Guess that explains why the Neverseen have had so many power shifts," Dex said.

"Maybe," Rayni agreed. "But I thought that was incredibly fair of her. She said her plans were always changing, so she would never expect anyone to commit to them fully. All she asked was for us to only sign on if we agreed about the problems we were facing—and to promise that someday we'd find a way to repay her for any kindness she showed us. And when I saw her in Loamnore, wounded and bound in shadows, she looked at me and mouthed, *You owe me.*"

"So you set her free," Tam finished for her. "Just like that."

Rayni nodded. "It was the only way I could keep my word."

"How noble of you," Linh grumbled. "Keeping your promise to a murderer!"

"No, I kept my promise to someone who'd made me feel like I mattered at a time when everyone else just wanted me to go away. Someone who gave me a place to stay and made it feel like a home after mine had been ripped apart. I know that doesn't erase the things she's done, but it meant too much for me to totally ignore it. I *did* owe her. So . . . I let her go. But now my debt's repaid—and no matter what you think, I *want* her locked away. That's why I'm *trying* to help you catch her. I've even been cooperative with the Council—and do you have any idea how hard it's been for me to not throw things at their heads every time they stop by to ask me more questions? But I've sat there, trying to be polite and helpful. The only thing I've held back is my identity."

"And the fact that you let Lady Gisela go," Marella noted.

"Technically, they didn't ask about that. But . . . I suppose you're right—and in case you're thinking it's because I'm afraid of being punished, it isn't. I just didn't want it to stop anyone from listening to me. You need my help. Without me, you never would've found the Neverseen's storehouse—and Sophie never would've realized how poorly you plan your missions."

"Maybe you're just pretending to be on our side so you can sabotage us," Marella suggested. "Maybe *that's* what you owed Gisela."

Rayni tossed her head back and laughed. "You think she needs *me* to sabotage you? You do that just fine on your own. In fact, you're doing it right now. Wasting all this time accusing me instead of letting me tell you my plan."

"Your *plan*," everyone repeated—though their tones covered a wide range of emotions.

Curiosity.

Skepticism.

Outright disdain.

"Yes," Rayni told them. "I have a plan. A really good one. I'd actually been hoping someone would come by today so I could tell you about it. Guess I should've known I'd have to endure lots more bickering and questioning first. Though . . . it *is* nice finally being free of that horrible hood." She took a long, deep breath. "In fact, let's be done with the rest of it, shall we?"

She stood slowly, like she wasn't sure if anyone was going to pounce on her for moving. When no one did, she unfastened her cloak, letting the dark, heavy fabric slide off her shoulders—which were much narrower than Sophie expected. In fact, everything about Rayni was much tinier than Sophie had imagined. Also more colorful. Without the black cloak, she was a petite vision in vibrant red, orange, and yellow, with flashes of gold. She looked like any normal, stylish girl wandering the streets of Atlantis or shopping in Slurps and Burps.

But she isn't a normal girl, Sophie reminded herself.

She might not be as skeptical as some of her friends, but she wasn't fully Team Rayni either.

Not yet, at least.

But she was still glad Tam said, "So what's this big plan?"

"Hang on." Rayni sank back onto her bed and settled against the pillows. "I might as well get comfortable, since I'm sure there's about to be a whole lot more arguing. I swear, that's the one thing you all are actually good at. Well, that and losing—but I'm trying to change that. *If* you're willing to let me."

"Let you do what?" Tam asked.

She snatched her cat statue back from him and kissed its tiny sparkly nose before she said, "Let me set up a meeting with Trix."

ELEVEN

TRIX.

The name echoed off the walls, turning the room colder and darker.

Maybe Tam had done something with the shadows. Or maybe the chills running down Sophie's spine were because Trix was the Neverseen's mysterious Guster.

"You want *us* to meet with *Trix*?" Tam clarified.

"Actually, I'd *prefer* to meet with him myself," Rayni corrected, "since that would go way faster and much smoother, but—"

"*No!*" everyone said in unison.

"Yeah, I already knew you were going to say that. That's why what I'm *actually* offering is to set up a meeting with Trix, me, and *some* of you. Not all of you. You, you, you, and you"—she pointed to Linh, Maruca, Stina, and Marella with the tail of her cat statue—"would turn it into a shouting match. And I'm betting you're still holding a grudge about Trix's role in your abductions"—she pointed to Dex and Wylie—"so that would make it super tense. Not sure how I feel about you two." She pointed to Fitz and Biana. "In my experience, Vackers tend to have a hard time understanding that some people don't have powerful families and all the privilege that comes with that. Trix also wasn't a huge fan of your brother. So the best option would be just Trix, Tam, and me—"

"*No!*" Linh cut in.

Rayni threw her hands up. "Let me guess: You're about to suggest that I'm plotting to kidnap Tam again—which makes no sense, since I'm the one who set him free in the first place. But whatever. Let me try to set your mind at ease, okay? If that was my goal, I would've done it right away and saved myself from being stuck in this boring, stuffy room with a grumpy ogre barricading the door for so many days. Plus, I'm pretty sure your brother could take me down in about three seconds."

"Two," Tam corrected—without the slightest hint of a smile.

Rayni raised one eyebrow. "*Anyway*, now that we've settled *that*, can I get back to the plan? I'd been about to add Sophie to my list of invitees before I was so rudely interrupted."

"Not happening," Sandor informed her.

"Pretty sure that's *her* decision." She pointed to Sophie with her cat statue. "And I know it might be a little awkward, since you also have a history with Trix—"

"You mean how he helped drug me and drag me out of a cave and then used his ability to stir up a huge wave and convince everyone I drowned?" Sophie asked.

"Yeah," Rayni mumbled, "like I said . . . *awkward*. Though, for what it's worth, he told me later that he felt really weird about all that."

Dex snorted. "Oh, he felt *weird*. That makes it totally okay, then."

"Fine, maybe 'weird' wasn't the best word. I think he actually said 'conflicted.' Is that better?"

"Sure, that changes everything! Who cares that he almost got us killed? He felt conflicted about it afterward!" If Dex rolled his periwinkle eyes any harder, his eyeballs might've dropped into the back of his head. "It's also *awesome* knowing you two were sitting around chatting about our kidnapping, isn't it, Sophie? Do you think they also placed bets on which of us would get murdered first?"

Rayni set aside her cat statue and folded her hands in her lap. "Okay. I guess I deserve that. But just so we're clear, I had no idea you two had been taken until after you'd already been rescued."

"Do you honestly expect us to believe that?" Fitz asked. "They were held captive for *days*."

"At a facility I didn't even know existed! That's how the

Neverseen work. Everything is compartmentalized. Everyone only knows tiny pieces—and only about things they're directly involved with—and I was new to the order back then, so no one told me anything. If you don't believe me, think about this: I didn't even find out that Gisela had been sent to an ogre prison until she'd been locked up for *weeks*."

"And yet you still stuck around, even though she wasn't there anymore?" Sophie asked.

"I thought about leaving. But . . . I had nowhere else to go—and I still believed the Neverseen were going to bring about some important changes. They also weren't asking very much from me. Brant moved me to one of their more isolated hideouts and gave me a stack of books on flashing and a bunch on healing techniques. I think he was hoping I'd become their version of Elwin—but that would take decades of study and practice. And Fintan would stop by sometimes and ask me questions about his weird Criterion thing, but he never told me what it was, or gave me an actual assignment. That's why I didn't know the Neverseen had anything to do with the gnomish plague. It's also why I didn't cross paths with Keefe while he was pretending to be a member. And I only heard about your abduction after you escaped," she told Wylie. "I also didn't know Gisela was going to try to destroy Atlantis. She wasn't back with the Neverseen until *after* she did that—and then she was working with Vespera, and Vespera's even stricter about how much everyone is allowed to know."

"Pretty convenient how you somehow *missed* all the worst things they've done," Marella noted.

"Not really. Gisela had made it clear to everyone that she brought me into the order to help with her son's legacy. So when she wasn't around, people didn't really know what to do with me. They didn't trust me enough to tell me anything or give me any assignments. And once Gisela was back, the only information she ever gave me was about her plans for Keefe."

"What else did she tell you?" Sophie asked.

"If you're hoping I know what she's going to do next—I don't," Rayni told her.

"But she *is* planning more for Keefe?" Sophie pressed.

"I'm assuming so. He's not working with her yet, is he?"

"He'll *never* work with her," Sophie promised.

"Yeah, I got that sense in Loamnore. But Gisela's not going to give up. She needs him to 'prove' something."

"Prove what?" Dex asked.

"No idea. She said it has something to do with our potential as a species—but she never told me any specifics."

"Of *course* she didn't," Stina grumbled.

"Hey, I would've loved it if Gisela sat me down and told me all her secrets—just like I'm sure you'd love it if that Mr. Forkle guy did the same thing with you. But he hasn't, has he? Pretty sure I can take those frowns as a no. So can you stop blaming me for not knowing everything either? I snooped around as much as I could—but I'm not a Vanisher, so my opportunities were limited. And I asked lots of questions, but most of the time they ignored me. There's a *lot* I don't know. That's why I need to talk to Trix."

"You seriously think Trix would be willing to meet with you?" Sophie had to ask. "I'm sure he's figured out that you helped us find that storehouse."

"That's *why* he'll meet with me. He'll want to know why I switched sides."

"Or he'll assume we're forcing you to help us and try to rescue you," Tam countered.

"Please. Trix knows I don't need rescuing! Especially from you all. No offense—but he's not exactly worried about any of you. You've never given him a reason to be—though he might be starting to wonder about the moonlark. He used to go on and on about how weird he thought it was that Brant and Fintan were paying so much attention to a little girl who hadn't actually done anything important. But now you're showing some real fight. I bet he'll be willing to listen to you now—at least to see what you're about."

"Do you even know where he is?" Tam asked, saving Sophie from having to figure out how to respond to that.

"Probably not. I doubt they're using any of the hideouts I'm aware of. But I'm pretty sure I know how to get him a message."

"*Pretty sure,*" Maruca repeated.

"Hey, I'm just being honest. If you want a one-hundred-percent guarantee, you're never going to get one. But I'm ninety-five percent certain I can make this happen. You pick the day, the time, and the place, and I'll put that all in a message and leave it for him. Then we just wait and see if he shows up."

"Absolutely not!" Sandor snapped.

"Wow, you really have *that* little confidence in your abilities?" Rayni asked. "I figured if you had control over the situation, you'd be able to arrange some solid security."

"I can arrange *brilliant* security," Sandor assured her. "But a wise bodyguard recognizes that the *best* way to protect their charge is to keep them away from danger."

"Yeah, but if you don't let Sophie be the moonlark, the Neverseen are going to win," Rayni argued. "I thought that was why she had you—so she could still do all the risky things she needs to do but have some extra protection."

"She's right," Sophie agreed, even though her stomach was getting all sour and sloshy. "You can't keep trying to put me in a bubble away from all the danger."

"I don't have to put you in the center of it either!" Sandor argued.

"Trust me, this isn't going to be dangerous," Rayni assured both of them.

"And *there's* your problem," Sandor snapped back. "I *don't* trust you—and even if I did, there are tremendous flaws in your plan."

"Like what?" Rayni asked.

Sandor laughed—which sounded more like a squeaky chipmunk than he probably wanted it to. "Where do I even start? How about the fact that you cannot control who finds the message, or guarantee that it won't fall into the wrong hands?"

"Doesn't matter. They won't understand it. Trix and I used to send each other notes all the time, since we were living in different hideouts. And we came up with our own shorthand to make sure no one could figure out what we were saying if the notes ended up somewhere we didn't want them to."

"Then what if this Trix person decides to simply tell the rest of the Neverseen about the meeting and bring them along to ambush us?" Sandor demanded.

"Trix would *never* do that," Rayni promised. "But that's also why I said you could pick the time and location. If you're as good as you say you are, you should be able to prepare for every possible scenario."

"Something *always* goes wrong when we do that," Fitz argued. "We've tried setting traps before—"

"This *isn't* a trap!" Rayni interrupted. "I want to make that *very* clear. I'm not going to help you lure Trix somewhere so you can try to lock him away."

"You don't get to make that decision," Stina informed her.

"Actually, I do, since I'll be the one writing the note. The only instructions I'm willing to give are for *a meeting*, where we can talk and either decide to work together—or go our separate ways. Anything beyond that is off the table—and I'll be able to tell if that's what you're doing."

Fitz snorted. "I doubt that."

"Please. You're not as clever as you think you are. I also love how you're all acting like I'm suggesting the most bizarre thing you've ever heard of. It's super common in any sort of conflict situation for the opposing sides to meet and see if they can come to an agreement."

"She's right," Ro admitted. "In fact, that's pretty much all you elves ever do, isn't it? You usually call it treaty negotiations. But it's the same thing."

Even Sandor couldn't disagree with that.

"Okay, but let me guess. You'll need to be alone when you leave Trix the message?" Marella said.

"If you're trying to imply that this is my big escape plan—uh, don't you think I would've suggested it a while ago?" Rayni countered.

"Not if you were waiting to earn our trust," Maruca argued.

"Right, because I'm sitting here, surrounded by so much warmth and support." She gestured to the many scowling faces.

"Why *are* you suggesting this now?" Tam asked. "You never mentioned it earlier."

"I hadn't thought of it earlier! I came up with it last night, as I was trying to figure out what our next move should be."

"There is no *our*," Linh told her.

Rayni rubbed her temples. "Hey, I'm not exactly excited to

be part of this cheerful little group either. I'm just *trying* to help—and I thought some of you were finally wanting to make some real progress." Her eyes locked with Sophie's. "I guess I should've known they'd get in your head. You still haven't realized that being the leader means making choices that won't make everyone happy."

"I'm *not* their leader," Sophie insisted.

"You're not," Rayni agreed. "But you need to be, or you all are going to keep wasting too much time. Leaders usually aren't very popular. But they get the job done. That's what you did when you set that fire. Don't let their doubts make you second-guess yourself. You made the right call. You know it. I know it. Maybe someday they'll see it—but even if they don't, you can't let their fears slow you down. This is going to get a lot harder before anything gets better."

The words might've been more comforting if they hadn't reminded Sophie of the speech Lady Gisela gave in Loamnore.

The thing about being the leader of a movement is that you have to be willing to do anything to further the cause.

"Can I at least finish explaining my plan before you rule it out?" Rayni begged.

"I don't see the point," Fitz told her before focusing his teal eyes on Sophie. "We've already learned the hard way that working with the enemy *never* goes well. Lady Gisela set us up. Alvar betrayed us. And you spent twelve minutes with Glimmer and turned super reckless."

"Wooooow." Rayni tilted her head to study him. "That was a *lot* of judgment coming from a guy who, as far as I can tell, hasn't actually done all that much to help your little group. You're basically Sophie's telepathic backup, aren't you? Is *that* why you're so bothered about what happened at the storehouse? She was supposed to *need* you, and she didn't?"

"Man, I wish Funkyhair had been here for that," Ro mumbled as Fitz's jaw clenched with an audible *crack*.

"Funkyhair?" Rayni asked.

"The guy who almost died because you made Tam blast him with shadowflux while you hit him with light so he could fulfill his *legacy*," Fitz snapped. "He's still not okay, by the way, in case you were wondering."

Rayni looked away, fussing with the gold beading on the edge of her tunic. "I told you—Lady Gisela promised me that what we did was going to help him."

"Well . . . so far it hasn't," Sophie mumbled, trying not to think about Keefe having to go through something like that *again* if he wanted to fix that.

"Maybe he just needs a little more time to adjust to the changes," Rayni suggested.

"Or maybe we should have Tam and Wylie blast *you* with shadows and light and see if it *helps* you," Fitz countered.

"Still bitter about my 'telepathic backup' comment, huh?"

No one laughed.

Not even Ro.

"Okay, I get it," Rayni said quietly. "Some of you are always going to hate me. That doesn't mean we can't still work together. Look at the hatefest going on between those two!" She pointed to Stina and Sophie.

"Uh, Sophie's annoying," Stina argued, "but she's not a killer!"

"Neither am I. And neither is Trix. He's actually super nice. He used to take me with him on his 'snack runs' sometimes, because I knew my way around Mysterium. The Neverseen don't have any gnomes, so their food is *terrible*, and Trix always went out of his way to make sure we had some better stuff to eat."

"Does that mean you know who he is?" Biana asked.

Rayni shook her head. "We always went at night, so we could still wear our cloaks without drawing attention. Most of the food stalls aren't locked, so you can just walk in and grab whatever you want."

"You mean *steal*," Wylie corrected.

"Nope! Trix always left money to cover everything we took. That's the kind of guy he is. I'm telling you, we can trust him— and I think he'd be willing to help us."

"You *think*?" Fitz repeated.

Tam had a more useful question: "Help us with what?"

"Finding Gisela. Or Vespera. Or figuring out what they're planning. Maybe all of the above."

Stina laughed. "Oh please—you expect us to believe he'll

suddenly be willing to betray everyone he's been working with because Sophie set one fire?"

"Hey, that fire sent a *huge* message! But I never said that was the *only* reason. Trix was never all that committed to the Neverseen's cause. He was there for Umber."

Umber.

Another name that turned everything dark and shivery.

Sophie could almost feel the echoes stirring under her skin, even though she'd worked so hard to put them to rest.

"I know," Rayni mumbled as Sophie curled her aching right hand into a fist. "Umber was . . . intense."

"I think you mean creepy and violent," Fitz corrected as he tested the strength in his left leg.

"Sometimes she was," Rayni admitted. "She could be a little unstable. I never got to hear her story. But Trix told me that what happened to her was brutal, and broke her in ways even he couldn't fully understand. Made her want to lash out at anyone who got in her way."

"Sounds like an awesome choice for a girlfriend," Fitz muttered.

"Hey, we can't all go for the cute blondes," Rayni countered. "Though it seems like there might be trouble in paradise."

Ro cackled. "Okay, I'm easing back into Team Glimmer again—though I guess I should probably start calling it Team Rayni. And as someone on your team, I gotta say, you need to give us some better reasons for trusting this Trix guy. Sneaking snacks is a cute story, but it doesn't exactly prove he wouldn't try to kill us."

"I told you—he's not a killer."

"Maybe not *yet*," Wylie argued. "But he clearly has no problem capturing people and bringing them to other people to torture."

"Actually, he did feel conflicted about that, remember? Plus . . . that was before Umber was killed." She curled her knees into her chest and wrapped her arms around them. "I was there when Vespera told him what happened, and . . . I've never seen anyone so devastated. He dropped to the floor, making these horrible, wheezy gasps as he trembled and sobbed. He wouldn't eat for days. Couldn't sleep, either. He just cried or stared blankly at the ceiling. And when he found out they left her body behind, his winds swirled into some sort of hurricane-tornado thing. Shattered all the crystal in the room." She pulled up her sleeve, showing a thin scar just above her elbow. "One of the flying shards gave me this."

"Oh yeah, he seems like a *great* guy," Fitz grumbled.

"Uh, your brother told me stories about your temper too—and you don't even have a good excuse. Besides, Trix didn't *mean* to make the storm. The shock and grief made him lose control of his ability—I'm sure you can relate to that," she said to Linh.

Linh looked away. But Rayni was right. Elemental abilities were known for being much more volatile—which was probably why the mist in the air was now coiling across Linh's limbs like cloudy snakes, searching for a reason to strike.

"Just so I'm clear," Tam said slowly, "you're saying that Trix will be willing to help us take down the Neverseen because he's mad about what happened to Umber—even though he was still doing plenty of horrible stuff for them after she was dead? I was there, remember? I didn't see him resisting any of his orders."

"Right, because he thinks it's what Umber would want him to do. But I can't imagine Umber would be happy knowing he's helping the people who left her trampled body behind without even making sure she was dead. And if I remind him of that, and tell him how quickly Lady Giscla broke all her promises to you in Loamnore without any remorse, I'm pretty sure he'll realize he needs to get out of there—and yes, I'm only *pretty sure* again. But I'm *positive* he would never do anything to hurt me. So worst case? He'll tell me no and go back wherever he came from and we'll have to figure out a new plan. But there's a *really* good chance he'll at least tell us something useful. Or better yet, switch sides, now that Sophie's shown some proof that you're learning how to fight back."

"Oh yeah, that's *exactly* what we want," Stina mumbled. "More Neverseen creeps getting a chance to betray us."

"You won't feel that way after you talk to him. Well . . . after *we* talk to him," Rayni corrected, pointing to herself, Tam, and Sophie—and then at Sandor as well. "I'm sure you'll be there too."

"I will—*if* everyone is foolish enough to move forward with this plan," Sandor grumbled.

"Me too! Me too!" Ro said, waving her hand.

"That's fine," Rayni told her. "Whatever it takes to make this meeting happen."

"You're not actually considering this, are you?" Linh asked her brother.

Tam shrugged. "It's not the worst idea I've ever heard. I also don't see anyone else coming up with any suggestions for how we might find Gisela."

Linh's cloud snakes coiled tighter. "Unbelievable! I swear, it's like they brainwashed you!"

"And that—right there—is why I can't talk to you right now," Tam snapped back. "Every time we disagree, you act like it's because they've *changed* me."

"You *have* changed!" Linh insisted. "The old Tam was *barely* willing to trust Sophie, even after she helped us over and over. And it took you forever to trust the Black Swan. In fact, you still have tons of doubts about them. But you trust *her*, even though she put bonds on your wrists and let a murderer go."

Tam blew out a long, exhausted breath and tugged his bangs over his eyes. "I get that there's a lot about this situation that's messed up. But that doesn't mean I don't know what I'm doing. The thing is . . . I realized in Loamnore that there's no clear right or wrong anymore. Everything's gotten too messy. After all, I blasted Keefe with shadowflux knowing it could kill him—"

"You didn't have a choice," Linh argued.

"Yes, I did. I could've resisted. In fact, I could've fought Lady Gisela before she even took me away—then I never would've been her captive in the first place. But she told me she would hurt you, so I cooperated. And I unleashed the shadows when she told me to—not just because of the bonds. But because I knew she'd try to kill you if I didn't. I chose *your* life over everyone and everything else—and I'd do it again if I had to. Some might think that makes me a hero. But it also makes me a villain."

Linh's cloud snakes evaporated. "You're *not* a villain."

"I'm not," he agreed. "That's my point. You can't judge someone solely by their actions anymore—not with how complicated everything has gotten. Glimmer let Lady Gisela go— and I definitely wish she hadn't. But . . . I kinda get why she did it. Enough that I'm not willing to totally write her off yet. Maybe I'll feel the same once I talk to Trix. Maybe not. There's only one way to find out. And we *need* to find out. We have to consider any possible advantage if we want to win this."

Linh closed her eyes, gathering a small sphere of water with her hands. "Fine," she said, studying her rippled reflection, "do what you want, Tam. Just . . . don't expect me to be a part of it."

"Woo! That's one vote in favor of the Trix plan!" Rayni cheered as Linh shoved as far away from her brother as she could get in the tiny room. "Who else is in?"

Stina, Maruca, and Marella moved closer to Linh.

Linh turned toward Wylie. "Are you coming with us?"

He chewed his lip.

Linh sighed. "Do you seriously think we should try to meet with someone who dragged you out of the Silver Tower, knowing you'd be tortured?"

"No," Wylie admitted. "But I also don't think it should be my decision."

"Hmm. Guess I'll count that as another vote in favor," Rayni told him.

"It isn't," Wylie warned. "I was about to remind everyone that this needs to be the Council's decision—just like *they* should be the ones to decide if you need to face any consequences for letting Lady Gisela go."

"So what I'm hearing is . . . you want a little payback," Rayni mumbled.

"You'd definitely deserve it," Wylie told her. "But that's not what this is about. I'm a Regent now, and a member of Team Valiant." He pointed to the pin securing his cape around his shoulders—three swirls of metal, representing the Prime Sources.

Sophie, Stina, Biana, and Dex all had the same pins.

"I swore an oath promising complete allegiance to the Council when I joined the team," Wylie added, standing up taller, like he wanted to remind everyone that he was the oldest among them. "I'd be violating that oath if I didn't let them know about all this and let them decide the proper way of handling it."

"*That* is an excellent point!" Stina said, patting her own Team Valiant pin. "I'm surprised our fearless leader didn't think of it. Actually, wait. No, I'm not."

Sophie wished she could use her telekinesis to shove Stina out the door.

But . . . Wylie *did* have a point.

"I guess we should meet with the Council," Sophie said quietly.

Rayni flopped back against her pillows. "Ugh. Worst. Decision. Ever."

"Afraid you'll be exiled?" Stina asked.

"You won't be," Tam promised. "I'll make sure the Councillors understand how their mistakes played a role in everything that happened."

Rayni laughed. "Like they'll care."

"They should. They've ruined a lot of lives, and our world is dissolving into chaos because of it," Tam argued. "They need to understand that if they don't start changing, the Neverseen are going to win."

"Yeah, I'm sure they'll be super ready to listen to all that," Rayni told him. "And then we'll all snuggle in for a great big group hug."

Tam smiled, but shadows also settled into his features, making him look as ominous as he sounded when he said, "Trust me, I can be *very* convincing when I want to be."

"And they can be *very* small-minded," Rayni countered. "But . . . do what you have to do. It's not like I can stop you."

"So . . . we're all going to Eternalia, then?" Biana asked, breaking the silence that followed. "Will we need an appointment with the Council?"

"Probably," Wylie said. "I'll reach out to my points of contact and set something up—but I don't think we should all go. Glim—uh—Rayni has a point about how much we argue. Add in twelve Councillors, and we'll be there for hours."

"Days," Rayni corrected. *"Months."*

"Hopefully not," Wylie told her. "But that's why I think it should just be Tam and me who go to Eternalia."

"And me," Sophie reminded him.

Wylie shook his head. "You don't know how the Council feels about the storehouse fire, do you? Have they talked to you about it?"

"Not yet," Sophie admitted.

"Then I don't think it'd be smart to have you there. Otherwise the whole conversation could end up being about that."

"Wylie's right," Tam agreed. "It might even make the Council more opposed to letting us meet with Trix."

"Maybe that's a good thing," Fitz argued, turning to Wylie. "I want to be there for this meeting. I may not be on Team Valiant—but neither is Tam, and—"

"It's not a Team Valiant thing," Wylie interrupted. *"I'm* going because it's the only way I can know for sure that this was properly reported to the Council. And Tam is going to speak in Glim—Rayni's defense."

"And who will make it clear that *most* of us think meeting with Trix is a terrible plan proposed by someone who let a murderer escape?" Fitz asked.

"No one will need to," Wylie told him. "All we need to do is present the facts. The Councillors are capable of asking their own questions and deciding for themselves."

"Are they, though?" Rayni said, mostly to herself.

"You sound scared," Marella noted.

"I'm not. The Council already ruined my life. There's nothing else they can do to me."

"Oh, I have a feeling there's a *lot* more they can do," Stina told her.

"I wouldn't sound so gleeful if I were you," Rayni warned. "Every time the Council talks about *my* family, it reminds them of the rumors about *yours*. And all it'll take is one tiny bit of proof slipping out, and you'll be right where I am—regardless of how powerful your mom is. Maybe it'll even be worse, since your dad is Talentless, so whatever trick they pulled had to be way bigger than tweaking one question."

"They didn't pull any tricks!" Stina insisted. "Plus, *I'm* not part of an illegal rebellion!"

"Maybe not at the moment. But how many times has the Council turned against the Black Swan? Do you really think it won't happen again?"

Stina's mouth snapped shut.

"Okay . . . ," Dex said slowly. "So . . . are we all agreed, then? Wylie will reach out to his points of contact and set up a meeting for him and Tam with the Council. And the rest of us will wait to hear how that all goes."

"And wait, and wait, and wait," Rayni mumbled. "That's all you do. Wondering the whole time why the Neverseen are always so many steps ahead of you."

"Actually, I have things some of us can work on," Sophie told them.

"There she goes, trying to boss us around again," Stina muttered. "This isn't Team Valiant right now!"

"And you're welcome to leave anytime!" Sophie reminded her. "All of you are. I'm not trying to tell anyone what to do. But if you *want* some ideas, I have a few projects."

"This ought to be good," Stina sneered—but her jaw fell slack when Sophie reached into her pocket and pulled out the two caches, letting the clear, marble-size gadgets roll around her palm.

"I took these from the Neverseen's storehouse," she explained as she offered the one with nine inner crystals to Marella. "That one is Fintan's cache from back when he was a Councillor. I have no idea if there's anything useful in it, since the Forgotten Secrets inside are probably all ancient. But it's worth finding out. Maybe you can convince Fintan to open it for you. You've been getting along pretty well with him, haven't you?"

"Uh, not *that* well," Marella warned. "It's more of a . . . *let me teach you to master your fire so you can prove it's possible and lift the ban on pyrokinesis* kind of thing. Not a *let me spill all my dark secrets* relationship. Plus, he's pretty unstable, so it varies lesson by lesson." But she still took the cache and held it up to the light, twisting it so the tiny crystals sparkled. "Do the different colors mean something?"

"No idea," Sophie admitted. "Guess you'll find out if he opens it."

Marella closed her fist around the cache. "You realize he's going to want something in return, right? And it's not like there's much I can offer him."

"Oh! I know what you can suggest!" Rayni sat up and leaned forward. "Say you'll ask the Council to create a statue of him filled with balefire. He used to go on and on about how everyone only remembers his unruly Everblaze and all the destruction it can cause—but he also created fire that can be calm and contained, and if people would focus on that, they wouldn't be so afraid of Pyrokinetics."

"You know what else would make them less afraid?" Marella asked. "If he hadn't killed people and burned down half of Eternalia. I remind him of that. A *lot*."

"Yeah, plus, I don't think the Council is ever going to make a statue of the person who murdered Councillor Kenric," Biana added quietly.

"I never said he'd *get* the statue," Rayni argued. "I said to tell him you'll *ask* for one. And honestly, the Council *should* consider it. Our world could use a reminder of what can happen when we try to force people to deny who they are."

"Yeeeeaaaaaaaah . . . pretty sure I'm not going to suggest that," Marella said, shoving the cache into her pocket. "But I'll try to come up with something better. Want to brainstorm with me?" she asked Linh, Maruca, and Stina.

"Anything that gets us out of here," Linh told her.

"What about the rest of us?" Biana asked Sophie. "Need help with the other cache? It was Kenric's, right?"

"Actually, I was thinking you and Fitz could talk to Tiergan about checking all the other stuff we took from the Neverseen's storehouse," Sophie told her.

Biana scowled. "You want us to read a bunch of boring scrolls?"

"I thought you'd be excited!" Sophie tried not to sound too smug when she added, "Weren't you saying earlier that the storehouse probably had—how did you put it? Vital 'evidence and intelligence, which probably would've told us everything we needed to take down the Neverseen'? This is your chance to find out if that's true."

"What are *you* going to do?" Fitz asked Sophie.

She tightened her grip on Kenric's cache. "I'm hoping Dex can help me figure out how to open this thing."

"I can try," Dex said. "But the security on caches is beyond crazy."

"I believe in you," Sophie promised.

She also *really* didn't want to have to bring the cache to the only other person who could open it.

"Won't you need my help with the cache?" Fitz asked.

It felt *very* good to tell him, "I don't see why."

Ro snickered.

"Hang on," Stina said as everyone started reaching for their home crystals. "Are we seriously going to let Sophie tell us what to do?"

"I don't hear you offering any suggestions," Ro pointed out. "You may not want Blondie to be your leader, but it sure is easier to complain than it is to come up with actual ideas."

"Whatever." Stina hooked her arms around Marella's, Maruca's, and Linh's shoulders. "Come on, let's get away from these losers."

Linh glanced over her shoulder at her brother. "You'll let me know what the Council says?"

"Of course." Tam kicked the toe of his shoe. "Are you going back to Choralmere?"

Linh nodded. "It's better there than . . ."

She didn't finish, but Sophie was pretty sure her last words would've been "staying with you."

Wylie cleared his throat. "I'll hail Councillor Ramira and Councillor Velia and let them know I need to arrange a meeting."

"You won't tell them why, though, right?" Tam asked.

"Only that it's about Glim—uh, Rayni. Well, actually, I should probably keep calling her Glimmer. I don't want to reveal too much until everyone's there, and you can weigh in."

"Thank you," Tam told him, glancing at Rayni, who was staring at her cat statue, pretending none of them existed.

Fitz sighed and stumbled toward the door. "Well . . . I guess Biana and I will go ask Tiergan to show us the storehouse stuff."

"Speak for yourself!" Biana held her crystal up to the light. "You can meet me at home with the boring scrolls."

"What if Tiergan won't let me leave with them?" Fitz asked.

"Then you can tell me everything you learn when you finish reading them!" She tossed her hair and winked as she leaped away.

Dex laughed. "She just left without poor Woltzer—again."

"I don't know how he doesn't constantly want to strangle her," Fitz said under his breath.

He called for Bo to let him out of the room and glanced at Sophie as the door opened. His eyebrows scrunched together, like he wanted to say something. But he left without another word.

Dex rushed to catch the door before it slammed shut. "I'll get Lovise and go home and grab some tools. Meet you at Havenfield?"

Sophie nodded. "Should we all check in tomorrow to catch each other up on what we're doing?"

"How about we just agree to update each other once we actually learn something?" Marella countered.

"I'm sure *we'll* make progress long before you," Stina added as she raised her home crystal and glittered away with Linh, Marella, and Maruca.

Wylie left right after, and Tam quickly followed.

"Well, *that* was even less fun than I expected," Rayni groaned as she flopped back into her pillows again.

"Will you . . . um . . . be okay?" Sophie asked, feeling strange leaving her all alone in her tiny bedroom.

"Oh, don't worry about me." She traced her finger down the spine of her sparkly cat. "I can survive anything. But if you don't get control of your group, you're heading for an epic disaster. And no one will be able to save you."

TWELVE

I'M SORRY," DEX SAID FOR THE FIFTH TIME as Sophie stared at the row of glittering castles in front of them, trying to find the courage to make her way over to the one with the pink flowers and knock on the front door. "It seems like I should be able to figure it out. But I'm afraid if I keep trying, the cache is going to erase itself."

"I told you, you don't need to apologize," Sophie promised him again. "I knew it was kind of a long shot. I just appreciate you trying."

"I still feel bad," Dex mumbled. "I can tell you really don't want to be here."

"Is that why we're still standing outside, watching the sparkly buildings sparkle?" Ro asked.

"Pretty much," Sophie admitted.

"Well, we either need to make our way *inside* or head back to Havenfield," Sandor told her after he ordered Lovise to take up a position behind them. "I don't like having you out in the open for this long. Especially near such high-profile targets."

"*Targets?*" Dex repeated.

"Yep! Gigantor's right." Ro craned her neck to check the tops of the towering Pures that lined the river that divided the twelve crystal castles from the rest of Eternalia. "If I were in the Neverseen, this is where I'd strike the hardest. Hit the Councillors at their fancy homes—or offices—or whatever these things are supposed to be. What better way to send the message 'We're in charge now!' than *that*, you know? What?" she asked when she noticed the way Sophie and Dex were gaping at her. "I said *if* I were a member of the Neverseen—not like I'm planning on becoming one! Besides, anyone who's studied basic battle strategy knows you have to take down the greatest symbols of power—preferably in a big, dramatic way—if you want the public to submit to your rule. Why do you think Gigantor wants to get us out of here as fast as possible?"

"Uh-huh," Sophie mumbled, not sure what to do with any of that information.

She went back to staring at the shiny castle.

"Are you nervous because of what Wylie said?" Dex asked as Sandor, Ro, and Lovise fanned out to cover more ground. "How the Council hasn't talked to you about the fire yet?"

That had nothing to do with the dread coursing through Sophie's veins—but it was a much safer answer than the truth.

"Do you think the Council will be upset?" she asked.

Dex shook his head. "You destroyed the enemy's storehouse. Why would they be mad?"

"I don't know. I wasn't expecting you all to be mad at me either—but I was clearly wrong about *that*."

Dex focused on his feet, kicking a loose pebble up the path. "I don't think anyone was *mad*—well, except Stina, but she's always mad about everything. And Linh was mostly mad at her brother. Not sure what's going on with you and Fitz—and I don't *want* to know," he added quickly. "But everyone else . . . well . . . I'm pretty sure they were mostly just scared."

Sophie turned to study him. "Are *you* scared?"

He kicked another pebble. "I know I shouldn't be."

"There is no *should*, Dex. You're allowed to feel whatever you feel."

"I guess. But . . . I've had a bodyguard for long enough that you'd think I'd be used to the whole sense-of-impending-doom thing. It's just beginning to feel real in a different way, you know? Like . . . remember when our biggest worries were whether or not we'd pass our midterms? And now I'm not even sure when it'll be safe enough for Foxfire to start having sessions again. And obviously I know you're the moonlark, and I knew you'd have to do all kinds of crazy, important things someday. But it's so strange hearing about you starting fires and scratching your own symbol into the ground. Even what Sandor and Ro were just saying, about how this place is a 'target' for the Neverseen. I never realized how lucky we all used to be, not having to worry about being attacked in our own cities."

"Someday we'll get that feeling back," Sophie promised.

"I sure hope so," Dex said quietly.

He turned back to face the row of castles, and Sophie realized how much his profile had changed since she'd first met him in Slurps and Burps. His rounded cheeks were gone, replaced with a sharper jawline, and his chin had a much more chiseled edge. Proof that her goofy best friend was slowly turning into a grown-up.

She just hoped his dimples would always be there when he smiled—and that she'd get to see that smile more often.

"Okay, it's time to listen to your bodyguards," Sandor said, clapping his hands and making Sophie and Dex both jump. "The sun will be setting soon, and we've stood here long enough. Either go knock on that door or take us home—now!"

Sophie reached into her pocket and squeezed Kenric's cache, reminding herself why she needed to be there. But she still had to tug out an itchy eyelash before she could force her legs to carry her up the crystal stairs.

"You're sure it's okay that you brought me with you?" Dex asked as Sophie made a ridiculously wimpy knock.

Sophie nodded. "We're going to need your help."

Plus, she couldn't handle another long stretch of alone time with Councillor Oralie.

Oralie would probably insist on making more excuses for why she gave her DNA to Project Moonlark and then totally abandoned her genetic daughter, lied to her for years, and left her stuck with a huge gap in her registry file. She might even take another stab at convincing Sophie that she was sorry for the problems Sophie would forever be stuck dealing with as a result of all the secrecy about her genetic parents.

Worse yet: She might try to tell Sophie that she truly does care about her again—and then Sophie would have to vomit all over the sparkly floor.

"I think you might need to knock a little louder," Dex said when no one answered.

"Allow me." Ro shoved past them and banged on the door with both fists.

Sophie cringed, counting the seconds, half hoping no one was home.

"Did you let Councillor Oralie know we were coming by?" Dex asked.

"She did *not*," a soft, fragile voice said as the door swung open.

And there she was.

Well . . . Sophie assumed it was Councillor Oralie. She'd kept her eyes down, so she could only see feet and legs at the moment. But Oralie was pretty much the only grown-up that

Sophie knew who would wear a ruffled pink gown and pink jeweled heels with diamond hearts on the toes just to hang around the house.

"Is everything okay?" Oralie asked. "I heard from Councillor Velia that Wylie has requested a full-Council meeting."

"We're not here about that," Sophie told her, taking a deep breath before forcing herself to look up. "And we don't have time to debate about letting my bodyguards come in."

Oralie's face was as annoyingly perfect as ever—all bright blue eyes and soft pink cheeks, framed by long blond ringlets. And even though Sophie had already done it several times, she couldn't help trying to spot some small resemblance between them.

Thankfully, she couldn't find anything.

Sophie cleared her throat and held out Kenric's cache. "We're here about *this*."

Oralie sucked in a breath. "Come in—quickly."

Sandor marched through first, scanning the shimmering foyer like he expected black-cloaked figures to drop from the chandelier.

"Woooooooooooooooooooooooooooooooow," Ro said, spinning in a slow circle. "I thought I'd reached maximum sparkle exposure with you elves. But this place is *unreal*. It's like glitter on top of jewels on top of *more* glitter on top of *more* jewels."

"I'm glad you're enjoying it," Oralie told her, "because I'll need you to wait here." She motioned to several throne-size armchairs with soft pink cushions. "You as well, Lovise. And yes, even you, Sandor."

"I go where Sophie goes," Sandor insisted.

"You *are* where Sophie is. Same building. It'll just be a slightly different room—and it's not up for negotiation. This is my house. I get to set the rules. And unfortunately, Dex, I need you to wait here as well."

"No—we need his help," Sophie told her.

Oralie shook her head, making her ringlets dance against the cream-colored bodice of her gown. "I already told you, *I* know how to open the cache. Sorry, Dex—it's nothing personal. I appreciate your willingness to assist us. I just want to keep you safe. Sophie doesn't always appreciate the dangers connected with Forgotten Secrets."

"Oh, I remember your little speech perfectly," Sophie assured her. "But Dex can handle it! Well . . . assuming he wants to," she added, realizing she should've double-checked that with him before she brought him. She leaned closer and whispered, "Sorry, I guess I should've asked if you're okay with this. There *is* a chance the memories could be a little intense, so I totally understand if you'd rather go home."

"No, I *want* to stay," Dex said, staring at the floor like he wished there were another pebble to kick. "But if Oralie doesn't want me here—"

"It's not her decision," Sophie interrupted. "I'm the one with the cache."

"And *I'm* the only one who can open it," Oralie reminded her.

"Eh. I'm sure we can figure it out on our own. I was just trying to save time—but if you're going to be stubborn . . ." Sophie shoved the cache into her pocket and turned to head toward the front door.

Oralie stepped in front of her. "Why are you being so difficult?"

Sophie could've given her a *long* list of reasons.

But she stuck with the one she could actually say in front of other people. "Because keeping things compartmentalized is what the Neverseen do—and I want us to be better than that! I realize there are risks, and trust me, I would never want to put any of my friends in danger. But I'm *so* sick of all the secrets! I'm also tired of trying to remember who knows what, and figuring out who I'm allowed to talk to. That's how our world has gotten into this mess in the first place—and I thought you agreed with me on that. Didn't you say it was time to start facing our world's darker truths instead of washing them away?"

"That doesn't mean I'm ready for the information in these caches to become public knowledge," Oralie argued.

"Dex isn't the public! He's a member of Team Valiant. And a superpowerful Technopath—which I'm pretty sure we *are* going to need." She held up the cache and pointed to the tiny inner crystals. "There are *seven* secrets in here—and I'm betting most of them are going to be as vague as the one in your cache. So we'll probably have to open another cache, and another, and another, to get to any sort of actual answer."

"Wait, you opened Oralie's cache?" Dex asked.

Sophie nodded. "A few days ago. There was only one memory—and it basically told us nothing. But it seemed like it might connect to something in Kenric's cache. That's why I had to track it down."

"Did tracking it down have anything to do with this fire I've been hearing about?" Oralie asked.

"It did." Sophie made sure she kept her head held high as she added, "The fire was an unexpected bonus. Why?"

"I'm not certain." Oralie looked down, trailing her fingers along the silken waistband of her gown. "Honestly, I have no idea what to make of your recent behavior, Sophie. Or this new attitude."

"For the record, I'm a *huge* fan of the attitude!" Ro informed her.

"There's no *attitude*," Sophie insisted. "I'm just trying to get things done without making our usual mistakes."

"Or considering the consequences," Oralie noted.

"Uh, I've pretty much set a record for near-death experiences—*and* I've had to watch all the people I care about risk their lives over and over and over. So I think it's safe to say that I'm *very* aware of the consequences. I just can't pretend that there's a way out of this mess without doing things that make us uncomfortable. The stakes are too high. So you can either help me—like you promised you would—or I can figure it out without you, like I've had to do for everything else."

Oralie reached up to rub her forehead—which was notably missing her pink-jeweled circlet. "Are you sure you want to expose yourself to these memories, Dex? They could be quite traumatic."

"They could also be super boring," Sophie countered.

"They could," Oralie agreed. "But I still need Dex to confirm that he understands the potential for danger. In fact . . ." She stalked toward him, placing her hands lightly on his shoulders and waiting for him to look at her. "Are you sure you want to do this, Dex? And by *this*, I mean exposing yourself to memories that may have been erased because the knowledge within them could shatter a person's sanity."

"Uhhhhh . . . sure," he mumbled, turning a little pale.

Sophie reached for his hand. "You can leave anytime, okay?"

He squeezed her hand tighter. "I know. But I'm not going anywhere."

Sophie tangled their fingers together and turned back to Oralie. "So . . . are we good?"

Oralie closed her eyes and adjusted her grip on Dex's shoulders. "I feel a lot of trepidation. But . . . he does seem emotionally prepared."

"I do?" Dex asked, then cleared his throat and said, "Right. Of course I do."

"Nice save," Ro told him.

His cheeks turned even pinker than the ruffles on Oralie's gown.

Sophie repeated her question. *"Are we good?"*

"I suppose," Oralie said through a long sigh. "But don't forget that I tried to warn you."

She dropped her arms and turned toward a long hall—then spun back to block Sandor when he tried to follow. "I still need you to stay here."

"If you're worried about my sanity," he told her, "there's no need."

"Actually, I'm worried about confidentiality. These are *elvin* secrets."

"Trying to hide your terrible decisions?" Ro asked. "Because I hate to break it to you, but we're already *super* aware of how poorly elves have been running things—aren't we?"

"Absolutely," Sandor and Lovise agreed immediately.

"And this is a *perfect* example of a poor decision," Sandor added. "Separating me from my charge and withholding information will only cause Sophie harm. Secrets hinder my ability to protect her."

"And yet I'm confident you have the skills to overcome any disadvantage," Oralie told him, pointing to one of the chairs.

"Give it up, Gigantor," Ro said. "Did you see that hair toss she just did? That's a classic we're-done-here move. You might as well get comfortable. She's not going to change her mind."

"I'm not," Oralie agreed, tossing her hair again.

Sandor gritted his teeth and turned to pace the room.

"We'll be fine," Sophie called over her shoulder as she followed Oralie down the hall.

Dex trailed after her, and neither of them spoke as Oralie's heels *click-click-click*ed across the floor through what felt like an endless series of shimmering rooms.

"Where are we going?" Sophie asked when they reached a winding staircase tucked deep into a shadowy corner.

"Somewhere quiet" was all Oralie told her.

Up and up they went, coiling around and around and around.

Sophie tried counting the steps but lost track after two hundred.

She lost her breath around the same time.

"Are we there yet?" she gasped.

"Close," Oralie promised—not sounding winded at all.

"*How* close?" Sophie asked after another two hundred steps. Sweat was streaming down her face—and of course Oralie was only glistening.

"*Very* close. In fact . . ." Oralie stopped in the middle of the next curve and licked a panel on the wall.

A hidden door sprang open, and she motioned for Dex and Sophie to follow her into a huge oblong room where everything was solid black—the floor, the walls, the ceiling. No sign of any windows or furniture, and the only light came from four round bulbs mounted in each of the corners.

"Wow," Sophie mumbled. "No pink."

"And no sparkles," Dex added.

"No *distractions*," Oralie clarified, gathering up her hair and coiling it into a loose bun. "My castle is designed to display the elegance and opulence that's expected of a Councillor. But my private office is meant for focus."

"Focus on what?" Sophie asked.

"Hang on." Oralie unfastened her sash, revealing that her gown was actually three separate pieces: a simple cream-colored tank top, a ruffled pink skirt, and plain black pants underneath.

The skirt whooshed to the floor, puddling at Oralie's feet like melting cotton candy, and Oralie kicked it into the corner—along with her heels.

"Wow," Sophie said again. "I didn't know you wore pants."

"There's a *lot* you don't know about me," Oralie said, padding across the room in her bare feet. Between the boring tank, black pants, and messy bun, she was almost unrecognizable. "Like I said, I come here to be free of any distractions—so I can relax and focus on this."

She leaned in and licked some sort of hidden panel in the middle of the wall, causing a soft whir to fill the air as projections flashed across every surface.

The floor and ceiling were covered in images, all of them jumbled on top of each other like messy stacks of photos—most of places and people that Sophie didn't recognize. But some were painfully familiar: the scorched buildings of Eternalia, the damaged force field around Atlantis, Silveny's broken wing, both Nightfall facilities, the Four Seasons Tree, the troll hive at Everglen, King Enki's ruined throne—basically the Neverseen's greatest hits, preserved in full, devastating color.

And the walls reminded Sophie of a brainstorming exercise she'd learned in her human elementary school. Hundreds and hundreds of words glowed as if they'd been written with pure white light, all tucked inside hand-drawn bubbles that were connected to other bubbles by thin lines that curled and dipped and tangled together and swooped across the room. Some words were crossed out. Others underlined. And some definitely caught Sophie's attention.

"Lodestar Initiative." "Criterion." "Archetype." "Legacy." "Stellarlune." "Elysian."

There were also names.

So. Many. Names.

All of Sophie's friends. Their families. All of the known members of the Black Swan—and the Neverseen. The other eleven Councillors. Sophie's human parents and sister. All of the Vackers. On and on and on.

Oralie had even listed two people that Sophie mostly tried her best not to think about: "Ethan Benedict Wright II" and "Eleanor Olivia Wright."

The bubbles for both names were tucked into a corner, connected only to each other, with a long line that led to a bubble with "Lady Gisela" inside—probably because she'd murdered them.

Thankfully, Oralie hadn't also connected them to Keefe.

"What is all this?" Dex asked, spinning around to take it in.

"My mind map," Oralie said, tracing her hand over a bubble with the name "Kenric Fathdon" inside. "Plus a collection of significant visuals, should I need clarity or inspiration. I'm sure it won't make much sense to you. But it helps me to draw it all out like this. It's the only way I can find all the different connections."

"Uh . . . why do you have a bubble with my name connected to a bubble that says 'ability restrictor'?" Dex asked.

"Because you created it."

"But I'll never make another one—*ever* again," Dex reminded her.

"That doesn't change the fact that you still know how to do it, which is all those bubbles are meant to imply. It's a record of your significant discovery, in case it ever comes into play again."

"It won't," Dex assured her.

"Perhaps not through you—but you're not the only Technopath in our world, are you? Do you really think the Neverseen don't have someone trying to build one for them? And if that happens, it seems prudent to make sure we never forget that you can make one as well, don't you agree?"

Dex gritted his teeth but didn't argue. Instead he pointed

to a bubble toward the bottom of one of the walls, with the name "Kesler Dizznee" inside and a bold line striking through it. "Why is my dad's name crossed out?"

Oralie tilted her head. "Ah. That was back when I was trying to figure out who was part of the Black Swan. Your father fit the profile—"

"Why? Because he's Talentless?" Dex jumped in.

"No, because he's known for expressing frustration with both the Council and our laws. Plus, there were certain anomalies with his registry feed. But after monitoring him more closely, I realized my assumption was wrong, so I crossed him out from that particular investigation. I still have him over there"—she pointed to the opposite wall, with the bubbles Dex had already asked about—"connected to you and your family, as well as to the work he does in his apothecary."

Sophie and Dex shared a look, and Sophie didn't have to read his mind to know he was thinking the same thing she was.

His dad wasn't part of the Black Swan—but his mom was a member of the Collective.

"Why do you have a line connecting Fallon Vacker to Elysian?" Sophie asked, changing the subject to something safer—and much more important. She crossed to the widest wall in the room to study Fallon's bubble, which had lines connecting it to almost every other bubble. "Does that mean he knows what it is?"

"I don't know," Oralie admitted, moving to Sophie's side. "That's why the line is dotted. See?" She pointed to the row of neat, glowing dashes. "But Fallon tends to be involved with most of our world's secrets, so I figured it was a safe bet to put in a placeholder."

"Are you going to ask him about it?" Sophie asked.

"Not unless I have to. His mind is . . . well . . . you saw how he was at Alvar's Tribunal. The past and present blur together into a mental mess. So I'm trying to see what I can discover on my own. If I get stuck, I'll set up a meeting."

"I want to be there if you do," Sophie told her.

"We'll see" was the most Oralie would promise.

"Um . . . what's Elysian?" Dex asked.

Oralie sighed and tucked a stray ringlet behind her ear. "Something I'd hoped I'd be able to keep between just Sophie and me—so I'm counting on your discretion. And I understand that you don't want to keep our information compartmentalized, Sophie," she added quickly, "but we need to be cautious—at least until we know more. Right now I have no idea what we're on the brink of uncovering, and I fear it may be something quite traumatic. When Kenric said the word in my cache, I could feel his genuine terror—and he wasn't someone who was easily shaken. So until we have at least some idea of what we're dealing with, can we agree to keep any knowledge of Elysian between the three of us?"

"That . . . might be a problem," Sophie mumbled, fidgeting with the panic-switch ring on her finger.

"Please tell me you haven't told any of your other friends—"

"Not yet," Sophie cut in. "But . . . I saw Lord Cassius yesterday, and he showed me a memory he'd recovered—one that Lady Gisela had tried really, really hard to erase. She spent the majority of the memory prying information out of him about Keefe's empathy because she was trying to figure out if the treatments she'd done to herself and Lord Cassius were working. But at the end she asked him if he'd ever heard anything about Elysian."

"Had he?" Oralie asked, making her way over to the bubble with Lord Cassius's name.

Sophie shook her head. "He asked if it was a star, and Gisela seemed to take that as confirmation that he didn't know anything."

"Hmm. Well, he knows the name now, so . . ." Oralie swished her finger through the air, and a solid glowing line appeared between Lord Cassius's bubble and the Elysian bubble.

"But he doesn't know what it is," Dex reminded her. "So shouldn't that be a dotted line?"

"He knows the name. That's enough to solidly connect him. In fact . . ." She swished her finger a different direction, and a solid line appeared, connecting the Dex Dizznee bubble to the Elysian bubble.

Sophie noticed there was already a line connecting her name to Elysian as well.

"Did you ask Lord Cassius not to mention Elysian to anyone else?" Oralie asked.

"No—I figured that would guarantee he'd bring it up to

everyone. I did try to downplay it, but he could tell I'd heard the term before and assumed that meant it was important."

"Sounds like I'll need to have a talk with him," Oralie said as she added a line between the Lady Gisela bubble and the Elysian bubble. "Did Lady Gisela say anything that might tell us what Elysian is, or at least what she thinks it is—aside from the fact that it isn't a star?" She swept her wrist and created a new bubble with "Star?" in it, then connected that to Elysian and crossed it out.

"Well . . . she said she'd been researching things like moon cycles and star and planetary alignments and the Prime Sources and shadowflux and quintessence."

"That was probably for stellarlune," Oralie murmured, adding bubbles with all those terms right between the Elysian and stellarlune bubbles—with dotted lines going to each. "Anything else?"

"Um . . . she mentioned a final riddle she needed to solve."

"Interesting." Oralie added another bubble with "Riddle?" inside and put a solid line from it to Lady Gisela and a dotted line between it and Elysian and stellarlune. "Is that everything?"

"Actually . . . no. Lady Gisela also revealed she's a Conjurer."

"You don't seem surprised," Dex noted as Oralie made the appropriate adjustments to her mind map.

"Well . . . I've long wondered if she had another talent, since she's always been far too haughty for someone who was one of the rare Polyglots with only one ability. But I wouldn't have guessed she's a Conjurer."

"What would you have guessed?" Sophie wondered.

"Given Keefe's new ability to give commands, I've been wondering if she was a Beguiler."

Sure enough, there was a bubble with "Beguiler?" inside connected to Lady Gisela's name.

Oralie crossed it out.

"Any idea why she would hide being a Conjurer?" Sophie asked.

"Not at the moment. But I'll definitely put some thought into it." Oralie stepped back, studying her updated mind map. "Is that everything you learned from the memory?"

"Yep!" Sophie ordered her eyes to stay *far* away from the stellarlune bubble.

Oralie smiled. "You're a terrible liar."

Sophie shrugged. "I can't be good at everything."

"No one can," Oralie agreed. "And I'm assuming that's your way of telling me that you're not going to share—which does seem odd, considering the speech you gave a few minutes ago about how you're sick of secrets. Aren't we supposed to be better than the Neverseen?"

Sophie *really* hated when her own words came back to haunt her.

"It's just . . . something I feel like Keefe deserves to hear first," she mumbled.

"I suppose I can understand that. So how about this? I'll let it go—for *now*—if you promise you'll fill me in if it becomes significant. And *if* you answer one question."

"That depends on the question," Sophie countered.

"It's simple enough. I just want to know if it has something to do with Keefe's new abilities—and I'm pretty sure the way you just flinched gave me my answer."

Sophie didn't see any point in arguing.

"While we're on the subject," Oralie said quietly, "is there *anything* about Keefe's abilities that you're willing to share?"

Sophie glanced at Dex, and he gave her a tiny head shake—so fast, Oralie shouldn't have noticed. But Sophie was pretty sure she had.

"Well . . . he ran away yesterday," Sophie said, trying to distract Oralie with a different bombshell. "That's why Ro's with me—in case you were wondering. Apparently he thinks the only way to guarantee that his mom can never exploit his new abilities is to hide. And no, we don't know where he is." There was no way she was telling Oralie that Keefe was somewhere in the Forbidden Cities. "We also don't have any way to track him down—and I tried transmitting to him, but he ignored me. So I asked Silveny to try calling for him, and we'll see if she can annoy him into cooperating."

"Hmmm," Oralie said, adding a new bubble next to Keefe's name with the word "Missing" in the center.

It shouldn't have made Sophie's eyes burn—but her tear ducts didn't get the message.

"I must say," Oralie murmured, "I'm not sure how to interpret the fact that you're here right now."

"What do you mean?" Sophie asked.

"Well . . . I know how important Keefe is to you—"

"He's my friend," Sophie jumped in, with maybe a little too much emphasis.

"I know," Oralie told her. "And yet you're here, working on Kenric's cache, instead of rounding up all your friends to form a search party—and I don't mean that as a criticism, by the way. I doubt Keefe needs to be rescued. I'm simply trying to determine if the reason you're letting him hide is your fear of Lady Gisela or your fear of Keefe's new abilities."

"Neither," Sophie told her. "I'm just . . . trying to respect Keefe's wishes—and I'm trying to focus on things that might help us get ahead of the Neverseen. We know Lady Gisela is interested in Elysian, so we *need* to figure out what it is." She held up Kenric's cache. "Please tell me this one will be easier to open than yours was."

"It definitely will be." Oralie stretched out her hand for the cache. "May I?"

Sophie only hesitated a second before handing it over.

Oralie held it closer to the wall, and the soft glow from the projections made the inner crystals twinkle as she spun the cache in a slow circle. "Kenric made some changes before he asked me to give it to you. He wanted to make sure you'd have a way of accessing the memories if you needed them—but he also wanted to make sure you couldn't do it without me. I guess he wanted us to work together."

"Huh," Dex said. "That was kinda risky. If something had happened to you, Sophie would be out of luck."

"Yes, I suppose that's true. Kenric must've been hoping it would encourage me to be cautious."

"And you never tried to open the cache before you gave it to me?" Sophie asked.

"I considered it," Oralie admitted. "But I knew Kenric would be able to tell if I did. And then he was gone, and the idea of watching his memories sounded far too painful. Even now . . ." She wrapped her arm around her middle, and Sophie noticed her hand was shaking.

"You don't have to stay," Sophie offered. "Once the cache is open, we can take it from there. I'm sure Dex can figure out how to update your mind map with anything we learn."

"I'm sure he could," Oralie agreed, closing her eyes and taking a deep breath. "But . . . I cannot keep running from these truths."

She tapped the side of the cache, then flipped it over and tapped a different place, rotating it three more times before tapping it again.

"Please tell me that *is* Kenric's cache," Sophie mumbled when nothing happened.

She'd asked Dex to verify, but he'd said there was no way to identify the original owner—and after all the drama with Keefe stealing the cache and then stealing back a fake, she couldn't help worrying.

"We'll know as soon as I complete the activation sequence," Oralie said, flipping the cache over and spinning it again before holding her finger over a specific place.

"Wow," Dex breathed as a tiny curved crack, similar to a broken piece of fingernail, appeared in the center of the clear crystal. "I couldn't feel any of those buttons—or that access point."

"You aren't supposed to. Caches are designed to be counterintuitive to a Technopath's senses and rely on tangible evidence rather than technology. In my cache's case, it needed several different kinds of DNA along with a password. For Kenric's, he chose to have it require only one thing—though I wish he'd picked something else. I worked so hard to break myself of this nervous habit."

She reached up, tugged on her eyelashes, and held out the one she pulled free.

"Huh," Dex said, "I've never seen anyone do that besides Sophie."

"Me neither," Oralie said. "Strange coincidence."

Sophie looked anywhere but at her. "So . . . we put the eyelash in that little slit?"

"We do," Oralie agreed, lowering the eyelash toward the cache and slowly sliding it in.

Sophie waited for a click or a beep. "Um . . . nothing happened."

"Actually, it did." Dex pointed to the colorful inner crystals, which were now twinkling like tiny stars. "It's waiting for us to select which memory we want to view."

Oralie lowered her finger toward the cache but stopped before making contact. "Which one do you want to start with?"

"Do the colors mean anything?" Sophie asked.

"I'm not sure. I'm told the color can reflect the mood of the memory—but I've only logged one, so I don't truly know."

Sophie studied the crystals.

One was blue.

One was red.

One was yellow.

One was pink.

One was purple.

One was orange.

And one was a color that meant something very significant to the elves.

"Let's start with that one," Sophie whispered, pointing to the crystal that probably held the most intense memory in the cache.

Green.

The color of death.

THIRTEEN

WHOA," DEX WHISPERED AS a small hologram flashed out of the cache and hovered above Oralie's palm—two familiar figures, standing in the middle of a forest. "Is that Councillor Bronte?"

"Looks like it." Sophie squinted at the tiny face of the notoriously grumpy Councillor. "Same scowl. Same sharp features and pointy ears. But . . . I didn't know his hair is curly."

"That's why he usually keeps it cropped short," Oralie explained. "He thinks the curls make him look too soft for a member of the Council."

"So why is his hair longer here?" Dex wondered.

"I'm assuming he's been away on a long assignment, and

that's why his cape and tunic also look wrinkled and dirty. But I can't say for certain. This memory is from before I was on the Council."

"How can you tell?" Sophie asked.

Oralie swallowed hard and pointed to the redheaded figure standing next to Bronte. "Kenric's hair. He always wore it in a ponytail like that—until I teased him about it at my inauguration. Next time I saw him, he'd cut it short, and he kept it that way."

"You did him a favor," Dex told her, flashing a dimpled grin.

Oralie didn't return his smile. She just stared and stared at Kenric, like she was a prisoner and he was the gateway to freedom.

Sophie cleared her throat. "So . . . how long ago was this?"

"It's hard to say. Kenric served on the Council for quite some time before I was elected."

"You can't tell by Bronte's ears?" Sophie asked.

"Not really. The only notable benchmark with our ears is when the points begin to take shape at the end of our first millennium—and even then, the change is barely noticeable. And all the growth after that is too subtle to use as any sort of gauge." Oralie laughed when she noticed the way Sophie was cringing. "Don't worry, you'll be used to it by the time yours start to form."

Sophie was pretty sure she would *never* get used to the idea of having pointy ears. But at least she apparently had nine hundred eighty-five more years before she had to worry about it.

Or was it nine hundred eighty-four?

She could never keep track of her age anymore. The elves were too vague about time.

"So, if you—" Sophie started to say, but the projection of Kenric cut her off.

"Why are you here?" he asked Bronte, crossing his arms. "I didn't call for help—and I have the situation under control."

"I'll be the judge of that," Bronte told him, turning in a slow circle as he studied the trees, many of which looked withered and yellow. "Why are you investigating this area?"

"King Dimitar brought it to our attention. He claimed we've been allowing the humans to expand into this land, even though it's supposed to be a Neutral Territory—and unfortunately he's right." Kenric pointed to the mountains in the distance. "That's the border over there. And *that*"—he gestured to a patch of brownish haze with the vague outlines of buildings peeking through—"is a well-established human city that cannot easily be relocated. Clearly we should've been paying closer attention. Especially since their pollution has already done tremendous damage to the surrounding landscape. I'm honestly not sure what solution would make sense at this point. Perhaps if we—"

"Has King Dimitar made any threats?" Bronte interrupted.

"Not directly. But he made it clear that if the humans are

allowed to remain, he'll consider it proof that the Neutral Territories are up for grabs. He gave us a week to get back to him."

"Why didn't someone hail me? I have more experience with the ogres!"

"You have more experience with *everything*, Bronte. You can't always claim seniority. Plus, you were away working on the mysterious investigation you refuse to tell us about. So Emery assigned this to *me*—and I'm more than capable of handling it."

"You're an adequate Councillor," Bronte told him—which was actually a compliment coming from him. "But you're out of your depth here. You have *no* idea what we may be dealing with."

"Then why don't you enlighten me?" Kenric snapped.

"Trust me—you don't want to know."

Most of the time Sophie couldn't tell that Bronte was thousands of years old—aside from his ears. But as he surveyed the forest again, his eyes filled with an ancient grief. "Where's the gnome you hailed Elwin about?"

Kenric frowned. "How did you—"

"Elwin alerted me right after he spoke with you. I've asked all the physicians to contact me if they ever hear any report of a sick gnome—and thankfully Elwin remembered."

"Why? Are you some sort of expert in gnomish illness?"

"Unfortunately, yes. But only of a very specific ailment."

"Which ailment?"

"He's talking about the drakostomes, isn't he?" Sophie mumbled when Bronte ignored Kenric's question.

"He must be," Oralie agreed.

"But that can't be what this is, right?" Dex asked. "I thought the gnomish plague was the first time the ogres ever used the drakostomes—well, except for what happened with the Four Seasons Tree."

"That was my understanding as well," Oralie said quietly. "But I suppose we're about to find out."

She pointed to the hologram, where the projection of Bronte was demanding to see the gnome immediately.

"It's a bit of a walk," Kenric warned as he motioned for Bronte to follow him.

The memory turned shaky for the next few minutes as they wove through the forest, scaling fallen logs and crossing a dried-up river before reaching a clearing where all the trees were bare—except one, which was covered in vivid green leaves and delicate white flowers.

Kenric knelt at the base of the thriving tree, and it took Sophie a second to notice the small body tangled in the roots.

She gasped.

So did Dex and Oralie.

In the memory, Bronte just shook his head.

"I'm assuming he was healing this tree," Kenric said, placing his hand on the healthy trunk, "and whatever poisoned the clearing ended up poisoning him. But Elwin will know for certain. He told me he had to stop by an apothecary for supplies before heading over. That's why I was back at the arrival point when you showed up, waiting to bring him here."

"I'm certain Elwin will hail you if he can't find us," Bronte assured Kenric as he studied the gnome's pale face. "But I fear he'll be too late."

"The gnome still has a pulse," Kenric argued, reaching for the gnome's wrist.

Bronte grabbed his shoulder to stop him. "*Don't* touch him! In fact, don't touch anything!"

"I already touched him when I checked his pulse earlier! And why would it matter? If this is a virus, they rarely pass between species—and given the state of this forest, it's pretty safe to assume there's a toxin at work, which we've already been exposed to just by being here."

"Trust me, there are no safe assumptions if ogres are involved," Bronte muttered, tearing his hands through his hair—and scowling when he felt the curls.

"What does *that* mean?" Kenric asked.

"Just . . . don't move. Stop talking. I need to think for a second." Bronte made his way over to one of the withered trees, sniffing the bark before crouching to study the roots.

"It's been about three hundred seconds," Kenric announced several minutes later. "So it's time to tell me what's going on. This is *my* assignment—"

"Not anymore. I'm officially taking over."

"You can't—"

"Yes, I can—and honestly, you should be thanking me, Kenric. I can't tell you how many times I've wished I erased this knowledge. I just didn't see how all of us could bury it while the ogres still knew everything."

"He was right," Oralie said as Kenric's projection demanded answers—and Bronte ignored him. "If Bronte had erased his memories of the drakostomes, we never would've known what was happening when the ogres unleashed the plague."

"And yet Councillors are still using caches," Sophie reminded her. "Aren't you?"

"We have to. There will always be *some* knowledge that's too dangerous for us to maintain. But . . . there must be a better way to find what's been erased. Maybe if everyone knows small pieces—"

"We'd be exactly like the Neverseen," Sophie finished for her.

"In a way, yes, we would. But we wouldn't be doing it to limit the power of our members. Merely to protect everyone's sanity, while also making sure we don't keep too much important information in one place."

"It'll still slow everything down," Sophie argued.

"I suppose." Oralie tucked another stray ringlet behind her ear as she turned to study her mind map. "There are no easy answers, Sophie. And very few perfect solutions—but I'm assuming you don't need me to tell you that. You're the one setting fires."

"*One* fire," Sophie corrected, ready to remind her that they were talking about two very different things—but the hologram Bronte had finished studying the roots and was making his way back to Kenric.

"The good news," he said, "is that this doesn't appear to be what I feared. I'll still need to collect a few samples to be absolutely certain—but I believe you're right. This poor creature fell victim to whatever human chemical wreaked havoc on this forest."

"And the bad news?" Kenric asked. "Since I'm assuming you have some."

"Unfortunately, I do." Bronte knelt next to the gnome, sighing as he studied the gnome's bare feet. "We're too late to save him—though I don't know that we ever would've been able to."

Kenric covered his mouth. "How can you be so sure?"

"Clearly, you're not familiar with gnomish anatomy. See these growths?" Bronte pointed to the gnome's toes, which were covered in strange, wispy tendrils. "Those are roots—or the beginning of them, anyway. And that only happens when—"

"A gnome is trying to shift," Kenric finished for him.

Bronte nodded grimly. "Gnomes will only try to shift when they have no other option, since it means surrendering their form forever. So he must've sensed the poison in his system, knew the damage was too great to recover from, and tried to finish the rest of his days as a tree. But his roots were too weak to take hold. Or perhaps the soil was too tainted. Either way, the roots have now dried up—and I'm sure if you check again, his last song will have fallen silent. I'm assuming that's what you felt. The song is rhythmic, like a pulse."

Kenric gently took the gnome's wrist and pressed two fingers against the pulse point.

Sophie's eyes welled with tears when he shook his head.

Dex sniffled.

Oralie looked away.

"The best we can do now," Bronte said, grabbing a rock and starting to scrape at the mud with it, "is help him return to the soil."

"You want to *bury* him?" Kenric asked. "But . . . what if you're wrong and there's a way to save him?"

"There isn't. But Elwin will be here soon enough to confirm—and to test us for any signs of contamination. We'll also need a full detox, but we can deal with that later. For now, we have a lot of digging to do. We owe this gnome a dignified burial as soon as possible." He pointed to another rock for Kenric to use.

"Shouldn't we at least hail someone to bring us proper tools?"

"And have another mind to wash and another detox to perform?" Bronte shook his head and dug the rock deeper, pushing aside a thick trench of soil. "I'd rather make do with what we have."

Kenric reluctantly set to work, and they both dug in silence—until Kenric stopped and turned toward the healthy tree. "We should make this a memorial, to honor the gnome's sacrifice—"

"That won't be possible," Bronte interrupted.

"Why not?"

"Because that tree—along with all the others—will have to be removed in order to make sure the toxin is completely eradicated."

"But . . . he gave his life to save it!"

"All the more reason to make sure all trace of it is gone. We know too little about human chemicals to risk leaving anything behind that could harm other gnomes."

Kenric stepped closer to the tree, trailing his hand down the bark. "Then we'll plant another to replace it. Maybe with a plaque—"

"There can be no memorial, Kenric. What happened here is tragic—but it must be kept secret. Think of the panic it could cause if others found out."

"But this gnome—"

"Is gone," Bronte finished for him. "We cannot change that. Our focus must be on protecting the living."

"That doesn't mean we can't honor the dead."

"In this case, it does."

"That's not your decision!"

"Yes, it is. I already told you, I'm taking over this

assignment—and you should be relieved. The Washer will spare you from this sorrow."

Kenric threw down his rock. "I don't want to be spared!"

Bronte sighed but continued scraping away another layer of soil. "You're letting your emotions take control—and I don't say that with any judgment. I understand how difficult these kinds of tragedies are to process. But that doesn't change the fact that this situation must be handled objectively, with a mind toward safety and preservation, which you're clearly incapable of at the moment. I also have questions for King Dimitar that only *I* can ask. So *I* will be taking over. And given the sensitivity of this situation, *you* will submit to the wash. You know the protocol, Kenric. You'd tell me exactly the same thing if our roles were reversed—and I would be *obligated* to comply."

"What's that?" Sophie asked as the projection of Bronte reached into his pocket and removed a small blue handkerchief.

"Standard procedure," Oralie murmured.

"This is wrong," Kenric said as he stomped over and snatched the square of fabric. "That gnome gave his life trying to clean up our mess—"

"It's not *our* mess," Bronte interrupted. "The humans polluted this forest."

"And we let them. We're supposed to be monitoring this planet, making sure things like this don't happen!"

"There is a *lot* to monitor, Kenric. We can only keep track of so much."

"Then we should ask for more help."

"From *whom*?"

Kenric dragged a hand down his face, leaving streaks of mud. "I . . . have no idea. But this gnome was a hero. He deserves to be remembered."

"He will be," Bronte promised, waiting for Kenric to meet his eyes before he told him, "by *me*."

Kenric frowned. "You're not going to erase—"

"Not in this case. So I can assure you, *I* will never forget what happened here. I'll even endeavor to discover the gnome's name and alert any of his friends and family of his passing."

"Somehow that doesn't feel like enough."

"It doesn't," Bronte agreed. "But . . . it will have to be."

Kenric moved back toward the tree and plucked a handful of the white flowers. He sprinkled the petals over the gnome as he murmured, "I'm sorry we failed to keep you safe. Hopefully we'll do better in the future."

"We'll certainly try our best," Bronte said quietly.

Sophie wanted to shout at both of them that they'd fail—that the ogres would unleash the plague and Calla would have to sacrifice herself to save her species. But talking to a memory was almost as pointless as erasing the memory in the first place.

"Rest well, Kenric," Bronte told him. "And make sure you lean against something solid."

Kenric rolled his eyes and sat, leaning against the healthy tree as he held the handkerchief against his nose and breathed in the sweet scent.

"Bronte *drugged* him?" Sophie asked as the memory blurred to black.

Oralie nodded. "That's the protocol. Whenever it becomes clear that something will become a Forgotten Secret, the Councillor making the call sedates the other, to give the Washer a clean edge to the memory."

"But that's not how your Forgotten Secret ended," Sophie reminded her.

"No, Kenric bent the rules that night. In more ways than one." The slight flush to her checks made Sophie wonder if Oralie was thinking about the moment when Kenric had almost kissed her.

Councillors weren't allowed to date or marry or have families of their own because it could bias their decisions. But Kenric had asked Oralie to resign with him so they could be together—and Oralie had refused.

Not because she didn't love him.

Because she needed to stay on the Council.

Partially for her own ambitions. And partially so she'd be in a position to protect Sophie.

Sophie still couldn't figure out what to do with any of that information.

"That poor gnome," Dex said, reminding Sophie what she

should be thinking about. "I can't believe there was nothing they could do to help him."

"We are powerless in many ways," Oralie said quietly. "That's why I warned you that these memories could be traumatic. You don't have to subject yourself to them—"

"Yes, we do," Sophie interrupted. "Or, I do at least."

"So do I," Dex jumped in. "But I'm confused. What happened to the first half of this memory? Shouldn't it have started with the moment Kenric got to wherever that Neutral Territory was—not when Bronte arrived?"

"Caches don't need to contain the *entire* memory," Oralie told him. "Only the significant information. The rest is erased."

"But what if they didn't realize that something was significant at the time?" Dex argued.

"That wouldn't happen."

Sophie snorted. "Riiiiiiiiiight. Because Councillors *never* make mistakes."

Oralie reached up to massage her temples. "Fine. I suppose I can't say *never*—because no one can. But I think you're forgetting that these decisions are being made by *Councillors*. I know your upbringing has made it hard for you to view us with the proper respect—but we are elected for our talent, intelligence, and experience."

"Really?" Sophie asked. "You're blaming my *upbringing*?"

"There's no *blame*. I'm just making sure you realize that it takes decades of hard work and sacrifice to prove ourselves worthy enough to be elected to the Council. We're not perfect—but we deserve more credit than you're giving us."

"I guess it'd be easier to agree with you about that if our world wasn't currently falling apart," Sophie snapped back. "Or if I hadn't been *created* so I could fix all your problems. Or—"

"Okay." Oralie held out her hands like a stop sign. "Let's just . . . move on. We still have six memories left, and at this rate we'll be here all night."

"Fine." Sophie crossed her arms as Oralie pressed the cache's pink crystal and a new hologram appeared—two figures again, this time sitting in a small, square room with mirrored walls and a table between them.

Kenric's hair was cut short, so it had to be a memory from after Oralie was elected to the Council. And the elf he was talking to had the matchmaker's crest fastening his white cape across his shoulders.

"I know what you're going to say, Behnam," Kenric said, "but you have nothing to worry about. This is purely a hypothetical conversation."

"That would be easier to believe if you weren't wearing your circlet," Behnam noted.

Kenric reached up and removed his amber-encrusted crown and set it on the table between them. "Better?"

"Wait!" Sophie leaned toward the cache to study the matchmaker. "Is that Behnam Aria?"

Now that she was looking closer, she could see the

similarities between Behnam and Glim—Rayni. Same shiny black hair. Same bronze skin. Same dramatic eyebrows.

Oralie nodded slowly. "How do you know him?"

"I don't." She had to stop herself from blurting out that he was Glimmer's father.

Tam and Wylie were supposed to be the ones to reveal that to the Council.

But she couldn't resist adding, "I've heard the gossip about his family."

"That was . . . a difficult situation" was all Oralie had to say about that.

Before Sophie could press her about it, the projection of Behnam told Kenric, "You realize that taking off your crown doesn't actually change anything, right? You're still a Councillor. And I still have rules and procedures to follow— rules and procedures which you're supposed to enforce, by the way. Not ask me to bend for you *hypothetically*."

Kenric sighed, tracing his fingers over the smooth stones in his circlet. "You're right, of course. But . . . between you and me, I'd get rid of those rules if I could."

Behnam glanced over his shoulder. "You should be careful who hears you say that. Especially here." He waved his arm around the room, and Sophie finally recognized it.

She'd been in an identical room when she'd gone to register for the match. And she'd sat in an identical chair when she'd discovered that she was *unmatchable*.

"What if I told you that neither of us was going to remember the rest of this conversation?" Kenric asked quietly. "Everything from this moment on will be erased."

Behnam's eyebrows lifted. "Then what's the point?"

"This way I'll be able to remember that I asked. But I won't know whether or not you answered. That'll be enough for me to finally let this go—while also ensuring that there's no proof of you bending any rules. It'll be almost as if it never happened."

"'Almost' doesn't usually count for much," Behnam noted.

"No, I suppose it doesn't." Kenric buried his face in his hands and took a long breath. "I realize this is a tremendous ask. I'm just . . . running out of ideas for how to move on—and I *have* to move on. Surely you can understand that."

Behnam steepled his fingers in front of his face and leaned back in his chair. "Who will wash my memory?"

"I will."

"And what will I get in return?"

"Do you need something?"

Behnam looked away. "I might. Someday."

Kenric tilted his head to study him. "Well, seeing as how I won't remember this part of our conversation, I can't guarantee anything beyond this: I've always liked you. I also trust you. That's why I came to you with this question. And I always strive to be a fair and ethical person. So if you ever find yourself in need, I'd like to believe that I'll do everything within my power to help. Do you believe that?"

Several long seconds passed before Behnam nodded.

"How did Kenric vote in Behnam's Tribunal?" Sophie had to know.

Kenric had been one of her favorite Councillors before he was killed. But she was getting pretty used to having people disappoint her.

"I can't discuss that," Oralie told her. "But . . . you should know that he was as fair and ethical as he always was." She swallowed hard before she added, "That verdict haunted him. It haunted many of us."

Sophie doubted Rayni would think that was enough.

She certainly didn't.

But in the projection, Behnam leaned forward and told Kenric, "Truthfully, I *do* understand why you need this answer. So I'll plug in the data for you—but I feel the need to remind you that it will always be impossible. She already collected all five of her lists. No more can ever be issued."

"No need to worry about that—she'll never ask for one," Kenric assured him with a smile that didn't match the sorrow in his eyes. "But I appreciate the reminder of how futile this all is."

"Is he talking about . . . you?" Sophie asked, stealing a glance at Oralie.

Oralie covered her mouth. "I . . ."

Her voice trailed off as Behnam picked up a small, clear

screen and started tapping different places—a process Sophie remembered all too well.

In her case, the screen had flashed red with the word "unmatchable."

But for Kenric, the light flashed bright white.

"Want me to say it?" Behnam asked. "Or just show you?"

Kenric swallowed hard. "Just show me."

Everyone held their breath as Behnam turned his screen to face Kenric.

The gadget showed two match lists side by side—one for Kenric and one for Oralie, followed by a series of names.

Sophie only had to read the top listings to find the answer Kenric had been looking for.

Kenric's number one match was Oralie.

And Oralie's number one match was Kenric.

FOURTEEN

I DON'T UNDERSTAND," ORALIE WHISPERED, closing her palm around the cache to block the projection. "This isn't a Forgotten Secret. It's . . . I don't know what it is."

"It's something Kenric didn't want to remember," Sophie mumbled. "But I'm pretty sure he didn't want to forget it either."

Oralie's laugh was equal parts bitter and broken. "Well, how nice of him to leave it in his cache for anyone to find."

"He probably figured he'd be the only one to see it, since that's how caches are supposed to work," Dex reminded her. "And by the time he decided to give it to you, he wouldn't have had any idea what was in there, right?"

"No, he wouldn't. But Kenric was usually far more cautious when it came to . . . these kinds of things." She cleared her throat, but her voice still cracked when she added, "Then again, I never would've imagined him going to a matchmaker with that question."

"Were you surprised by the answer?" Sophie had to ask. "I know you're probably going to say it's none of my business—and . . . I guess it isn't. I've just seen the matchmakers ruin so many lives by following their rules that I'm curious if this time, when he bent the rules, he actually got it right."

Oralie wrapped her arms around her waist and bowed her head, as if she were trying to curl into herself. "All I'll say is this. Kenric and I . . . we had a very special connection. Add in the fact that Empaths and Telepaths are frequently matched with each other, and . . . no, I wasn't surprised to see his name at the top of my list, or mine at the top of his. But . . . we also wanted different things—and no matchmaker would ever be able to account for that."

Sophie could think of a *lot* more questions. But she knew how much they would hurt Oralie—and even as angry as she was, she wasn't ready to sink that low.

"Why are Empaths and Telepaths usually matched together?" Dex asked.

Oralie cleared her throat again and dabbed the corners of her eyes. "The abilities complement each other. Both are introspective—but in very different ways, which allows each partner to find a deeper understanding of the other."

"Huh," Dex said, glancing at Sophie. "I guess that means you probably would've been matched with—"

"I won't be matched with anyone," Sophie jumped in, before he could say the name she definitely wasn't ready to think about. And she made sure Oralie was listening when she added, "I'm unmatchable, remember?"

Oralie looked away.

So did Dex.

Sophie sighed. "We should move on to the next memory— and hopefully it'll tell us something about Elysian. We haven't learned anything useful so far."

"We haven't," Oralie agreed, wiping her eyes again as she stood up taller. "But before we move on, I need to ask a favor. I know you're tired of secrets, Sophie—and I can't make you keep this one. But this . . . It's . . ."

"I get it," Sophie said, even though Oralie didn't deserve any favors. Some things should be allowed to stay private. "I'm not going to tell anyone."

"Neither will I," Dex promised.

"Thank you." Oralie smoothed the front of her pants and tucked a loose ringlet behind her ear—collecting herself a little before she held out the cache. "Okay. So . . . which memory do you want to view next?"

"Why don't you pick this time?" Sophie told Dex. "Maybe you'll have better luck finding what we need."

He studied the cache for a beat before choosing the red crystal.

The new hologram showed Kenric with short hair again. And this time the other figure was Oralie.

"Do you remember this?" Sophie asked as the real Oralie sucked in a breath.

"I . . . don't know." She spun the cache in her palm, studying the scene from every angle. "I think we're in Kenric's readying room in the Seat of Eminence. The walls had wood paneling like this, and I'll never forget that ugly red armchair—or the horrible plaid ottoman. But I've only been to his readying room once—and I wasn't wearing that dress."

"Are you sure?" Sophie squinted at the pink ruffles. "It looks like all your other sparkly gowns."

"But it isn't. That one was woven from fresh rose petals, and the shimmer comes from dewdrops. I could only wear it once before it withered away. A gnome made it for me, to thank me for helping her find a home inside our Sanctuary. She wanted me to have something special to wear at my first-year reception. The Councillors hold a banquet to celebrate when someone completes their first year after being elected," she explained when she saw Sophie's confusion. "And mine was at the Seat of Eminence, so that must be why I'm in Kenric's readying room. But I have no memory of going there that night. In fact . . . I don't remember much about the banquet, either—though I did have a glass of fizzleberry wine, and that always makes my head a little fuzzy."

"Kenric blamed fizzleberry wine for your other memory he erased," Sophie reminded her.

"He did." Oralie frowned at his projection. "The fuzziness does feel familiar, so maybe this is the memory we've been waiting for."

"Let's hope," Sophie said as Kenric pointed to his red armchair and said, "Have a seat."

"No, I won't be staying long enough for that." Oralie's gown made a soft swishing sound as she stalked closer to him. "I just came by to tell you that you can stop pretending to be my ally. I know you want me off the Council."

"I do?" Kenric lowered himself into the chair and propped up his feet. "That's news to me."

"Oh please. Clarette told me during dinner that you were the lone holdout vote during my election—which you would've heard if you'd stayed past the first course tonight. But clearly you couldn't stand to watch me be celebrated."

"No, my stomach wasn't feeling well, and I assumed you wouldn't appreciate it if I vomited during your fancy dinner."

"Yet you seem perfectly fine now."

"Because I hailed Elwin! He told me which elixirs I should take—and he warned me that one of them would have me burping like an imp for over an hour, so I figured everyone would prefer I not come back for dessert."

She leaned closer, placing her hand over his. "You're a better liar than most. But I can still tell. So why don't you try the truth this time? It's obvious you don't like me—and that's fine. I'm not a fan of you, either."

Kenric's lips twitched with a smile. "Is that so?"

"Yes. You're arrogant and boring. And you have terrible taste in everything." She crinkled her nose at his orange tunic— which did clash with his bright red hair.

Kenric's smile widened. "If you were a better Empath, I doubt you'd denounce my taste in *everything*."

She yanked back her hand. "I'm the best Empath you'll ever find."

"Someday you might be—if you stop letting your personal biases and ambitions cloud your judgment."

"Excuse me?"

"And there it is," Kenric said, pointing to the hand she'd placed over her heart. "The wide-eyed innocent act you love to hide behind."

"There's no act!"

"Really? So you parade around in pink and ruffles because you want to be taken seriously?"

"No, I dress this way because I like the way I look."

"Pretty sure it's because you like to be *admired*." Kenric stood up to face her. "You like to be showered with attention. And you want everyone to think you're sweet and pretty and caring. But the person you care about most will always be yourself."

"Wow," Sophie said, glancing at the real Oralie. "I never realized you and Kenric hated each other in the beginning."

"We definitely did. It took years for us to respect each other—and even longer before we figured out that most of our resentment was a defense mechanism to help us fight our deeper feelings."

Dex shook his head. "Love is so weird."

"It can be." Oralie wiped her eyes.

In the memory, her projection stepped into Kenric's personal space. "Well, I guess I should thank you for finally dropping the polite act. I always prefer to deal with my enemies honestly."

"We're enemies now?" Kenric asked. "Is that how it works with you? If someone doesn't fall all over themselves to impress you, they're a villain?"

"No. But if they actively work to hurt me, they are. I've always wondered why it took so many days for everyone to reach a consensus, since Emery had told me I was the only Empath up for consideration. But apparently it was you—and I came here to ask why, but I'm pretty sure I already know the answer."

Kenric laughed. "Do you, now?"

"It's so strange," the real Oralie murmured. "I knew Kenric voted against me becoming a Councillor—but I don't remember confronting him like this. In fact, I remember him coming to me a few weeks after my banquet, wanting to clear the air."

"Then why would he erase this memory?" Dex asked.

Sophie heaved an enormous sigh. "I bet he wanted a do-over, so you wouldn't hate him so much—which probably means this memory is another waste of time."

"Maybe not. If that was Kenric's goal, he failed completely. We didn't speak for months after that talk."

"Why did he vote against you?" Dex asked.

"He never told me."

But apparently, he had.

The projection of Kenric took a step back and said, "I know what you're thinking, Oralie—and no, not because I'm listening. You're much easier to read than you think you are—and you're wrong. I voted against you because I didn't think we should elect someone who rushed through her assignments so she'd be available for tasks that would garner more attention."

The projection of Oralie looked ready to slap him. "I have *never* rushed through an assignment!"

"Oh really? So you didn't declare Lady Fayina dead within two days of her disappearance—without finding a body—and then find yourself conveniently free to work one-on-one with Councillor Emery on something else?"

"Wow," the real Oralie whispered, "I had no idea he once thought *that* little of me."

Her projection looked just as offended. "I don't owe you an explanation for *any* of my decisions. But if you'd seen how devastated her family was—and how badly they needed closure—perhaps you'd understand why I felt the need for urgency. Especially if you'd also looked at the abundance of evidence I found suggesting that she fell from a cliff. My swift decision allowed her husband to arrange a planting in the Wanderling Woods so everyone could start grieving and healing."

Kenric crossed his arms and turned away. "Fine. I suppose your actions may have been justified in that case."

"They were in *all* my cases," the projection of Oralie corrected. "Which is why everyone else was eager to vote in my favor—while you voted against me three times."

"Why does that bother you so much? I eventually gave you my vote—you have the circlet on your head to prove it."

Oralie's projection reached up to trace her fingers over the pink tourmalines. "It bothers me because you still do everything in your power to prevent me from doing my job! I've been here a year now, and I still haven't been given any serious assignments. Every time my name comes up, you convince the others it would be too traumatic for an Empath."

"Because it might be!" Kenric argued. "You have no idea what horrible things come to light during these kinds of investigations—and you'll be affected more than anyone else."

"That doesn't mean I can't handle it."

"It doesn't mean we should risk it either. Especially when

we have eleven other Councillors who are more than capable."

"*I'm* capable. And I'm tired of being treated like I'm weak!"

"I don't think you're weak, Oralie. In fact, I'm fairly certain you're stronger than all of us. But your ability will always make you more vulnerable to certain things."

"*How?*" she demanded.

Kenric sighed and slumped back into his armchair. "The only way I can give you an example is if you let me erase your memory of this conversation afterward."

"How convenient. And let me guess—you'll *also* need to erase everything Clarette told me about you."

"I would—but I have no problem with you knowing about that. In fact, you have my word that I'll come to you and confess. Take a reading if you think I'm lying." He held out his hand. "And just think: If you take this deal, you'll get your answer *and* you'll get to yell at me all over again. I'll even make sure you're holding a beverage, in case you want to splash it in my face!"

"He could be quite charming when he wanted to be," the real Oralie said quietly as she watched herself reluctantly agree. "And . . . I guess that explains why he washed this memory."

"I just hope the example he gives you is about Elysian," Sophie mumbled as Kenric's projection stood to pace.

He crossed the room four times before he swiped a hand down his face and said, "During my last investigation, I learned that we've been imprisoning someone for thousands of years—someone whose crimes were so horrible, they've been completely stricken from any kind of record. We found evidence of a plot to break her free, and it was my job to ensure that it never happens."

"Is he talking about Vespera?" Sophie asked.

A crease formed between Oralie's eyebrows. "He must be."

Her projection looked equally confused. "Is there more to this little example? Because I don't see the problem."

"That's because you're not considering what will happen if it turns out that I failed. I couldn't find any specifics about the plot—who might be behind it, when they'll strike, what they're planning. *Nothing*. Best I could do was amp up security. And if it ends up not being enough, I'll have to know that a monster is back out in this world because of me."

"No, you won't. It'll end up in your cache."

"Not immediately. They'll have to tell me why my memory is being washed. And if I manage not to shatter from the guilt right then and there, that horror will still linger with me forever. Emotions can't be erased. They can only be buried or misdirected—which is *much* harder to do with an Empath. And I know you're probably standing there thinking it won't matter because you're too brilliant and gifted to ever fail at anything. But take it from someone who's been at this job a whole lot longer than you. You'll do the best you can. But you *will* fail. And until you truly accept that, you shouldn't go anywhere near a serious assignment."

"Does that mean Kenric tried to stop the Neverseen from breaking Vespera out of Lumenaria?" Dex asked as both figures in the memory fell silent.

"He must have," Sophie mumbled.

And he failed.

Which made her strangely relieved that Kenric was gone.

At least he never had to know.

In fact, part of her wished she hadn't seen that memory.

Now she couldn't help thinking about how different things would be if Kenric had done his job.

Mr. Forkle's twin would still be alive.

So would Lumenaria's guards.

Her human parents never would've been taken and tortured.

Biana's arms wouldn't be covered in scars.

The troll hive at Everglen never would've—

"Careful," Oralie told her, resting her hand softly on Sophie's shoulder. "That's a dangerous emotional road you're traveling."

It was.

But she couldn't help it.

Just like she couldn't stop herself from asking the question that made her feel like there was suddenly no air.

What if *she* failed?

She was the moonlark.

Everyone was counting on her.

What if she let them down someday?

Or worse yet: What if she already had?

FIFTEEN

I THINK WE'RE FINALLY GETTING SOMEWHERE," Oralie said after she pressed the next crystal—orange this time—and a new hologram flared to life.

The memory was much darker than the others, lit only by the soft moonlight highlighting the silhouettes of three shadowy figures who were gathered in what appeared to be an overgrown garden. Kenric and Oralie both wore long silver cloaks that shimmered as they moved, making them look almost ghostly as they approached the painfully familiar blond elf with pointy ears who was crouched next to some sort of droopy, gnarled plant.

The real Oralie pointed to the hood covering her projection's circlet. "This must be the missing half of the memory we found in my cache—when Kenric dragged me out of bed in the middle of the night and brought me to Fintan to ask him about Elysian."

"I thought he had you ask about stellarlune," Sophie reminded her.

"I guess that's true. He slipped and mentioned Elysian later—but the two must be connected. And even if they're not, Kenric wouldn't have erased this from both of our minds and recorded it here if it weren't important."

Sophie wasn't so sure about that, given how little they'd learned from the last few memories—but she was *trying* to stay positive. "Is seeing this triggering anything for you?" she asked.

Oralie shook her head. "Right now everything still feels fuzzy and disconnected. But hopefully a little more time will help it sync up." She watched herself try to untangle her cape from some sort of thornbush, tearing the hem in the process. "Huh. I'd wondered how that got damaged! I told the gnome who repaired it that I must've snagged it on one of my jeweled shoes without realizing—but that didn't really make sense, since I would've noticed that."

"It must be so weird, seeing yourself do things you don't remember," Dex mumbled.

"It definitely is," Oralie agreed.

It was even weirder watching Kenric smile at the elf who murdered him.

Fintan didn't smile back.

His thin features looked particularly harsh with all the shadows, and his raspy voice made Sophie shudder when he said, "I'm assuming you're *not* here to watch my Noxflares bloom."

"We aren't," Kenric agreed. "Though I've been told that you'd be up late working on something tonight and was curious to find out what it was."

"Were you, now?" Fintan's lips curled into something that looked like a snarl. "Well, you'll have to tell me more about this mysterious *informant*—but not right now. There's no way I'm letting you ruin this moment. I planted this seed nearly five hundred years ago, and I've spent centuries nurturing it and protecting it—preparing for tonight, when my Noxflares will finally bloom after absorbing enough light from their two hundredth blue moon. And just so we're clear, I did all that on my own—no gnomes are ever allowed inside this garden. I like proving that elves are just as capable of coaxing life out of the ground as any other creature."

"Probably because he knew he was going to help the ogres unleash the plague and force the gnomes into slavery in Ravagog," Sophie muttered, wishing she could stomp his ugly plant into pulp.

"Yeah, and a gnome could've made his garden *way* better," Dex added. "It looks like it's mostly thorns and weeds. Plus, I'm pretty sure his special plant is actually a vine. Doesn't it look like it's all tangled up? And are the leaves supposed to be black?"

Oralie leaned closer. "I think they're actually a very deep purple. Or maybe they're . . ."

Her voice trailed off as the projection of Kenric told Fintan, "I've never heard of Noxflares."

"Neither have I," the projection of Oralie admitted.

Fintan sighed and rubbed his temples, streaking his face with mud. "I swear, the educational standards for Councillors keep getting lower and lower. Noxflares have never been *common* knowledge, but two people in your positions should know that they emit a unique form of bioluminescence when they bloom—a light that *only* exists for that rare moment in time. It doesn't travel—it absorbs. And you can't bottle it or preserve it. You have to be there to witness it—which I suppose is why the knowledge has been lost. No one has any patience anymore. They want what they want the *second* they desire it. But some of us are still willing to wait for the opportune moment." He smiled with the last words, as if he'd made a private joke—then pointed to his plant. "Should be any minute now . . ."

Everyone stared at the Noxflares.

And stared.

And stared.

"Is it—" Kenric started to ask, but Fintan shushed him.

"Here we go," he breathed, pointing to the shadowy stems, which were stirring slightly. He leaned closer and whispered, "You can do it. I believe in you."

The stirring grew more noticeable, the leaves flapping like butterfly wings.

Or maybe they weren't leaves.

Maybe they were petals.

"That's it," Fintan told the flowers, stroking their stems like he was petting a cat. "It's time to show us what you can do."

"Is he . . . singing to the plant?" Dex asked as Fintan started humming. "I mean, I know the gnomes do that—but this is Fintan, you know? I'm more used to him threatening to kill people and stuff."

"It's definitely strange," Sophie agreed. "He almost seems . . . kind."

Or he did, until Kenric dared to step closer. Then Fintan reeled toward him, screaming, "STAND BACK OR YOU'LL SCARE THEM!"

Oralie cleared her throat. "I'm assuming this is why I called Fintan 'particularly unstable' when I spoke to Kenric in the other half of this memory."

"Let's hope that's all it is," Sophie mumbled, trying not to relive her other terrifying encounters with an unstable Fintan. But a chill prickled down her spine anyway.

Fintan turned back toward his plant and leaned closer, whispering, "There you go. Keep going. Keeeeep going. Keeeeeeeeeeeeeep going."

The petals trembled harder and harder—then slowly curled

open, morphing into spiky blossoms that reminded Sophie a little of water lilies.

"Is that it?" Dex asked as a soft, orangey glow radiated from the center of each of the flowers.

"I think it might be," Sophie said—but the Noxflares were ready to prove her wrong.

Their petals stretched wider and flashed so bright, everyone had to turn their faces away.

Fintan's raspy laughter filled the room as Sophie rubbed her eyes and blinked hard, trying to regain her vision.

When everything came back into focus, the flowers had thankfully dimmed to a twinkling flicker, and the ground around them was covered in strange puddles of glowing orange.

"The light is heavier than any other light I've ever experienced," Fintan murmured, dipping his fingers into the flashing liquid. "*Almost* tangible. I've always wanted to find a use for it—I even asked Luzia once, but . . ." He turned and stared into the distance.

"But . . . ?" Kenric prompted.

Fintan reached up to wipe the mud off his face, and Sophie was surprised that none of the orange glow had stuck to his skin. "But what?"

"That's what I was asking you," Kenric reminded him.

"You were?" Fintan watched the last drops of orange disappear into the ground. "I'm not sure why. . . ."

"Is he avoiding the question?" Sophie asked.

"I don't think so," Oralie told her. "His mind is Ancient, and Ancient minds tend to wander."

"Right, but he also mentioned Luzia Vacker," Sophie argued.

Luzia was responsible for the illegal troll hive at Everglen—and she'd worked closely with Vespera before Vespera was arrested.

"I know what you're thinking," Oralie told her. "And I can certainly ask Luzia about Noxflares. But I can't imagine she's going to tell me anything significant. The Noxflares aren't the reason this memory was recorded. They're just flowers."

"Rare flowers that only Councillors seem to know about," Sophie countered, squinting at the Noxflares in the hologram. They looked . . .

. . . pretty boring.

And kind of ugly.

But it was still worth double-checking.

The projection of Kenric cleared his throat, drawing everyone's focus back to him. "Well, my friend," he told Fintan. "That was truly incredible."

Fintan huffed out a breath. "*Friend?* Is that what we are?"

"I'd like to think so," Kenric said.

"Mmmm. So then, am I supposed to assume that this is a *friendly* visit—even though you showed up unannounced, in the middle of the night, and brought your lovely little Empath along to keep me honest? Perhaps others would be fooled by your pleasantries, Kenric. But I've lived far too long to be charmed anymore. So let's try for honesty, shall we?" He folded his hands in his lap and turned to face Kenric fully. "You're here because the Council was less than thrilled with the report they received about me and sent you to give one of your infamous heart-to-hearts."

"What were his 'infamous heart-to-hearts'?" Sophie asked, trying to match Fintan's ominous tone.

"I have no idea," Oralie admitted. "Though . . . Kenric could be quite intimidating when he wanted to be."

Sophie couldn't picture that.

Kenric had always been the easiest Councillor to be around—by far.

But . . . she hadn't seen him very often.

He'd also known that she was Oralie's biological daughter, or suspected it anyway, which might've motivated him to be extra nice to her—even though it also meant he was yet another person constantly lying to her.

"What report is he talking about?" Dex asked, saving her from falling too much farther down that uncomfortable rabbit hole.

Oralie's projection had the same question.

Fintan rolled his eyes. "Oh please. We all know the Council sporadically assigns Regents to monitor Pyrokinetics and report us if we dare to spark any flames. I'm sure a Regent was the mysterious informant who told you I'd be up late tonight.

In fact, I'd wager they're hiding behind one of the trees over there—and if they are, they may as well come out!" He raised his voice with the last words and waved at the shadows.

No one stepped forward.

"Well, either they're too cowardly to show their face—or they begged for a new assignment after they tattled on me," Fintan grumbled.

"Or they were never there to begin with," Kenric suggested.

Fintan snorted. "You expect me to believe that you're *not* monitoring me?"

"No. You're right about that," Kenric told him, and Sophie noticed that the projection of Oralie looked surprised by his honesty.

The real Oralie mostly looked amused.

"But we use dwarves, not Regents," Kenric added. "I figured you of all people would assume as much. Weren't you the one who added 'monitoring and observation' to the dwarven treaty? Or was that Fallon's doing?"

"It was me," Fintan said quietly. "But when I made that arrangement, I never thought you'd use it to monitor people for *existing*—which is what you're doing to me. I have no control over my craving for flame. Fire will *always* call to me—and yet I still try my best to comply with your unjust rules. I resist every call when I'm in public—no matter how great the struggle. I resigned from the Council and allowed myself to be relegated to a Talentless status. But when I'm home, in the privacy and isolation of my own property, I should have the right to be myself. I'm harming *no one* when I do this."

He flicked his wrist and the Noxflares burst into flames.

Sophie, Dex, and Oralie stumbled back from the hologram—even though it was only a memory.

Oralie's projection faltered as well.

But Kenric held his ground. "I'm not sure how destroying a five-hundred-year-old plant is supposed to prove you're not causing any harm," he noted.

"Once again, you show your ignorance! Noxflares are fire-resistant. In fact, some believe that they need to burn in order to . . ." Fintan's eyes glazed over as he studied the blaze.

"In order to what?" Oralie's projection asked.

Fintan ignored her, reaching into the fire and plucking out a burning flower by the stem. The petals should've been ash by that point, but instead they'd turned as white as the flames dancing along their sharp-looking edges.

"Something's missing," Fintan whispered, holding the flower so close, Sophie could see the fire reflecting in his pupils. "I need to . . ."

"What you need to do," Kenric said when he didn't finish, "is put out that fire before it spreads."

Fintan shook his head. "These aren't hungry flames. They'll stay right where I want them. That's why I chose them. But . . . something's missing."

"Yes, you said that already," Kenric reminded him after a long stretch of silence.

Fintan closed his eyes. "I'm still trying to find the answer."

The fire crackled and sparked.

"Any luck?" Kenric eventually asked.

"Am I boring you? You're welcome to leave anytime. Or feel free to start the lecture I'll be ignoring."

Kenric laughed. "Actually, I don't have a lecture for you. Quite honestly, Fintan, I don't care if you use your ability when you're at home. I even told the others I thought they were being ridiculous when I learned that they'd arranged to have you monitored here—ask Oralie if you don't believe me."

"He did," Oralie said—though her projection simply nodded. "*That* I remember. It caused quite the heated debate between him and Noland—and there's nothing like a shouting match with a Vociferator."

Dex snorted. "I bet."

"As far as I'm concerned," Kenric continued, "you can burn your whole house down if you want to—as long as no one gets hurt. And while I can't guarantee that someone else won't be coming by to discuss your report at some point, I *can* assure you that it's not why I'm here."

"Then why *are* you here?" Fintan's flames stretched higher with the demand.

Kenric glanced at the projection of Oralie, waiting for her nod before he said, "We came to ask a very simple question."

"I see. And are you planning on sneaking into my mind if I refuse to answer? Because I have *excellent* defenses."

"I'm sure you do," Kenric told him. "But there's no need—this should be fast and painless for everyone."

He motioned for Oralie to move closer—but a circle of flames erupted around her.

"I never agreed to have my emotions read!" Fintan snapped.

"So strange," the real Oralie murmured, waving her fingers through the hologram's flames. "I have no idea how I stood there so calmly. I've always hated fire. Even before . . ."

No one needed her to finish that sentence.

And yet, her projection managed to smile as she crossed her arms and told Fintan, "Those who protest my readings tend to have something to hide."

Fintan smirked. "Who doesn't?"

Kenric placed his hand on Fintan's shoulder—and his grip looked more threatening than reassuring as he said, "You have no reason to be concerned, Fintan. So why don't you put out those flames and prove you're truly as harmless as you claim?"

"There's no need," the projection of Oralie told him before Fintan could respond.

She fanned out the sides of her cloak, making the silvery fabric flutter as she gracefully levitated over the fire and set herself down next to Fintan.

"For the record," she said, gripping Fintan's shoulder even

harder than Kenric was, "Empaths don't need permission for readings."

He gritted his teeth. "Maybe not—but you would be wise to get it from me."

The flames on the Noxflare he was holding turned purple and surged higher.

He tilted his head to study the flower, brows crunching together. "Something's still missing."

"Yes, well, the sooner we leave, the sooner you can figure it out," Kenric told him. "Should we get on with the question?"

When Fintan ignored him, he added, "I promise, this won't be an interrogation. It's barely even an investigation at this point. I've already exhausted every possible lead. Now I'm just managing the final containment."

"Containment," Fintan repeated, spinning the flower between his fingers. "And how exactly am I going to be *contained*?"

"Honestly? You're the end of a completely pointless list— that's why we're here so late. It's been an incredibly long day, and I'm pretty sure you'll be as clueless as all the others I've had to waste time talking to. But I can't go to bed until I have your answer. So how about you do us all a favor? The sooner you let Councillor Oralie read your response to her question, the sooner we can go home—and you can burn your flowers in peace."

"How about we make a deal?" Fintan countered, waving his hand to extinguish the circle of flames he'd tried to trap

Oralie with. "I agree to answer your question if you agree to do something for me."

Kenric shook his head. "I don't make deals."

"You should. I could be a valuable ally."

"I don't need allies."

Fintan's vicious smile returned. "Someday that may change."

"Was that a threat?" Dex asked.

Sophie had been wondering the same thing.

She also couldn't help wondering if Kenric would still be alive if he'd taken Fintan's bargain.

"What do you think Fintan wanted from him?" she whispered.

"I can't begin to imagine," the real Oralie told her. "But I'm sure it would've been something Kenric couldn't give."

Kenric must've known that as well, because he told Fintan, "How about we keep things simple? Answer the question, and I'll see if I can convince the others to scale back on their surveillance of you."

"You won't be able to," Fintan argued.

"Probably not. But at least I'll give it a try. Otherwise, I guess we'll all have to settle in for a long night." He bent to feel the grass, humming a pleased note. "Not bad. I've squatted in far more uncomfortable places, waiting for someone to cooperate. And I never mind an excuse to practice my Ogreish."

He grunted several sounds, spraying spittle.

"What did he just say?" Dex asked when Sophie giggled.

"He said Fintan's garden smells like a pooping skunk," she told him.

Fintan's hand curled into a fist, snuffing out the flames on his flower. "Just . . . make this quick."

"*Happy* to," Kenric promised, glancing at Oralie's projection. "Ready?"

She nodded and closed her eyes.

I need you to ask him about stellarlune.

"Whoa, what was that?" Dex asked as the words echoed around the room.

It took Sophie a second to realize that Kenric must've transmitted in the memory.

"They're talking telepathically," she said as Oralie's thought echoed back.

What's stellarlune?

Something he's hopefully never heard of, Kenric told her.

Does that mean you're NOT convinced that this is a waste of time? she asked. *Were you trying to make him lower his guard?*

Kenric's eyes twinkled. *Mostly, I was trying to get us out of here. Not sure I can handle any more gardening advice.*

You're going to tell me what this is about the second we're back at my castle, Oralie told him before she asked Fintan—out loud—"Have you ever heard of stellarlune?"

"Stellarlune?" Fintan repeated, dragging out the syllables. "Can't say that I have."

Is he telling the truth? Kenric transmitted.

It's hard to tell. I feel a lot of tension and unease—but he's also very suspicious. And annoyed. And . . . confused.

Try pressing him, then.

The projection of Oralie sighed and repeated her question—but halfway through, the words turned muffled and distant.

"Is that the end of the memory?" Dex asked when the hologram warped and faded.

"I don't think—" the real Oralie started to say, until vivid white flames burst out of the cache.

"They're not real!" Sophie shouted—not that it stopped her from scrambling back with the others. Or from imagining that she could feel the fire scorching her skin.

Dex shielded his eyes. "I don't understand. Did Fintan attack them?"

The fire morphed into giant burning flowers.

"No, I think Kenric is trying to read Fintan's mind right now," Sophie told him.

"But why did the projection get so huge?" Dex asked.

"Ancient minds are known for being vast," Oralie explained. "I'm sure this is what it felt like for Kenric."

"Ugh, is that what it was like when you were in Fintan's head?" Dex asked Sophie.

Sophie fought back the searing flashbacks. "Worse. He uses fire as a defense mechanism."

"I'm not sure if that's what this is," Oralie murmured.

"I remember Kenric said in my cache that Fintan's mind felt calmer because I was there, and he was able to slip past Fintan's guard. I think that's what we're seeing—Fintan's mind must've been fixated on the Noxflares. Listen."

Mixed with the hisses and crackles of the flames, they could hear Fintan's mental voice repeating, *Something's missing. Something's missing. Something's missing.*

"Or he's trying to keep his mind distracted because he knew Kenric was using his telepathy," Sophie countered. "See how we can *barely* hear what Kenric's saying?"

It seemed like Kenric had taken over the questioning, but he sounded miles and miles away. The only word Sophie could make out was "stellarlune."

Fintan's mind didn't change.

The giant Noxflares kept burning, and he kept mumbling "something's missing"—until Kenric finally pulled his consciousness free.

Then the fire flowers vanished, and the projections of Kenric, Oralie, and Fintan sharpened back into focus, the three of them still standing in the same positions they'd been in—though Fintan was now massaging his temples.

"For *hopefully* the last time," Fintan said, "*no.* I've never heard of stellarlune!"

"I believe you." Kenric glanced at Oralie. "I'm assuming your reading verifies that."

"He definitely seemed confused," Oralie agreed.

"I hope you also felt every drop of my annoyance," Fintan muttered.

Oralie shrugged. "I've felt worse."

Kenric grinned. "Well, the good news is, we can leave you alone now, Fintan. I just need one more thing before we go."

He reached into his pocket and held out a blue handkerchief.

Fintan's laugh seemed to turn the room colder. "You *must* be joking."

"I'm not." Kenric pressed the fabric into Fintan's free hand. "You know the protocol."

"I also know that I'm no longer a Councillor."

"And yet I'm sure you still recall what I'll have to do if you resist," Kenric said quietly—with an expression that suddenly made Sophie understand what Oralie meant about Kenric being intimidating when he wanted to be.

Fintan curled his fist around the blue handkerchief. "If you erase my Noxflares—"

"I'll send a message to the Washer instructing them to preserve that part of this evening," Kenric assured him. "The Noxflares truly were a sight to behold. No one should ever have to lose that memory."

"I'm not convinced that anyone should have to lose *any* memories," Fintan snapped back. "But I'm not in charge—at the moment."

Kenric was too busy tapping the message into his Imparter to catch the way Fintan's tone changed with the last words.

They sounded more like a promise than a lament—and once again Sophie wished she could shout warnings at the memory.

But it was far too late for that.

"Make sure you're sitting," Kenric reminded Fintan. "And I'd recommend putting out these fires before the Washer gets here."

Fintan didn't acknowledge him.

He just stared at his Noxflares, murmuring "something's missing" as Kenric held up his pathfinder and he and Oralie glittered away.

"Let's stop the memory here," the real Oralie said as the scene shifted and her projection now stood facing Kenric. "This is where the crystal in my cache started, and . . . I can't watch that again."

Sophie couldn't blame her.

Plus, if the scene played on, Dex would find out that Oralie was her biological mother.

But once again, they'd finished a memory and learned *nothing*—except that Kenric either lied when he told Oralie he'd slipped past Fintan's mental defenses, or he'd been fooled by a pretty simple trick.

Sophie couldn't decide which was more depressing.

"You'll tell me what Luzia says about the Noxflares?" she asked, wanting to make sure Oralie wouldn't forget.

"Of course," Oralie promised, pressing the next crystal on the cache.

The blue memory had a slight delay—long enough that Sophie started to wonder if the cache had stopped working.

Then two new holograms appeared.

Kenric again—of course—still with short, ponytail-free hair.

And the other figure was someone that Sophie never would've expected.

In fact, she blinked several times to make sure her eyes weren't playing tricks on her.

But no.

There was Kenric, sitting in a cluttered library.

And in the armchair across from him sat *Prentice*.

SIXTEEN

WERE KENRIC AND PRENTICE friends?" Sophie asked, pretty sure she already knew the answer.

"Not that I was aware of," Oralie told her. Which was probably why Prentice seemed a little nervous. He kept crossing and uncrossing his legs and tapping his fingers against his knees.

But all Sophie could think was *He looks so . . . different.*

Most of the times she'd seen Prentice, he'd either been unconscious, imprisoned, or unstable—and even now that he was free from Exile and she'd been able to heal his broken mind, he often seemed . . . somber.

She understood *why.*

He'd lost his wife, years of his life, and all his memories.

But she wished he could go back to being the fidgety elf in the projection in front of her, flashing a smile that seemed to make his dark skin glow as he watched Kenric pour some sort of clear liquid into two silver goblets.

"You certainly know how to keep someone in suspense," he told Kenric.

Kenric laughed. "It's part of our training after we're elected to the Council. That, and how to keep these obnoxious circlets from slipping off our heads."

"I can see how that might take some practice," Prentice teased. His deep blue eyes studied the room. "Do they also teach you to rely on mysterious locations? I never realized this library existed."

Kenric handed him one of the goblets. "Actually, no one does. I cut the crystal that leaped us here myself—and it's the only one of its kind. Humans abandoned this building ages ago, and I found it moldered and rotting during one of my assignments, back when I was still an Emissary. The architecture is so wonderfully different from our style—all carved wood and cut stone, without a jewel or crystal in sight. And I loved the way nature was slowly reclaiming everything. It felt like someone should find a way to preserve that strange balance and create something truly special." He pointed to the moss covering the stone floor, and the vines weaving around the bookshelves—then up to the leafy branches poking through the domed roof. "Only took a few tricks I learned from the gnomes to make the forest and the structure coexist. Then I just had to bring over my books and some comfy chairs—and add a few illusions to ensure that no one could ever find this place unless I wanted them to. Now it's my personal oasis. I call it Hushwood."

"Did you know about Hushwood?" Sophie asked Oralie.

Oralie fussed with one of her loose ringlets. "He mentioned something about an oasis a few times—but it always sounded like a joke. And he never offered to bring me there."

But he'd brought Prentice—who seemed equally surprised.

"Why are you showing me this?" he asked.

Kenric propped his feet on what looked like a polished tree stump. "I'd hoped it might illustrate how much I trust you."

"And why would I need to know that?" Prentice took a sip from the goblet—then winced and set it aside on another tree stump.

Kenric downed his drink in one gulp. "Because I have a proposition of sorts, for the most talented Keeper I've ever met."

"The *most* talented," Prentice repeated, tucking several of his dreadlocks behind his ears. "That is some heavy flattery. Sounds like this is going to be a *big* proposition."

"It is," Kenric agreed.

"Then I should warn you that I don't have the kind of

availability that I used to. I've scaled way back on assignments since Wylie was born."

"As you should. Family must always come first. Why do you think Councillors aren't allowed to have them?" Kenric smiled as he asked the question, but it didn't match his pained expression. He cleared his throat. "How old is Wylie now?"

"Three. And he's becoming more of a handful every day—but Cyrah and I are loving every minute of it." Prentice reached into his pocket and showed Kenric a projected picture of the three of them.

Wylie was a blur of flailing limbs, and Cyrah and Prentice were both cracking up—and their obvious joy made Sophie's eyes sting.

"I can't decide if he looks more like you or his mother," Kenric noted.

"It's hard to tell," Prentice agreed. "But he gets his laugh from Cyrah. And his knack for finding trouble from me."

Sophie frowned, trying to do the mental math. "Wait—if Wylie was three, wasn't Prentice already working with the Black Swan during this memory?"

"I'm not sure that we know exactly when he swore fealty," Oralie told her. "But he might've been, since he was arrested a few years later."

She said the words so casually, as if she weren't talking about the moment that had ruined Prentice's life.

The Council had ordered a memory break—and Prentice

had had to sacrifice his sanity in order to keep Sophie's existence secret. And Oralie had known exactly what Prentice was
hiding.

She'd also known that the Black Swan wasn't the enemy. But
she'd let Prentice take the fall, claiming she had no choice in
the matter. After all, the only way to spare Prentice would've
been to reveal the very secrets he was trying to protect.

But that didn't make Oralie's actions any less of a betrayal.
Especially since she was also trying to preserve her position on
the Council.

And it reminded Sophie of one of the mysteries surrounding Prentice's arrest that she'd completely forgotten about:
why Prentice had called swan song.

Everyone assumed he'd used the Black Swan's code for
imminent danger because he'd somehow uncovered the
Lodestar symbol and feared the Neverseen would be coming
after him. But the explanation didn't totally make sense, as
Prentice could've told someone what he'd learned—both to
help prove his innocence and to make sure the information
didn't get buried if he ended up in Exile.

Instead, he had kept everything to himself.

Almost as if he hadn't known who he could trust.

And now Sophie was watching Prentice sit with Kenric in a
secret library, about to discuss some sort of "big proposition."

"You okay?" Dex asked.

Sophie blinked, realizing he was staring at her—and that

she was breathing very, very fast. "Yeah. I'm just . . . trying to decide if I should tell Wylie and Prentice this story."

In the memory, Prentice was telling Kenric about how Wylie had wandered off during his first trip to the Sanctuary, climbed to the top of a giant pile of T. rex poop, and then refused to come back down. And when Prentice levitated up there to get him, Wylie leaped into his arms before he was ready and sent them both crashing into the manure.

Dex laughed. "I'm sure they'd love to hear it."

They would. And Wylie and Prentice could definitely use another happy memory of the two of them.

But then Sophie would have to explain how she knew—and she needed to hear more about Kenric's proposition first.

Prentice wanted more information as well.

"I appreciate your bringing me here," he told Kenric, "and the compliments. But I think it's time to tell me what you want."

Kenric poured himself a second drink and downed it before he stood to pace. His heavy boots made a squishing sound on the mossy floor as he said, "You're right—and there's no subtle way of saying this, so I'll just have to put it out there. I brought you here because I'm hoping you'll be willing to serve as my Keeper." He let that sink in before he added, "*Off* the record."

Prentice leaned back, dragging a hand down his face. "That's a very strange request coming from someone with a cache tucked away in the void."

"You mean this?" Kenric pulled his cache out of his pocket and tossed it to a wide-eyed Prentice. "Isn't it funny how much faith we put in such an unimpressive-looking gadget? I've been told to protect it above *everything* else—as if our world could crumble over what's hidden inside. And for years I've faithfully recorded my Forgotten Secrets in this tiny crystal ball and wiped all trace of them from my mind. But recently I've realized . . . I have no idea what's hidden behind those colorful jewels. So how does that do me—or anyone else—any good?"

Prentice didn't have an answer.

He just held up the cache and studied the glints of color.

There were only six secrets at that point. The blue crystal was missing—which made sense, since it was the memory they were currently watching.

But that meant Kenric had stopped recording things in his cache soon after this conversation—either because he didn't have any secrets that needed to be saved, or because he'd saved them somewhere else.

Prentice handed the cache back to Kenric. "When you say 'off the record'—does that include your updates to the rest of the Council?"

"It does," Kenric agreed, shoving his cache back into his pocket. "I'd prefer that no one knows what I'm working on until I've proven it's a success. My fellow Councillors can be . . . resistant to change."

Prentice snorted. "That's putting it mildly."

"It is—and I understand their reasons to some extent. Ruling this planet has proven to be far more complicated than I ever imagined. From the outside, everything we've built—our treaties and laws and systems—seem as sturdy as the castle in Lumenaria. But the reality is much more like this library: dozens of opposing forces all coaxed into a careful peace." He reached up and tucked a drooping vine back into place before it could latch onto any of his books. "The slightest shift could send it all crashing down, so caution must be key. But . . . we can't use our fear of change as an excuse to ignore our problems either."

"And *caches* are the problem you want to focus on?" Prentice asked, standing to face him. "Forgive my bluntness, but . . . there are much bigger issues."

"Are there?" Kenric countered. "I don't see how. Not when you consider that every Councillor—both former and current—has a cache full of secrets, and *none* of us knows what's actually recorded in them. There could be crimes. Wars. Disasters. All manner of devastation. And when I suggested we find out, I was . . . outvoted. Everyone was too afraid of the toll it might take on their sanity and preferred to remain ignorant."

"I remember that," Oralie murmured. "Kenric called a special meeting—probably not that long before he brought Prentice to Hushwood."

"I'm guessing there was a lot of arguing?" Dex said.

"Actually, it was one of those rare instances when our vote

was both quick and unanimous. Well . . . unanimous save for Kenric."

"So that means *you* voted against him," Sophie couldn't help pointing out.

Oralie looked away. "I did. At the time, I saw no reason for us to dig too deeply into our past. It seemed like a waste of our time and energy. Obviously I was wrong—though I still believe that caches serve some purpose."

Kenric clearly disagreed.

"We call them *Forgotten* Secrets," he told Prentice, "and we tell ourselves that erasing them is necessary to preserve our sanity and our world. But there are truths that we can't afford to forget. After all, isn't the point of preserving the past to *learn* from it? Otherwise we could be repeating the same mistakes over and over."

"And how is a Keeper a better solution?" Prentice asked.

"Well, for one thing it means relying on someone with a brain—and a heart—instead of a tiny gadget that none of us ever even look at because we're too afraid."

"Yes, but that brain and heart also make the Keeper vulnerable," Prentice reminded him. "Rule number one of our training is to never let ourselves be burdened with information that could destroy our sanity—"

"I have a plan for that," Kenric interrupted. "My training as a Washer has taught me how to hide memories in a very specific way, where the person holding them remains completely unaware—but the memories can easily be triggered if the need arises. And I, as your partner, would know the triggers. They would be carefully selected words or phrases containing enough of a clue about the secret that I'd be able to recognize any need to call for it, yet remain completely in the dark otherwise. So we'd both be thoroughly protected but also have the information much more readily available—and I realize how simplistic that explanation sounds. I assure you, I've put a great deal of thought into how to make this work. But it'd be much easier to show you what I mean—assuming you agree to give this a try, of course."

"Even if your plan works," Prentice said, noticeably *not* agreeing, "the Keeper would be a target for anyone seeking privileged information."

"Another reason why I'd keep your role off the record," Kenric told him. "The Council would eventually be informed—but only them."

Prentice shook his head. "We all know how easily information can leak."

"Not if you and I are the *only* ones who know we're working together. I'd tell the Council that I have a Keeper—but not your identity. And I would sooner let my sanity shatter than expose you."

Sophie could tell by Kenric's expression—and his tone—that he truly believed he could protect Prentice. But his confidence couldn't silence the horrible thought that had started whispering in the back of her mind the moment she'd watched Kenric mention his "proposition."

What if Kenric was the reason Prentice was arrested?

Or part of it, at least?

If Prentice had been serving as Kenric's Keeper—and the other Councillors had no idea—they might've seen or heard something that made them suspicious of him.

And even if Prentice never actually worked with Kenric, someone could've found out that Kenric had made him an offer and started watching Prentice more closely.

She could be wrong, of course.

But she couldn't deny the possibility.

And either way . . . Kenric was yet another person who *should've* come to Prentice's defense and didn't. Which made Sophie want to grab the cache and smash it into a million pieces—and not to protect Kenric.

She wasn't sure he deserved that.

But she didn't want to put Wylie or Prentice through any more painful revelations—especially since there was no one who could answer their questions.

Kenric was dead.

Prentice's memories were gone.

And nothing would ever change that.

"Seriously, are you okay?" Dex asked, pointing to Sophie's white-knuckled fists.

She relaxed her grip. "Yeah. I just . . . wish we knew if

Prentice agreed to Kenric's plan. But with the way these memories are going, I have a feeling it's going to cut off before we get that answer."

Sure enough, Kenric told Prentice—almost on cue—"In case you're wondering, I'll be wiping this conversation from my mind the second you leave. That way it'll be as if it never happened—unless you decide to accept my proposition. If you do, just mention *Hushwood* the next time you see me, and it'll trigger this memory."

"And then what?" Prentice asked, turning to trace his fingers along the spines of several of the thickest books.

"Then we test my plan for protecting your sanity—using totally innocuous information to ensure there's no risk, of course. And if it works the way I expect, you and I will start the process of transferring what's in my cache into your head. Assuming *that* goes smoothly, you'd then become the place I record any new secrets—and I'd recommend that the rest of the Councillors select their own Keepers and start doing the same."

Prentice spun back to face him. "You say that as if there's an abundance of Keepers to choose from. I can only think of a handful of Telepaths with the skill for this kind of responsibility—and it's nowhere near twelve. And even if we did find someone for every Councillor, it would be glaringly obvious who was chosen, and we'd all become targets."

"Not if the Councillors are the only ones aware of the new

Keeper program," Kenric argued. "Everyone else would believe we're still relying on caches. And I'm sure there are other precautions we can take as well. You and I could work all that out together—but let's not get ahead of ourselves. I'm well aware that you haven't said yes—and I wouldn't want you to at the moment."

Sophie heaved a heavy sigh.

"This is not a decision to be made lightly," Kenric continued. "Go home, hug your wife, play with your son, and give this a good long think—and if you decide you're not interested, that's totally fine. You won't get any pressure from me. As I said, I won't even remember that I approached you about this."

"Won't that mean you'll just find another time to ask me?" Prentice wondered.

"I suppose that could be a good way to wear you down." He laughed when Prentice scowled. "I'm kidding! I have a way to prevent that. I would never want you to sign on unless you were one hundred percent behind the idea. The only way this will ever work is if you have complete trust in me—and I in you."

"Well," Prentice said slowly, fidgeting with his dreadlocks, "it sounds like I have a lot of thinking to do."

Kenric nodded. "Take your time. As I said at the beginning— you're the most talented Keeper I know. You're worth the wait."

Prentice didn't smile at the compliment.

Instead he stepped closer and told Kenric, "No amount of talent will ever make me infallible."

"And I would never expect you to be," Kenric promised. "This role doesn't require perfection. Only a willingness to do your best—*if* you decide you want to try."

"That's a big *if*," Prentice said, removing his pathfinder from his cape pocket.

He held the crystal up to the light and glittered away without another word.

The hologram disappeared as soon as he was gone.

Sophie turned to Oralie. "Are the Councillors using Keepers now? Don't say you can't tell me—"

"We're not," Oralie cut in. "As far as I know, Kenric never made the suggestion. I'm assuming that means Prentice chose not to take him up on his offer—or that their tests to protect his sanity failed."

Or that they were still working everything out when Prentice was arrested . . .

Sophie was tempted to ask Oralie if she'd had the same revelation about Kenric's possible involvement in all that. But . . . what was the point?

Nothing could change what had happened.

All it would do is stir up more pain.

Which was why she told Dex, "I don't think we should tell Wylie about this."

"I agree," Oralie said—so quickly, it made Sophie wonder if she *had* made the connection.

Not that it mattered.

"Should we move on to the next memory?" Oralie asked.

"I almost don't see the point," Sophie grumbled. "It's not like we're actually learning anything useful."

"Well . . . now we know that Kenric didn't like caches," Dex reminded her, "and was trying to find a better solution."

"And that only makes me wonder why he bothered giving me his cache in the first place," Sophie countered.

"Really?" Dex said. "I thought that was pretty clear, since he obviously believed the secrets inside were super important. He was probably counting on you to find out what they were and use them to save the world or something."

"I guess," Sophie said quietly. "But that'd mean a whole lot more if he'd been right."

"How do you know he wasn't?" Oralie asked.

"Because nothing we've seen is going to help anyone save *anything*!" Sophie snapped.

"You don't know that," Oralie insisted. "This is the challenge with Forgotten Secrets. We don't have any context for the moments we're witnessing, so it's difficult to measure their value. But remember: Kenric recorded each of these memories for a very specific reason. We just need more time to understand why."

"Yeah, but we don't *have* time," Sophie argued. "We need to know more about stellarlune and Elysian *now*."

"Then I guess it's a good thing we still have two more memories," Oralie told her, pressing the cache's yellow crystal.

When the hologram appeared, they were once again staring at projections of Kenric and Oralie, both wearing their jeweled circlets.

"This better not be another scene from your star-crossed love story," Sophie muttered under her breath.

"It's not," Oralie assured her. "This is the other missing memory I told you about—when there was someone in my house who I can't remember, and Kenric told me I drank too much fizzleberry wine."

"But you aren't at your house," Sophie reminded her. She pointed to the background, which looked like some sort of meadow—or maybe it was a field.

Sophie could never remember the difference.

All she knew was that Kenric and Oralie stood in the middle of a wide stretch of windswept grass. A few unruly trees with red, orange, and yellow leaves were scattered around them—and in the distance Sophie could make out the bank of a rocky river.

"It's not my castle," Oralie agreed. "But I remember the jerkin Kenric's wearing. Look at those stripes—have you ever seen anything so hideous?"

Sophie couldn't care less about Kenric's wardrobe.

"Where are you, then?" she asked, not surprised at all when Oralie told her she didn't know.

She was even less surprised when Oralie's projection asked Kenric the same question, and Kenric told her, "I can't tell you that."

"That's absurd," Oralie's projection snapped. "If you can bring me here, then surely—"

"Honestly?" Kenric interrupted. "*I'm* not even supposed to be here. No one is. According to every map and record I've checked, this place doesn't exist. It doesn't even have a name."

"Then how did you find it?" Oralie's projection wondered.

"By following a convoluted trail of evidence that I've slowly pieced together over the last several months. And then walking a *very* long time."

"But we leaped here," she reminded him.

"We did—because I decided to cut a crystal when I realized I needed another opinion. But I'm going to have to destroy it as soon as we get back. Well . . . maybe I can wait until I wrap up this investigation. It depends."

"On what?" Oralie's projection asked.

"You tell me. Does anything about this place feel . . . strange? And I'm not talking about any of the things I just told you about it. I mean, when you really take this place in . . . does anything seem off?"

Oralie turned in a slow circle, squinting at the scenery. "Well . . . I suppose it's a little too quiet." She made her way closer to the river and pointed to the water crashing against the dark rocks. "You'd think a river like this would be roaring at us, for how fast it's flowing. But it sounds more like a trickling stream."

Sophie strained her ears, but all she could make out was a faint gurgle—more like the sound a faucet would make.

Kenric nodded. "That was one of the details that helped me find this place. Something had mentioned 'whispering rapids,' so when I found this river, I followed it here."

"And I'm assuming you won't tell me where you uncovered this information," Oralie's projection said.

"It's classified," Kenric agreed.

"Of course it is," Sophie grumbled.

Oralie's projection sighed and headed for one of the trees, which looked even more wild and overgrown up close. Thick blue vines wrapped around the gnarled trunk, and the tree's leaves were all wrinkled, like crumpled pieces of paper.

Oralie reached up to feel one, and it didn't crunch the way Sophie would've expected. "Was there also a clue about silent foliage?" she asked.

"Nope. Nothing weird about the trees—though I've never seen anything quite like them. But I did find a mention of these."

He pointed to something near his feet, and Sophie assumed Kenric must've been drawing Oralie's attention to the way the bright blue vines were tangled around the roots. But then Oralie knelt closer, and Sophie noticed hundreds of tiny yellow moths—or butterflies—resting on the vine's pointy leaves.

Kenric clapped, and the insects launched into the air, fluttering around their heads.

"I've never paid attention to insects," Oralie said, fanning several away from her eyes. "Are these *special* butterflies?"

"No idea," Kenric admitted. "But see how they have red on their faces? I found a mention about that, too—'butterflies kissed with red.'"

Dex chuckled. "Whoever wrote these descriptions was trying way too hard to sound deep and poetic."

Sophie nodded, wishing she had *any* idea who that could've been.

"Have you collected a specimen of these 'kissed butterflies'?" Oralie's projection asked Kenric.

"I've tried." He pulled a tiny net from his pocket and made a quick swipe—and all the butterflies zipped away. "So far I haven't had much luck."

He swiped again and again—nearly losing his balance the second time.

"I swear these things are laughing at me," he muttered.

Oralie's projection failed just as epically when she tried.

"I doubt it matters," Kenric said, taking back the net after Oralie accidentally smacked him in the head while trying to catch one fluttering past his nose. "None of this stuff is what I meant when I asked you if this place seemed off. I meant as an Empath. What do you *feel* when you read the air?"

She closed her eyes, slowly waving her hands back and forth. "I feel . . . wind."

Kenric shook his head. "Clearly you're not concentrating."

"I'm not," she agreed, "because I have no idea what this is all about! It might help if you gave me at least *some* explanation."

"I couldn't even if I wanted to. Like I said, I've been following a long string of random clues, and somehow they led me here. And . . . there's something weird about this place. But I can't figure out what it is. That's why I took such a huge risk and brought you here for an opinion. *Please*, Ora, I need your help."

Oralie's projection released a much heavier sigh.

She also squeezed her eyes tighter, making creases streak across her forehead as she murmured, "I do feel . . . *something*. But I don't know how to describe it. It's almost as if this meadow has . . . a mood."

"A *mood*," Kenric repeated, nodding slowly. "That sounds about right. I feel it too—but the only word I could come up with for the sensation was *awareness*."

"What does *that* mean?" Sophie asked.

"And why does it sound so creepy?" Dex added.

"I don't know," Oralie told them. "But it really does."

Past Oralie seemed far less shaken. "I've heard stories," she told Kenric as she turned to scan the meadow, "that there are certain rare forms of energy that can mess with our senses. Perhaps one of them is here and that's what we're both picking up."

"It's possible," Kenric agreed. "But . . . what energy? I can't find any source—can you?"

"Perhaps it's the water?" Oralie took a few steps closer to the river. "The force of the current might be unusually strong. That could even be the reason the rapids are so quiet. The energy may be muffling the sound."

"Maybe." Kenric didn't sound convinced.

Sophie wasn't either.

But no one had any other explanations.

"Is any of this triggering anything for you?" Sophie asked the real Oralie.

"I wish," she admitted.

And sadly, there wasn't much left of the memory.

Kenric and Oralie both wandered around the meadow, searching for anything else that could explain what they were feeling. But there was nothing except the trees and the vines and the river and the butterflies. And when the sun sank behind the distant mountains, Kenric decided it was time to go.

The scene shifted as they leaped back to Oralie's sparkly castle and Kenric led her to one of the armchairs, handing her a glass of fizzleberry wine as Oralie asked a bunch of questions he ignored.

"That must be the visitor I can't remember," the real Oralie said when someone knocked on her door a few minutes later.

Sophie held her breath as Kenric went to answer, silently pleading for it to be someone important.

But when the figure strode into the room, their face was a blur.

Sophie blinked and rubbed her eyes, but nothing snapped into focus. "Why can't we see who it is?"

"I think they're wearing an addler," Dex told her.

The real Oralie groaned. "You're probably right. Which means it must be the Washer Kenric called to make sure I wouldn't remember any of this. They often wear addlers to protect their identities."

The hologram blinked away a second later.

"That's it?" Sophie snapped. "*That* was the big mystery? A Washer stopped by and erased your memory—and all you'd done was go to some weird, unmapped meadow with a river?"

"I understand your frustration," Oralie told her.

"Pretty sure you don't," Sophie jumped in. "Otherwise you'd be flinging that cache at the wall as hard as you could."

"No," Oralie said calmly, "the reason I'm not trying to destroy the cache is because there's still one memory left."

"I'm sure it'll be as useless as the others," Sophie muttered.

"Hate to say it, but I agree," Dex added.

"Well, we're going to check it anyway." Oralie pressed the final, purple crystal and triggered another hologram—one that was very different from the others.

There were no figures this time.

No background, either—because it wasn't a scene.

It was a single, still image.

Five squiggly, hand-drawn lines coming from five different directions, all weaving and intersecting around something that was either a star or a flower, with a rune scrawled underneath.

Dex groaned. "Oh good! Another mysterious symbol—because we don't have enough of those!"

He turned to Sophie, waiting for her to echo his frustration.

But Sophie could only stare.

And the more she studied the symbol, the more her brain seemed to prickle with a strange sort of familiarity.

Somehow she *knew* she'd seen it before—even though she was also *positive* that she hadn't. Which could only mean one thing.

A long time ago—before she knew about elves or caches or the giant conspiracies she was caught up in—the Black Swan planted that same image into her brain, along with all their other secrets.

SEVENTEEN

YOU'D BETTER NOT BE IGNORING ME!" Sophie shouted, pounding on the round, gilded door set into the side of a rolling hill—a place that would forever remind her of a hobbit hole. "WE NEED TO TALK!"

The door stayed annoyingly closed.

She pounded harder.

"Soooooooo . . . as much as I'm enjoying Blondie's current meltdown," Ro told Dex, "it might be good if I had *some* idea of what's going on—so, uh, where are we? Why did Blondie come charging into our sparkly waiting room, haul us outside, and teleport us to this very shiny door? And who does she think is hiding behind it?"

"I believe I can answer that," Sandor said in a tone that sounded much calmer than Sophie would've expected after she'd brought him to the middle of nowhere late at night, without asking permission or giving him any time to take the proper security precautions. He sent Lovise to patrol the moon-lit meadow before he told Ro, "This is Mr. Forkle's private office—or the one we're aware of, anyway. So I'm assuming she found something in the cache that she wishes to discuss with him."

"Does that mean one of the elf-y secrets was actually useful for a change?" Ro asked.

"No idea," Dex told her. "All I know is it's some sort of sym-bol, and it must be connected to the Black Swan."

"It's not *connected* to them," Sophie corrected. "I just know they know about it—otherwise *I* wouldn't know about it."

"Uhhhhh . . . you lost me," Ro said.

"Me too," Dex admitted.

Sophie wasn't in the mood to explain.

Instead, she dug out her Imparter and told it, "Show me Mr. Forkle! Show me Magnate Leto! Show me Sir Astin!"

None of his aliases responded.

She'd expected as much, since she'd tried the same thing when she was still in Oralie's mind-map room—and her Imparter had stayed just as silent. That was why she'd dragged everyone to the only place she could think of where she might be able to track him down: Watchward Heath. But of course he wasn't there—unless he was cowering in his strange, egg-shaped office, waiting for her to leave. . . .

She tucked her Imparter away and pounded on the door again—adding a couple of kicks for good measure. "DON'T FORGET THAT YOU MADE MY INFLICTING WAY STRONGER NOW—AND I HAVE NO PROBLEM USING IT!"

"Hate to say it," Dex mumbled, "but I don't think he's here."

"I'd be happy to bust down the door if you want to double-check," Ro offered. "Then we could snoop around and dig up all the Forklenator's secrets."

"It's not worth it." Sophie slumped to the ground and wrapped her arms around her knees. "The only thing in there is a weird 3-D map of the planet."

"Oooh, we should totally smash that!" Ro clapped Sophie on the shoulder and gave her a gentle shake. "Come on, Blondie—you look like you need to unleash some of that pent-up angst!"

She definitely did.

Sophie had forgotten how unsettling it was to have her brain remember something that wasn't actually one of *her* memories.

It'd been years since she'd triggered any of the secrets that Mr. Forkle had planted inside her brain. In fact, she often forgot that there was still information tucked away. And sometimes she worried the reason the memories never popped up was because the Black Swan hadn't properly prepared her for the problems they were facing.

But *this* felt even worse.

It was just so . . . pointless.

If the Black Swan knew the symbol was important, why hide it in her mind and never bother telling her anything about it?

What good did *that* do for anyone?

"We could go back to Tiergan's house," Dex suggested. "I'm sure he knows how to reach Mr. Forkle."

He must.

But he'd probably want to know why she needed to talk to him.

And if she told him, he'd also want to know about all the other memories in Kenric's cache—and then he'd have ten zillion questions and Sophie would end up burying her face in a pillow and screaming herself hoarse.

"All right," Sandor said, sheathing his sword and marching over to Sophie. "It's late. No one's here. And we're far too exposed. So it's time to go home—and no, this is not up for debate. I've been *very* patient with you thus far—but I've reached my limit."

"Uh-oh. He brought out a 'thus,'" Ro noted. "Pretty sure that means there's a sweaty goblin stranglehold in your future if you don't cooperate."

"Worse," Sandor warned.

"I should probably head home too," Dex said quietly. "I'm sure my parents are starting to worry about how long I've been gone—and I don't even want to think about what kind of a disaster I'm going to find when I get there. I wouldn't be surprised if Bex figured out how to phase into my room. I set up an electrical field to zap her if she tries—but it's going to take something *much* stronger to actually block her."

"Oooh—I have some amoebas that'll do the trick!" Ro reached into her corset and pulled out a small black packet. "Smear these little buggers all over your walls, and if she makes any sort of contact, she'll end up covered in pus-squirting boils."

Dex looked tempted for a second—but then shook his head. "I'd probably forget and lean against the wall or something. Plus, Bex would just run around squirting pus on everybody."

"Sounds like your sister and I need to hang out," Ro said as she tucked the packet of amoebas away.

"You'd regret that," Sophie told her. "The triplets are a whole other level of chaos—especially now that two of them have manifested."

She glanced at Dex as soon as the words left her mouth, hoping the reminder wasn't too painful for him.

But he nodded and told Ro, "You should see what they did to poor Lovise this morning. I found her stuck to the wall with ice bonds, and Bex was about to force-feed her the elixir my dad's been keeping locked up while he works out the kinks. I'm not sure what it's *supposed* to do—but right now it makes weird, stringy boogers pour out of your nose."

"Sounds like fun!" Ro insisted.

"Just so we're clear," Lovise grumbled as she stomped back over to Dex's side, "they only trapped me because I'm not allowed to use my weapons."

"You're not," Sandor agreed. "But let me know if you need backup."

Lovise cracked her knuckles. "I can handle it."

"Better idea!" Ro jumped in. "How about we all head to the Dexinator's house and expand our little slumber party? Take these triplets on in force!"

Dex glanced at Sophie. "Uh . . ."

"Sophie's going back to Havenfield," Sandor cut in, "where I have full control of the security. And speaking of which, it's time to go."

"Will you be okay?" Dex asked as Sophie stumbled to her feet.

"Of course she will!" Ro draped her arm around Sophie's shoulders. "This is Blondie we're talking about! She's going to head back to her sparkly bedroom and figure out everything she needs to know about the annoying new symbol all by herself—and even if she doesn't, we won't care because there will be food! Have I mentioned I'm starving? Seriously, *how* do you go so long without eating?"

Sophie wanted to argue that she ate as often as everybody else—but now that Ro had mentioned it, she couldn't actually remember the last time she'd eaten.

There'd been so much going on that food had been the last thing on her mind.

Her stomach made a loud, sloshy growl to punish her.

"Sounds like we all agree it's time for a midnight snack!" Ro told her. "And let's hope there are more of those swirly pastry things."

Sophie locked her knees as Ro tried to drag her away from the round door. "Wait—I need to make sure Mr. Forkle knows I'm looking for him. Does anyone have anything I can use to leave a note?"

Dex didn't.

Neither did Sandor.

"Ugh, hang on," Ro said when Sophie tried to see if she could scratch a message into the dirt with the toe of her boot. "Try this."

She pulled a small red tube out of her corset and handed it over.

"Really hoping this is lip gloss," Sophie said, "and not more scary microbes."

"It's *lipstick*," Ro corrected. "I don't do shiny. And given the fact that you were threatening to go all Inflictor-rage a few minutes ago, I would've thought you'd be down for a little bacterial punishment—but that's not what this is. And don't say I never did anything for you, because that's my favorite lipstick color. It should be pretty hard to miss if you write your little message across the ugly door."

That was definitely a better plan than kicking at the ground.

Now Sophie just needed to figure out what to say.

She thought of all the notes the Black Swan used to leave for her—and the few she'd left for them—and somehow her final message ended up sounding a lot like Keefe:

> *We need to talk—NOW!*
> *You have a lot of explaining to do.*
> *And if you try to ignore me,*
> *I'll fill your office with sasquatch poo.*

Ro applauded. "Niiiiiiiiiiice! Definitely worth the lipstick sacrifice—but can we please go get some food now?"

"I just need to do one more thing," Sophie said, realizing her note needed a signature.

She used the last of the lipstick to draw her moonlark symbol underneath, hoping it wouldn't weird Dex out.

"That looks supercool," he told her.

"Really?" Sophie asked. "You're not just saying that?"

"Nope. I love the way you drew it midflight. Makes it look extra intimidating, like *do not mess with the moonlark!*"

Sophie smiled.

And she was tempted to leave the conversation there.

But . . . after the big confrontation that morning, she had to ask, "Does that mean you aren't bothered that I made my own symbol?"

Dex fidgeted with his cape. "I was never *bothered*. It just felt . . . like a big, scary change—but I get it now. In fact, I totally agree with what Ro told Oralie earlier. I like this new Sophie attitude."

"You do?"

Sophie still wasn't sure she *had* a new attitude.

Dex flashed a dimpled grin. "Yeah. You're really taking charge."

Was she?

She wasn't trying to.

"I just want to actually *solve* things, you know?" she mumbled. "I'm sick of waiting for answers and getting nowhere."

"Me too." Dex's smile faded. "I'm sorry I got a little freaked out about the storehouse fire this morning. I shouldn't have—"

"It's okay," Sophie interrupted. "I know it was a big deal."

"It was," he agreed. "But . . . I'm glad you were brave enough to do it. And I hope if I'm ever in that kind of situation, I'll be brave enough too."

"I'm sure you will be," Sophie promised. "You're one of the bravest people I know."

"Awwwwwwwwwwwwwwwwwww, you two are so cute!" Ro jumped in. "You're *almost* making me want to root for Dexphie—but I'm still Team Foster-Keefe through and through. Plus, I think the Dexphie ship already crashed and burned, didn't it?"

Sophie groaned, hoping the darkness hid her burning cheeks.

She'd never regret using her first kiss to prove to Dex that they worked much better as friends—but that didn't make reliving the awkwardness any less humiliating.

Dex cleared his throat and fumbled for his home crystal. "Well . . . uh . . . I should go. Will you let me know what you find out from Mr. Forkle?"

"Of course."

Ro clapped her hands as Dex and Lovise glittered away. "Okay, Blondie, let's go get some pastries!"

Sophie glanced back at the door, checking her message one last time—and part of her wondered if she should camp out there to make sure Mr. Forkle couldn't ignore her.

But Sandor would have a heart attack.

Plus, there were things she needed to follow up on.

So she leaped everyone back to Havenfield, and Sophie was glad to find the alicorns all snuggled up under the Panakes tree. She gave Wynn and Luna a good nuzzle before she turned to Silveny to see if she'd managed to make contact with Keefe.

Silveny sounded equal parts annoyed and worried when she admitted, *NOT YET! NOT YET! NOT YET!*

Sophie stroked Silveny's velvet-soft nose and tried not to imagine any of the different ways that Keefe could be in trouble. The much more likely explanation was that he just didn't want to be found—and Sophie was mostly okay with that.

Or maybe he couldn't hear the alicorns' transmissions after all.

But she still told Silveny, *Don't give up on him yet.*

NEVER! Silveny promised. *NEVER! GIVE! UP!*

A fresh chant of *KEEFE! KEEFE! KEEFE!* filled Sophie's mind as she headed inside to check in with Grady and Edaline, who'd sadly made equally little progress.

Grady hadn't learned anything about the missing islands, and Edaline didn't have any new theories about Gisela using her conjuring. But they both promised they'd keep working on it.

"What about you, kiddo?" Grady asked. "You've been gone a pretty long time. Anything we need to know?"

"I'm not sure yet," Sophie admitted. "But hopefully I'll get more answers soon."

"We're also *starving*," Ro added, turning to Edaline with big, pleading eyes. "Any chance you could do your elf-y snappy thing and make more buttery baked goods appear? Preferably more of those berry swirly-dos?"

Edaline laughed and snapped her fingers. "I'll do you one better. It's all waiting for you in Sophie's room—and I added a new savory recipe to the mix. I call them toasty turnovers."

"LOOK OUT!" Ro tossed Sophie over her shoulder and charged up all the stairs to Sophie's room in a matter of seconds. "AHHHHH—IT'S EVEN BETTER THAN I IMAGINED!"

Sophie held on for dear life as Ro sprinted for her bed.

When she finally managed to twist around, she could see three enormous platters lined up near the edge—one piled with sweetberry swirls, another with little moon-shaped hand pies that had to be the toasty turnovers, and the third with a mix of mallowmelt and butterblasts.

Ro plopped Sophie on her feet. "Better grab some quick, Blondie. I don't care how long it's been since you've eaten— this is everyone for themselves."

Sophie snatched two of the toasty turnovers—which turned out to be filled with gooey melted cheese and tasted like the best pizza pockets *ever*—and then made sure she grabbed a sweetberry swirl before Ro could devour them all. One bite was all she needed to understand the ogre princess's obsession. It was like eating the soft, buttery center of a warm cinnamon roll—but stuffed with juicy berries and topped with triple the icing.

When she finished the last bite, her stomach was officially at maximum capacity, and she stumbled over to her desk to get away from the pastries before she made herself sick.

"Calling your sister again?" Ro asked, shoving two butter- blasts into her mouth.

"Nope!" Sophie had nothing to tell Amy—which was also why she didn't hail any of her friends.

They'd agreed to wait until they'd actually learned some- thing.

Instead, she dug out her memory log and sank down on the floor next to her bed, staring at the silver moonlark embossed on the teal cover.

"Oh look, it's your disappointing diary!" Ro said, showering

Sophie with mallowmelt crumbs. "I found that when I searched your room this morning—and don't look so scowl-y. It's not like there was anything good in there. I *thought* it'd be filled with mushy ramblings about Captain Perfectpants. But nope! Just boring symbols and images—though what was up with all the fires and screaming people?"

"Those were projections of my nightmares," Sophie mumbled, flipping past them as fast as she could. "This is a memory log, not a diary. Alden gave it to me back when he first realized that the Black Swan had hidden secrets in my mind, hoping it would help me keep track of what I'd remembered—and maybe trigger more."

It hadn't worked as well as they'd hoped.

But Sophie finally had another memory to add.

She turned to a fresh page and concentrated on the symbol they'd found in Kenric's cache.

"Okay, that's one of your freakier mind tricks," Ro said as the black squiggly lines slowly spread across the top of the page, like they were being painted by an invisible hand.

Sophie filled the bottom section with the symbol that had already been in her head—and now that she had them next to each other, she could see that they weren't one hundred percent identical.

The one from Kenric's cache was more obviously hand-drawn, and the squiggly lines stretched a lot farther past the points where they intersected.

The memory the Black Swan had given her also had a rough, dark halo around it, as if she were actually looking at a burned scrap of paper with the symbol printed on it.

But they were definitely still renderings of the same thing.

"I can't tell if that's a star or a flower in the center," she said, studying the page from different angles.

Ro leaned closer. "Uh, you realize that's not a symbol, right?"

"What do you mean?"

Ro dragged her claw along the squiggly lines. "Haven't you ever seen a map before? These look exactly like rivers."

Sophie tilted her head, trying to see what Ro was describing.

"It's easier to tell on this one," Ro said, tapping the bottom image, "since it looks like it's actually a piece from a burned map. But the one up top looks like whoever made it was either looking at the same map as they drew it—or traced part of it."

"What's this, then?" Sophie asked, pointing to the flower-star thing in the center.

"Probably a marker for what everyone wanted to find. Isn't that one of your fancy runes underneath?"

Sophie nodded, wishing she'd thought to ask Dex or Oralie about it. She'd been too focused on the fact that the image was already in her head.

"I can't read it," she admitted. "The Black Swan trained my mind to read their cipher runes, so I can't recognize the regular ones."

But Grady and Edaline could—and Sophie wasted no time

racing down the stairs and showing them her projections.

Grady pointed to the curves at the ends of the rune and reminded her that only the *most* ancient runes had all those flourishes—which might've been why Dex and Oralie hadn't translated the rune either.

Thankfully, Edaline knew how to read it.

"That's an *E*," she told Sophie.

"I'm assuming that's significant?" Grady asked when Sophie sucked in a huge breath.

Sophie nodded, tracing each of the five squiggly lines with her finger.

Five *rivers*, she corrected—which all intersected at different points, creating a unique island of land that was marked on a map with an *E*.

Sophie had wondered if Elysian was a place from the moment she'd first heard Kenric say the word in Oralie's cache. She'd grown up reading myths about the Elysian Fields—and human legends tended to be rooted in shades of truth.

So if she was understanding the markings correctly—and she was pretty sure she was—all she had to do was find where those five rivers connected, and she'd find Elysian.

EIGHTEEN

UGH, SCROLLS ARE SERIOUSLY *THE worst*," Sophie grumbled, wrestling with a particularly stubborn piece of paper that kept rolling back up the second she tried to smooth it out on the kitchen table. "Why do we still use them? Even humans moved on a few centuries ago. Now they have this handy thing called Google Maps—you should really check it out."

Grady laughed and set his bottle of lushberry juice on the scroll to help weigh one end down. "Scrolls make it easier to control who's able to view the information. Remember: our world is designed to be found only by those allowed to have access."

"Yeah, well, there has to be a way to be mysterious *and* efficient," Sophie argued.

"I'm with Blondie," Ro jumped in, waving one of the scrolls like it was a sword and she was challenging Sandor to a scroll duel. "In the Armorgate we have these grids that . . . Actually, I'm not sure if I'm allowed to tell you about those—especially with a goblin around." She poked Sandor's side with her scroll-sword—and he did *not* look amused. "But they're way cooler than these dusty things."

"Pretty much anything is," Sophie muttered.

Ro groaned as Edaline strode into the kitchen carrying another armload of paper—and Sophie was right there with her. She was tempted to run back upstairs, grab Iggy, and let the destructive little imp do some serious shredding.

When she'd asked Grady and Edaline if she could check all their maps, she'd had *no* idea what she was getting herself into.

The entire kitchen table was now buried under scrolls.

So were the empty chairs.

And most of the floor.

Now she understood why Grady and Edaline had insisted she get some sleep before she started her search for the mysterious rivers.

"This shouldn't be so hard," she'd said, letting her eyes go out of focus so she could see the lines of the rivers without as many distractions. So far, she hadn't found even *one* match.

Some maps didn't have any rivers—and most of the ones that did only showed a small portion. It would've been *really* nice if she could've clicked a "zoom out" button—but nope!

She lifted Grady's lushberry juice and moved the current scroll to her "not it" pile, which looked depressingly small compared to the mountain of scrolls she still needed to search—and that was just the maps that Grady and Edaline had in their offices. There had to be thousands of others sitting in dusty libraries throughout the Lost Cities, and she'd have to start tracking them all down if she couldn't find what she needed.

"I'd be happy to help," Edaline offered, planting a kiss on the top of Sophie's head as she dumped the new batch of maps onto the table. "We have a Spinosaurus arriving in the next minute or two, and I'll need to get it settled into a pasture—but I should be free in a few hours."

"Thanks," Sophie said, trying not to think about how numb her butt was going to be by that point. The kitchen chairs were *not* as comfortable as she would've liked.

"I'm ready to jump in anytime too," Grady said as he helped Sophie weigh down the next scroll. "But I'll be way more useful if you tell me what this is all about."

Sophie became very interested in examining the newest rivers.

She wasn't sure how much she was allowed to share about Elysian, so she was keeping everything extremely vague. They knew she was looking for rivers that matched the pattern of her projections, and that it had something to do with the letter *E*—but nothing else.

"You can trust me," Grady promised. "I won't—"

Sophie was saved by a ground-shaking *ROAR!*

"That's my cue," Edaline said, rumpling Sophie's hair before she rolled up her sleeves and headed out to the pastures.

"Holler if you need me!" Grady called after her.

"Eh, it's one Spinosaurus," Edaline shouted back. "It'll be easy."

The next *ROOOAAAR* seemed to suggest otherwise.

"Don't worry," Grady told Sophie. "Edaline's the dinosaur whisperer."

Sophie watched through the windows—and the Spinosaurus did seem to calm when Edaline approached with slow, careful steps and outstretched arms.

The scene reminded her a little of the first time she'd sat in Havenfield's kitchen staring at the creature-filled pastures through the wide windows—back when taming feathery dinosaurs seemed as impossible as feeling at home in this glittering house with these beautiful strangers.

So much had changed since then.

Now this was her *family*—her *world*.

And she had to make sure the Neverseen couldn't destroy it—even if it meant checking every map in existence.

She reached for the next scroll, coughing when it unleashed a giant plume of dust. "Maybe I should hail Dex and see if he can think of any gadgets that might speed up this process."

"What about that 3-D map thing you said the Forklenator has in his office?" Ro asked. "Would that be useful?"

"It depends on what you're looking for," a familiar wheezy voice said behind them.

Scrolls went flying as Sophie spun around to find Mr. Forkle standing in the kitchen doorway, looking as wrinkled and puffy as he always did after he ate a few ruckleberries—but there were deep shadows under his eyes that usually weren't there.

"Hope it's okay that I let myself in," he said, glancing at Grady before shifting his focus to Sophie. "Apparently I have a *lot* of explaining to do."

Sophie had to stop herself from apologizing.

She had every right to demand answers—especially now that she knew how important the triggered memory was.

"Where were you last night?" she asked.

He sighed. "*That* is a very long story—and I'm assuming you called me here to discuss something else. But I should warn you: If you're planning to ask me to use Watchward Heath's cameras to track down where young Mr. Sencen is hiding, I've already tried."

"You have?" Sophie asked.

She'd actually forgotten all about his ability to sort through those recordings, targeting a specific face.

Mr. Forkle nodded. "Of course. While I respect Mr. Sencen's desire for privacy at the moment, it seemed prudent to at least check and make sure he wasn't causing any interspeciesial incidents. So I did a search for his likeness and found three scattered images that must've been captured not long after he left. One showed him in a desert, at the base of one of the pyramids we helped the humans build long ago. In the next he was on a boat floating near an enormous curved waterfall, seeming quite jealous of the blue coverings all the humans were wearing to prevent themselves from getting drenched. And in the last he was in the midst of a rather exhausted-looking crowd in front of an unimpressive castle in what I believe humans call a 'theme park'—and he was looking right at the camera, as if he knew exactly where it was. I believe he did indeed learn how to identify our surveillance, because his face hasn't shown up since, so clearly he is going to great lengths to not be found."

"Huh," Sophie said, fighting the urge to pummel him with follow-up questions. She needed to stay focused. "Well . . . good to know, I guess. But that's not why I needed to talk to you."

"Yes, I'm now assuming your reason must be related to whatever inspired this project you're working on." He waved his hands at the abundance of scrolls. "What are you hoping to find?"

Sophie scrounged under the piles of paper and dug out her memory log, pointing to the maps she'd projected. *"This."*

Mr. Forkle's jaw fell open. "Where did you find that?"

"Nope! You're here to answer *my* questions—and I want to know why you buried a map in my brain and never bothered to tell me about it."

"You say that with such accusation," he murmured, shuffling closer and squinting at the squiggly black lines from Kenric's cache. "I assure you, there was no ulterior motive. I simply had no idea if it would ever become relevant."

"Uh, you must've had *some* clue if you took the time to

plant the memory in my head in the first place!"

"That's not necessarily true. I don't think you understand how these memories are meant to work."

"How could I? It's not like you gave me an instruction manual! The memories just started popping up out of nowhere one day—which almost got me exiled, if you remember."

"Oh, I remember. And I'd known it was a risk to provide you with such volatile information—but I was afraid you would be at too great of a disadvantage if you were brought to the Lost Cities with no knowledge of the challenges you'd be facing. And since I also couldn't overwhelm your conscious mind with facts and details that would make little-to-no sense while you were still living among humans, the best solution I could find was to take everything I'd learned—no matter how vague— and bury each piece as a separate memory that would trigger if it proved to be relevant, and remain hidden if not. That way you'd have what you needed precisely when you needed it, and not be distracted by anything irrelevant. The main downside was that I couldn't predict *when* something would trigger— or if it ever would. After all, if I knew the full significance of the information I was sharing, or exactly how it fit into the enemy's plans, I could've ended this mess ages ago."

"But you *had* to know that certain things were more important than others," Sophie pressed.

"In a few cases, yes. I strongly suspected that one of our enemies was a Pyrokinetic, so I had a feeling you would need the formula for frissyn someday, as well as the names and locations of the unmapped stars. But nearly everything else was truly a guessing game. Our understanding of our enemies was very blurry back then."

Ro coughed. "Still seems pretty blurry now."

"It can be," Mr. Forkle agreed. A deep, shadowy sorrow settled into his features, and he blinked it away before he added, "But we've still come a long way."

"I'm sure we'd have gotten a lot farther if you'd caught me up on all the information that never triggered," Sophie muttered. "You should've walked me through every single memory once I was in the Lost Cities—or at least after I swore fealty to the Black Swan!"

"To what end?" Mr. Forkle countered. "So you could be distracted by things that clearly weren't important?"

"Uh, Elysian is *super* important!"

She covered her mouth—wishing she could snatch the words back, but it was too late.

"What's Elysian?" Grady asked.

"And who told you about it?" Mr. Forkle added.

Sophie glanced at Ro and Sandor, wondering how bad it would be to say any more in front of them.

Ro rolled her eyes. "Oh please, like Gigantor and I can't figure out on our own that this Elysian thing is the place you're looking for on these maps—and you learned about it in that Councillor dude's cache."

"*Kenric's* cache?" Mr. Forkle clarified. "You accessed his Forgotten Secrets?"

Sophie nodded. "Dex and I met with Councillor Oralie yesterday and watched all seven memories—most of which were too vague to really tell us anything."

Ro snort-laughed. "Now, *there's* a shock."

"Believe me, I'm just as sick of it as you are," Sophie told her before she turned back to Mr. Forkle. She pointed to the top projection in her memory log. "This was the only thing that seemed like it might actually be important. And as soon as I saw it, it triggered the version you planted in my memory."

"And now you're convinced that I've somehow denied you the answer to everything because I didn't show you the map earlier," Mr. Forkle guessed.

"I don't think it's the answer to *everything*," Sophie corrected. "But Elysian *is* crucial."

"What makes you so certain?" he asked.

"Because it's connected to stellarlune!"

"Stellarlune," Mr. Forkle repeated, dragging out each syllable. "You'll have to forgive me—sometimes the abundance of strange terms gets the better of me. Stellarlune is one of Lady Gisela's projects, isn't it? Pertaining to Mr. Sencen's 'legacy'?"

Sophie nodded. "She told me in Loamnore—before she had Tam and Glimmer blast Keefe with shadows and light—that stellarlune is about using the natural forces of our world to bring out someone's full potential. But it must be bigger than that, because Kenric actually looked into it at some point. There was a memory in his cache of him bringing Oralie to Fintan's house to ask him if he knew anything about stellarlune."

"What did Fintan say?" Mr. Forkle asked.

"He said he'd never heard of it—and Oralie believed him. Kenric also couldn't find anything when he tried reading Fintan's mind—though it kind of looked like he got fooled by Fintan's mental defenses. In fact, I should probably see if Marella can ask Fintan about it again."

She added *Have Marella ask Fintan about stellarlune* to her mental to-do list.

"Did Fintan say anything else?" Grady asked.

"Well, he talked a lot about these weird flowers called Noxflares—have you ever heard of them?"

Grady and Mr. Forkle both shook their heads.

"Should we have?" Grady asked.

"I'm not sure. Oralie's going to ask Luzia Vacker about them, since Fintan also mentioned her."

Mr. Forkle frowned. "How does any of this connect to Elysian?"

"I was about to get to that part," Sophie told him. "After Kenric and Oralie left Fintan's house, Kenric accidentally mentioned Elysian—and the way it came up made it clear it had something to do with stellarlune. He also told Oralie it's essential to keep everything about Elysian fragmented, so I'm assuming that's why he recorded the map without any context. Just like you did."

"Yes, but in my case, that scrap of paper was the full extent of my knowledge," Mr. Forkle argued. "I found it inside an apartment in Atlantis that I'd suspected was being used by the rebels. The place had been cleared by the time I snuck in—but I found that scorched bit of map in a pile of ash."

"Do you think Fintan was the one who burned it?" Sophie asked.

He shrugged. "It could just as easily have been Brant."

"Or anyone else," Grady reminded them. "Pyrokinetics aren't the only ones capable of setting fires to destroy evidence."

"True." But Sophie still added another item to her to-do list: *Have Marella ask Fintan if he's ever seen a map with five rivers.*

Mr. Forkle reached for her memory log and traced his wrinkled fingers over the lines. "You have no idea how determined I was to find out where this led. In fact, one of my offices was buried in scrolls like this for *years*. It's one of the reasons I asked Tinker to build the 3-D map you saw in my other office—which definitely sped up my search. I've now been to every river, every creek, and every stream on this planet—so I can say with absolute confidence that no such place exists."

"Then why would Kenric save the map in his cache?" Sophie argued.

"Probably the same reason I gave the memory to you." Mr. Forkle turned away, staring out the window, where Edaline was now riding the Spinosaurus around one of the pastures. "After I'd ruled out all the rivers, I started to wonder if the map wasn't actually a map at all, but rather a blueprint for a place that someone wanted to build."

"Like a new hideout?" Grady wondered.

"Possibly," Mr. Forkle told him. "Though redirecting rivers seems like an awful lot of hassle for something like that. So for a while now I've wondered if what we're *really* looking at"—he held up her memory log to show everyone—"is a plan for a human sanctuary."

Grady muttered something under his breath that Sophie was pretty sure she'd get in trouble for saying—and she was tempted to mutter the same thing.

"I know," Mr. Forkle told them. "I would love to be wrong. But it makes sense, doesn't it? We hollowed out a mountain range to construct the first sanctuary, so it seems quite plausible that someone would want to reroute rivers in order to build another. Perhaps they feel the rivers will serve as a natural barrier between humans and the rest of the planet."

"Wait," Ro cut in. "You're going to relocate the humans?"

"First of all, *we* have nothing to do with any of this," Mr. Forkle told her. "And no, no one will be relocating the humans. Building a human sanctuary was simply an idea proposed by a small group of—"

"Not *that* small," Grady jumped in.

"No . . . I suppose the group was far larger than it should've been," Mr. Forkle admitted. "It was a segment of our nobility, along with their supporters, who believed that human weapons and pollution had become too massive of a problem to continue without intervention, and that as a result humans no longer deserved to have free rein of the planet. They felt that the only solution was to restrict humans to a designated sanctuary, where they could be monitored and controlled for everyone's safety—including their own."

Ro blinked. "Uh, don't hate me for saying this, Blondie, but . . . that sounds like a pretty solid plan."

"It does," Sandor agreed.

Sophie reeled toward them. "Seriously? How can you—"

"Because humans threaten the stability of everything," Sandor told her.

"And they have *way* too much land!" Ro added. "*My* people are restricted to *our* territory."

"As are mine," Sandor agreed. "As are the dwarves. And the trolls. Even you elves stay within the limits of your cities and properties. And yet, humans aren't held to the same limitations. They're allowed to live wherever they please."

"And they're not even held to a treaty!" Ro added. "Seriously, *what* were your ancient Councillors thinking?"

"I can't say for certain," Mr. Forkle said quietly, "but I doubt anyone—even *your* ancient leaders—expected humans to spread throughout the planet the way they have. Nor that they'd develop so many chemicals, pollutants, and weapons. It's definitely a problem that needs to be addressed—but in a way that accounts for the fact that humans can be clever, and loving, and *many* other wonderful things. Relocating them to a sanctuary would be far too devastating."

"It would," Sophie agreed—scowling at Sandor and Ro. "You're talking about uprooting everyone's lives, cramming them together, and forcing them to live like prisoners—"

"Which is why the Council rejected the idea," Mr. Forkle reminded her. "Someday, we *will* find a solution to the human conundrum," he promised Sandor and Ro. "But a sanctuary isn't the answer—and most supporters of the plan eventually came to agree with the Council's ruling. *But* . . . it's possible that someone in the Neverseen is still hoping to move forward with the idea, and this"—he pointed to the symbols in Sophie's memory log—"is their plan for how to build it."

"That does sound plausible," Grady admitted.

Sophie couldn't deny that it did. *But* . . .

"If Kenric had found proof that someone was planning to build a human sanctuary, would he really store that kind of thing in his cache?" she asked.

"What better place would there be to keep such an ugly secret?" Mr. Forkle countered.

"Maybe somewhere he would actually be able to remember it, so he could make sure it never happened," Sophie snapped back.

Unless *that* was one of the reasons Kenric had asked Prentice to serve as his Keeper . . .

"Don't forget," Grady said, reaching for Sophie's hand to stop her from tugging on her eyelashes, "it's also possible that Kenric didn't understand what the map meant either, and simply stored it in his cache in case it ever became important."

"Which would also make a whole lot more sense if the Councillors actually knew what's in their caches," Sophie grumbled. "But they don't. And Kenric not only knew that—he was trying to find a better solution for it. There was even a memory in his cache where he talked to . . ."

She stopped herself before saying Prentice's name. If she hadn't, Mr. Forkle would've had the same questions that she'd had about whether Kenric was involved with Prentice's arrest—and it would completely derail the conversation.

"Are you going to finish that sentence?" Mr. Forkle asked, raising his eyebrows.

Sophie shook her head. "I know you're going to want to see all of Kenric's memories—and I'll show you eventually. But I called you here because I'm trying to find Elysian."

"I thought you called me here because you believed I was hiding things from you," he corrected. "And now you're planning to hide things from me."

Sophie's smile felt more like a smirk as she told him, "Funny how that goes, isn't it?"

If his eyebrows lifted any higher, they would've flown off his head. And his lips twitched with a smile of his own. "Fine. We can focus on Elysian—*for now.*"

"Good," Sophie told him. "Because I still think this is a map leading to it. Why else would it be labeled with that?" She pointed to the ancient rune.

"An *E* could stand for *lots* of things," Mr. Forkle reminded her. "The fact that 'Elysian' starts with one could simply be a coincidence."

"It could," Sophie hated to admit.

But it didn't *feel* like a coincidence.

It just . . . made too much sense.

The map. The rune. The human myths about Elysian Fields.

It all fit together *so* perfectly.

The only thing that didn't fit was Mr. Forkle not being able to find the rivers—and he couldn't possibly have visited every square inch of the planet.

He only would've gone to places his maps told him to check.

"The 3-D map Tinker built for you," Sophie said. "Is it basically like a big amalgamation of every map she had access to?"

"I know what you're thinking," Mr. Forkle said instead of answering. "And I can assure you, Tinker was given an *extensive* collection of maps to work with."

"That doesn't mean it covered absolutely everything," Sophie argued. "Especially since Kenric talked about Elysian like it was *beyond* top secret. I'm sure any map it's on is only available to the Council—and maybe only to some of them. In fact, that's probably why Kenric's map looks like he had to draw it himself. Maybe he had to copy it! Or . . ."

"You okay, kiddo?" Grady asked when her voice trailed off.

"Yeah . . . I just . . . I need to think for a minute."

Pieces were clicking together in her head so fast, she couldn't keep up with it.

She snatched back her memory log, flipped to a blank page, and closed her eyes, replaying everything to make sure it all fit the way she thought it did—and then replayed it again just to be safe.

"Okay," she said slowly, "hear me out for a second. In one of the other memories in his cache, Kenric took Oralie somewhere with a *river*. And he told Oralie the place wasn't on *any* maps. In fact, he said he'd only found it by following 'a convoluted trail of evidence' that he'd spent months piecing together—and then walked for a *very* long time. He said he'd had to cut his own crystal so he could bring Oralie there without putting her through all that—and that he'd have to destroy the crystal afterward. But maybe he also made his own map—and *that's* the map in his cache!"

"If that were the case, why would I have found a more official version of that same map in one of the Neverseen's hideouts?" Mr. Forkle asked.

"Well . . . maybe the Council made a version for the record, and the Neverseen copied it or stole it," Sophie suggested.

"That's a big 'maybe,' Miss Foster—and I don't see how we'd verify any of these theories."

"Well . . . what about this?" She squeezed her eyes tighter, letting the dark rocks and white misty rapids paint across the page, along with the grassy field and the red-orange trees. When she'd captured every detail, she held the memory log out to Mr. Forkle. "Have you ever been *here*?"

He frowned. "Truthfully? I have no idea. It looks like many of the other rivers I've visited."

"But it's *not*," Sophie assured him. "One of the clues that Kenric followed mentioned a river with 'whispering rapids.'"

"I'm not sure I know what that means," Mr. Forkle admitted.

"You would if you'd heard it. Oralie noticed the difference right away—and so did I. The current was so fast, the crashing water should've sounded as loud as a waterfall. But all you could hear was a muffled trickle—so if you've never heard a river like that, you've never been to *this* river."

Mr. Forkle reached up to rub his temples. "Okay, so maybe I've missed a river during my search—but before you get too excited, remember: we're not looking for *one* river. We need *five*—and I don't see four others there, do you?"

"But we don't know the scale of the map!" Sophie argued. "The rivers could be far enough apart that you wouldn't see more than one at a time when you're at ground level."

"I suppose. . . ." Mr. Forkle squinted at the dark water. "Did Kenric tell Oralie why he brought her there?"

"He said he wanted to see if she felt what he felt—and she did. She called it a *mood* and he called it an *awareness*, but they both agreed that they were feeling the same thing. And when Oralie tried to figure out what was causing it, she said . . ."

Ro elbowed her when she didn't finish. "Come on, Blondie—don't just leave us hanging!"

"Sorry." Sophie's hands shook as she tucked her hair

behind her ears. "I . . . I think I just figured it out."

"Figured what out?" Sandor, Ro, Mr. Forkle, and Grady all asked in unison.

"Everything," Sophie whispered. "Well . . . not *everything*—but everything about this."

Ro coughed. "You're losing us."

She probably was. But her brain was sprinting like a runner near the finish line, and she was scrambling to keep up.

She took a deep breath before she said, "In the memory, Oralie told Kenric that she'd heard stories about rare power sources that could affect someone's senses—and she wondered if that was happening to them. They couldn't find a power source to prove her theory—but they didn't look for very long either. And if she was right, *that's* how stellarlune and Elysian are connected!"

"Not sure I follow," Grady admitted.

"Neither do I," Mr. Forkle said.

"Yeah, we're gonna need you to back it up a whole lot more," Ro told her. "Walk us through it, Blondie. We want to be with you—you just gotta lead us there."

"Fine," Sophie said, trying to think of a better starting point. "In Loamnore, Lady Gisela said stellarlune was about harnessing natural forces. And Lord Cassius recently recovered a memory where she gave him this whole speech about how the Council supposedly took away a tremendous source of power and then tried to bury any proof of its existence. She said she was going to take that power back—and then she asked him what he knew about Elysian. So maybe that means she's trying to find Elysian because it's where that power source is hidden, and she wants to steal it and use it for the last step of stellarlune!"

"Whoooooaaaaaa," Ro breathed. "That *does* make sense. But hang on—did you just say there's another step to this stellarlune thing?"

"It's possible," Sophie said, too excited to care that she'd let that detail slip. She turned to Mr. Forkle and Grady. "Come on— you *have* to admit that what I'm saying connects all the pieces."

"It does . . . ," Mr. Forkle said carefully. "But just because something makes sense doesn't mean it's true. Take it from someone who's made that mistake far too many times. This puzzle doesn't have finite edges. The pieces can be turned all different ways—and they may *seem* like they fit, but—"

"These *do*."

She refused to let him make her doubt herself.

Truth felt different.

This felt different.

She had to be right.

And if she was . . .

"We need to find Elysian," she told him, "and grab that power source—whatever it is—before Lady Gisela finds it and tries to use it on Keefe."

Mr. Forkle dragged a hand down his face. "Even if you're right, Miss Foster—"

"I *am*," she assured him.

"Perhaps. Perhaps not. Either way, you seem to be forgetting the *how* in this equation. We have no idea where Elysian *actually* is, do we?"

"No," Sophie said, feeling her shoulders slump.

"Oooh, I have a question!" Ro said, raising her hand. "Is there a reason you can't teleport us there?"

"Sophie can only teleport to places she's been," Grady explained. "Right?"

"No, I can only teleport to places I've *seen*," Sophie corrected, not sure if she wanted to hug Ro or smack herself for not thinking of it the second she'd remembered the memory with the river.

Instead she jumped to her feet, dropping her memory log as she grabbed Sandor's and Mr. Forkle's hands and pulled them out of the room.

"Not without me!" Ro said, snatching Mr. Forkle's other hand as Sophie ran for the front door.

"Or me!" Grady added, latching onto Sandor.

"We shouldn't be doing this," Sandor warned. "We have no idea what threats might be waiting for us."

"I'm sure we can handle it," Sophie told him, picking up speed as she made it outside to the pastures.

Faster and faster she ran, until her feet barely touched the ground and everyone turned weightless. Then thunder crashed and a dark, jagged crack split the scenery ahead.

"Here we go," she breathed as she charged into the void. "Next stop: Elysian!"

NINETEEN

SOOOOOOO, UH, WASN'T THERE supposed to be a river here?" Ro asked, turning in a slow circle to study the mossy trees surrounding the small clearing as Sandor drew his sword and dropped into a crouch. "I mean, I tuned out some of your little debate because, wow, can you all overthink everything—but I definitely remember rivers coming up a *lot*."

"They did," Sophie said, leaning on Grady as she rubbed her throbbing temples. "I . . . had to change plans."

No matter how hard she'd concentrated, the void had refused to split open when she'd pictured Elysian—even though her mind could see every detail perfectly.

The dark rocks.

The white-capped water.

The long, windswept grass.

The fall-colored trees with blue vines tangled among their roots.

Even the tiny yellow butterflies with the red faces.

It was all so clear.

So real.

As if all she had to do was reach out and touch it.

But every time she'd tried, the darkness stayed thick and suffocating and endless.

Sophie had only been trapped in the void one other time—when she'd learned the hard way that she couldn't teleport through the solid rock walls of the Sanctuary. But Elysian was a wide-open field next to a river—she shouldn't have had any problems.

And yet, deep in the pit of her stomach, she'd known that if she didn't change course, they were never going to see daylight again—and as she'd fought back the headache and panic and claustrophobia, she could only think of one possible explanation.

Maybe she couldn't teleport somewhere she'd only seen in a cache.

The Forgotten Secrets might leave out some crucial piece of information that her mind needed in order to home in on the location.

The good news was, she had a pretty easy way to test her theory.

She just had to picture one of the other locations she'd seen in Kenric's cache and see if the void finally opened up.

And since the thought of going to Fintan's garden—or the forest where Bronte had buried the dead gnome—made her insides feel like they were filled with creepy-crawlies, she'd made Hushwood her new destination.

She hadn't expected it to work—especially since she'd only seen the *inside* of Kenric's secret library. But somehow the second she'd pictured the vine-covered bookshelves and the branches poking through the domed ceiling, the void had cracked wide open and she was able to drag everyone into the light and skid to a stop in the misty clearing.

Her knees wanted to collapse with relief and exhaustion, but Grady managed to keep her on her feet as she gasped for breath and studied the building in front of them.

The stone walls were crawling with vines, and long branches disappeared into the domed roof, making it hard to tell where the forest ended and the structure began—exactly like she'd imagined.

But she *wasn't* imagining it.

Hushwood was really there.

So why couldn't she teleport to Elysian?

"There must be some kind of security," she said mostly to herself as she straightened her shoulders and tried standing on her own. "Maybe a force field."

"Here?" Mr. Forkle asked as he made his way over to one

of the narrow windows and peeked through. "I don't feel any trace of one—though I'm not a Psionipath, so my senses aren't as attuned to them. Where are we, by the way? It looks like some sort of library."

"It is. It's another place I saw in Kenric's cache. He called it Hushwood." She moved toward the front door, noting the way the ferns were slowly closing off the path—as if nature was trying to take over again, now that Kenric was no longer around to tame it.

"Are we in the Forbidden Cities?" Grady asked, keeping pace with her. "This looks like their style of architecture."

"I think we must be," Sophie told him. "In the memory, Kenric said he found Hushwood during one of his assignments before he became a Councillor, and he loved it so much that he decided to turn the abandoned building into his own secret library. Even Oralie didn't know about it."

But Prentice had.

She had to bite her tongue to stop herself from blurting out the rest of the story.

"I guess that explains the illusions surrounding this place," Grady said, pointing to the edge of the clearing—and it took Sophie a second to notice what he meant.

The trees were all rippling ever so slightly, like she was staring at them through a heat wave. And the shadows were all scattered in different directions.

"Illusions or no," Sandor said, "I don't like it here. The trees block my view of anyone approaching."

"And here I thought goblin senses were supposed to be all fancy and powerful," Ro said, tossing her pigtails. She sniffed the air and shrugged. "*My* senses say we're good."

"Mine do too," Sandor argued. "But my *brain* is also very aware that our safety can change in an instant. Have you forgotten that the Neverseen can light leap?"

"Nah. I'm just not worried about it. That's the difference between you and me. You'd rather hide and I'd rather fight." Ro unsheathed two of her daggers and shouted, "You hear that? If you're out there—bring it on!"

No one appeared.

"See?" Ro twirled her daggers. "Like I said—we're good. And if that changes, we're *still* good." She slashed at the ferns, sending tiny leaves fluttering everywhere.

"I have no problem fighting," Sandor growled, slashing one of the ferns neatly in half with his sword. "But we're facing enemies who'll cower behind force fields and attack children without mercy—and I'll do anything in my power to keep my charge far away from them. Perhaps that's why *your* charge felt safer running away without you."

Ro stalked closer. "If you think you're a better fighter than me, I'm always up for a spar."

"NOPE!" Sophie rushed between them. She'd already had to watch Keefe spar with King Dimitar—she wasn't about to relive the bloodshed. "We don't need any proof that you're both very big, very scary bodyguards."

"But if you could only have one of us," Ro pressed, "who would you pick? And it's okay, Blondie. No one will blame you when you choose me."

Sophie rolled her eyes and glanced at Sandor, expecting him to look just as annoyed. But his expression was . . . intent.

Like he actually wanted to hear her answer.

She turned and headed up the mossy steps to Hushwood's front door, calling over her shoulder. "If I had to pick between my bodyguards right now, I'd pick Flori!"

Grady laughed.

"Why did you bring us here?" Mr. Forkle asked as he rattled the locked door. "Is there something important inside?"

"I have no idea." Sophie peered through one of the windows. "I was just trying to figure out why I couldn't teleport to Elysian. I thought it might be because Forgotten Secrets leave out details that block my ability—but if I was able to get us here, that can't be the reason. The only other explanation I can think of is that Elysian is protected somehow. Probably by some sort of force field—which would at least prove I'm right about how important it is."

"Would it?" Mr. Forkle asked as he turned to study the clearing. "I'm not sure we can jump to that conclusion."

"How else do you explain it? I should've had *no* problem bringing us to that river—just like I had no problem bringing us *here*. But every time I tried, it felt like I was slamming against an endless black wall. So there *had* to be something blocking me—and if there was, someone must've set up that barrier. Why would they do that—unless they're trying to protect something hidden there?"

"I can think of several reasons," Mr. Forkle said, ticking them off on his fingers. "Simple privacy. Basic safety. Or perhaps the barrier is a remnant from a different time."

"Well, I guess the only way we'll know for sure is if we find another way to get there," Sophie argued. "I can ask Oralie to give me access to any classified maps the Councillors keep on record. Hopefully one of them will show Elysian—and if that doesn't work, I can search their caches and—"

"Whose caches?" Mr. Forkle interrupted.

"I don't know. I guess it'd probably make sense to start with Bronte's, since he's served the longest—and if his cache doesn't have anything, I'd just go Councillor by Councillor. We'll probably need to track down Fallon's cache too—and any other former Councillors. I'm sure it'll be tedious—but it's something we need to do anyway. I can't believe *no one* knows what's in the Forgotten Secrets."

"Let's not get ahead of ourselves," Mr. Forkle said, using his sleeve to wipe the sweat beading on his brow.

The clearing wasn't warm—but it was very, very humid.

Sophie could feel her tunic sticking to her skin, no matter how much she fidgeted.

"You said yourself that most of the memories in Kenric's cache were too vague to really tell us anything," Mr. Forkle reminded her.

"Yeah, but that was before I understood what I was seeing. Oralie said the challenge with Forgotten Secrets is that we don't have any context for the memories—and she was right. I didn't know Kenric and Oralie were in Elysian when I first watched that memory, because I hadn't seen the map yet. So who knows if I'll discover that the other memories were super important too, once I find what they're connected to? And the best place to find those connections is in the other caches."

"You may be right," Mr. Forkle told her. "But I hope you realize that the Council isn't going to approve letting you view their Forgotten Secrets. Not only could it be harmful to your sanity—but you're not a Councillor."

"But I'm a Regent. And the leader of Team Valiant. And I already know Kenric's and Oralie's Forgotten Secrets. So it's not like I'm just some normal kid, either. And if it makes them feel better, they could give me some sort of official title. I could be their personal Keeper."

Mr. Forkle tilted his head to study her. "Is that what you want? To be the official Keeper of all the Lost Cities' secrets?"

Sophie shook her head. "Not really."

Grady moved closer, taking her hands. "Good. That would be *way* too huge of a responsibility."

"I know," she said as she focused on Hushwood's window, staring at the armchairs that Kenric and Prentice had sat in while Kenric asked Prentice to play a similar role.

Prentice had looked just as shaken as she felt.

And yet she found herself whispering, "But . . . it kind of makes sense, doesn't it? The Black Swan made my mind basically impenetrable, so I'd be able to protect the secrets. And if I'm going to be the moonlark . . . I need to know what the Council's hiding. Especially since the Neverseen seem to. They knew about the drakostomes. And Vespera's Nightfall experiments. And now they're looking for Elysian. I wouldn't be surprised if tons of their other plans are connected to Ancient secrets. So how are we ever supposed to win if we don't know as much as they do?"

"And how are *you* supposed to stay sane with a head full of traumatic memories?" Grady asked. "The Forgotten Secrets were erased for a reason."

"I *know*." Sophie rubbed her arms, trying to calm the prickles. "But hiding from them is just as dangerous. The cache system is broken—"

"It is," Mr. Forkle cut in. "And I plan to emphasize that the next time I meet with the Council. But *this* is not the solution."

"Then what is?" Sophie demanded.

"I don't know," he admitted. "But I *do* know we'll figure it out."

"Before or after the Neverseen destroy everything?" Sophie asked.

"Preferably before." He offered her a weak smile before he moved to study a sensor along the doorframe. "We'll need to find a way to access this library. It's possible that some of the answers lie in these tomes. Kenric may have kept a journal—or made notes in the margins of the books he studied."

Ro dragged out her groan. "Ugh, I call 'Not it!' for that job."

"So do I!" Sophie added.

Mr. Forkle sighed. "You kids have so little appreciation for research."

"Maybe that's because I spent most of my childhood reading human encyclopedias," Sophie reminded him. "And then I found out it was all a complete waste of time and everything I'd learned about the world was wrong."

"Not *everything*," Grady said, pulling her into a side hug. "Humans definitely have a strange way of seeing the world— but they still hit some of the basics. And their myths and legends can be quite entertaining."

"You're also using that knowledge far more than you think," Mr. Forkle added. "You understand and relate to humans in a way the rest of us never will, which makes you a powerful resource *and* a much-needed ally."

"Maybe," Sophie said, sinking down on the mossy steps. "But none of that helps us right now. If we're going to beat the Neverseen, we have to get ahead of them—which means we need to find Elysian before they do."

Mr. Forkle sat beside her. "You keep talking about Elysian as if your theories are a proven fact. They aren't—and I'm surprised you don't see the danger in making those kinds of assumptions. You know better than anyone how easy it is to be misled. The Neverseen are master manipulators."

"But Elysian has nothing to do with the Neverseen," Sophie reminded him. "Well . . . except for the fact that Lady Gisela's trying to find it. All the mysteries around it are connected to the Council."

"And our Councillors are equally skilled at manipulation," Mr. Forkle argued. "How often are they dealing with crises and having to go about their day as though nothing is happening? How often are they wildly divided on a decision and yet presenting themselves as a united front?"

"Yeah, see, that's the problem with elves," Ro jumped in. "You're more concerned about appearances than reality. Your entire world could be about to crumble, and you'll act like that's okay because it's sparkly!"

"And I'm trying to change that," Sophie said, standing up again. "I'm not making *assumptions*. I'm trying to uncover the *truth* about Elysian using whatever clues I currently have. If the Council hid something there, we need to know what it is, where it is, and why they hid it—*before* the Neverseen find it."

"I'm not saying you're wrong," Mr. Forkle said quietly. "I just worry that you're missing the bigger picture. Elysian is—"

"The best lead we have at the moment," Sophie finished for him. "If you'd seen the look on Kenric's face when he mentioned it, you'd agree with me."

"And I'd be happy to view that memory, Miss Foster," he told her, "as well as the other memories you've been withholding from me."

"*Withholding?*" Sophie repeated, much louder than she meant to.

A couple of birds launched from one of the nearby trees, startled by the outburst.

"You're talking to me about *withholding* information," she said, keeping her voice lower, "when *you* put tons of secrets in my head and never told me about any of them?"

"I already explained why I did that."

"Yeah, but that doesn't change the fact that you left me sitting on one of the biggest secrets in the Lost Cities—for *years*. And now that I finally know about it and am *trying* to look into it, all you want to do is downplay it—probably to hide your mistake!"

"Have I mentioned lately that I adore Blondie's new attitude?" Ro asked. "Because it just keeps getting better and better."

"Meanwhile *I* fear that her new confidence is turning into recklessness," Mr. Forkle said quietly.

"*Recklessness?*" Sophie shouted—sending more birds scattering.

She watched them disappear into the clouds, wishing she had wings—or that Silveny was there and she could jump on her back and fly higher and higher and higher, until everything looked like tiny insignificant dots.

Grady pulled her closer, but Sophie twisted free.

She didn't need comfort.

She needed to understand.

"*How* am I being reckless?" she asked, looming over Mr. Forkle. "If this is about the storehouse fire, I already sat through your lecture and answered all your questions—for hours. Plus, you called that a victory!"

"It *was* a victory," Mr. Forkle assured her. "I still maintain that you could've exercised a bit more caution about certain things. But I was referring to other errors in your recent judgment."

"Like *what*?" Sophie demanded.

Mr. Forkle dragged a hand down his face and stood. "For one thing, there's the meeting your friends have approached the Council about."

"Wait—what meeting?" Grady asked.

"Do you want to tell him?" Mr. Forkle said to Sophie. "Or should I?"

Sophie rolled her eyes. "It's not like it's a secret. I just figured I'd wait until I knew if the Council approved it—which is pretty much as *un*reckless as you can get, by the way. If I was being reckless, I would've just told Glimmer to set it up and not told anyone what we were up to."

Grady turned slightly pale. "Please tell me you're not trying to set up a meeting with the Neverseen."

"*I'm* not," Sophie corrected. "Glimmer is."

"But you're planning to be there when it happens," Grady pressed.

"That's the current plan," Sophie admitted, "but it might

change. And the meeting is only with Trix. Glimmer seems to think he might be willing to help us find Lady Gisela because he was never all that loyal to the Neverseen. I guess he was only there for Umber, and Umber's dead now, so he doesn't have any reason to stay."

"But he *has* stayed," Grady argued. "Umber died months ago. And wasn't she the one who attacked you with shadowflux and left you shattered and full of echoes?"

Sophie couldn't help shuddering as she nodded. "Believe me, I definitely have lots of reservations about this plan—but I figured it was at least worth considering. And if you're going to launch into a big speech about how trusting our enemies never goes well, don't bother. My friends have already covered that *really* well."

"They have," Ro agreed. "You have no idea how much angsty arguing I've had to suffer through—and no one's even thrown any punches to at least make it interesting."

"Sandor's also covered all the security risks," Sophie added. "And I'm sure I'll hear a *lot* more about it if the Council approves the meeting."

"You will," Sandor assured her as he drew his sword and moved to patrol the border of the clearing.

"And if the Council doesn't agree to this plan?" Mr. Forkle asked. "Will you pursue the meeting with Trix anyway?"

"I don't know," Sophie admitted. "If it's our *only* lead, then yeah, we'll have to. But why do you think I'm working so hard to find Elysian? Do you think I wanted to get up at the crack of dawn and start searching through a mountain of maps, trying to find the right rivers? Or why I'm willing to fill my brain with Forgotten Secrets?"

"You say that as if it's supposed to reassure me," Mr. Forkle said, turning back toward Hushwood and trailing his hand down the mossy stones. "All it does is prove that you've lost sight of the bigger picture."

"*How?*" Sophie demanded.

"Several ways. But most importantly, tell me this. . . . Why are you so focused on Elysian? And don't try claiming it's about the look you saw on Kenric's face when he said the word—we both know it's not. Just like we both know it's also not about the alleged power source you believe is there, or the fact that something prevented you from teleporting us to that river."

"Um, yeah, it is," Sophie insisted.

He shook his head. "No, it's not. It's because you believe Elysian is connected to stellarlune. And stellarlune affects young Mr. Sencen."

Sophie fell back a step, her brain flooding with denials—arguments—explanations.

It took her a second to land on a better reaction: "What's wrong with *that*?"

"'Wrong' isn't the right word," Mr. Forkle corrected. "I'm not saying that Keefe isn't important—"

"Uh, it kinda sounds like you are," Ro noted.

Mr. Forkle swiped away more sweat. "No, I'm saying he's *one* person—whose life isn't actually in danger at the moment. Despite all her threats and bluster, Lady Gisela has made it quite clear that she needs her son alive—"

"So she can run experiments on him that might kill him!" Sophie argued, tempted to grab her home crystal and leap away right then—because seriously, what more did she need to say? But she went ahead and added, "Even if Keefe survives all that, who knows what creepy new abilities he'll have, or how his mom will try to exploit him? She could turn him into a weapon—"

"That will *never* happen," Mr. Forkle interrupted. "Keefe is *far* too stubborn."

"He may not have a choice," Sophie snapped back. "Tam didn't. She put ethertine bonds on his wrists and used them to control him. So who knows what Lady Gisela's planning for Keefe? She's been building toward this his entire life—do you think she hasn't created some backup plans in case he refuses to cooperate? That's why I'm not trying to find him right now! I wish I could, since he's not exactly safe in the Forbidden Cities. But . . . it's better for everyone if he stays hidden until we either find the power source his mom is looking for—or better yet, if we find his mom and make sure she can't do anything to hurt him. *That's* why I want to find Elysian. We know she's looking for it—so if we get there first—"

"If you're about to propose setting a trap," Mr. Forkle

interrupted, "tell me this: Have any of our traps actually worked?"

"Not with *that* attitude," Ro grumbled.

Mr. Forkle glanced at Grady. "You see my point, don't you?"

Grady stepped back, holding out his hands like stop signs. "This is between you and Sophie. I'm not getting in the middle of it."

"Wise choice," Sandor told him, moving to Grady's side. "I'm staying out of it as well."

"Fine," Mr. Forkle said, turning to pace. "Let's try this another way. I need to know, Miss Foster, that you understand that we've reached a stage in this conflict where hard choices are going to have to be made. As are sacrifices. And compromises. We're all going to hate every minute of it. But we can't let that anger and frustration stop us from making the best decisions possible. Or let our feelings cloud our judgment. I'm not saying we'll abandon young Mr. Sencen. Nor am I saying we won't investigate Elysian. I'm simply saying that we can't lose sight of the larger problems—like the fact that the Neverseen are continuing to make significant strides toward destabilizing the other intelligent species. Surely you remember what that means—or do you need me to repeat the conversation we had in my office?"

"Nope, I remember," Sophie mumbled, crossing her arms. "You think the Neverseen need all the intelligent species to either be weakened, distracted by internal conflicts, or siding against the Council before they can make their move to take over. Otherwise there's too great of a risk that one of the other species might take advantage of the Lost Cities' turmoil and make their own move to overthrow us."

"Huh," Ro said, studying one of her daggers. "I never thought about it like that."

"It's easy to overlook," Mr. Forkle said with a meaningful glance at Sophie. "Which is what the Neverseen are counting on. As we speak, they're preparing to deal another drastic blow—and they're hoping we won't notice. But we *have*."

"You mean to the trolls," Sophie guessed, remembering what Lord Cassius had told her about the stalled treaty negotiations.

"No, our relationship with the trolls may be balanced on a blade's edge," Mr. Forkle said quietly, "but we've been in a stalemate for long enough that it's lost its urgency. Empress Pernille has grown apathetic to the whole situation, which is usually what happens right before we're finally able to reach a compromise."

"Then who are the Neverseen going after?" Sophie asked. "The goblins?"

Sandor's squeaky laugh echoed off the trees. "My queen would *never* ally with them."

"I agree," Mr. Forkle said. "Though, technically, the Neverseen don't need her as an ally in order to deliver a blow. All they'd need to do is force her to pull her support from the Council—and while you're probably about to assure me that she would never do that, either—"

"I was," Sandor agreed.

"But you can't guarantee that," Mr. Forkle argued. "Queen Hylda's loyalties are first and foremost to her subjects—as they should be. So if she ever found herself in a situation where she feared for her people's safety, she wouldn't hesitate to call back all the soldiers serving here in the Lost Cities and use them to fight her own battles. Which would of course be the logical thing to do—but it would leave the Council utterly defenseless."

Sophie glanced at Sandor, hoping he'd be able to deny all of that.

He pressed his lips together and looked away.

"Exactly," Mr. Forkle said—a little smugly. "Though it should be noted that the goblins are not the blow I meant either—at least not at the moment. I just used them to illustrate how truly volatile things are getting. And to prove why we absolutely must focus our energy on the intelligent species. That's why I was out so late last night—well, one of the reasons anyway. You asked where I was—"

"And you brushed me off, telling me it's a long story," Sophie reminded him.

"It *is* a long story. And much of it doesn't pertain to this conversation. But I spent part of the night following up on a tip I'd gotten about the location of the rebel ogres who've been missing since the battle at Everglen. Unfortunately, they were gone by the time I arrived—but I was able to confirm the rumors I'd heard about their current mission."

"If you mean Cadfael and his remaining band of cowards," Ro told him, "you don't need to worry about them. Cadfael's no friend to the Neverseen. He'll never forget the soldiers he lost because they unleashed those freaky mutant trolls."

"That may be," Mr. Forkle told her. "But he doesn't have a lot of options. He already betrayed your father. And King Dimitar has special punishments for traitors."

"He does," Ro agreed. "Which is why Cadfael is going to keep his head down and stay hidden."

"That would be the wise course," Mr. Forkle said quietly. "But it's *not* the path Cadfael has chosen to take. My sources tell me he's planning an attack any day now."

"Relax, Blondie," Ro said when Sophie sucked in a breath. "I can handle Cadfael without even messing up my hair. He won't get anywhere near any of your sparkly cities—or your elf-y friends."

"I'm glad you feel so confident," Mr. Forkle told her. "But it won't be that easy. Cadfael isn't planning to attack us—or the Neverseen." He held Ro's stare as he told her, "He's aiming to overthrow your father."

TWENTY

ARE YOU OKAY?" SOPHIE ASKED,
trying to translate Ro's expression.

The ogre princess's jaw had fallen slack.

Brows raised.

Eyes stretched as wide as they could go.

Was it shock?

Fear?

Sophie couldn't tell.

All she knew was that Ro didn't blink when Sophie waved
a hand in front of her face. Nor did she respond when Sophie
repeated Ro's name.

Sophie glanced at Grady and Sandor, wondering if either
of them had any idea how to snap an ogre warrior out of a

trance without getting sliced into itty-bitty pieces.

They both shrugged.

She turned back to Mr. Forkle and cleared her throat. "Um . . ."

Ro sprang to life, tossing her head back like she was ready to unleash some sort of primal scream.

Instead she burst into a hysterical fit of giggles.

"Sorry," she said, gasping for air between snickers. "I know you're all *very serious* right now—but . . . I can't stop picturing Cadfael challenging my father to a spar for the throne. He . . ."

Her voice dissolved into more laughter—and Sophie wished she understood what Ro found so funny.

Cadfael used to be one of King Dimitar's Mercadirs—a title reserved only for his *best* warriors. He was also one of the tallest, buffest, scariest ogres that Sophie had ever seen—and he carried two *huge* swords.

Yes, King Dimitar was *also* incredibly terrifying, but . . . when Keefe challenged him to a sparring match, *Keefe won*. It wasn't a battle to the death, so King Dimitar had to hold himself back—and Keefe had used his elvin skills to throw Dimitar off his game.

But *still*.

"I can't!" Ro gasped, loud enough to send a few birds soaring into the sky. "There would be *So. Much. Flexing*. Cadfael would be like"—she curled her arms and clenched her fists to make her biceps bulge as she deepened her voice and said—"'I am Cadfael the Annihilator—'"

"The *Annihilator*?" Sophie had to interrupt.

"Yep! Cadfael insists on adding the title when he's trying to be formal—he's *that* ridiculous. Anyway, he'd be like"—she flexed harder and shifted her voice again—"'I am Cadfael the Annihilator, and I challenge you to a spar for the throne!' And my dad would be like"—she yawned extra loud and changed her voice again—"'If you insist.' And then Cadfael would strut toward him like this"—she giggled as she marched through the clearing like a bodybuilder competing for Mr. Universe—"and my dad would roll his eyes, crack his knuckles, and tell him, 'Let's get on with it!' And then they'd both draw their swords, and Cadfael would circle him like this"—she flexed her leg muscles with every step as she made a slow circuit around Kenric's secret library—"aaaaaaaaaaaaaaaaand about five minutes later, Cad would be headless, and my dad would be doing the victory dance I keep telling him to stop doing because it has way too much butt-wiggling. So, seriously, Blondie—there's no need for that cute little forehead crinkle." She pointed a claw toward Sophie's forehead as she added, "The Forklenator must've gotten some bad information."

"I assure you, I did not," Mr. Forkle told her.

"Oh, but you did," Ro insisted. "I'm not saying Cadfael wouldn't *love* to be king. But he loves *being alive* even more. And he's not great at sparring. He doesn't have the patience for it. He's all grunt and no style, swinging his weapons with the most predictable moves ever."

"That *could* be a strategy," Grady suggested. "Tricking his opponents into thinking they're prepared for the next blow because they've been able to anticipate all the others—only to attack in a way that's completely unexpected?"

"If that's his plan, it's failed him over and over," Ro told him. "*Every* time he and I sparred—I won."

"Yeah, but . . . wasn't he your boyfriend?" Sophie asked, even though she was pretty sure she was going to end up with ogre bacteria in her dinner because of it.

Ro's smile collapsed into a scowl. "Why would that matter?"

"Well . . ." Sophie reached for her eyelashes, trying to think of the most delicate way to put it. "I don't have a lot of experience with . . . relationships"—she looked anywhere except at Grady—"and ogres might be different. But in human movies they often showed one character intentionally losing at something, so they didn't make their boyfriend or girlfriend mad."

Ro's smile returned. "Uh, one of the reasons I lost interest in Cadfael was because I could beat him so easily—and he knew that. So if he'd wanted to keep me happy, he would've practiced night and day trying to stomp me into the ground— not that he'd ever be able to because I'm far too awesome."

"Yes, well, even if that's the case," Mr. Forkle told her, "sparring isn't the only method for overthrowing your father. My sources actually indicated that Cadfael's planning an attack on Ravagog with the intent to take out your father during the battle."

Ro blinked as she processed that.

Then she cracked up again.

"Uh, Cadfael may be arrogant, but there's no way he'd try taking on my father's *entire army*," she said when she'd gotten ahold of herself. "He knows he'd get captured in, like, a minute—*and* he knows what kind of death he'd face as a traitor. I'll spare you the details, but . . . it's a very long, very painful way to go."

Sophie shuddered.

"Whatever you're imagining, Blondie? It's so much worse."

"I'm sure it is," Mr. Forkle said quietly. "But . . . desperation is a powerful motivator—and as I said earlier, Cadfael doesn't have a lot of options."

"Yeah, but if he has to choose between living on the run or dying as a traitor, that's a no-brainer," Ro argued.

"Is it?" Mr. Forkle asked. "From what I've heard, Cadfael is furious that his family has been disgraced by his defection. He's also convinced that your father's rule is failing the people he cares about. That was why he allied with the Neverseen in the first place. And now that the Neverseen have *also* failed him, he's planning to take matters into his own hands—and it's well known that Cadfael's quite gifted when it comes to battle strategy."

"He *is*," Ro agreed. "But all the strategizing in the world won't make up for the fact that it'd be him and a handful of his traitor buddies taking on the most dangerous army on the planet—"

Sandor coughed.

"Cough all you want, Gigantor. I'm not saying goblins are wimps or anything. But your fighting style is . . . cleaner."

"I believe you mean that ogres fight dirty," Sandor corrected, stalking closer to Sophie's side, "which I'd agree with. But that makes you more *ruthless*—*not* more dangerous. And if we ever found ourselves at war—"

"You won't," Mr. Forkle cut in. "Though I fear the Neverseen may try to make that happen—which is why we cannot take these threats so lightly. If Cadfael attacks Ravagog—"

"I'm telling you, he'd never do that," Ro interrupted. "He's smart enough to know that being outnumbered a thousand to one in a city that was designed to give my father every possible advantage is a terrible, *terrible* life choice."

Mr. Forkle heaved a sigh. "I think you're forgetting that people can make choices we would never expect. For instance, I assumed you'd treat any threat to your father's life with the seriousness it deserves."

"Please, this isn't a *real* threat! Even if you're right—even if Cadfael does surprise me and actually try attacking Ravagog— he *will* be captured. That's a guarantee. And if he tries for a spar instead, he *will* lose."

"I wouldn't be so certain," Mr. Forkle warned. "He's been training quite extensively. Every boulder in the abandoned camp had clearly been used for sharpening blades. There were also sword gashes in the tree trunks, as well as gouges that were likely from daggers. And the ground was trampled in patterns that would only make sense if they were practicing hand-to-hand combat."

"Wait—is *that* why you're so convinced Cadfael's going after my father?" Ro asked. "Because that's standard protocol for our warrior camps. We keep our weapons primed and sharpened, we use downtime to practice our aim, and we run regular drills to keep our muscles loose."

"Good to know," Mr. Forkle told her. "But that's not what led me to realize that your father's life is in danger. Cadfael's group strayed into dwarven territory, and Queen Nubiti assigned a group of her best soldiers to shadow them through the earth, assuming the ogres were planning an attack on Loamnore. But the more the dwarves listened, the more they realized that *they* weren't the target. That's when Queen Nubiti reached out to me and told me what they'd overheard. I rushed over as soon as I could—but by the time I got there, the ogres had moved on. They'd left no trail of any kind—even the dwarves couldn't find a path—which likely means they've switched to a stealthier mode of transport to prepare for their attack."

"Or they caught the scent of dwarves eavesdropping on them through the ground and wanted more privacy," Ro noted, stomping her foot on the mossy stones, like she was warning any nearby dwarves to back off.

"I suppose," Mr. Forkle said. "But the dwarves also over-heard numerous discussions of an uprising."

"Okaaaaaay, but . . . Cadfael could start an uprising *any-where*," Ro reminded him. "Even here in Sparkle Town—and don't look so panicked, Blondie. I'm just trying to make my point. Trust me, if Cadfael's planning an uprising, it'll be against the Neverseen, to get some payback for the soldiers he lost thanks to their horrible planning."

"I thought the same thing," Mr. Forkle told her. "But the dwarves said the ogres spent a great deal of time discuss-ing how their target was 'weakened by the river.' And given Ravagog's recent floods . . ."

Sophie cringed, bracing for Ro to remind her that she was partially responsible for destroying half the city.

But Ro either didn't catch the reminder—or she let it go.

"Um, after *all* the map-debating I had to listen to today," she said, "I can't believe I have to remind you that Ravagog's not the only city near a river. Shoot, there's a river running right in front of your sparkly castles—but *you* don't look too worried about an uprising against your Council."

"That river doesn't weaken anything," Mr. Forkle argued.

"And the Councillors have goblins guarding them—and their city." Sandor slashed his sword through several ferns, sending branches flying. "No harm will come to anyone while they're on duty."

"Is that why you told Blondie we were too exposed when

we were standing in front of those castles?" Ro asked, smirking when Sandor didn't have an answer. "That's what I thought. I—"

"Wait!" Sophie said, stumbling closer to Mr. Forkle. "What if the *river* they were talking about is in Elysian? And what if the *uprising* they're planning is actually Cadfael going after the power source hidden there? Or maybe that's just the first step and whatever they're going to do with the power source—once they get their hands on it—is part of their *uprising*? Either way, this could all be about Elysian!"

Mr. Forkle dragged a hand down his face. "Such is the danger of vague clues. It's far too easy to find connections to the things you *want* to focus on and think you've fit all the pieces together—when you actually have everything backward."

"I could say the same thing to you!" Sophie snapped— sending more birds scattering. "Just because my theory is different from yours doesn't mean I'm wrong and you're right."

"No, but the extra information I have—and haven't been able to share because of all these interruptions—*does*," Mr. Forkle assured her.

"And what's that?" Sophie demanded.

He swiped away the sweat beading at the back of his neck before he told her, "Cadfael mentioned a score he needed to settle."

"Exactly," Ro jumped in. "And he has a score to settle with the *Neverseen*."

"He has a much bigger score to settle with your father," Mr. Forkle argued.

"Does he, though?" Ro asked. "If anything, they're even. You're just doing the same thing you accused Blondie of doing. You like your interpretation better because it fits with what *you* want everyone to focus on—the whole Neverseen-trying-to-destabilize-the-other-species thing."

"And I don't actually see how this has anything to do with that," Sophie had to point out. "Cadfael's not working with the Neverseen anymore."

"Oooh, good point, Blondie! What do you have to say about *that*, Forklenator?"

"I suppose I can see how that's a little confusing," he admitted. "But you must remember that the Neverseen put all this into motion in the first place. They lured Cadfael and the other ogres into betraying King Dimitar, knowing it would force an uprising if they ever wanted to return. I'm sure they were mostly hoping to keep the ogres on their side—but knew that if the relationship dissolved, the ogres would still serve their ultimate goals."

Ro glanced at Sophie. "Eh—still seems like a stretch, doesn't it?"

"It does," Sophie agreed.

"No, the *stretch* is believing your father's military—and your father himself—are invulnerable to attack. All it would take is one mistake—one miscalculation—and . . ." Mr. Forkle snapped his fingers. "Everything you know could fall to Cadfael. And I've now given you a chance to warn your father so he can prepare. But apparently you'd prefer to argue with my reasoning."

"Oh, is *that* what this is?" Ro asked. "You want me to run home screaming, 'Look out, Daddy! The big bad traitors might be coming to get you!'?"

Mr. Forkle's lips twitched with a hint of a smile. "If you think King Dimitar would listen to a warning like that . . . go right ahead. But I'm sure it would be just as effective to relay the information somewhat less dramatically. The point is to give your father a chance to decide for himself how much he needs to prepare."

Ro crossed her arms. "He'll think this is all as ridiculous as I do."

"Perhaps. But then it's *his* choice, rather than you gambling with your father's life and—"

"Whoa," Ro interrupted, drawing one of her daggers. "Let's be clear about something. Having confidence in my father's skills isn't a gamble. It's a fact. He trains too hard and prepares too carefully, in case something like this ever happens. So I guarantee: He. Would. Win."

"I hope you're right," Mr. Forkle murmured. "But I don't understand why you're so against passing along a warning—especially since you have no official charge to protect at the moment. Sandor is perfectly capable of handling Miss

Foster's security, and young Mr. Sencen is nowhere to be found. So really, the only thing keeping you here is your stubborn insistence that Cadfael isn't a threat—and if he turns out to be, you'll have to live with the knowledge that your world has fallen and you did nothing to prevent it."

Ro gripped her dagger tighter. But when she opened her mouth to argue, she couldn't seem to find any words.

Mr. Forkle seized his advantage. "I'd warn your father if I could. But we all know my message won't reach him. So if you refuse, I'll have to ask Bo."

"Bo," Ro repeated, spitting the name like it tasted rotten.

Mr. Forkle nodded. "I considered going to him first—since he tends to be more cooperative and won't be needed to guard Glimmer for much longer."

"Why not?" Sophie asked. "Have you heard something from the Council?"

"Nothing definitive yet. But it stands to reason, now that Glimmer's being more cooperative. I hear she's even revealed her true identity—though no one's shared that story with me *yet*. I'm sure they will soon enough." He raised his eyebrows at Sophie before turning back to Ro. "In the meantime, I'm sure Bo would be eager to return to Ravagog to protect his king."

"I bet he would," Ro muttered, stabbing a nearby fern. "He's always very *Sir, yes, sir! It's an honor to serve!*" She swept her arm in the Mercadir salute—then mimed gagging. "I'm pretty sure that was the first thing he said after we finished our wedding vows. You should have Funkyhair add that to his *Ballad of Bo and Ro* when he gets back—it'll really amp up the romance."

Sophie wasn't sure how to respond—especially while Ro was still stabbing innocent foliage.

Bo and Ro had . . . an *interesting* relationship.

King Dimitar had arranged their marriage in an attempt to prevent them from killing each other in the final spar. But if he'd hoped they'd grow to care for each other someday, he'd definitely miscalculated.

Mr. Forkle knew that. Which was probably why there was a glint in his eyes when he asked Ro, "Should I head to Solreef to speak with Bo about this?"

Ro heaved the world's most dramatic sigh.

"That's up to you," she said, re-sheathing her dagger and straightening up to her full height. "*I'll* be in Ravagog passing along your ridiculous warning. I'm sure my father and I will have a good long laugh at the absurdity of it. But since I'm apparently not needed around here, I'm also going to do what I probably should've done a while ago. I'll track down Cadfael and find out what he's really planning—and I'll make sure it *never* happens."

TWENTY-ONE

I CAN'T BELIEVE YOU'RE LEAVING," SOPHIE mumbled as she watched Ro retrieve her belongings—which basically meant gathering up all the weapons that Ro had hidden around Sophie's bedroom without anyone realizing.

There'd been a dagger tucked among the frilliest gowns in her closet.

Another stuffed behind her highest, sparkliest heels.

Plus packets of scary-sounding bacteria slipped between the thickest books on her bookshelves.

"Aw, no need for the sad eyes, Blondie," Ro said as she retrieved more microbe-filled packets, which she'd somehow secured to the bottom of Iggy's cage. "Same goes for you, little dude." She scratched Iggy's cheeks through the bars, filling the room with the sound of his squeaky purr. "You keep being your stinky, awesome self—and don't let anyone change your fur color while I'm gone. I'm sure it'll only take me a few days to track down Cad and his goons, and I want my style buddy here when I get back."

Sophie had a feeling it was going to take *much* longer.

And if Cadfael really was trying to find Elysian . . .

She sighed. "I should be going with you."

Ro snort-laughed. "Be glad Gigantor's downstairs discussing security with the Forklenator. If he heard you say that, you'd be barricaded in here for the rest of eternity. And I appreciate the offer. But every time you go to Ravagog, you and my father have all kinds of drama—and I'm so not in the mood to be in the middle of that mess. Plus, you'd slow me down too much on my hunt for Cad."

"Uhhh, *how*? Of the two of us, I'm the only one who can light leap and teleport!"

"Yeah, but your elf-y travel tricks aren't going to work for tracking down traitors. I need to be on the ground, letting my senses find their trail—and you'd be all, 'My feet hurt and it smells bad in these tunnels and I haven't seen sparkles in days! *How will I survive without sparkles?*'"

Sophie rolled her eyes as hard as she could. "I could handle it."

"You probably could. *But* I'd have to protect you when Cadfael makes his big move, and *that* would be a problem."

"Big move?" Sophie repeated, not liking the way that sounded.

Ro nodded. "The best way to catch a band of arrogant warriors is to let them trap themselves. You find them. Wait until the end of the day and let them realize you're nearby—but make it seem like you have no idea they saw you. Then you set up camp for the night and look like a distracted, easy target—and when they make their big move, you turn their ambush against them."

"But Cadfael knows you," Sophie reminded her. "Won't he be able to tell you're setting a trap?"

"Not the way I'm planning to do it." Ro's smile showed all of her pointed teeth. "I'm going to make him think I'm not there for them at all. I'm just a panicked mess, frantically trying to track down my runaway charge before anyone finds out I let him get away. Cad will be so eager to mock me for failing as a bodyguard that he'll basically hand his group over to me."

It wasn't the worst plan Sophie had ever heard—though she wasn't sure how Ro was going to make Cadfael think she was hunting for Keefe.

But it was the word "group" that made Sophie's heart pause.

"How many will you be up against?" she asked, trying not to calculate the odds of one against three—four—five.

Maybe more.

"Awwwwwwwww, look at you! Tugging on your eyelashes because of little old me! That's sweet of you, Blondie. But seriously, I'm good. You're clearly forgetting that I'm a princess."

"What does that have to do with anything?"

"Well, let me put it this way," Ro said as she retrieved another dagger from under Sophie's bed. "When I was a kid, if someone wanted to manipulate my father, what do you think they were going to try? Attacking *him*, and probably getting their head chopped off in the process? Or capturing his seemingly much-less-dangerous little daughter?"

"Wait—you were kidnapped?"

"*I* wasn't. But the daughter of a previous king was. So my parents had me in special princess training from the moment I could walk, and it was all about how to handle that kind of situation. What to do if you're outnumbered—when to fight, when to flee. How to turn disadvantages into advantages. I have moves these losers have never seen—even Cadfael. Add in all my warrior training—and my general amazingness—and yeah. I got this. I'll have zero problem taking them all out."

Sophie's insides tangled as she watched Ro slash the dagger at imaginary enemies. "Does that mean you're going to . . . ?"

"Kill them?" Ro guessed, slashing the dagger again. "I don't actually know—and no, that's not because I have any lingering feelings for Cadfael. You betray your people, you deserve to die—no excuses. So if they force my hand, I *will* end them. *But* I know my father would prefer to talk to Cad while he's still breathing."

"So would I," Sophie admitted.

"About that Elysian thing?"

A lump the size of Eternalia lodged in Sophie's throat as she realized her little slip might soon have *big* consequences.

She needed a deep breath before she could find enough voice to ask, "Are you going to tell your father about Elysian?"

"I take it that means you don't want me to?" Ro asked, sliding the dagger into one of the sheaths strapped to her thigh.

"Well . . . I'm sure the Council won't be happy that I mentioned it to you," Sophie said. "And I don't care if they're angry, but . . ."

"You don't trust my father," Ro finished for her.

Sophie didn't see any point in denying it. "I mean . . . he tried to drag me off to one of his work camps to punish me for reading his mind. And then he unleashed the drakostomes on the gnomes and tried to make them into his slaves—*and* tried to kill us all when—"

"Okay, okay, I get it," Ro jumped in. "Like I said, I don't want to be in the middle of your drama. But I guess I can *sorta* see why you might have a few reservations about him knowing your weird elf-y secret. Especially with how paranoid your Council is. The thing is, though . . . he's not just my father. He's my *king*. And if Cadfael *is* planning something with Elysian, my king needs to know."

"Yeah. I get that. I just wish we knew more about Elysian, you know? I only have theories right now—and I'm sure your father will come up with a ton of assumptions of his own. And it could be that all of us are wrong and we'd have all kinds of problems for no reason."

Ro twirled one of her pigtails as she considered. "Okay. How about this? I won't tell him unless it becomes relevant. But the *second* it does . . ."

"That's fair," Sophie agreed.

"Then you've got yourself a deal!" Ro held out her hand for a handshake.

Sophie tried not to wince from Ro's extra-strong ogre grip. "If you *do* find Cadfael—"

"Not *if*," Ro corrected. "*When*. And I'm way ahead of you. I have *lots* of questions for him about what exactly he's been planning for his little uprising. Plus, I want to know all about his time playing the Neverseen's pathetic little errand boy. I'm betting he knows something about the next few moves they're planning. So I'll be doing everything in my power to bring him in still breathing. Same goes for the rest of his group. They have a lot to answer for."

"Okay, but . . . how are you going to haul them all back to Ravagog by yourself?"

"Psh—that's the easy part. We have this amazing, super-lightweight, completely unbreakable cord in the Armorgate." Her eyes turned a little dreamy. "I'll bring a couple of coils with me to bind them up and drag them all home—and I'm *so good* at dragging stuff! I'm actually surprised I've never dragged

Hunkyhair anywhere, now that I think about it. Guess I'll have to put that at the top of the to-do list for once we're both back in Sparkle Town. Right, Blondie?"

Sophie tried to smile. But hearing Ro talk about being back in the Lost Cities—especially with Keefe—felt a lot like the last day of her human schools, when everyone would promise to stay friends even though they knew they probably wouldn't.

Ro fished a dagger out from the other side of Sophie's bed and slipped it into a notch in the back of her corset. "Okay, I think I got everything."

She turned in a slow circle, checking the room one more time—and her eyes narrowed when her gaze made it back to Sophie.

"Hmm. I'm guessing if Hunkyhair were here, he'd be fanning his face to keep away all the Foster-feelings in the air. I see the forehead crinkle, so I can tell there's plenty of worry going on. And *obviously* you're devastated about having to spend a few days without me—which, who wouldn't be? But . . . you're also looking extra tense and fidgety. What's *that* all about? And don't say 'nothing' or I'll pelt you with pillows."

Sophie sank down on the edge of her bed. "I'm just . . . feeling a little useless. You're going off to hunt down Cadfael, and I'm doing what? Looking through a bunch of maps? And I doubt I'll even find anything, because the only rivers on them will be rivers Mr. Forkle already checked. So I guess I could try to convince the Council to let me look through their caches—but I'm pretty sure Mr. Forkle's right and they're going to tell me to go away because I'm not a Councillor. So you know what'll probably happen? Mr. Forkle will figure out how to get into Hushwood and he'll bring me there and make me search through all of Kenric's boring books."

"That *does* sound like the Forklenator," Ro said.

"Doesn't it? And even if I do that, we all know I'm not going to find anything because Kenric was too afraid of Elysian to keep any records. He even said he was going to destroy the crystal he made—"

"Do you really think he did?" Ro interrupted. "Gotta say, if it were me, and I'd made a secret crystal to a place that no one was supposed to know about, you can bet I'd hang on to that bad boy in case I ever wanted to go back. Wouldn't you?"

The word "no" crawled toward Sophie's lips, since the old her would've destroyed the crystal immediately so she wouldn't have to worry about getting in trouble—or losing it.

But now . . .

"I'd probably keep it too," she admitted.

"Yeah, you would!" Ro held up her hand for a high five.

Sophie left her hanging. "But I don't know if Kenric would."

Clearly, he was willing to bend some rules if he had a secret library in an old human building. And he'd reached out to a matchmaker about Oralie and him. *And* he'd talked to Prentice about being his personal Keeper.

But he was different when it came to Elysian.

He didn't tell Oralie anything about it. He kept everything fragmented. *And* he still erased his memories of it and stored them in his cache, even though he thought the cache system wasn't working.

"Well . . . at least that's something you can do if Forkle drags you to Hushwood," Ro said. "*He* can read the boring books while you dig around and see what else you can find. Maybe you'll get lucky and stumble across that crystal."

"Maybe."

"Wow, your excitement is *overwhelming*."

"Yeah, well, we both know I'm not going to find it. We never find anything we need."

"Not true. You found those cache things, didn't you?"

"I guess. But it took forever. And I've never found the missing starstone."

"The missing what, now?"

"It's a light-leaping thing. I'm sure you've heard us talk about it before."

"Maybe. But you realize I tune you all out a lot, right? Especially if you're talking about something that sounds sparkly."

Sophie rolled her eyes again. "Well, the quick version is that Lady Gisela forced Wylie's mom to make a bunch of starstones for her. Then the Neverseen killed Wylie's mom for knowing too much, and *then* Lady Gisela realized that Cyrah never gave her one of the starstones."

"Don't you hate when that happens? They really should've timed their murder better. What? I'm kidding!" Ro plopped down on the bed next to Sophie. "Fine. I guess we're being *serious*. So the starstone thingy's still missing, and you're pouting because . . . it's important?"

"Who even knows anymore? The Neverseen kidnapped Wylie, hoping he knew where it was—but he didn't. So clearly *they* think it's important. Or they used to, at least. But with our luck, if we ever find it, it'll probably go somewhere pointless, like a hideout Gisela destroyed after the starstone went missing."

"Wow. Someone sure is being Miss Negativity right now."

Sophie shrugged. "Isn't that how it always goes?"

"Not *always*," Ro insisted. "But I do get why it feels that way. I guess I just liked Feisty Foster better than Sulky Sophie."

"Yeah, well, I woke up feeling like I *finally* had a plan. Yes, it meant searching a zillion maps—but it was worth it because I was going to find Elysian! But now apparently that's impossible—and I can't even teleport there for some reason, which probably proves Elysian is super important, but who cares because I'll never be able to get there. So now the only sorta useful thing I can do is check in with other people, hoping they're having better luck with their projects than I am, even though they probably aren't or I would've already heard from them with an update."

She kicked the flowered carpet so hard, petals went scattering.

"If you want to trash this place, I'm happy to stick around a little longer and help," Ro offered. "Especially if you let me smash your talking mirror. That thing turned on when you were sleeping yesterday, and seriously, you're lucky I didn't shatter it right then. That snotty little girl-head told me I should move my nose stud to the other side of my face because it's my better nostril!"

"That sounds like Vertina," Sophie grumbled—and part of her definitely wouldn't be sad if Ro stomped the outspoken spectral mirror into teeny, tiny pieces.

But . . . Vertina almost seemed like she was alive sometimes.

She wasn't, of course.

She was just a fancy bit of programming.

But she also had *thoughts* and *opinions*—and even seemed to care about certain people.

So destroying her—or even shoving her back to a forgotten corner to gather dust—felt . . . wrong.

"Hmm," Ro said, turning to face Sophie fully. "I don't know what you're thinking about right now. But you've turned the same pale-green color you were when you were asking me if I was going to kill Cadfael. And Hunkyhair always turns the same shade when we talk about ending Mommy Dearest. So I think I figured out something you can work on while I'm gone—probably the *most* important thing you can do, honestly." She reached behind her and unsheathed a dagger hidden in a compartment on one side of her breastplate, offering

Sophie the hilt. It was smaller than Ro's other daggers, with a zigzag blade that had intricate swirls etched into the dark blue metal, matching the pattern of her tattoos. "That's one of the first weapons my father gave me. Take it, and learn how to—"

"I've already done battle training," Sophie reminded her.

Ro snorted. "You've learned form and basic safety—which are important. But trust me, you aren't prepared to properly wield a weapon if the situation demands it. That's why I need you to take this"—she shook the dagger—"and learn how to *conquer your elf-y instincts*. I know you probably think you already have. But the lovely greenish hue to your skin says otherwise. And in some ways that's good—weapons come with tremendous responsibility. But you know what's at stake here. And one second of hesitation—one single moment of doubt or fear—could be the difference between ending this victorious or having Lady Creeptastic win."

"Trust *me*, if I get a chance to take Lady Gisela down, I won't hesitate."

"You say that," Ro told her. "But you're hesitating right now—and all I'm asking you to do is practice."

"Practice *how*?" Sophie asked.

"Well, the first step is taking the dagger—so how about you do that, huh?" Ro waved the hilt under Sophie's nose until Sophie's fingers closed around the cold metal. "Good, your hand isn't shaking."

"I would hope not. I'm just holding a knife."

"*Dagger,*" Ro corrected. "Knives are what you use to cut up your dinner. Daggers are designed to be lethal in the right hands—which is why, in my experience, most elves *can't* hold one without shaking at least a little. Even Hunkyhair flinched the first time I handed him my best stabbing blade—which surprised me. I figured if he could spar with my father, he must be different—and he *is*, but . . . it's still more of a struggle for him than it is for you. He's driven by anger and fear and all kinds of other emotions that make all of this extra intense for him. Whereas you're sitting there all cool and calm and collected. Steady hands. Steady gaze. You're one of a kind, Blondie!"

Sophie looked away.

She'd already discovered during her other battle training that she was kind of a natural when it came to violence.

Her brain just didn't know what to do with that unsettling realization.

"Don't be scared," Ro told her. "Be proud. And be ready, because you'll probably have to be the one to take out Lady Creeptastic."

The dagger turned a million pounds heavier.

"Don't get me wrong," Ro said quietly. "I'm still planning to be there—and if I am, I'll happily be the one to take care of her. But I have this funny feeling that it's going to come down to you. So you need to make sure you're ready when that moment comes."

Sophie wanted to argue—or teleport somewhere far away. Preferably a place with lots of pretty scenery and cuddly animals.

But she'd had the same gut feeling for a while now.

She was the moonlark, after all.

She'd have to be the one to end this.

"It's going to take some major work to get you ready," Ro warned.

"Okay, but what kind of work?" Sophie asked, watching the light hit the dagger's blade, which made the swirled carvings glow white against the blue metal.

It looked very sharp.

And absolutely terrifying.

"I think the fancy term is 'desensitization,'" Ro told her. "But that takes all the emotion out of what you're learning— and emotion *should* play a role in something this serious. So I prefer to think of it as *bonding*."

TWENTY-TWO

YOU WANT ME TO BOND WITH A *dagger*," Sophie clarified.

"Yep!" Ro told her, flashing another pointed-tooth grin. "I want it to be your new BFF. So you're going to start by naming it."

Sophie gave her biggest eye roll yet. "I'm not naming a dagger."

"Why not? I name all of mine. You're holding Lutguardia. And this"—she unsheathed another dagger—"is Alewar. And these"—she patted the four daggers strapped to the front of her left thigh—"are Durward, Elek, Hekie, and Gerrt. And these"—she pointed to her right thigh—"are Rodge and—"

"Okay, I believe you," Sophie interrupted. "I don't need to know all their names."

"You're missing out. They're awesome. But let's see if you can do better."

"I'm *not* naming a dagger," Sophie repeated.

"Oh, but you are. If you don't pick something, I'll choose for you—and imagine how it'll go over when I tell everyone your dagger's name is Captain Hunkyhair."

"Uh, you'll be gone, remember?"

"I'll make sure I tell everyone before I go. So you'd better pick quick. Otherwise we're going with Captain Hunkyhair in three . . . two . . ."

"Ugh, I don't know," Sophie mumbled, searching her brain for any sort of name that made sense for a weapon.

She'd read enough fantasy during her human years that things like Excalibur, Sting, and Mjollnir popped up as options—but she was never going to bond with a name like that.

Then again, she doubted she'd bond with a dagger called Luke or Kelly or Eddie, either—because it was a dagger!

"Ticktock, Blondie. I'm serious. Your time should already be up, but I'll give you five more seconds."

"Uh . . ." Sophie tried to think of movies, video games, TV shows, books—anything with a character she'd liked, preferably who carried a weapon.

Percy? Leia? Legolas? Wolverine?

They all felt too silly and weird.

Maybe she needed to come at it a different way.

What did she *want* from the dagger?

"Twoooooooooo," Ro said. "Onnnnnnnnnnnnnne. Okay, I guess that means it's officially—"

"Gah—how about Hope?" Sophie blurted out.

"Hope?" Ro repeated, and her eyebrows shot up so far, they looked ready to lift off her head.

Sophie's cheeks warmed. "You're the one who made me pick a name!"

"I did. And you went with . . . Hope."

It was better than having to call it Captain Hunkyhair.

And she could always rename it if she thought of something better—or not, because it was a dagger and this whole thing was totally ridiculous.

"I'm not judging you," Ro promised when Sophie opened her mouth to tell her that. "I think it's actually kinda deep. A dagger called Hope. Leave it to an elf."

Sophie crossed her arms. "It was the only thing I could think of."

"I'm glad you did. And I think you and Hope will be very happy together—which is good, because you're going to be spending a lot of time with each other. You need to carry Hope with you everywhere—and I mean *everywhere*. The bathroom. The shower. When you go to bed. When you get up. And at least once a day, I want you to practice doing this."

She grabbed Sophie's wrist and guided her arm through a stabbing motion. Then another. And another.

Stab.

Stab.

Stab.

"Not bad," Ro told her. "But I can definitely feel resistance. Which is why I'm having you do this. Bonding with Hope will only get you so far." She guided Sophie's arm through several more stabs. "Pretend you're shredding those maps you wasted time going through this morning. Or the boring books you know the Forklenator is going to make you read. Or if you need a little post-breakup therapy, you could always imagine you're going to town on any gifts from Captain Perfectpants. I'm assuming he gave you some."

"A few," Sophie admitted.

She hadn't really let herself think about the Cognate rings engraved with her and Fitz's initials. Or the teal heart necklace. Or even the boring riddler pen he'd given her for her first midterms gift.

She didn't want to be bothered by any of them.

But then she remembered the look on Fitz's face when he'd stood there in her circle of friends, lecturing her about the storehouse fire and Glimmer, and . . . she couldn't help imagining the blade slicing through each trinket.

Stab.

Stab.

Stab.

"Better," Ro said. "Your muscles are finally starting to relax. But you'll need to do this every day for it to become instinctive—and *that's* the goal. Once this motion feels like second nature, and you're used to having Hope with you everywhere, your elf-y brain will be able to bypass any doubts and worries if you go to use the dagger as a weapon. And if the blade hits home, it'll feel like you're just doing this."

Stab.

Stab.

Stab.

Sophie closed her eyes, trying to keep her head clear—but she could still imagine how different it would feel to hit a real target.

And that was good—she didn't want to take any of this lightly.

This wasn't a game.

Sandor made that clear when she'd trained with him.

But she also had to make sure she was prepared—and clearly she wasn't there yet.

"You know what to aim for, right?" Ro asked, almost like she knew what Sophie was thinking. "Gigantor went over that with you?"

Sophie nodded.

Her mouth was too dry for her to answer.

"Good. I know some ways to make aiming second nature

too," Ro told her. "But we'll get to that once I'm back. This will keep you busy enough until then. Is your arm sore yet?"

Sophie nodded again, surprised that such a small motion could make her muscles burn that fast.

"Awesome. That's how you know when to stop. You'll be able to go a little longer each time, and pretty soon, you'll be like, *Psh, I could do this all day.*"

Sophie highly doubted that.

She let her arm drop to her side, and the dagger slipped from her tired grasp, stabbing into the floor with a soft *thud*—right through the heart of one of the flowers.

She stared at the floral carnage.

"Clearly we need to find you something to use as a holster," Ro said, retrieving the dagger as she stood and marched toward Sophie's closet.

"There's nothing in there," Sophie called after her.

"Sure there is!" Ro disappeared—and there was a whole lot of rustling. She returned several minutes later holding a long silk sash covered in tiny topaz flowers like it was a giant snake. "Victory!"

"Uh, the dagger can slice right through that," Sophie warned.

"Yes, *Hope* can. Don't think I haven't noticed that you're not using the lovely name you chose. Quit that—the name's vital to this process! And you'll need to ask someone to help you make a permanent holster. I just want you to get the feel for Hope's new home right now." She twisted the fabric a few different ways, forming a knot in the center of two wide loops. "Ta-da! Sparkly shoulder holster! Get over here, let's try it on."

Sophie did as she was told, and Ro slid the loops up her arms and positioned the knot right between her shoulder blades.

"You don't think a hip holster would be better?" she asked, showing Ro how far she had to arch her back in order to reach the dagger.

"You'll get used to it," Ro assured her. "And you can make the permanent holster hang lower—but not too low. It's important to keep Hope on the same level as your heart."

"Why?"

"Because you're bonding!"

Sophie groaned.

"Fine. If you want a more practical reason, think of it this way: Your cape will keep Hope hidden, so you won't have to feel like everyone's staring at you, or judging you, or afraid of you for carrying a weapon—and the Neverseen won't know you're ready for them."

"I guess," Sophie mumbled, flinching as Ro slipped the dagger into place.

Even through the fabric of her tunic, she could feel the chill of the metal seeping into her skin.

"You've got this, Blondie. You just have to believe. In fact, I'll let you in on a little secret." Ro leaned closer, whispering in Sophie's ear. "I freaked out the first time it hit me that I'd be ending lives."

"Really?" Sophie asked. "I thought you were basically born with a blade in your hand."

"I was. But training is very technical. It's all about how to hold each of the different weapons, and where to put your feet during a fight, and proper form, and moves and countermoves. So the reality of what I was learning didn't really sink in for a while. And then one day I realized that someone was going to stop living because of *me*, and I remember staring at my sword, hoping my dad wouldn't notice that my hand was shaking. But of course he did—because he notices everything—and he put his hand on my shoulder, and I thought I was in trouble. But instead, he told me to remember one thing. They're words I still have on repeat in my brain every time I'm fighting." She leaned in again to whisper, *"It's them or me."*

The words sank into the pit of Sophie's stomach like big sour lumps.

"Say that to yourself every chance you get," Ro told her. "Because in a battle, it's the only thing that's true. If you don't take them down, they *will* take you down. You believe that, don't you?"

Sophie's mind flashed through all the wounds she'd had Elwin treat—all the times she'd almost died and somehow pulled through.

It's them or me.

She nodded.

"Then say it," Ro told her.

Sophie cleared her throat. "It's them or me."

"Eh, your voice is a little squeaky—but keep at it and you'll get there. And don't you dare shove Hope in a drawer the second I leave because all of this feels super ridiculous to you. Give it a chance, okay?"

Sophie sighed. "I'll try."

"You better. When I get back, I expect to see some serious progress!" Ro scanned the room again. "All right, I guess my work here is done—for now. Eat lots of pastries while I'm gone—and try not to have too much fun without me. Oh, and before I forget . . ." She reached into her corset and pulled out a thin gold packet. "If Hunkyhair shows up before I'm back, spread some of this on your skin immediately."

Sophie backed up a step. "What does it do?"

"Nothing to be afraid of. And look, it's shiny! You love shiny!" She shook the packet, making the gilded paper glint.

"Yeah, I think I'll pass."

"Wow, an elf who can resist sparkles. You really *are* one of a kind! But you can relax. This is basically a biological version of that little talky square thing you love so much. Every colony of Linquillosa shares a single consciousness—whether they're near each other or not. So the microbes in this packet"—she shook it again—"are connected to the ones living here." She traced a line on her thigh, right below her daggers. "The second you rub some on your skin, the Linquillosa I'm carrying will have the same reaction—"

"What kind of reaction?" Sophie asked, imagining hives or scabs or pus or . . .

"Kind of a tickly feeling? And your skin will turn a bluish-purple color—but it's not a bruise. It's just the Linquillosa being like, *Whoa, it's bright here!* And mine will turn blue too, like *We're used to it, but we feel you!* And I'll know it's time to get my butt back to Sparkle Town."

Sophie scratched her arms, already feeling itchy. "How about I just give you an Imparter instead?"

Ro shook her head. "I love how you elves think your technology is better than everybody else's."

"Well, I mean, it doesn't require rubbing bacteria on my skin, so . . ."

"Harmless bacteria," Ro insisted. "Which can't be dropped or broken or lost like your little talky square thing. *And* the Linquillosa give their message silently, so if you happen to reach out when I'm within earshot of Cadfael, I won't have to worry about you giving me away."

Sophie had to admit that the Linquillosa had a few advantages.

She reluctantly took the golden packet—but she *really* hoped Ro came back quickly so she wouldn't have to use it. "How do I clean it off?"

"With this." Ro pulled a green packet out of her corset—but held it out of Sophie's reach. "Nope! No erasing the message until I'm back."

"But that could be weeks! If you're still hunting Cadfael—"

"I won't be. Like I said, I should be able to catch him in the next few days. And odds are, Hunkyhair won't come to his senses before then—but if he *does*, catching Cadfael can wait! No way am I missing the big Team Foster-Keefe reunion—or all the . . ."

She made a very loud smooching sound, and Sophie tried to decide if she should crawl under her bed or reach for her dagger.

"Scowl at me all you want, Blondie—I see that adorable blush!"

Sophie pulled her hair around her face. "That just means I'm sick of this conversation."

"Does it, though?" Ro asked. "Pretty sure there's a whole lot more to it than that."

"Yeah, I'm trying to decide if I should use you for stabbing practice," Sophie muttered.

"I'd actually love to see you try that—but no changing the subject. I can hear your heart beating about a hundred times faster than normal right now. And your breath is all hitched. And your voice is all high pitched and squeaky. So clearly you're feeling excited and fluttery and—"

"I don't know what I'm feeling!" Sophie shouted.

It might've been the truest thing she'd ever said.

She crossed her arms and focused on her feet, not sure she could handle the way Ro was staring at her.

She was still trying to process everything that had happened between her and Fitz. And now Keefe was gone—and all he'd left was a hasty letter saying something that might not even mean what Ro thought it meant and . . .

"Hmmmm," Ro said, dragging out the sound. "Looks like we've gone from the Great Foster Oblivion to the Great Foster Confusion. Guess I should've expected that. The good news is, it's easy to fix. You just need to—"

"I don't *need* to do anything!" Sophie spun back around to face her. "Except figure out how to stop the Neverseen. *That's* what matters. Everything else is just . . ."

"Just what?" Ro asked.

A zillion words zipped through Sophie's mind, but none of them fit.

"It's all right," Ro told her. "You don't need to have it all figured out. Hunkyhair's not even here right now. But . . . he will be someday. You know that, right? I realize his letter was super melodramatic—but he *will* be back. He won't be able to stay away."

"I'm sure his mom will trick him into coming home eventually," Sophie mumbled.

"Probably," Ro agreed. "But that's not what I meant, and you know it."

"I don't know anything."

Another very true, very real confession.

"Okay. I get it. And I'm definitely not trying to pressure you.

You're a smart girl—you'll get there when you're ready. *But*. You do also have a history of being . . . a little quick to deny certain stuff. So even though Hunkyhair would probably clobber me for telling you this, I feel like I should make sure you know one thing, okay?" She waited for Sophie to hold her gaze before she told her, "He meant what he said in his letter—and he meant it exactly the way you thought he did before you tried to talk yourself out of it."

Sophie wasn't sure why she sucked in a breath.

She just needed more air.

In fact, she really needed to sit—but somehow sitting felt like it was admitting something and . . .

"Easy there, Blondie," Ro said, guiding Sophie back to the edge of the bed. "I know it's a lot to process."

It really was.

She sank onto her mattress, wishing she could ask why Ro sounded so certain.

Or why Keefe never said anything before.

But . . . she wasn't sure what she'd do with any of that information. Especially while Keefe was far away—and currently ignoring her when she tried to transmit to him, and . . .

Ro laughed. "Elf-y drama is so adorable."

"Is this all just a game to you?" Sophie snapped.

"Absolutely not. I told you, I'm Team Foster-Keefe through and through. You two would be perfect together."

"Oh please."

"No, I mean it. You balance each other. He helps you lighten up, and you help him focus. He boosts your confidence, and you keep his ego in check. You both dive headfirst into danger, but somehow you're able to help each other play it a little smarter. *And* you both act more like yourselves when you're together. I could keep going, but I don't want it to seem like I'm trying to pressure you. This one's your call. The only thing is . . . you *are* going to need to start figuring out what you feel, okay? And when you do? If you're not on the same page? You have to let him know."

Sophie wrapped her arms around her stomach.

It felt like she had a bunch of creatures stuck in there, fluttering and squirming and twisting and trembling.

Or maybe the shaking was her.

"He's held on to these, like, teeny, tiny threads of hope for so long that he'll never let go on his own," Ro said quietly. "You have to tell him—and I know it'll be scary and hard, but you have to. You won't even lose him as a friend, if that's what you're worried about. He's willing to follow your lead. If you just want a buddy, he'll be the best friend he can be. But if you want more, well . . . I'll let you be the one to imagine what that would be like. I'm going to go, before I start making up a ballad about Blondie and Hunkyhair. But it sure would be epic."

Would it?

Or would it be an even bigger disaster than she and Fitz turned out to be?

She was still unmatchable—and that wasn't going to change.

Though . . . when she'd told Keefe about that, he hadn't seemed to care.

But he might, once it actually affected him.

"Ha, I can practically hear your brain spinning," Ro said, clapping Sophie on the shoulder. "And I get it. But . . . maybe try listening to your *heart* before you decide, okay? It's still racing and racing—which seems like it's trying to tell you something. And on that bombshell, I'm officially out!"

She gave a dramatic bow and turned toward the door.

"Wait," Sophie called, trying to focus on something easier than the noise in her head. "Don't you need me to teleport you closer to Ravagog?"

"Nah. I don't need your elf-y tricks to get to *my* world. It'll be nice to be home." She waved over her shoulder as she headed for the stairs.

Before she slipped out of sight, she called out one more thing.

"Go Team Foster-Keefe!"

TWENTY-THREE

SOPHIE WASN'T SURE HOW LONG SHE
sat there staring blankly at her empty doorway.

Could've been minutes.

Could've been hours.

It didn't matter.

No amount of time was going to quiet the chaos in her
head.

All it did was raise a whole lot of terrifying questions.
Because even if Ro was right about Keefe's feelings—and
Sophie decided she wanted to see what would happen—this
was so much bigger than just the two of them.

Like . . .

What would Grady and Edaline think?

Sophie still didn't know if she was actually allowed to date—much less date That Boy.

And even if she was, there would surely be all kinds of annoying new rules and restrictions to deal with. Plus, Edaline would probably follow them around with a sappy, embarrassing smile, and Grady would make them sit through a series of horrifying Dad Talks.

And what would her friends say when they found out?

There'd been a time when Sophie had wondered if Biana had a crush on Keefe—and even though it seemed like Biana had gotten over it . . . what if she hadn't?

Better question: *How would Fitz react?*

Keefe was Fitz's best friend—and Fitz's temper could be . . . challenging.

The possibilities for drama were endless.

Sophie's insides twisted into knots on top of knots as she imagined the awkward conversations.

And the stares.

And the gossip.

There would be So. Much. Gossip.

She wanted to hide just thinking about it—and Keefe would probably *love* the attention.

Did that prove they weren't compatible?

Or was she just looking for an excuse because she was scared?

And *why* was she so scared?

Keefe would honestly be . . .

. . .

. . .

. . . a really awesome boyfriend.

He was thoughtful. And supportive. And he could be incredibly sweet—when he was actually being serious instead of joking around with everybody.

Though . . . maybe some of his jokes with her hadn't *just* been teasing.

Had some of it also been . . . *flirting?*

If Ro were still there, she probably would've been nodding and shouting about the Great Foster Oblivion.

And maybe she was right.

Maybe Sophie had been too insecure to let herself see what was right in front of her.

Or too distracted by her crush on Fitz.

The last thought made her inner knots twist so much tighter.

She'd liked Fitz for so long that she'd never even *thought* about liking someone else—and she was still trying to get over all of that.

But . . .

Did she want to risk missing out on something that might be . . . really great?

Keefe's face filled her mind, flashing his trademark smirk.

"OKAY—ENOUGH!" Sophie said the words out loud, hoping it would snap her brain out of it.

She needed to stop thinking about this, or she was never going to be able to sleep, or eat, or think coherently again—and she certainly wasn't going to be able to come up with a new plan for how to find Elysian, or how to stop the Neverseen, or how to solve any of the very serious, very important, very real problems they were facing.

She couldn't afford to lose focus because of a cute boy.

Even if he was really, really, *really* cute.

Keefe might not be as classically handsome as Fitz—but he didn't need to be. In fact, there was something extra appealing about his crooked smile and artfully messy hair.

It made him less serious.

Less perfect.

Less intimidating.

Plus, he was smart.

And funny.

And kind.

And a good listener.

And . . .

. . . a superpowerful Empath who could read her emotions through the air without even trying.

Which meant the next time she saw him, he'd be able to feel everything she was feeling.

Maybe he could help her make sense of it.

Or maybe he'd run away screaming.

Or maybe she'd die of embarrassment.

Or maybe he'd take her hand, and she'd stare into his ice blue eyes as he stepped even closer and . . .

"STOP!" she said, realizing she was forgetting the most basic, fundamental reason this entire thought process was a giant waste of time.

Keefe was gone.

He ran away—and he needed to stay away until he knew more about his new abilities and Sophie figured out how to capture his mom and make sure Lady Gisela could never hurt Keefe or anyone else ever again.

That's what she needed to be thinking about—not replaying all her memories, trying to figure out if Ro was right about Keefe liking her.

She was the moonlark.

Keefe had a legacy connected to stellarlune.

They both had more than enough to deal with on their own.

But . . . didn't that mean they also understood each other better than anyone?

Her mind flashed to their window slumber parties in Alluveterre, when she was trying to keep Keefe from falling apart after all the hard truths he'd learned about his mother.

Then to Keefe's hilarious visits to the Healing Center after the Neverseen shattered her hand and left her haunted by echoes.

Keefe could send gentle breezes into her mind to keep her calm and steady.

And his thoughts had clung to hers while he was fighting to stay alive in Loamnore.

Didn't all of that prove they had a connection?

"SERIOUSLY, STOP!" she told herself again.

Hadn't she already learned her lesson with Fitz?

Adding those kinds of feelings to a friendship pretty much ruined everything.

It didn't matter that Ro believed it wouldn't.

That didn't make it true.

In fact, it could just as easily be that Ro was wrong about *everything* and Sophie was now stressing about all this for no reason.

But . . . if that was the case, why would Keefe have added that line to his letter?

Better question: Why was she so busy worrying about how *Keefe* felt?

He'd already made that pretty clear.

Yes, her insecure brain wanted to deny it—but the words were there, in ink on a page.

The only thing she needed to figure out was how *she* was feeling.

Her mind raced through more memories, seeing them through a very different lens.

Like the night she flew with Keefe and Silveny to have the Black Swan heal her abilities. She and Keefe were still fairly new friends at that point—but when he'd wrapped his arms around her, she'd felt . . . safer.

Maybe even a tiny bit fluttery.

If she hadn't been so distracted by other things, would that feeling have grown?

And couldn't it still grow now?

Because if she was really, *really* honest—and really, *really* brave—she had to admit that the idea of being with Keefe sounded . . . kind of amazing.

Yes, it was scary.

And yes, there were risks.

But . . . wouldn't it be worth trying?

"OKAY," she said, talking to herself out loud again. "We're officially done thinking about this."

She had to stop—because Keefe was still gone and the Lost Cities were still in danger, and until either of those things changed, there was no point obsessing about this stuff.

She jumped to her feet when her brain still tried to circle back anyway.

Maybe if she moved—changed scenery, did something productive—it would help.

She stumbled over to the stairs, taking deep, calming breaths.

This is good, she told herself. *I'm fine. Everything is fine.*

It would've been easier to believe if her legs weren't so shaky, and her palms weren't so sweaty, and her heart wasn't *thump, thump, thump*ing so loud that Ro could probably hear it all the way in Ravagog.

But she made it downstairs without stumbling and even seemed to be picking up some momentum.

See? she told herself. *This is what you need.*

No thinking.

Just moving.

One foot in front of the other.

Again and again and again.

She stepped outside, and the blast of fresh air and sunshine cleared her head even more—but what she really needed was a good, solid distraction.

She headed into the pastures, searching for Grady and Edaline—and finally spotted them with Sandor and Mr. Forkle, way at the edge of the property, near the gorgodon's enclosure.

Perfect!

Feeding the Neverseen's mutant beast was always an adventure. Maybe she could help.

Or she could brush Verdi's teeth.

Or give the verminion a bath.

At this point, she'd even happily take a bunch of Mr. Forkle's pointless busywork.

Bring on all the boring books!

Okay, remember, everything is normal, she told herself as she made her way over to the gorgodon's enclosure. *There's absolutely nothing out of the ordinary going on.*

She twisted her features into what felt like a perfectly regular smile—but something must've been off, because Grady took one look at her and asked, "What happened?"

"Nothing!" The voice squeak gave away her lie, so she cleared her throat and tried again. "It just . . . feels weird without Ro here."

"I bet." Edaline draped an arm around Sophie's shoulders. "I'm sure she'll be back. I just wish I'd known she was leaving. I would've packed up some sweetberry swirls for her to snack on in the tunnels."

"Tunnels?" Sophie asked.

"Ro left the same way you've seen her father appear before," Mr. Forkle explained. "The ogres have their own network of shallow underground paths to speed their travel."

"And now she's added an access point *here*," Sandor grumbled, glaring at a spot several feet away, where the earth looked recently churned. "I'll have to reorganize the patrols again to make sure it's properly guarded."

"Probably wise—though it looks like you have things well under control," Mr. Forkle told him. "Your new adjustments to the security are quite impressive."

"They are," Sandor agreed, standing a bit taller. "Which is why Sophie should remain within Havenfield's borders. Returning to Foxfire would be far too dangerous."

"Wait—what?" Sophie asked, spinning toward Mr. Forkle, all thoughts of boy drama evaporating. "Please tell me you're not expecting me to go back to school right now."

"It's not entirely up to me," Mr. Forkle said. "But, for the record, I agree with the Council's decision to resume sessions at Foxfire. It's imperative for our world to return to some form of normalcy."

"But things *aren't* normal," Sophie argued, glancing at Grady and Edaline, surprised they looked like they were on board with the whole back-to-school plan. "The Neverseen are still out there! We don't have time to—"

"Learn?" Mr. Forkle finished for her. "That sets a rather dangerous precedent, don't you think? After all, what more fundamental need could anyone have than to receive a proper education? The Neverseen have already disrupted your studies—and the studies of every current Foxfire prodigy— for far too long. Allowing that to continue only hands them another victory they didn't earn."

"I know you don't want to hear this, kiddo," Grady jumped in as Edaline tightened her hold on Sophie's shoulders. "But he's right. The more we let the Neverseen affect our lives, the more we send the message that they're the ones with the power."

"We need to reassure people that life in the Lost Cities has not been changed by these conflicts," Mr. Forkle added. "They need proof that our world is strong, and stable, and that the things they value aren't going to disappear."

Sophie pulled away from all of them. "So . . . you want to lie."

"It's more about giving people hope," Edaline said quietly. "Which they need now, more than ever."

"And since Foxfire is one of our proudest institutions," Mr. Forkle said, "we're starting there."

"What about Exillium?" Sophie countered. "How come it's okay to keep that school closed?"

"Actually, Exillium never shut down," Mr. Forkle corrected. "The Coaches opted to continue their lessons despite the recent turmoil, believing the program provided a form of stability. And I believe their choice was far wiser than ours. Shuttering Foxfire has been incredibly disheartening for everyone. It's also denied our prodigies the opportunity to gain necessary knowledge and experience—and to form friendships and socialize. So we will deprive you no longer. Scrolls will be going out tomorrow morning announcing that Foxfire will resume sessions next week—with two extra hours added to each day to help make up for the learning time that's been lost."

"*Two extra hours?*" Sophie repeated, unable to keep the whiny tone out of her voice.

"Yes," Mr. Forkle said firmly. "Morning orientation will begin one hour earlier, and the day will close one hour later, adding an extra hour to both the morning and afternoon sessions. That way your Mentors will have the time they need to make up for all the missed lectures. The current plan is to return to the normal schedule once all the lost hours have been made up—but it's possible everyone will prefer the extended sessions."

"Somehow I doubt that," Sophie muttered.

"You'd be surprised," Mr. Forkle insisted. "I think you've forgotten that attending Foxfire is an incredible honor. In fact, it wasn't that long ago that your biggest worry was not being allowed to continue your sessions there."

"Yeah, well, that was before I realized I had people trying to kill me—and everyone I care about—and take over the world," Sophie reminded him.

"All the more reason a return to Foxfire will be helpful," Mr. Forkle said. "It'll provide a much-needed break from those worries."

"A break." Sophie tried not to laugh. "The Neverseen aren't going to be taking any breaks—"

"Probably not," Mr. Forkle agreed. "But you're not the only one working to stop them."

Sometimes it felt like she was.

She almost said that—but she had a feeling it wouldn't go over very well.

Instead, she took a slow breath and tried to keep her voice even as she said, "We all know the stakes are too high right now for me to spend hours every day learning about old treaties, or how to bottle clouds, or competing in splotching matches, or—"

"I wouldn't underestimate the value of those lessons,

Miss Foster," Mr. Forkle cut in. "The knowledge you're receiving is vital."

"For *what*? It's not going to help me find Elysian. Or Lady Gisela. It's not even going to help keep the peace between all the intelligent species like you keep telling me to focus on."

"You don't know that," Mr. Forkle argued.

"You might even find that allowing yourself to focus on something a little less overwhelming frees up your mind to solve the other problems with your subconscious," Grady suggested.

Sophie had to fight hard to not roll her eyes. "Right, I'm going to find the answers to everything while tuning out a boring lecture."

Grady shrugged. "Stranger things have happened."

"But even if that *doesn't* occur," Mr. Forkle added quickly, "I think you're forgetting that you have a very long life ahead of you, beyond all of this—"

"Maybe not," Sophie muttered. "If the Neverseen win—"

"They *won't!*" Mr. Forkle's tone somehow sounded both calm and ominous. "Take it from someone who was fighting these battles long before you existed—long before there was even a plan for your creation. I realize these challenges feel all-consuming at the moment—"

"Because they *are!*" Sophie snapped. "If they weren't, I doubt the Black Swan would've gone through with Project Moonlark. But you did. And I'm here. So put me to use! Don't send me off to school to waste time—"

"A good education will never be a waste," Edaline said gently.

Mr. Forkle sighed when Sophie scowled. "I realize this isn't what you want to hear, Miss Foster. But if you can't manage to muster any excitement, perhaps you can at least take comfort in knowing you're not the first child to wish they didn't have to go to school—nor will you be the last."

Sophie gritted her teeth. "I'm not a child. And I'm not pouting because I want to stay home and play video games or something. I'm trying to save the world—which is the job *you* gave me, by the way."

"I gave you many jobs," he told her. "One of which is to lead."

"Exactly, so let me lead—"

"I'm trying to. But you seem to have forgotten that the best way to lead is by example. If you want to save our world—and I mean *truly* save everything the Lost Cities stands for—you'll show everyone that you aren't going to let the Neverseen stop you from having a normal, happy life. Show them you're planning for a future beyond all of this. Show them it's safe—"

"But it isn't! Or have you forgotten why Sandor's been extra obsessed with changing all the security around here? I burned down the Neverseen's storehouse—and ever since I did, everyone's gone on and on about how the Neverseen are going to retaliate against me."

"And you've insisted on continuing to take risks," Mr. Forkle reminded her.

"Yeah, but refusing to sit around at Havenfield all day is different than parading around a *crowded* school that just reopened because the Council wants to pretend that everything is normal. If you want to reopen Foxfire, go right ahead. But I shouldn't be anywhere near there. It just turns the school into a perfect target."

Sandor nodded, like he agreed.

Even Grady and Edaline looked a little unsure.

But Mr. Forkle dragged a hand down his face. "You don't need to concern yourself with that anymore, Miss Foster."

"Why not?" Sophie asked.

"Because there was another reason you couldn't reach me last night," he said quietly. "The Neverseen have already retaliated—and they chose their target very strategically. They destroyed Brumevale."

TWENTY-FOUR

WHAT'S BRUMEVALE?" GRADY asked, beating Sophie to the question.

But then her memory connected the name.

"It's one of the Black Swan's hideouts," she mumbled. "Way up in the sky."

She'd had to climb an endless floating staircase in order to get there—then stepped through a shroud of mist onto some sort of cloud-covered ridge high over the ocean, where a lonely white lighthouse stood silhouetted against the endless blue horizon.

That was the day she'd found out that Mr. Forkle had a secret twin brother, and that the two of them had been sharing one life—the day he'd walked into Brumevale's sitting room after dying in her arms and she'd had to wrap her mind around the fact that Mr. Forkle was somehow both dead and still alive all at the same time.

"Brumevale's not a hideout," Mr. Forkle corrected. "It's a place for reflection. Though . . . I suppose I should say it *was* a place for reflection."

Was.

The ground seemed to tremble with the word.

Edaline reached for Sophie's hand. "What happened?"

"Honestly, I'm not certain," Mr. Forkle admitted. "No one should've been able to set foot in Brumevale without our permission. I remember thinking that installing any sort of security there was a complete waste of time—but Tinker *insisted* we add sensors to all our properties after we put Project Moonlark into action. Clearly she's wiser than I am. We would've had no idea that anything was amiss if Wraith hadn't gotten the alert—though, sadly, by the time he made it to Brumevale, the Neverseen were gone."

"You're sure it was them?" Grady asked.

Mr. Forkle nodded, and his gaze shifted to Sophie. "They took a cue from our moonlark and left their symbol in the ruins."

The ground trembled a little harder.

Ruins.

Signed with a symbol.

Following her cue.

"Was anyone hurt?" Edaline asked, tightening her grip on Sophie's hand.

"Thankfully, no. Brumevale has been empty since my last visit." Mr. Forkle frowned. "It's strange to think that it truly was my *last* visit. I knew I wouldn't be returning for a while, but . . . I never expected this."

He turned away, and his eyes looked slightly glassy.

The trembling amped up again, and when Edaline pulled Sophie close enough for Sophie to lean against her, Sophie realized that *she* was the one shaking.

She sucked in a breath and forced herself to focus on the gorgodon, watching it groom its massive wings. There was something soothing about the way it cleaned each feather before smoothing it back into place.

Such a calm, normal act from such a fearsome beast.

"Was it a fire?" Grady asked.

"Surprisingly, no," Mr. Forkle told him. "You'd think the Neverseen would've gone that route. But perhaps they're tired of flames, now that Brant and Fintan are no longer with them. Whatever their reason, they chose to cause an explosion unlike anything I've ever seen. Parts of the tower completely disintegrated. The rest twisted into a whole other form, as if it absorbed the force of the blast and took on the shape of the energy. I don't understand how they accomplished it—but Tinker's working to figure it out. Whatever weapon they used—"

"Weapon?" Grady interrupted.

Mr. Forkle nodded. "No natural force could've caused this kind of destruction. *Nothing* could be salvaged."

"Nothing," Sophie whispered, choking on the word.

Tiergan had told her that Brumevale was *ancient*—standing proudly above the clouds for millennia.

And now there was *nothing* left.

Because of her.

"No one was hurt," Edaline reminded her, wrapping her other arm around Sophie to hold her even tighter. "That's what's important."

"Exactly," Mr. Forkle agreed. "Towers can be rebuilt."

They could.

But Sophie remembered something she'd learned during her brief visit to Brumevale. "What about the moonlarks?"

A pair of moonlarks had built their nest on Brumevale's roof. Mr. Forkle had lowered the windows to let her hear the songs they were singing to their fledglings, offering encouragement and guidance from afar.

"Well," Mr. Forkle said quietly. "I can't say for certain. But we found no traces of any bodies. Not even any fallen feathers. So I'm assuming the moonlarks flew away before the explosion."

Sophie closed her eyes and tried to believe him.

But a tiny doubt wriggled deep into her heart.

A weight she was sure she'd always carry.

And she *deserved* to carry it.

"This was not your fault, Miss Foster," Mr. Forkle said, waiting for her to make eye contact. "I've always known we'd face these kinds of tactics someday. The harder we fight, the harder the Neverseen will strike back. It's going to be nothing but moves and countermoves until we finally reach a conclusion. Perhaps you motivated them to retaliate—but if so, that works to our advantage. The more we force our enemies to change their plans, the more mistakes they'll make. And honestly, choosing Brumevale as a target shows their haste."

"But you said they chose it strategically," Sophie reminded him.

"They did. But they were clearly so focused on striking back quickly that they didn't consider that destroying Brumevale affects us very little. It was mostly a place we went to for a respite—or to think." He turned away, watching the sunlight glint across the ocean. "It was also one of the few places my brother and I felt safe enough to be together for any sort of extended period of time. But those days are gone anyway."

Sophie felt her knees wobble again as her mind filled with images of red-stained rubble, and the other Mr. Forkle's weak plea for Oralie to take care of his moonlark before his voice fell silent forever.

Somehow losing Brumevale felt almost as huge as that loss, even though it was only an empty tower.

Maybe she just hated that the Neverseen had gotten to take something else away.

Or maybe it was because Brumevale had been so quiet and peaceful.

It was a place that didn't belong in any sort of battle—though it might not have always been that way.

"Tiergan told us that Brumevale had a 'complicated history,'" she said quietly.

Mr. Forkle nodded. "I've heard that as well. Supposedly it was once the scene of some sort of tragedy, but I don't know the specifics. No one does. The story's been lost over the centuries."

Sophie frowned. "Tiergan made it sound like he knew."

"Did he?" Mr. Forkle asked. "Or did he simply dodge your questions? Tiergan's particularly adept at misdirection."

"He . . ." Sophie's voice trailed off as her mind replayed the exact words Tiergan had used.

He'd said the person affected should be the one to tell her about Brumevale's history—which was technically true whether he knew who they were and what happened to them, or not.

Either way, it didn't matter because she'd thought of a much more important question: "Do you think what happened in Brumevale's past is connected to the Neverseen?"

"I suppose anything is possible. But I doubt it. From what I understand, Brumevale was built by an Ancient couple that have since passed away. They never had any children, and no one claims any ties to their family line. That's why I was able to take over the property without any issue. Only a handful of people even know Brumevale exists—and even fewer know how to find it. I'm sure you remember how difficult it was to journey there. And there are no direct paths. The mist filters too much of the light, preventing anyone from leaping to the actual lighthouse. Everyone must take the stairs—which are hidden by the clouds. You have to know exactly where they are in order to reveal them."

"I wonder how the Neverseen were able to find it, then," Edaline said.

"We're trying to figure that out," Mr. Forkle told her.

"Any theories?" Sophie pressed.

"None I'm willing to share at the moment—and not because I'm trying to keep you in the dark. It's simply unwise to call out suspects without any evidence of their involvement."

"Does that mean you think it's someone we know?" Grady asked.

"Someone in the Black Swan?" Sophie added.

"It's hard to say," Mr. Forkle told them. "Though I don't believe anything was said or done maliciously, if that's what you're worried about. Secrets have a way of slipping through cracks, especially as our order grows larger and larger. I'll know more after I look into it further."

Somehow, that didn't feel very reassuring.

If the Black Swan had a leak—even an unintentional one— that could get *very* bad *very* quickly.

"So is that why the Neverseen chose Brumevale as a target?" Grady asked. "It was the only hideout they knew about?"

"Perhaps," Mr. Forkle said. "Though I suspect they also wanted to send a message—likely in response to the storehouse fire. Which, again, is not your fault, Miss Foster. In a way, we should be celebrating that you rattled them enough to make them hastily strike back on a fairly useless target."

"But what's their message?" Grady wondered.

"I think I know what it is," Sophie mumbled, wrapping her arms around her stomach. "You came up with the idea for Project Moonlark in Brumevale, right?" she asked Mr. Forkle. When he nodded, she added, "Then I bet they wanted to remind me that I'm just an experiment. And . . . experiments can fail."

Edaline held her tighter.

Mr. Forkle shook his head. "Actually, I believe the message was meant for all of us. They wanted us to know that there will be no more rest—and that nothing we care about is safe."

"Oh great, because *that's* better," Sophie muttered.

"It's not," Mr. Forkle admitted. "But it's simply a message, and messages can be ignored."

"We *can't* ignore the fact that they destroyed Brumevale," Sophie argued.

"We can and we will," Mr. Forkle insisted. "*We* do not make hasty, reactive decisions. We stay the course. Investigate. Strategize. And—"

"Waste a ton of time," Sophie cut in. "Which is why we're always too late."

"It's easy to think that," Mr. Forkle told her. "But that doesn't make it true."

"Then how do you explain why the Neverseen are always ahead of us?" Sophie demanded.

"Taking the lead only matters at the finish line, Miss Foster. And whenever we finally get there, you'll see how our caution and preparation give us a clear advantage."

Sophie wanted to believe him.

But it was hard to feel hopeful knowing the Neverseen were probably celebrating their big victory right now and the Black Swan was planning to do nothing.

"Is this why you waited so long to tell me about Brumevale?" she asked, pulling away from Edaline to stand on her own. "Because you knew I'd want to strike back?"

"No, Miss Foster. I held off mentioning it because you weren't ready to listen until now. You were too focused on the revelations that caused you to leave me that note—and I say that with no judgment. Not everything needs to be your concern."

"Um, if the Neverseen are retaliating because of something *I* did, I should definitely be concerned about that!" Sophie snapped.

"Why?" Mr. Forkle asked. "They've made their move. They won't strike again until we give them a reason."

"You don't know that," Sophie argued. "And if we don't strike back, they'll think we're weak."

"Let them. Remember: Every time the Neverseen speed up their timeline, it works to our advantage. They aren't ready to put their plans into action yet—and we're working to keep it that way. Why do you think I insisted that Ro return to Ravagog to warn her father? And why do you think I'm advising you not to pursue any sort of meeting with the Neverseen's Guster?"

"What does that have to do with anything?" Sophie asked.

"Meeting with the enemy is always risky. And now that things have grown increasingly volatile—"

"Glimmer thinks Trix isn't loyal to the Neverseen," Sophie interrupted.

"I'm sure she does. But that seems rather hard to believe when you consider that a Guster is most likely behind what happened in Brumevale," Mr. Forkle countered.

Sophie's knees turned wobbly again. "But . . . you said no natural force could cause it."

"Not the explosion—but I'm sure you remember that wind is necessary to reveal the staircase. And given how quickly the Neverseen were able to destroy the tower after setting off the sensors, it seems likely they also used their Guster to float their weapon into position."

Sophie's heart screeched to a stop.

She glanced at Edaline. "Unless they conjured the weapon . . ."

Mr. Forkle's eyebrows raised. "Sounds like there's something you haven't told me."

"There is." Sophie explained about Lord Cassius's memory, and how Lady Gisela slipped and revealed she's a Conjurer. "You have to admit that makes sense," she said when she finished.

Mr. Forkle turned toward the ocean again. "It's a definite possibility—though it seems strange that she would suddenly start using the ability after going to such lengths to hide it for all this time."

"Maybe she assumed we'd blame Trix," Sophie suggested. "Or maybe all her injuries from Loamnore weakened her too much and she needs to start using the ability. Or maybe her plans are close enough to coming together that she's ready to reveal it now."

"If that were the case, she'd reveal it in some sort of dramatic display," Mr. Forkle assured her.

"Fine—so it was one of the other reasons I gave," Sophie pressed. "Or something else we haven't thought of yet. It doesn't matter. What *does* matter is that we need to find Lady Gisela more than ever—and I don't hear anyone coming up with a whole lot of actual plans for how to do that. So if the Council agrees to let Glimmer reach out to Trix—"

"You should tell them you've reconsidered," Mr. Forkle told her. "And not risk falling into one of the Neverseen's traps."

"But *we'd* be setting the meeting," Sophie argued. "We'd control all the variables."

"You can never control *everything*," Sandor warned.

"And yet you think you're controlling everything here," Sophie reminded him, waving her arms toward Havenfield's pastures.

Sandor shook his head. "No, I'm controlling everything I possibly can, and relying on my training to cover the rest."

"So we'll rely on *our* training," Sophie countered.

Sandor heaved a squeaky sigh. "The little training you have will not be enough."

"He's right," Grady said quietly.

Sophie wanted to argue, but her less-than-stellar practice with Ro's dagger was a little too fresh in her mind. She could feel its weight between her shoulders—a constant reminder of all the work she had ahead.

But she wasn't ready to give up either.

Now that she'd hit a dead end on Elysian, Trix was pretty much their only chance of finding Lady Gisela and stopping whatever she was planning.

And then . . . Keefe could come home.

Sophie wished she could reach into her head and slap her brain for adding that last part—and maybe smack her heart, too, since it had changed rhythm.

The Neverseen destroyed Brumevale, she reminded herself. *That's what this is about.*

"We'll take every possible precaution," she assured Mr. Forkle. "The fact that we're waiting for the Council's approval should prove that."

"All the precautions in the world won't make it a wise course of action," Mr. Forkle told her. "Hopefully the Council will agree."

"Does the Council know what happened in Brumevale?" Grady asked.

"Wraith went to update them. But I haven't heard their response. I found a rather demanding note scrawled across my office door and headed straight here—as ordered." He sighed when Sophie didn't return his smile. "I know you're frustrated, Miss Foster—"

"Of course I am! The Neverseen are exploding towers, and all you want me to do is go back to school and pretend everything's normal!"

"No, I want you to return to Foxfire and show everyone that you refuse to be shaken—and that you won't allow them to interfere with your life any longer. Send the message that the moonlark isn't afraid."

When he put it that way, it didn't sound *as* bad.

But . . .

"What if the Neverseen see *that* as a move against them?" she asked. "And decide to retaliate again—at Foxfire this time?"

"I don't see that happening—but I would never trifle with the lives of my prodigies," he added quickly. "That's why I'm already working on adjustments to the security. Foxfire will be as safe as it can possibly be."

Which wasn't the same as it actually being *safe*.

But Sophie wasn't sure if anywhere was safe in the Lost Cities anymore.

Especially if the Neverseen had some sort of new weapon causing mysterious explosions that were so destructive, *nothing* was salvageable.

And if the Black Swan had someone sharing their secrets—accidentally or not—they were even more vulnerable than they realized.

"I should be helping you try to figure out what happened with Brumevale," Sophie told Mr. Forkle.

"How? Investigating the explosion is a job for a Technopath. Possibly also an alchemist. So if anything, I may have to reach out to Mr. Dizznee—but I doubt it'll come to that. Tinker is more than capable of handling it."

"What about the leak?" she pressed.

"I'd be careful using that term," Mr. Forkle warned. "That's a situation that requires subtlety and patience—both of which you seem to be running a bit low on at the moment. So why don't you stick to what you do best?"

"If you say research or homework—"

"No, I was going to say *inspiring*. How many of your friends have eagerly joined our cause because of you? And how many do you think might be struggling with the same fears and doubts right now? Show them they can take this chance to enjoy a small return to normal."

"What if you agree just to give it a try?" Edaline suggested when Sophie sighed. "If it feels like it's causing any problems, you can stop anytime." She reached for Sophie's hand as she added, "I think it'll be good for you. I feel like you might need a distraction."

Sophie's cheeks burned as Keefe's face filled her mind—and once again she wanted to strangle her brain.

Clearly she *did* need a distraction.

But she also needed to stay focused.

"Fine," she grumbled. "I'll *try* going back to Foxfire—but I'm not going to stop looking for Elysian. Or Lady Gisela. Or the rest of the Neverseen."

Mr. Forkle smiled. "I would expect nothing less."

TWENTY-FIVE

UGH—WHAT *IS* THAT?" SOPHIE ASKED, scraping her tongue against her teeth, trying to remove the horrible flavor coating her taste buds.

She'd foolishly assumed that the DNA sensor on her locker would taste *good*, since it was their first day back at Foxfire and Magnate Leto had given this big speech during orientation about how it was a day for celebration.

But he must've left Elwin in charge of the locker flavor, because it tasted like sour milk mixed with pickle brine.

"I don't know," Dex said as he tore through his locker's shelves. "But I thought I had some Prattles in here for gross-flavor days, and I can't find them."

"Want some of these?" Biana asked, holding out a brightly colored box of something called Fizzlers as she appeared next to Dex. She laughed when Sophie stumbled back so fast, she conked her head on the tail of the jeweled dragon statue in the middle of the Level Four atrium. "Are you seriously still startled by Vanishers?"

Sophie rubbed the back of her head. "Uh, you appear out of nowhere—so *yeah*. And just so you know, it's not a good idea to sneak up on me right now. Sandor's in mega-overprotective mode."

She pointed over her shoulder to where Sandor had his sword raised and a throwing star aimed right at Biana.

Lovise had drawn her sword as well.

"Where's *your* bodyguard?" Sandor demanded.

Biana shrugged. "I'm sure he's on his way. What? I can't help that I move through the halls way faster when I'm invisible."

Sandor and Lovise both sighed.

Biana didn't seem to notice as she handed the box of Fizzlers to Dex.

"You're officially my favorite person in the entire world!" he told her as he shoved a handful of the tiny, bubblelike candies into his mouth.

Biana tossed her long dark hair. "I get that a lot."

Dex's cheeks dimpled with his grin—and Sophie had to stop herself from reminding him how much he'd complained when she first became friends with Biana.

He'd come a long way from his days of despising the Vacker family.

Then again, Biana had come a long way as well.

She was still as gorgeous and stylish as ever, with sparkly eye shadow bringing out the shimmer in her teal eyes and the perfect amount of lip gloss on her heart-shaped lips. But she'd discovered a new kind of confidence over the years, which was somehow both a bit humbler *and* much more empowering. She'd even chosen to wear a short-sleeve shirt under her green Level Four vest, leaving most of her scars exposed.

"So why is Sandor in mega-overprotective mode?" Biana asked as Sophie tried one of the Fizzlers, which was squishy like a gummy bear and tasted like a chocolate-covered strawberry—with a crackly *pop-pop-pop* at the end. "Because of the fire thing? Or something else?"

"It's . . . a long story," Sophie told her, realizing it probably wouldn't be smart to talk about the explosion at Brumevale with so many prodigies within earshot. "But you might not want to ditch Woltzer for a while."

"Really?" Biana asked. "That bad?"

"Yeah," Sophie mumbled. "Things are getting super real, super fast."

Biana turned toward one of the hallways, where her bodyguard now stood leaning against the green glass wall. "Sounds like I need to hear this long story."

"I'll tell you later," Sophie promised. "In fact, we should

probably do a group catch-up at some point—if you want," she added, hoping she wasn't sounding too controlling. "Maybe during lunch, if we can find a quiet table?"

"That shouldn't be a problem." Biana lowered her voice before she added, "Did you notice the *huge* gap everyone left around me during orientation?"

Sophie hadn't.

She'd kept her head down during Magnate Leto's speech, in case he decided to single her out so she could *inspire* people.

She also hadn't sought out any of her friends, since things had been so tense the last time she saw them.

But now she felt terrible that Biana had been all alone.

Sophie wondered why Fitz hadn't been with his sister—but before she could ask, Biana said, "I guess everyone is still getting over the whole bloodthirsty-mutant-trolls-in-my-backyard thing."

She tossed her hair again, like it didn't bother her—but it had to be hard going from being the Lost Cities' version of teen royalty to having people go out of their way to avoid her.

Especially since it wasn't Biana's fault.

She hadn't known about the illegal troll hive at Everglen, or the creepy experiments the trolls were doing to create the ultimate soldiers. But the Neverseen had broadcast the whole brutal battle to everyone at the Celestial Festival—and watching huge, ravenous trolls devour everything in their path was the kind of thing people probably weren't going to forget.

Biana cleared her throat. "*Anyway*—what sessions are you both heading to?"

"Actually, I can't remember," Dex mumbled, glancing at Lovise like he thought she might know.

"I'm here to protect, not guide," Lovise reminded him.

Dex scowled. "Guess I should probably find my old schedule, then."

He went back to digging through his locker as Sophie told Biana, "I have elementalism."

"Ugh, I'm jealous," Biana grumbled. "I'm stuck with elvin history, and I'm pretty sure the extra hour is going to melt my brain. Whoever decided to extend our sessions should have to suffer through them with us."

"Right?" Sophie asked. "Mr. Fork—er, Magnate Leto—actually thinks we're going to *like* the longer sessions so much, we'll want to keep them."

Biana crinkled her nose. "Yeah, put me down for a 'no' on that."

"Me too!" Dex paused his locker search. "Did Forkle like the note you left for him?"

Sophie grinned. "'Like' isn't the right word—but it worked."

"What note?" Biana asked.

"Also a long story," Sophie told her.

Biana pouted. "I knew I should've snuck along with you. You totally kept the good project for yourself."

"Hey, you were the one who went on and on about what

might've been in the storehouse," Sophie reminded her. "I thought you'd be excited to go through the stuff we salvaged."

"Suuuuuuuuure." Biana looked away, fidgeting with the dragon-shaped clasp on her cape as she added, "Sorry, by the way. I know we kind of ambushed you about everything."

"You did," Sophie agreed.

But after what happened in Brumevale, she couldn't be quite as irritated about it.

She fidgeted with her own cape pin as she told Biana, "I know it's getting scary. But . . . we have to fight back as hard as we can."

Biana nodded. "I know. I promise I won't be so shocked the next time you take a stand."

The next time.

Sophie hated those words.

But there *would* be a next time.

And another.

And another.

Until she finally found a way to end this.

No.

Until the Neverseen were dead.

She needed to stop thinking in vague, easier terms.

Prison wouldn't be an option—Vespera, Gisela, and Gethen had all escaped from prisons.

Any permanent solution was going to involve death.

And the more she made herself accept that, the more she'd be ready to make it happen.

Especially if she was diligent about Ro's lessons.

She adjusted her uniform's half cape, making sure the straps she'd slung around her shoulders were covered. Flori had been kind enough to make her a holster from a leathery kind of tree bark. But it felt wrong bringing a dagger to Foxfire, so Sophie left Hope back in her room and wore the holster without it so she could still get used to the feel.

Hopefully that wouldn't turn out to be a mistake.

"Anyone else think it's weird being back here?" she asked, keeping her voice low so only Dex and Biana could hear.

All the other prodigies in the atrium were happily gossiping and swapping out books from their lockers, as if it were a perfectly normal school day. Maybe that proved Mr. Forkle was right, and getting back to routines would be a huge morale boost for everyone. But Sophie couldn't stop checking every corner and shadow—and her brain kept reminding her how much time was *tick, tick, tick*ing away.

"It *is* weird," Biana admitted. "Especially since Keefe isn't here."

Sophie became extremely interested in finding her elementalism notebook—but it didn't stop her mind from racing down a ridiculous worry spiral, wondering why Biana was the one bringing up Keefe.

Did that mean Biana still liked him?

Sophie had managed to go four whole days without think-ing about him.

Well . . . without thinking about him *much*.

But now that she was back at Foxfire, it was basically impos-sible.

Everything reminded her of him—which felt extra silly since they weren't in the same grade Level, so even if he'd been there, he'd be far away, in the Level Six wing.

But . . . she'd have seen him at orientation.

And study hall.

And lunch.

And PE.

Her breakfast tried to crawl back out of her stomach when she realized she was going to have to see Fitz in all those same places—plus their joint telepathy session.

What if he could tell . . . ?

Tell what? she asked herself. *That she was CONSIDERING the idea of liking another boy? Would that really be THAT big of a deal?*

Yes.

She'd be kind of a mess when Fitz started liking someone else.

In fact, just admitting that it was going to happen someday made her chest feel like she had a T. rex standing on it.

It really wasn't fair that she could feel so many conflicting emotions all at once.

"Uh . . . hello?" Biana said, waving a hand under Sophie's nose. "You okay?"

Sophie blinked. "Yeah. Sorry. I was just, uh . . ."

Nope—her annoying brain couldn't give her a single useful excuse.

Biana tilted her head to study Sophie. "Anything I should be worried about?"

Sophie searched for an honest answer. "Not for the next three hours."

Biana groaned. *Three hours—whyyyyyy?*

"Found it!" Dex said, holding up his schedule. He scowled after he read it. "Oh joy. Multispeciesial studies."

Sophie sighed. "This is such a waste of time."

"Probably," Biana said. "But . . . it's happening. And if we don't start heading to our sessions, we're all going to end up in detention."

Detention—another place Sophie used to run into Keefe.

He always found a way to sit by her. And sometimes he'd lean in and whisper in her ear or . . .

"STOP!"

Her cheeks felt like they were going to spontaneously combust when she realized she'd said the word out loud.

"What's wrong?" Biana and Dex asked—as everyone else turned to stare at her, and Sandor, Lovise, and Woltzer scanned the atrium for threats.

"Sorry, I, uh . . . just realized I need your help finding my session," she mumbled, knowing it was the worst excuse ever. "I can't remember which way I'm supposed to go—all the halls look the same."

"The elemental wing is that way," Biana said, narrowing her eyes as she pointed to one of the nearly identical glittering green hallways.

"Thanks." Sophie grabbed the first book she could get her hands on and slammed her locker shut, fleeing down the path Biana had shown her.

"Try not to blow up the school!" Dex called after her, making several prodigies laugh.

It was an old joke.

A good one, given her previous disasters.

But after Brumevale, it felt way too real.

So did her elementalism session.

Her Mentor had chosen to have her practice bottling *wind*.

Sophie was as terrible at the assignment as ever. Apparently she was *never* going to get used to doing stuff that defied everything she'd been taught in her human science classes. And after she shattered her seventh bottle, she got grumpy and asked her Mentor why she had to learn the skill, since there were Gusters who could do it for everyone.

He told her it was because "the wind is unpredictable—just like those who control it."

Which shouldn't have sent chills crawling down the edge of her spine.

She'd already known the elemental abilities were harder to control. That was why Linh's hydrokinesis was always such a struggle for her.

But now they were trying to set up a meeting with Trix.

And almost as if her Mentor knew—even though he couldn't possibly—he lowered his voice and murmured, "In my experience, you can never trust a Guster."

TWENTY-SIX

EITHER YOU LOST A BATTLE WITH A hurricane," Marella said, making Sophie jump as she set down her tray at the seat across from her, "or you're searching for the answers to life in that soup."

"Kind of both," Sophie admitted, pushing aside the bowl she'd been stirring and stirring and stirring.

Her Mentor's comment about Gusters had destroyed whatever concentration Sophie had managed to scrape together for wind-collecting—and after she'd shattered her dozenth bottle, he mumbled something about three hours being far too long, wrote her a pass, and told her to go to lunch early.

So she'd headed to the cafeteria on the second floor of

Foxfire's glass pyramid and grabbed a table in the farthest corner, taking occasional bites of the strange purple soup she'd chosen from the food court—which tasted like liquefied tacos.

She hadn't noticed that other prodigies were finally starting to join her—though Sandor clearly had, since he'd drawn his sword.

"I take it this means you're still pretty bad at elementalism?" Marella asked.

Sophie nodded. "Some things never change."

"And some really do." Marella plopped into her chair and turned to study the still mostly empty tables. "Who knew the nervous girl I rescued from the social disaster of sitting with a bunch of awkward boys playing with their spit would turn out to be this fierce rebel warrior who likes picking fights with our enemies."

Sophie checked to make sure no one was listening. "Uh, you realize I don't *like* any of this, right?"

"You sure? I get it if you kinda do. Just like part of me will always love doing this." She snapped her fingers to create a tiny blue flame and let it flicker over her palm for a beat before she closed her fist to snuff it out. "But that doesn't change the fact that I never wanted to be our world's newest sorta-known, sorta-secret Pyrokinetic—and I definitely didn't want to take my ability lessons from a murderer who loves to tell me how much I remind him of himself." She nodded when Sophie shuddered. "Yeah, it's not cool. So I understand

the whole trying-to-be-who-you're-expected-to-be-and-still-be-
you struggle—and how quickly it all gets into your head and
makes you either want to laugh, cry, scream, run away, or
just . . . burn everything."

Sophie sat up taller.

Marella laughed. "I love how saying that freaks everyone
out! You should see how pale you just turned!"

Sophie rolled her eyes.

"No, seriously, you're whiter than a yeti! You started picturing me switching sides and setting everything on fire, didn't
you? Was I cackling? Wearing a black, hooded robe? Ooh, were
we fighting? Was it an epic struggle between the moonlark and
her fiery former friend?"

"Former?" Sophie asked.

"Well . . . in *that* scenario," Marella told her, trying and failing to smooth out some of the wrinkles in her green uniform.

"And in *this* scenario?" Sophie pressed, pointing back and
forth between herself and Marella.

Marella leaned back in her chair, twisting one of the braids
scattered through her blond hair—which looked much shinier
than usual for some reason. "I'm sitting with you, aren't I?"

"True," Sophie said slowly. "So . . . does that mean we're
good?"

"Depends." Marella cracked open a can of tangerine-flavored
air and took a long open-mouthed breath of the orange-tinted
mist that plumed around her.

"On what?" Sophie asked.

"Well, for one thing, I'm curious—are you only hanging out with me right now because you want to know how it went when I talked to Fintan about his cache?"

"Technically *you're* hanging out with *me*," Sophie reminded her. "I was already sitting here when you sat down. And you're the one who brought up Fintan—not me. I didn't even know if you'd had a chance to talk to him yet."

Marella shrugged. "Fair enough. But you're dying to ask about it now, aren't you?"

"Not really—because a *friend* would never hold back something important. So you'll tell me when you're ready. Or you have nothing worth telling. Either way, there's no point asking you about it. Especially since you're clearly trying to test me right now, and I'm not going to fall for it."

"Huh," Marella said, taking another long inhale of tangerine. "You really are *much* feistier now. I can't decide how I feel about it."

"How you feel about what?" Maruca asked as she set her tray in front of one of the chairs next to Marella.

"Sophie's new attitude," Marella said, fanning the last of the flavored air toward her mouth.

Stina snort-laughed and strode over to Marella's other side. "That's easy. I'm definitely *not* a fan."

"Then clearly I'm doing something right," Sophie told her.

"See?" Marella said as Stina huffed into a chair. "It's like she's been hanging around Ro too much and picked up a case of the Snarky Comeback. Where *is* Ro, by the way? Did she decide to go hunting for the Keefster?"

Sophie was proud of herself for not reacting to the name. "No, Mr. Forkle sent her back to Ravagog for . . . something. And then she's going to try to do something else before she comes back."

"Wow, way to answer a question without actually answering it," Marella told her. "Clearly you've also picked up some avoiding skills from the Forkle."

"Or I'm just waiting until everyone else gets here," Sophie countered. "Otherwise I'm going to have to keep repeating myself over and over."

"I guess." Marella opened another can of flavored air— watermelon this time. "I'll save my update until then too."

"Works for me." Sophie reached for her cold soup and went back to stirring—ignoring the way Stina leaned in and whispered something in Marella's ear that made Marella giggle. "So . . . ," she said to Maruca, "have you seen Wylie lately?"

"I thought we weren't doing updates until everyone was here," Stina jumped in.

"I wasn't asking if Wylie heard anything from the Council," Sophie argued. "I asked if she'd seen her cousin."

"I have," Maruca jumped in before Stina could make any snippy retorts. "My mom had him over for dinner last night. She *claimed* it was because he needs a good home-cooked meal every once in a while. But I know it was really because she wanted to know if he thought it'd be safe for me to go back to Foxfire—and of *course* he said it probably wouldn't be, because he's annoyingly overprotective. I wanted to clobber him when he added that I should have a bodyguard now that I spend so much time with you all."

"That can be arranged," Sandor offered.

Maruca shrugged. "Why do I need one? I can do this."

She snapped her fingers, and a dome of flickering light with a faint bluish tint formed around their table.

It would've been way more impressive if it hadn't sputtered out immediately.

Maruca scowled. "Ugh, the blue force fields are way more finicky. That's why most Psionipaths don't bother with them. But they're supposed to be stronger, so I'm determined to figure it out. It'll be good to get back to my ability sessions—especially with an extra hour to practice."

"That *will* be nice," Biana said, coming up behind Sophie— with Woltzer actually at her side. "But the extra hour of elvin history was *miserable*."

"The extra hour of multispeciesial studies was pretty awful too," Dex said as he took a seat next to Biana—making a clear divide between Sophie's group and Marella's group on either side of the table. "My Mentor kept going on and on about the trollish treaty, and how we're about to witness history when the trolls finally sign a new one—and all I could think was

Why do I have to learn any of this if it's all about to change? And Lovise was totally snoring."

Lovise didn't deny it as she took a position against one of the glass walls next to Sandor and Woltzer.

"Huh," Maruca said as she swirled several long blue noodles onto her fork. "I kinda liked the extra hour in my Universe session. But it was all dark and cozy in there, so I just angled my notebook to hide my face and took a nice long nap."

"I liked *my* session as well," Stina informed them. "But clearly I'm the only one here who appreciates the opportunity to learn something."

"Oh please," Marella told her, "you came from cryptozoology! You probably spent three hours cuddling with gremlins."

"*Actually*, we were working with genies, and they're quite challenging to get out of their shells," Stina corrected.

Sophie *really* wanted to ask about the fact that genies were apparently *real* in some form—but she couldn't bring herself to admit that Stina knew more than her about something.

"Besides," Stina told Marella, "*you* just came from alchemy, and it looks like you spent most of the morning gilding your hair."

"Which is why you don't hear *me* complaining about my session either," Marella said, tossing her head to make the shinier strands glint.

"Oooh, that looks awesome!" Biana told her.

Marella grinned and flipped her hair again. "My Mentor

said I could practice transmuting metals on anything I wanted, so I figured I'd take some inspiration from the Song twins and try rocking metallic highlights. Where are they, by the way? Think Linh is blasting Tam with tidal waves?"

"She *should* be," Stina said, taking a spoonful of something that looked like neon Jell-O. "But she's over there in the lunch line, all by herself."

Everyone turned that way, and sure enough, there was Linh in her green Level Four uniform, holding a tray piled with pastries.

Maruca sighed and poked at the pink-speckled fruit on her own tray. "Next time I should let Linh choose my lunch."

"Same," Sophie said, pushing her cold purple soup aside again.

"Who else are we missing?" Marella asked when Linh joined them a minute later, taking a seat on Marella's side of the table. "Wylie doesn't go here anymore, so it's just Shade Boy and Fitzy, right?"

"I doubt Tam will bother joining us," Linh muttered as the air turned misty around her. "He's probably leaping back to Solreef to eat lunch with Glimmer."

Sophie frowned. "Are we allowed to leave campus during lunch?"

"Nope, they keep the Leapmaster locked down until after study hall," Fitz said—and Sophie's pathetic heart still did a little flip at the sound of his crisp accent.

Maybe it was a habit.

Or maybe it was some sort of weird nostalgia since they were back in such a familiar place.

Or maybe it had something to do with the way the jerkin of his white Level Six uniform stretched across his broad shoulders.

Whatever it was, the feeling was very short-lived.

Sophie's heart turned heavy and prickly when Fitz ignored the empty seat next to her.

"Oooh, does this mean we're going to get some Fitzphie drama?" Marella asked as he sat on her side of the table and Grizel joined the other goblins.

Fitz rolled his perfect teal eyes. "No, it means I heard we're doing a group update—and I'm assuming we're going to discuss it all telepathically to make sure no one overhears us. So it's easier for me to help Sophie if I can make eye contact."

Marella laughed. "Where's Keefe when we need him to make a joke about Fitzphie staring into each other's eyes?"

Far away, Sophie reminded herself.

Which was good.

She clearly needed more time to figure out how to navigate this emotional mess.

"You okay?" Dex leaned in and whispered. "You look a little twitchy."

Sophie cleared her throat, begging her voice to hold steady when she told him, "There's just a lot going on. I'll explain as soon as Tam gets here."

"I'm here."

Tam seemed to melt out of the nearby shadows, making everyone jump.

The mist thickened into clouds over Linh's head. "How long have you been hiding there?" she demanded.

"I wasn't *hiding*." Tam gestured to his vivid green uniform—which was pretty hard to miss. "I was trying to figure out if it was safe to join you."

"Well, it's not," Linh told him.

"You sure about that?" Tam tugged his bangs lower on his forehead. "These are my friends too."

Linh's clouds darkened. "Because of *me*! You never wanted to trust anybody! You just wanted to sulk in the shadows—until Little Miss Neverseen came along. What is it about her, Tam? Is she, like . . . the light to your darkness?"

Stina snickered.

Tam's eye roll was legendary.

"Okay, I like where this is going," Marella jumped in. "I'm always a big fan of any Tam-Linh drama. *But* you two are kinda making the whole cafeteria stare at us right now. Plus, my new gold highlights need a little more time to set before they can handle a Linh temper-drenching."

"I'm not going to lose my temper," Linh assured her—even though her storm clouds were multiplying. "I just want to see if Tam can explain why Glimmer's so annoyingly special to him."

Tam's shadows stretched across the floor, and his dark voice flooded all their minds as he shadow-whispered, "Her name is Rayni. And she's not SPECIAL. But . . . she reminds me of you. Even before she gave us her whole backstory, I could tell she'd been alone for a while. And it made me wonder what you would've been like if I'd stayed in the Lost Cities."

"Oh, so you think you're *saving* her like you *saved* me?" Linh snapped, not seeming to care that the rest of the cafeteria could hear her.

Tam shook his head and replied with another shadow-whisper. "No. You never needed saving. But you did need a friend. And so did Rayni—but she made the wrong ones. So I just want to see what happens when she has some better influences."

"You're going to regret it," Linh insisted.

"Maybe," Tam told her. "Or maybe I'll be really glad my twin sister taught me how to trust people."

"Don't put this on me," Linh warned.

Marella cleared her throat. "So . . . you two done being all dramatic for the moment?"

"*I* am," Tam said, tossing his bangs out of his eyes as he set his tray down on Sophie's side of the table.

Linh's storm clouds slowly evaporated, and she focused on taking a huge bite of a butterblast.

"Good," Marella said. "Lunch is, like, halfway over at this point, so we should probably get to the whole update thing."

Sophie nodded. "Who wants to go first?"

"Oh please, we all know you do," Stina grumbled.

"At least Sophie *has* updates," Dex snapped. "What have *you* been doing? Following Linh, Marella, and Maruca while *they* do important stuff?"

Stina crossed her arms. "Like you haven't been doing the same thing with Foster."

"Actually, Dex has been a huge help," Sophie jumped in. "And I'm fine going first. But even if someone else wants to, Fitz is right that we should do this telepathically. So I need everyone's permission to open my thoughts to all of yours."

Everyone agreed—except Stina, who only shrugged, but Sophie took that as a yes. She stretched out her consciousness, wrapping it around the group like it was a huge, soft blanket, and when she could feel each of their thoughts, she imagined a series of doors between their minds—then sent a big mental blast and shoved them all open, connecting everyone together.

Impressive, Fitz transmitted, and Sophie's heart did another silly little flip at the compliment. *You okay? Need a boost of energy?*

I think I'm good, Sophie promised, reaching up to rub her temples. *The hard part is over.*

Well, if you change your mind, you know where to find me.

He grinned with the offer—his movie-star smile—and Sophie hoped her face wasn't turning red.

Okay, she transmitted to everyone, taking a long breath to steady her concentration. *A lot of this is classified. In fact, I'm not even sure if I'm allowed to say anything about it. So I need you to promise that you're not going to repeat it to anyone.*

Not even to Wylie? Linh asked.

I guess that's true, Sophie realized. *Someone should probably update him.*

I can do it, Linh and Maruca both offered at the same time.

I'll let you all figure that out, Sophie told them. *But other than Wylie, no telling anyone else, okay?*

She waited until everyone had agreed, then quickly told them everything she'd learned about Elysian. And the map in Kenric's cache. And the place with the river she couldn't teleport to.

She also shared Mr. Forkle's fears about Cadfael, and Ro's plan to find the rebel ogres after she warned her father.

And even though Sophie knew it would cause a huge freakout, she told them what happened in Brumevale.

Naturally, her head was a *very* noisy place for a while.

She did her best to provide answers and tried to calm everyone's fears—but there was only so much she could say.

Now I get why you told me to keep Woltzer close, Biana's brain mumbled.

Yeah, Sophie agreed. *And if any of you want bodyguards, I'm sure Sandor can arrange that.*

Great, so I have to have a giant goblin following me around because you decided to go on a fire spree, Stina grumbled.

You don't HAVE to do anything, Sophie told her.

And this wasn't Sophie's fault.

Sophie sucked in a breath when she realized the thought came from Marella.

Oh please, Stina started to say, but Marella cut her off.

No, I mean it. It's fine to be scared. But it's not fair to blame Sophie. She didn't ask to be caught up in the middle of a rebellion.

Maybe not, Stina argued. *But she didn't have to make it worse, either.*

You think it wasn't going to get worse anyway? Marella asked. *You think the Neverseen will just decide, "You know what? We've caused enough drama. Let's turn ourselves in and apologize"?*

Marella's right, Linh agreed. *I think we all need to get used to the fact that things are going to keep escalating.*

And what we SHOULD be focusing on, Dex added, *is the new weapon the Neverseen are using. I'll reach out to Tinker as soon as I get home and see what I can find out.*

What about the leak? Biana asked.

The "possible" leak, Sophie clarified.

Yeah, fine, Biana conceded. *But I hope I'm not the only one who's not cool with Forkle's whole "let me handle it" plan for that.*

I'm not either, Tam chimed in.

Neither am I, Fitz said. *But what are we going to do about it? We don't even know who everyone in the Black Swan is.*

That doesn't mean we shouldn't try to come up with our own plan, Biana argued. *Especially since it's not like we have a whole* lot else to work on right now, do we? We're all at dead ends, right?

I'm not, Tam said. *The Council just hasn't gotten back to me. I'm still hoping they'll agree to the Trix meeting.*

Okay, but until they do, you're stuck waiting, right? Biana pressed. *And Fitz didn't find anything useful in those scrolls you took from the storehouse.*

They were all about how to create the gorgodons, Fitz agreed, *which might come in handy if the Council ever decides that the Timeline to Extinction applies to a genetic experiment the same way it does to other species. But otherwise, it won't do much good.*

Biana nodded and turned to Sophie. *You don't have any plans to find this Elysian place, do you?*

Not unless I can convince the Council to let me open all their caches, Sophie admitted. *Or if Fintan will show us what's in his.*

All eyes shifted to Marella.

She took another big breath of flavored air. *Yeah, big shocker, he said he'd be happy to open his cache if I can convince the Council to let him out of his icy prison for a day—which I'm obviously not going to do. I can see the hunger in his eyes every time he talks about fire. He'd definitely try to torch everything if we give him a chance.*

I'm guessing that means he wasn't a fan of our offer to bring him all his favorite meals? Maruca asked.

Nope! He pretty much laughed in my face, Marella grumbled.

And I'm guessing Dex can't just bypass the security on the cache? Fitz asked.

I can try, Dex told him. *But honestly, I doubt I'll be able to. I couldn't get anywhere with Kenric's cache—and there's always the risk that I'll trigger the cache's defenses and make it erase itself.*

Then there has to be something else we can offer Fintan, Biana decided.

We could always try Rayni's brilliant idea and offer to build him a statue in his honor, Stina suggested with a heavy layer of sarcasm.

Wait! Sophie said, glancing at Dex as an idea took shape in her head. *Fintan was in one of the memories in Kenric's cache, sitting in this garden he grew all by himself—without any gnomes—and he went on and on about these special flowers called Noxflares. I guess he spent over five hundred years growing them. So I wonder if he'd cooperate if you offered to bring him a few of those flowers. I bet they're still growing at his old house.*

You really think he'd care that much about a plant? Marella asked.

He might, Dex told her. *He seemed SUPER attached to them.*

It couldn't hurt to try, right? Sophie pressed. *Worst he can do is say no.*

I guess, Marella said, definitely not sounding convinced. *I'll try asking him the next time I see him.*

So . . . is that it, then? Stina asked when everyone's thoughts went silent. *None of you have learned anything from your little assignments. Ro's hunting traitors that have managed to stay hidden for long enough that it's pretty safe to assume they're going to stay that way. The Black Swan is trying to figure out what* happened in Brumevale—and Dex is going to ask Tinker for an update, but we all know she won't tell him anything. Marella's going to offer Fintan some weird flowers and hope he decides, "Who needs freedom when I can have foliage?"—and we all know how that's going to turn out. Did I miss anything—aside from the fact that some of you weirdos are still hoping the Councillors will prove they've lost their minds and let you meet with Trix?

Uh, I want to work on finding out who the leak in the Black Swan is, Biana added.

Okay, but I don't hear an actual plan for how you're going to do that, so I can't imagine you're going to get anywhere, Stina insisted. *Same goes for trying to find this Elysian place.*

Well, THERE'S a great attitude, Dex grumbled.

But I'm not wrong—am I? Stina challenged. Her smile turned bitter when everyone stayed quiet. *That's what I thought. Great job, Foster! Way to give us a whole lot of nothing!*

That's not fair! Biana jumped in. *I don't see you having any brilliant ideas.*

You also don't see me handing out projects, or calling for lunch meetings, or making my own symbol, Stina reminded her. *If she's going to insist on leading us, she could at least do a good job!*

She's doing the best she can, Dex snapped, and Sophie was surprised to see everyone at the table nod their agreement—except Stina.

Maybe she is, Stina told them as she stood and towered over them. *But it's still not good enough.*

She stalked out of the cafeteria—and Sophie didn't bother trying to stop her.

"We . . . should probably start heading to our sessions," she mumbled.

She severed the connections between everyone's minds—but Fitz's transmission slipped past her mental barriers.

You okay?

I'll be fine, Sophie promised.

I'm sure you will be, he agreed, *but clearly you're dealing with a LOT. And . . . I'm here if you need to talk.*

He leaned closer and raised his eyebrows, like he was waiting for her to take his cue and brain-dump all her worries on him.

But . . . there really wasn't anything else to say.

And while a tiny part of her wished she could cry on his shoulder like she had the day she'd said goodbye to her human family—she wasn't a little girl anymore.

So she shook her head and told him, *Thanks. But I'm really okay. Hopefully the Council will approve the meeting with Trix soon and—*

You REALLY still want to go ahead with that? Fitz interrupted. *After what happened in Brumevale?*

I definitely have my reservations, Sophie admitted. *But I don't see any other options, do you?*

No—but you don't make a bad choice just because you don't have any good ones, he argued.

Sitting around and doing nothing isn't any better, Sophie insisted.

It's safer, he countered. *Mistakes get towers blown up.*

Mistakes.

Sophie wasn't sure if her mind actually repeated the word, or if it was just echoing around her head.

And she probably should've let it go, but she had to ask, *You still think I made a mistake when I burned down the Neverseen's storehouse, don't you?*

Fitz dragged a hand down his face. *"Mistake" isn't the right word—*

But it's the one you just used, she reminded him. *And I'm pretty sure it's what you meant.*

Several beats passed before he transmitted, *Maybe it is. I just . . . think you should wait for a plan that everyone agrees with this time.*

You mean a plan YOU agree with, Sophie corrected.

Well, yeah—I'm a part of this too.

That doesn't mean everything revolves around you.

I never said it did—and for the record, it doesn't mean everything revolves around YOU, either. Just because you're the moonlark doesn't mean you're smarter than everyone. You still have a LOT to learn.

You think I don't know that?

Fitz sighed. *I think you're scared. And angry. And you want to end this quickly. And I get that. But sometimes it feels like you don't realize that it's only a matter of time before something you do gets someone killed.*

Sophie's jaw fell open.

"Uh . . . would you two like to share your little telepathic convo with the rest of us?" Marella asked.

"Yeah, it looks kind of important," Biana added.

"It's not," Sophie said as she built the thickest, highest wall around her mind to block any more of Fitz's transmissions.

Fitz pinched the bridge of his nose like he had a headache. "I guess it isn't."

Marella whistled. "Wow. Major Fitzphie drama."

Fitz gritted his teeth. "Stop calling us Fitzphie! That's not a *thing!*"

The words echoed around the cafeteria.

Everyone was glancing from Sophie to Fitz.

And Sophie knew she needed to say something.

She even choked down the sharp, cold lump in her throat.

But she still couldn't find her voice.

So she stood and walked away.

TWENTY-SEVEN

IS IT OKAY IF I SIT HERE?" SOPHIE ASKED, trying not to think about the fact that she was in the middle of a very crowded cafeteria and definitely *not* standing in front of the table where the rest of her friends were sitting.

She wasn't sure if anyone had noticed—she'd kept her head down as she'd grabbed whatever food was closest in the lunch line and focused on her feet the whole walk to the seating area.

But she was hard to miss, thanks to her seven-foot goblin shadow.

Plus, she'd definitely heard whispers when she'd sat by herself during study hall the day before—and when she stood alone during orientation.

Dex and Biana had also been shooting her concerned looks

all morning, after she chose to play with a different team during PE.

Sophie felt bad for ignoring them. But . . . she wasn't ready to talk about what had happened, and she knew they'd have *lots* of questions.

She was also pretty sure that if she got anywhere near Fitz right now, she'd end up sucker punching him.

Her grip tightened on her tray, the metal warping slightly from the extra pressure.

After how hard she'd fought to keep her friends out of danger—and how much they'd all *insisted* on being involved—she couldn't believe that Fitz had accused her of trying to get someone killed.

Did that mean he also blamed her for the injury to his leg?

And the scars on Biana's arms?

And—

"Uh, did you hear me?" a familiar voice asked, snapping Sophie out of her mental rage-fest.

She blinked and found Jensi staring up at her with his eyebrows squished together.

"Sorry," she mumbled. "What did you say?"

"I said of course you can sit here." He waved his hands toward the empty seats all around him. "Take your pick."

Sophie breathed a sigh of relief and sank into the chair across from him. "Thanks."

"Sure. Anytime."

She could feel him studying her as she picked at the plate of leafy greens she'd assumed was some sort of salad—but when she took a bite, it tasted exactly like sweet-and-sour chicken.

And she was fully prepared to be bombarded with Jensi's trademark rapid-fire questions, usually delivered at a pace that made her wonder how much sugar he'd eaten.

But he stayed uncharacteristically silent.

After a few more bites, Sophie peeked at him through her eyelashes.

He looked different than the last time she'd seen him.

His round face had sharpened around the jawline, and she had a feeling that when he stood up, he'd be taller than she remembered.

But the real change was his smile.

Jensi's huge grin usually stretched from ear to ear. But when their eyes met, his lips barely lifted at the corners.

"Sorry," she said again, realizing her sulking was probably making him uncomfortable. "I'm just . . . having a weird week."

"I get it," Jensi told her, poking at the doughy-looking blob he'd chosen for his lunch. "Right there with you."

"Really?" Sophie asked. "Everything okay?"

He shrugged.

Poke. Poke. Poke. Poke. Poke.

"Want to talk about it?" she asked.

He shrugged again.

"That's not actually an answer," Sophie pointed out. "But

I don't want to bug you. In fact, if you want me to leave you alone—"

"No—please stay!" Jensi put a hand on her tray like he thought she was about to grab it and go. "I hate eating alone."

Sophie frowned.

She'd assumed the rest of his friends were still going through the lunch line. But a quick scan of the cafeteria showed his usual group—who had the unfortunate tendency to wear their hair in long, greasy ponytails—gathered at a table on the other side of the room.

She also confirmed that people definitely *had* noticed where she'd chosen to sit. Including her friends—though Fitz's head was down, and he seemed to be focusing very intently on whatever he was eating.

She hoped it tasted really, really gross.

But she shoved that petty thought aside and tried to find the most sensitive way to word her next question. "Did something . . . happen?"

Jensi went back to poking his lunch. "No. That's the problem."

"I'm not sure what that means."

"Yeah, I figured as much when you wanted to sit with me."

"Why wouldn't I want to sit with you?"

She knew she'd never been the kind of friend that Jensi deserved—but that hadn't been intentional. They'd just . . . drifted apart as everything got scarier and scarier.

"I don't know," Jensi mumbled—but clearly he had a reason.

Sophie thought about calling him out on it, but she wasn't sure if she should pry—especially since there were so many people who might overhear them. So she went back to eating her sweet-and-sour-chicken-flavored leaves, wondering if anyone else realized what they tasted like.

Elves were vegetarians, so none of them had ever eaten chicken—much less breaded chicken tossed with pineapple and peppers and onions in a sticky red sauce.

And now that she was thinking about it, how did humans come up with a dish that tasted exactly like a gnomish plant?

Was it just a bizarre coincidence?

Or had the first sweet-and-sour-chicken maker somehow tasted one of these leaves and felt inspired to create something just like them?

Jensi groaned. "Ugh, I can practically hear you feeling sorry for me right now."

"Not even close," Sophie said, deciding not to tell him she'd actually just spent way too much time thinking about human takeout food. "I don't even know what I'm supposed to feel sorry for—but I'm not saying that to pressure you. I get how it feels to have people trying to force you to open up when you still need more time to process what's going on."

"Is that why you wanted to sit here?" Jensi asked.

"Kind of. I might also be fighting the urge to dump my lunch on someone's head."

"Stina?" Jensi guessed, his voice picking up a little of his usual energy. "Sorry—you don't have to tell me. I just saw the way she stormed off yesterday—pretty sure everyone did."

"Great," Sophie grumbled, pushing the leaves around her plate. "But honestly, I'm kinda used to Stina. At this point, I think I'd be more freaked out if she actually said something nice to me."

Jensi laughed. "Yeah, that would be pretty weird." He poked his lunch a few more times before he asked, "So . . . are you mad at Fitz, then?"

Sophie sighed, wishing her chest didn't feel so tight and prickly. "Let's just say I'm dreading my next session."

Actually, "dread" wasn't a strong enough word.

She would rather drink a giant glass of imp spit than spend three hours doing one-on-one telepathy training with Mr. Fitzphie's-Not-a-Thing.

In fact, she was tempted to head to the Healing Center instead.

No one would question it—and Elwin would probably let her stay there until study hall.

She was his most frequent patient, after all.

"Well . . . if it helps," Jensi said quietly, "I'm dreading my next session too."

"What's your next session?" Sophie asked.

He poked a giant hole in the dough ball before he mumbled, "Ability detecting."

"Why would . . . ?"

Sophie's voice trailed off as she answered her own question—and she barely stopped herself from blurting out, *You haven't manifested?*

"You can say it," Jensi muttered. "I know I probably *should* start ditching at this point."

"That's not what I was going to say," Sophie assured him.

"Yeah, well . . . everyone's thinking it. I bet I'll be the only Level Four in there."

"There's no way that's true."

"It might be." His words picked up speed again. "Everyone I can think of has already manifested—but even if there *are* a few other desperate Level Fours left, we're pretty much at the cutoff. I don't think I've ever heard of anyone manifesting in Level Five."

"That doesn't mean it hasn't happened," Sophie reminded him. "Besides, we're not even to midterms in Level Four yet."

"Yeah—but that's because Foxfire was on hiatus for a while. Now they're extending our sessions to make up for lost time—and I'm pretty sure they're going to skip the whole midterm break—so I still only have a few months left."

"Okay . . . but . . . a *lot* can happen in a few months. I mean, think of how much went on when we were in Level Three." She started ticking things off on her fingers. "I found Silveny right before school started—and then the Neverseen tried to steal her a bunch of times. Alden's mind also shattered, and

I had to have my abilities reset so I could heal him. Then the Council ordered me to heal Fintan's mind, and he killed Kenric and burned down half of Eternalia. So the Council tried to force me to wear that horrible ability restrictor thing, and Dex had to throw it in the fire so we could fight the Neverseen on Mount Everest. And then a bunch of us got banished and had to live with the Black Swan. Then the ogres unleashed the gnomish plague, and we had to sneak into Ravagog. And Keefe ran off to infiltrate the Neverseen and barely got out of there before they took down Lumenaria." She frowned. "Wow, was all of that really only in one school year? No wonder it felt like we were in Level Three *forever*! But I think I'm getting sidetracked. My point is, I know time has a way of feeling both frustratingly slow and way too fast around here. But things can change overnight. Especially when it comes to manifesting, since that's the kind of thing where one day, out of nowhere, you're just like, *Whoa, look what I can do now!*"

"I guess." Jensi shoved his lunch aside. "But it's starting to feel like it's never going to happen—and I swear it doesn't make any sense! My parents were each other's top matches, so I should be guaranteed to get an ability—that's what the match is *supposed* to be for! And it worked for my brother— he's a Phaser. But so far . . . nothing! Meanwhile, all my friends have manifested—I'm seriously the only one who hasn't—and they're all starting to look at me like, *What's wrong with you?*

That's why I'm sitting over here—in case you were wondering. The thought of listening to them go on and on about their ability sessions when I have to suffer through *three hours* of being tested for stuff—and having my Mentors give me a sad head shake when it doesn't work—made me want to hide in my PE locker for the rest of the afternoon. I'm still tempted—it's super roomy in there."

"It is," Sophie agreed.

Their PE lockers were more like private dressing rooms.

But she hated that Jensi felt like he needed to hide.

"None of my friends have even glanced over here since I sat down," he added quietly. "I think they're relieved that they don't have to sit with me—and do you know what the worst part is? They're not even cool! I keep telling them they need to stop with the ponytails—but do they listen? Nope. *And* they spend, like, half of every lunch blowing spit bubbles."

Sophie couldn't help laughing. "Well . . . for what it's worth, I'm glad I got to sit with you—and I hope we can do it again."

"You don't think you'll be back with your other friends?"

"I . . . have no idea." She wasn't sure how long she could get away with avoiding them before there was major drama. "But even if I am, you're welcome to sit with us—you know that, right?"

He gave her another shrug—which made her realize she didn't actually know why Jensi had gone back to sitting with his old group.

They'd never talked about it.

And now probably wasn't the best time to bring it up.

But she had to at least make sure he knew. "None of them are going to care that you haven't manifested."

He snorted. "Pretty sure Stina will."

"Actually, I doubt it. Her dad's Talentless, remember?"

He flinched at the word—and Sophie wanted to kick herself for using it.

"Sorry—I—"

"It's fine," Jensi cut in. "I might as well start getting used to it. It's probably my future."

Sophie wanted to deny it, but . . .

She couldn't guarantee that he'd manifest.

Or that people wouldn't judge him for it.

Or that he wouldn't get kicked out of Foxfire.

The whole system was so incredibly unfair.

It made her want to stand outside the Councillors' castles screaming, *Why don't you fix this?*

Instead, she scanned the cafeteria again, searching for the biggest, loudest commotion—and sure enough, there were Lex, Bex, and Rex in their blue Level Two uniforms.

Lex had made a small blizzard's worth of snow around their table, and his friends were pelting each other with snowballs as Bex bragged about how she was the champion because she could let everything phase right through her.

Meanwhile, Rex . . .

. . . was sitting at the very edge of their table, hunched over his plate, not talking to anyone.

He was probably also dreading the moment when his siblings would head to their Froster and Phaser sessions and he'd have to head to ability detecting.

How many rude prodigies had already teased him about being the only Dizznee triplet without a special ability?

How many had reminded him that his dad was Talentless and his parents were a bad match?

How much hope was he losing every day he didn't manifest?

"Hey . . . so . . . can I . . . uh . . . ask you a question?" Jensi asked.

"Of course." Sophie turned back to give him her full attention.

Jensi looked down, and his twitchy fingers started tearing his lunch into teeny, tiny pieces. "Well . . . I heard that Marella had someone from the Black Swan trigger her ability—the same guy who's triggered some of yours—and even though she ended up a Pyrokinetic, which obviously isn't ideal, it's still an ability, so . . . clearly it worked."

None of that was a question. But Sophie knew where he was going with it. "You want me to ask Mr. Forkle to try triggering you?"

Jensi tried squishing the doughy bits back into a lumpy blob. "Do you think he'd be willing to?"

"I honestly don't know. He can be pretty grumpy—and if he does agree, I'm sure he'll give you the same speech he gave Marella, about how abilities come from our genetics and he can't do anything to change that."

"I know," Jensi mumbled. "And, I mean, obviously I *hope* it'll help—but if it doesn't . . . it'd be nice to at least feel like I did everything I possibly could, you know?"

Marella had said pretty much the same thing. That was what convinced Mr. Forkle to try triggering her.

"I'll ask him," Sophie promised—and as relief flooded Jensi's features, she realized there might be someone else she could ask.

Well . . . *if* Keefe's new ability really worked the way they thought it did.

And if he ever came back . . .

Then again, what would happen if he felt the same thing he'd felt with Rex?

"You okay?" Jensi asked, his smile fading. "Is it bad that I asked you to talk to him? Because if it is—"

"It's not bad at all," Sophie assured him. "It's a good idea. It just might take a little while before I can make it happen. There's kind of a lot going on."

Jensi nodded. "Anything I should know about?"

"Hopefully not."

"Well . . . if there's any way I can help, let me know—even though I know I'm pretty useless—"

"No, you're *not*," Sophie interrupted. "Abilities aren't everything. I get how weird that sounds coming from me, since I have a bunch of them. But . . . how many times have I almost died? How many times have my friends gotten hurt? How many times have the Neverseen escaped? If abilities were as awesome as everyone thinks they are, none of that should've happened."

Unless it was because she kept making "mistakes."

"Thanks," Jensi mumbled, smushing his lunch into a flat pancake. "I appreciate the pep talk. And . . . thanks for not looking at me like I'm defective."

"You're *not* defective," she promised. "I mean it."

He put his head down on the table, muffling his voice when he told her, "We'll see."

She'd thought that was his way of dropping the conversation, but after a few seconds he said, "I wonder how it'll go once it's official. No one ever talks about that part. Like—at some point—will I get called into Magnate Leto's office, and my ability detecting Mentors will be in there waiting for me, and they'll all announce that it's time to give up? Or will it be bigger than that? Think an Emissary will show up at my house with some sort of scroll saying the Council has declared me Talentless?"

"I think you should try not to worry about this stuff," she told him.

But as Jensi sat back up and started cleaning up the mess

from his lunch, she couldn't stop her eyes from wandering back to the Dizznee triplets.

Rex, Bex, and Lex had always looked and acted so similar that they might as well have been identical.

But Rex didn't seem to fit anymore.

His mischievous smile was gone. His shoulders were slumped. He looked pale—with shadows under his eyes.

And he didn't even know for sure that he was going to be Talentless.

When he found out, he'd never be the same.

And now Sophie couldn't help wondering who would have to tell him.

Would it be Dex?

That'd crush both of them—and Rex might not even believe him.

He'd probably need to hear it straight from Keefe—which made a whole new kind of dread course through Sophie's veins.

Keefe wouldn't just have to watch the tiny glints of hope fade from Rex's eyes.

He'd *feel it*.

He'd also feel Rex's panic.

And anger.

And all the other bitter emotions that would come with the revelation.

And given how sensitive Keefe's empathy had become,

the emotions would completely overwhelm him.

Or worse . . .

Keefe had warned her that Empaths had to be careful—that feeling too many intense emotions could make the sensations all blur together until everything started to feel the same and they basically went numb.

That was what had happened to Vespera.

Was Keefe heading down that same path?

Probably—if his mom got ahold of him.

Or the Council.

But even if none of that happened . . . Keefe's empathy was so much stronger now.

He could feel *everything* people were feeling—without even trying.

So . . . would he ever be able to come back to the Lost Cities?

Or would he need the third step to stellarlune in order for it to be safe?

And if he *did* need that, how long could his senses be bombarded while she was stuck with dead end after dead end trying to find Elysian?

Especially since being around humans might actually be even harder for him.

Human emotions were way more intense—just like their thoughts. And Sophie knew how brutal it had been for her when she hadn't learned how to control her telepathy.

The noise.

The headaches.

The inescapable anxiety.

Was that what Keefe was dealing with now, on an emotional level?

"Wow, you just turned as green as our uniforms," Jensi said as the chimes announced the end of lunch. "You really *are* dreading your next session."

Sophie nodded, letting him believe the easier explanation.

But she now had way bigger worries than spending a few awkward hours with Fitz.

Or, she thought she did, as she tried to give Jensi her most supportive smile and they both dragged their feet toward their sessions.

But barely a minute after she and Fitz took their seats in the weird silver chairs in their telepathy room, Tiergan told them, "I don't know what's going on between you two, but I don't have to be an Empath to sense the tension. You've barely looked at each other since you've stepped into this room. And I realize that arguments and temporary fall-outs can happen—but the Cognate connection is incredibly fragile. So we must work to preserve your relationship as quickly as possible."

"Let me guess," Fitz said, crossing his arms. "You want us to do another trust exercise."

"I wish it were that simple." Tiergan turned to pace the dim, round room, and his plain black cape seemed to fade into the shadows as he told them, "Sadly, you two seem to be beyond *exercises* at this point."

"What does *that* mean?" Sophie asked.

"It means it's time for something I'd rather hoped I'd be able to spare you from." He clapped his hands to turn off the remaining lights before he said, "You need a full Cognate Inquisition."

TWENTY-EIGHT

I'M SURE I'M SUPPOSED TO ALREADY KNOW this," Sophie mumbled through the darkness, "but . . . what's a 'full Cognate Inquisition'?"

"Better question," Fitz jumped in, using a smug tone that made her wish one of the buttons on her telepathy chair would turn Fitz's into an ejector seat and launch him out of the room. "Why were you hoping to spare us from it?"

"A Cognate Inquisition," Tiergan told them, "is a process designed to highlight the weaknesses in your connection and help you address any issues. It requires a much more complete level of honesty than either of you are used to—which is why I tried to spare you. Some Cognates are able to maintain certain degrees of privacy, and I'd hoped you would be among them, since I can tell that's important to you."

"To some of us more than others," Fitz mumbled.

Sophie rolled her eyes.

"Comments like that are not helping your situation," Tiergan warned Fitz. "I don't think either of you understands the gravity of what you're facing. You're heading rapidly toward a breaking point—and once the Cognate connection shatters, it cannot be repaired. So we must take action now. Otherwise you'll be back to working alone."

When he put it that way, working alone actually sounded pretty awesome.

In fact, Sophie almost wished she could drop her Cognate ring in Fitz's lap before fleeing the room as fast as her legs could carry her.

Maybe Tiergan could tell, because he told her, "You'll regret it if you give up."

"You sure about that?" Sophie grumbled, mostly under her breath.

"Are you *really* thinking of quitting?" Fitz asked.

"I don't know," she admitted, surprised at the hurt that flared in his eyes. "It's just . . . a lot of pressure."

"It is," Tiergan agreed. "But it's worth it."

"That'd be easier to believe if you actually had a Cognate," Sophie told him.

"I suppose that's true. And this is usually when I'd lament the fact that I never found a suitable partner. But . . . the truth is . . . there *was* someone I could've paired with. I was simply too stubborn to acknowledge the connection—and, I suppose, a little too afraid. I'm like you, Sophie. I value my privacy. So I ignored anyone who suggested giving it a try. And then . . . it was too late."

He turned away, fussing with the edges of his cape, and Sophie knew she should probably drop the subject there.

But she had to know. "Are you talking about Prentice?"

Several seconds passed before Tiergan nodded.

"I'll always wonder if I could've helped him more if we'd been Cognates," he said quietly. "I might've even been able to drag him free from that darkness."

"Is the connection really that powerful?" Sophie whispered.

Sure, she and Fitz had pulled off some cool tricks since they'd started training together—but she'd assumed a lot of that power had come from the genetic tweaks to her telepathy and Fitz was mostly a backup.

"It's a game changer," Tiergan promised, turning back to face her. "In fact—I can prove it to you, if you want."

He undimmed one of the lights, casting the room in a gray-ish glow as he opened a hidden compartment in the arm of Sophie's chair and pulled out a small, almost fluffy-looking gadget.

The bundle of stringy silver threads reminded Sophie of a Koosh ball, and he pointed to a sphere tucked into the center. "This measures the force of your mental power. All you have to do is concentrate on the sensors as hard as you can—think you're up for it?"

Sophie nodded, and he held the gadget a little closer to her forehead.

"Ready whenever you are," he told her. "Three . . . two . . . one."

She closed her eyes and imagined her thoughts slamming against the gadget like a sledgehammer in one of those Test Your Strength carnival games.

When she opened her eyes, bright blue numbers had appeared in the center.

291.

"Well done!" Tiergan said, shaking the gadget to reset it. "I've personally never tested higher than 274." His eyes shifted to Fitz. "Ready to see how you measure up?"

Fitz leaned toward the orb, gripping the arms of his chair as his whole face scrunched with concentration. "Ready."

Tiergan counted down, and . . .

263.

Fitz scowled. "Can I try again? You kept it farther away from me than you did for Sophie."

"That shouldn't matter." But Tiergan reset the gadget and held it closer to Fitz's forehead.

The veins in Fitz's temples looked ready to burst as Tiergan counted down again. And . . .

264.

"That actually *is* impressive," Tiergan promised when Fitz's shoulders slumped. "Most Telepaths register between 230 and 240—and before you start looking too smug," he told Sophie, "let's see what happens when the two of you work as Cognates. You'll need to open your minds and push together this time— think you can handle that?"

"*I* can," Fitz said, raising a questioning eyebrow in Sophie's direction.

She definitely did *not* want him anywhere near her thoughts at the moment.

But . . . she was also kind of curious.

"I'm game," she decided, sitting up as tall as she could.

"Excellent!" Tiergan held the gadget between them, showing Fitz that it was perfectly in the center. "Let me know when you're ready."

Sophie made sure she was thinking about a giant pile of gorgodon poop as she let Fitz into her head.

Fitz, meanwhile, was focused entirely on rallying his strength.

"Ready," they both announced together.

Tiergan counted down again—and when he got to "one," they both launched their consciousness at the gadget, striking the sensor with a blast that felt like mental lightning.

419.

Sophie slouched back in her chair and closed off her mind again. "Huh. I guess we really are stronger together."

"You are," Tiergan agreed. "But this is much worse than I feared."

"Why?" Fitz asked.

Tiergan reset the gadget again. "Four hundred nineteen is the kind of reading I'd expect if I was testing myself with either of you—not testing two Cognates—since regular Telepaths tend to find that their mental strength gets slightly diluted when they pool their power with another mind. You two should've been at least as high as the sum total of your individual levels—so a minimum of 554 or 555. And even *that* is low for your capabilities. I'm sure when you two are truly in sync, your reading is above seven hundred—and with proper trust and training, I wouldn't be surprised at all if you were the first Cognates to register over a thousand." He let that sink in before he added, "I realize that maintaining a Cognate relationship can be exhausting—particularly at your ages, when you're still trying to figure out who you are as individuals. But . . . it *is* worth preserving. Think of what you could accomplish with that kind of power at your disposal. The possibilities are endless—and will likely be vital given the challenges our world is facing. I'd hate to see you throw all of that away simply because it's getting difficult."

It was more than *difficult*.

It was starting to feel *impossible*.

But Sophie choked back the words.

After all, if she was willing to try bonding with a dagger,

she should probably also be willing to at least *try* to keep going with Cognate training.

What if it did turn out to be crucial for taking down the Neverseen?

She slumped back in her chair and sulked for a second before she asked, "Okay, assuming I'm on board for this Cognate Inquisition—and I'm not saying for sure that I am—what exactly would we have to do?"

"It's actually a fairly simple process," Tiergan told her, "broken into three steps. We'll tackle the first one today—"

"Why not all three?" Fitz interrupted. "We have an extra hour, remember? And if we need more time, I'm sure Magnate Leto would approve us skipping study hall for something this important. And then it'll all be fixed and—"

"The process doesn't work that way," Tiergan told him. "Think of the first step like . . . exposing wounds. You need to see how deep they stretch and how many places have been affected. And for anything that's been festering for a while, you need to let it bleed a little so it has a chance to properly heal."

"Greeeeeeeeaaaaaaaaaaat," Sophie muttered. "This is sounding better and better."

"It won't be fun," Tiergan agreed. "Particularly for you. But as I've said, it's also quite simple. I'll guide both of your consciousnesses to a little-known space in each of your minds called the Core of Verity—the one place in your head with nowhere to hide. No thoughts can be guarded. No defenses remain. It will be just the two of you, surrounded by pure, unedited truth in its most basic form."

"Uh, that's a *really* bad idea," Sophie mumbled.

Fitz groaned. "Here we go."

"What does *that* mean?" Sophie demanded.

"It means I get it—you like keeping secrets," he told her. "But I don't see how we're ever going to move past it. I thought our biggest barrier was that you didn't want me to know that you like me, but—"

The sound that slipped out of Sophie's mouth was half startled bird, half wounded whale.

Words.

She needed words.

But her brain was giving her nothing.

And her hands were shaking.

And her eyes were burning.

And . . .

"What?" Fitz glanced between her and Tiergan—who looked like he wanted to crawl under something and hide. "Why is it bad to say that you like me? You know I like you too."

"Do I?" Sophie snapped, finding a tiny sliver of her voice.

"Uh, I would hope so, since I've said it a bunch of times."

"Yeah, well, you also told the whole cafeteria that Fitzphie's not a thing," she reminded him.

"Fitzphie?" Tiergan asked, then shook his head. "Never mind, I don't want to know."

"You don't," Sophie agreed.

"Why?" Fitz asked. "Why is it all still a big secret? And if it *is* a secret, why am I the bad guy for telling Marella to stop bringing it up? You were the one who told me you weren't ready for a boyfriend right now because there was too much going on and . . . Oh." He collapsed back against his chair and smacked his hand against his forehead. "Okay. I guess I get it. I'm being a jerk."

"Finally, something we agree on," Sophie muttered.

Tiergan coughed—then cleared his throat. "I think . . . perhaps this conversation should be saved until it's just the two of you—preferably in the Core of Verity."

"I agree. But . . . that's not my call." Fitz glanced at Sophie. "You up for it? Or did I make it too weird?"

"I don't know." Sophie curled into another Sophie-ball.

Fitz sighed. "I get that I lose my temper sometimes and say the wrong thing. I'm trying to work on it. But . . . I hope you know that none of that changes how much I care about you. I just . . . don't know how to make you believe that—and I *really* don't know how to make you trust me enough to be honest with me."

Sophie had no idea what to do with most of those words.

They all seemed to tangle around each other into a giant mess in her brain.

"The thing is," she said quietly, "total honesty isn't as awesome as everyone thinks it is. I would know. I spent seven years with humans after my telepathy manifested, hearing every unguarded, brutally honest thought from every person around me. So I can say—for a fact—that some things are better left unheard. We all think stuff that isn't nice. Or want things we shouldn't. And sharing that *doesn't* bring anyone closer. I never saw my parents the same way again after I heard them wish I could be more like my sister. It didn't matter that they were just feeling overwhelmed because I clearly didn't belong and none of us understood why. It still hurt. Same went for every horrible thing the other kids at school thought about me. Even random strangers could be cruel. So . . . yeah, I'm not excited to hear your unguarded thoughts, because I know it's going to feel like I'm getting punched in the heart—and I'm sure my brain goes places you won't be a big fan of either."

"Like where?" Fitz asked.

Keefe's face filled her mind.

She shook her head—hard—until the image faded. "I just . . . don't see how any of this is going to help. Think about what happened yesterday—and I'm not talking about the Fitzphie comment. Did your other truth outburst bring us closer? Or is it the reason Tiergan's making us do this horrible exercise in the first place?"

Silence followed.

Ten seconds.

Twenty.

Thirty.

Tiergan cleared his throat again. "Okay, I don't know what was said yesterday—and I don't *want* to know. I'm not actually sure how I ended up in the middle of this conversation. But clearly this *emotional attachment* between you two is the root cause of many of your trust issues—"

"There's no rule that says Cognates can't date," Fitz jumped in. "I asked my dad."

He did?

Sophie couldn't decide if that was really sweet or really . . .

. . . strange.

What would Fitz have done if Alden had told him "no"?

Would he ever have confessed that he liked her?

Or would he have chosen Cognates above all else?

"Anyway," Tiergan said before her mind went too far down that uncomfortable mental path. "What I was trying to say is that ignoring your issues won't make them go away. *That's* why I'm suggesting a Cognate Inquisition. You can either address the barriers between you—or let your partnership crumble. Those are the only choices. And before you decide, it might help if I explained the process a little more clearly." He turned to Sophie, and his olive-toned skin turned a shade paler as he murmured, "I'm so sorry you were forced to endure such a painful mental barrage for so many years. I can see now how it haunts you—and I wish I'd put that together sooner. I don't blame you at all for being reluctant to expose yourself—or Fitz—to that level of unfiltered honesty again."

"Neither do I," Fitz added. "I should've realized how much that affected you. And if the Inquisition thing sounds like too much, I want you to know that I get it—okay?"

"Thanks," Sophie mumbled, hugging herself a little tighter. "I just . . . never want to live through anything like that again."

"You won't have to," Tiergan assured her. "A Cognate Inquisition actually works differently. The Core of Verity has no true coherent thoughts."

"But . . . you said, 'No thoughts can be guarded,'" Sophie reminded him.

"I did. And that was a poor wording choice on my part, so let me try again. You'll still be able to communicate with each other by transmissions—but you'll be in complete control over those. And the unguarded thoughts I was referring to are actually *reactions* that come in the form of a specific sensation— a temperature shift, telling you whether the thought has any significance."

"Uh, not sure I get what that means," Fitz admitted, and Sophie was glad she wasn't the only one who felt confused.

"Perhaps it would help if I gave some examples," Tiergan suggested. "So, Fitz, if you were in Sophie's Core of Verity, and you thought about mallowmelt—and I'm correct in assuming that there's been no dramatic mallowmelt incident between the two of you—then Sophie's mind would feel cold and still, telling you that the subject of mallowmelt is safe and doesn't need any further consideration. But if you were to think about whatever regrettable thing you said yesterday, you'd feel a sear-ing heat against your consciousness to let you know that there's a barrier there between you. And you'll both know which reac-tions were felt, so there will be no misunderstandings. Then the next step—"

"Let me guess," Sophie jumped in. "Step two is where Fitz asks me about anything that felt warm and I still have to tell him everything—"

"Wrong," Tiergan interrupted. "You're describing step three. That's why this isn't a one-day exercise. Step two is when you both go home and decide how you feel about these new discover-ies, specifically from a mindset of *What do I need to know in order to work together?* You'll both be surprised at how many of the issues require no further discussion. It's remarkable how often simply knowing a problem exists is enough to allow your mind to move past it—and I realize that might sound confusing. So, going back to my previous examples, if it turned out that there *had* been some sort of dramatic mallowmelt incident between you two, you both would likely decide upon further reflection that you'd rather eat other desserts around each other than dig any deeper into it. And by making that conscious choice to let the subject go, the barrier would be lifted even without any sort of uncomfortable discussion."

"Okay, but . . . what if Fitz decides he doesn't want to let something go?" Sophie asked. "Would that mean I'd *have* to tell him?"

"Yes and no. You'll have to tell him the truth—but truth can be as simple as saying, 'I can't talk about that right now.' Then it would be up to Fitz to respect your privacy."

"So why can't he just respect my privacy now, without having to go through all of that?" Sophie had to ask.

"Because the goal is to achieve a deeper understanding of each other—which is far more elusive than simple acceptance. Fitz can *accept* that you prefer to keep something secret, without *understanding* how-important that secret is to you—and that won't create the level of trust required for a Cognate. So working through this process and allowing him to feel the intensity of your reactions will help him understand you on a whole other level. And it will be the same for you. That's why I'm imploring you to at least give it a chance—but of course the ultimate decision is yours."

More endless silence followed as Sophie imagined all the ways this could get *very* ugly very fast.

"Before you decide, I'm curious," Tiergan said, holding up the fluffy gadget again. "I'd love to see what your reading is, now that you two have cleared the air at least a little."

"Totally up to you," Fitz told her.

Sophie fought the urge to tug on her eyelashes as she nodded and opened her mind to his.

The second she did, his thoughts flooded her head.

Before we do this, he transmitted, *I just want to say that I'm sorry for what I said yesterday. I don't think you're making mistakes. I just . . . don't want anyone else to get hurt—*

Neither do I, Sophie interrupted.

His eyes locked with hers. *I know. And I'm sorry for making you think I doubted you. I don't. Not even a little. I know you're trying your hardest and that there are a ton of things you can't control. And I'm with you—even for the scary decisions. And I'm not just saying that because I want to stay Cognates. I'm saying it because . . . I care about you. I'll always care about you, Sophie. And . . . I hope you know I don't just mean that as a friend. It's okay if that's all you're ready for right now. But I just . . . wanted to be clear, so there's no more confusion on where I stand, okay?*

Her foolish, reckless heart switched into flutter mode after all of that—even as her brain tried to scream reminders of how hard dating Fitz had been.

"Okay," Tiergan said, holding the sensor evenly between them. "Ready whenever you are."

Sophie forced herself to focus on the task, holding Fitz's stare as they concentrated on the sensor and sent a blast that felt more like a full lightning storm than a couple of bolts.

Tiergan whistled as he showed them the number.

634.

"Still a long way from your full potential," he said. "But it's quite remarkable that you've made that much progress without even completing the Inquisition."

"Does that mean we don't have to do it?" Sophie had to ask.

Tiergan smiled. "Sadly no. But I hope it reassures you that it *will* be worth it. I have no doubt that if you stick with this, you two will do absolutely incredible things."

Incredible things.

Sophie sure hoped that was true—because she had a feeling this was going to be a whole new level of miserable.

And yet, she turned to Fitz and said, "Okay, I'm in. Bring on the Cognate Inquisition."

TWENTY-NINE

ROUGH DAY?" EDALINE ASKED, frowning when she found Sophie already in bed, wrapped in her softest blankets and buried under a pile of pillows.

It was still the middle of the afternoon.

But hiding in a fluff cocoon and strangle-hugging Ella had seemed like the only reasonable way to recover from a three-hour Cognate Inquisition.

Sophie honestly wasn't sure how she'd made it through study hall.

"Have you ever had that embarrassing school nightmare?" she asked as Edaline sat on the bed beside her. "The one where you realize everyone's staring at you because you forgot to wear any clothes?"

"Can't say that I have," Edaline admitted.

"Huh. I wonder if it's a human thing." Sophie buried her face between Ella's floppy blue ears. "I kinda feel like I just lived through the real thing—though not the whole missing-clothes part, obviously. Just . . . feeling so exposed."

In fact, given the choice between "Cognate Inquisition" and "going to school in her underwear," Sophie probably would've chosen the underwear.

Edaline scooted closer, tucking Sophie's hair behind her ears. "Want to talk about it?"

"Not really."

There wasn't much to say.

She didn't have any answers.

Just questions.

And feelings.

So.

Many.

Feelings.

All squiggling and squirming inside her, like the pit of her stomach was filled with slimy larvagorns.

"All right," Edaline said slowly. "Any chance you'd be willing to at least narrow down the problem a little, so I know how much I need to worry? You don't even have to talk—just nod if

I guess right, okay?" She waited for Sophie to agree before she said, "So . . . is this a friend-drama kind of situation? Or . . . are you stressing about your grades? Or . . . are you feeling frustrated because you still haven't heard back from the Council?"

Sophie didn't nod for any of the options.

She probably should have, though, because then Edaline wouldn't have lowered her voice and asked, "Is this . . . boy-drama related?"

"It's always boy-drama related these days," Sandor grumbled.

"Hey—I thought you were supposed to stay out of this stuff because you don't want me trying to hide things from you!" Sophie snapped back.

Sandor shrugged. "If Ro were here, she'd say a whole lot worse."

She would.

But Sophie still whipped a pillow at Sandor's head.

Of course he managed to duck.

Annoying goblin reflexes.

"You're just trying to get back at me because of the whole Sandor Smoochypants thing, aren't you?" Sophie asked.

"DO NOT REPEAT THAT NAME!"

"Fine. Captain Smoochinator it is!"

"I feel like I missed something," Edaline said as Sandor ground his teeth so hard, they made a cracking sound.

"You did," Sophie told her. "Grizel kissed Sandor goodbye today as we were waiting for our turn to use the Leapmaster. So now everyone's calling him Sandor Smoochypants or Captain Smoochinator—but wait. Should it be General Smoochinator? What's your rank again?"

Edaline laughed when Sandor muttered about teenage elves being worse than mutant trolls.

"Clearly I need to have another talk with Grizel about her lack of professionalism," he added.

"Uh, you might want to be careful with how you phrase that if you want to still have a girlfriend at the end of the conversation," Edaline warned. "And if you and Grizel want to spend some time together somewhere a little less conspicuous, we can set you up a cute little date spot out in the pastures—"

"I know the perfect place!" Flori called from out in the hallway. "There's a clearing just beyond the gnomish grove where night-blooming vines have formed a special kind of canopy. The ground is also blanketed with bioluminescent toadstools, so as soon as the sun sets, it becomes incredibly romantic."

Sandor heaved a squeaky sigh. "That won't be necessary."

"You sure?" Edaline asked. "You'd score some major boyfriend points."

"I'm *positive*," Sandor assured her. "I don't have time for distractions."

Edaline shrugged. "Well, the offer stands if you change your mind—and word to the wise? I wouldn't tell Grizel she's a 'distraction.'"

"Or at least wait until I'm there so I can watch her clobber you," Sophie jumped in.

Sandor stomped toward the door. "All right, I've had enough of this. If you need me, I'll be in the hall."

"Thanks, Smoochypants!" Sophie called after him, along with a few kissing sounds.

Sandor slammed the door so hard, it rattled the windows.

Edaline grinned. "Well, I guess that's one way to get a break from your bodyguard. And now that we don't have an audience, maybe you'll finally tell me what brought on all this angst. Don't think I didn't notice how quickly you changed the subject."

Sophie pulled the blankets tighter. "It's not *angst*. Today's telepathy session was just . . . *intense*."

It didn't help that she'd had to go first in the Inquisition, since it turned out that her impenetrable blocking made it impossible for Tiergan to guide Fitz to her Core of Verity. The most Tiergan could do was show her the way through Fitz's mind, and then leave it up to her to lead Fitz down the same paths when it was his turn.

The journey was *super* disorienting.

They had to pass through Fitz's subconscious, which felt like entering some sort of bizarro world.

Up was down.

Right was left.

Shadows were light.

Windows were doors.

And everything was a blur—except the faces.

She only recognized some of them.

Friends.

Enemies.

But at the center of it all, standing high on a pedestal, was . . .

Her.

She looked powerful.

And pretty.

And totally perfect.

Exactly the way she would've wanted to be seen.

And yet, it felt kind of . . . wrong.

Kind of fake.

Kind of impossible.

And she couldn't help wondering if that was how Fitz actually saw her—or if that was just how he wanted her to be.

Or did he not even realize he thought of her that way, since she was in his subconscious?

She considered asking him about it when she reached his Core of Verity—which was a cramped, shadowy alcove with prickly edges—but she couldn't figure out how to phrase the question.

Or maybe she just didn't want to know the answer.

She still didn't want to know *anything*.

But that kind of thinking was apparently destroying their Cognate connection, so she'd forced herself to work through the Inquisition—and it was just as painful as she'd imagined.

She tried to ease her way in, starting with subjects where she could predict Fitz's reaction:

The time she let Alvar get away.

The fact that she wanted to meet with Trix.

The storehouse fire.

Unsurprisingly, all three sent a blast of scratchy heat whipping around her—like being caught in a desert sandstorm.

But the last one felt a little cooler than the other two.

Maybe it proved that Fitz had meant his apology and just needed more time to put it behind him.

Or maybe it meant he'd never *fully* get over it.

She'd have to ask him about it during the third step of the Inquisition, even though she was pretty sure she wouldn't like his answer.

She needed to trust the process.

So she kept throwing out whatever random topics she could think of that might be causing any barriers between them:

Returning to Foxfire.

Opening Kenric's cache.

Finding Elysian.

Solving any remaining mysteries about stellarlune.

His leg injury.

Biana's scars.

And Fitz's mind mostly stayed cool and calm—until she mentioned *Project Moonlark.* Then the temperature shifted.

The warmth was softer than the first surges—but it also kept building and building. Almost like Fitz was trying to keep control of his temper and losing the battle.

Which made Sophie wonder . . .

Could he be . . . jealous?

He'd kinda been the Golden Boy everyone talked about—until she came along.

Did that bother him?

It seemed like it might—especially when she decided to try tossing out the word "leader."

Then the heat bubbled over, searing her consciousness—and Sophie wanted to scream, "I DON'T EVEN WANT TO BE IN CHARGE."

She was so tired of dealing with all the drama and resentment that came with a role she'd never actually asked for—and she'd thought Fitz, of all people, would understand her struggle.

It hurt that he didn't.

And she couldn't see how talking about it later was going to make her feel any better.

But . . . Tiergan had been convinced that this was the only way to save their connection.

She had to keep going.

Which meant she couldn't leave Fitz's mind without saying the word that had changed everything between them.

The word that had torn through their fledgling relationship

like an angry gorgodon, leaving them broken and flailing in its dusty wake.

Unmatchable.

She'd braced for the blast of heat—but she still wasn't ready.

It was like drowning in boiling lava.

And all of Fitz's confessions and reassurances seemed to melt away.

This was more than a barrier.

This was a giant, insurmountable chasm.

No way around it.

No way to go back, either.

It made her want to run far, far away—or maybe collapse into a heap and cry.

But then Fitz's thoughts whispered into the darkness.

He promised they'd figure it out. Reminded her how much they'd been through. Begged her to not give up.

We're in control, he told her. *We get to choose. So let's choose* us.

She didn't know if he meant as Cognates or friends.

Or something *more.*

But in that moment, it didn't matter—because she could at least see a path forward again.

It was narrow.

And treacherous.

But it was *there.*

They just had to take it.

And she wanted to.

She didn't want this to be the end of everything.

So she slowly pulled her consciousness back and gave herself a few deep breaths to regroup before she guided Fitz through her mind to continue the Inquisition.

She had no idea what he saw in her subconscious along the way. But his mental voice sounded shaky when he reached her Core of Verity.

Do you need a break? she asked.

No, I think I'm okay, he told her. *That was just very . . . unsettling. And it showed me where I need to start. But I hope it won't be too harsh. I think I need to see how much I've hurt you over the years—and I don't know how to do that without repeating all the things I wish I never said. Will you be okay if I try that?*

Um . . . sure, Sophie told him. *I mean . . . I lived through it all once, right?*

True—though that makes me want to punch myself even more. But I'll deal with that later. Just promise me you'll let me know if it's too much, okay? I don't want this to feel like back when you were living with humans. We can stop anytime—just say the word.

Thanks. She hugged herself even tighter and took a couple of steadying breaths. *So . . . we should probably get this over with.*

He hesitated for a few seconds. Then ran through all the hurtful things he'd told her each time he'd lost his temper— and she was surprised at how perfectly he remembered what he'd said.

The harsh words definitely still stung.

But sometimes she could feel a cool, soothing rush that proved she'd forgiven him.

For the rest . . . there were burning flashes of lingering resentment.

That's what I figured, Fitz mumbled. *And . . . I'm so sorry, Sophie. I know we're not supposed to actually talk about anything until the third step—but . . . I need you to know that I WILL make all of this up to you. Please give me a chance to set it all right.*

She didn't know what to say to that.

Thankfully, he didn't seem to be expecting an answer.

Instead, his thoughts grew much quieter—more tentative—as he asked if she wished he'd never brought her to the Lost Cities, since it had caused so many pains and problems.

Of course not, she'd assured him as her mind turned cold and shivery.

She'd had no idea he still worried about that.

I mean, yeah, it'd be nice if there weren't quite so many people trying to kill me, she admitted. *But this is my home. I wouldn't want to be anywhere else.*

I wouldn't want you to be anywhere else either, he told her—and his tone made her whole face burn.

But the heat turned a lot more unpleasant when he went back to the Inquisition and brought up her biological mother.

He clearly still didn't understand why Sophie was protecting someone who signed her up for an experiment and abandoned her.

And Sophie would never be able to explain.

She also knew the only reason he cared was because he didn't want her to be unmatchable.

So the impasse between them felt even more impossible.

Fitz must've sensed that, because he pivoted to a new subject—one that Sophie definitely hadn't expected.

He asked her about Dex—or, specifically, the very awkward kiss that she and Dex had shared. And he seemed surprised by the cool breeze of her reaction—almost like he thought she might have feelings for Dex.

Sophie had wanted to laugh—but then Fitz reminded her that she'd never actually kissed *him*.

They'd come breathlessly close.

But Silveny had interrupted.

And now . . . they weren't together like that.

I don't know if I should tell you this, he thought quietly, *because I would NEVER want you to think that I'm pressuring you to do anything you don't want to do. But . . . we're supposed to be honest, right? So I have to say . . . I really want to kiss you. Not right now or anything,* he added when she sucked in a huge breath. *Just . . . when you're ready.*

Her mind somehow turned icy cold and scorching hot all at the same time—and the conflicting temperatures swirled so fast, it made her dizzy.

She could almost hear his smile when he told her, *Good to know you're not totally against the idea.*

She definitely wasn't.

In fact, a tiny—much braver—part of her wanted to grab him right then and *finally* kiss the boy she'd liked forever.

But the rest of her felt really, *really* queasy. And that seemed like something she shouldn't ignore.

After all, if kissing someone was a good idea, she probably shouldn't have to worry about vomiting on them afterward, right?

Anyway, Fitz had said, dragging her back to the moment, *it seems like we'll have a lot to talk about in the third step.*

Yeah . . . it seems like we will, Sophie mumbled, relieved that she could feel him pulling his consciousness back.

But just when she'd thought she might be free from any more stressful questions, he paused to bring up one final subject.

Keefe.

And her brain turned into a burning sun.

Fitz recoiled from the intensity of it, and she tried to come up with a joke or an excuse—anything to convince him there was a perfectly normal explanation for what they were both feeling.

But the heat had fried her brain.

She couldn't think.

Couldn't move.

She barely remembered to breathe.

And Fitz stayed equally silent.

Tiergan finally saved them, letting them know their session was ending.

But Sophie had no doubt they *would* be discussing Keefe during the third step.

She just didn't know *when.*

She asked Tiergan about the timing before she left, wondering if he'd be scheduling a meeting before their next telepathy session. But all he'd said was "You'll let me know when you're ready. Might be hours. Might be days. Might be much longer. Take your time to really think about what you need before we revisit any of this again."

So now she was stuck staring down a ticking time bomb, waiting for the explosion to happen—which was probably why she'd gotten home and crawled straight into bed.

She knew she should be using those precious non-school hours for something productive—but she couldn't stop replaying the Inquisition, trying to figure out what everything meant.

And wondering if Fitz was doing the same thing.

And worrying about what assumptions he was making—especially about Keefe.

And the whole thing was just . . .

Ridiculous.

She needed to stop.

But she didn't know how.

Her brain just kept spinning and spinning and spinning.

"Okay," she mumbled, realizing Edaline was still sitting

patiently by her side, despite how long she'd been ignoring her. She closed her eyes and sank deeper into her pillows before she said, "Maybe I *am* having some boy drama."

"Wow," Edaline breathed, "I can't believe that worked!"

Sophie frowned. "What did?"

"Well . . . I realized that getting you to open up is a lot like trying to tame a dinosaur, so I wondered what would happen if I just sat here nice and quiet and let your brain work through whatever it needed to on its own without feeling threatened or pressured—let you see that I'm not scary and not trying to trick you or trap you. I figured if *that* didn't work, I could try rewarding you with some treats. Or chasing you through the pastures."

Sophie wasn't sure she loved that comparison—but she could still feel a smile curling the edges of her lips.

Edaline grinned back. "So, will my cute little dinosaur bite my head off if I ask for a few more details? Like . . . is this drama the kind of thing where I need to go on a mama–T. rex rampage and scare some sense into a mean boy?"

Sophie laughed. "Nope. No T. rex rampages necessary. I actually think we worked everything out. Well . . . for now. It's this whole big process with all these steps, so there's still more awkwardness ahead. But supposedly once we're done, everything will be good again."

"And by 'good,' you mean . . . you and Fitz will be dating again?" Edaline asked. "Sorry, I know I just made this all very specific—and you don't have to tell me if you don't want to. But this is the kind of thing where it could be really bad if I end up jumping to the wrong conclusion, you know?"

Sophie did know.

And she appreciated how respectful Edaline was being.

So she tried to give her an honest answer.

"I have no idea what we'll be," she admitted. "Tiergan's having us do all this to save our Cognate connection. But . . . Fitz told me he still likes me, so . . . I don't know."

"Hmmm," Edaline murmured as Sophie burrowed deeper into her pillows. "Can I ask you something?"

"Only if it's not going to be super embarrassing," Sophie told her.

"Fair enough," Edaline agreed. "But let's give it a try, okay?"

Sophie made a squeaky noise that sort of sounded like agreement.

Edaline dug through the pillows until she found Sophie's hand and gave her a gentle squeeze. "I'm just wondering . . . what do *you* want? Do you *want* to date Fitz?"

Sophie glanced toward her door, wondering if she should teleport far away. Instead she asked, "Am I even allowed to date?"

Edaline nodded. "If it's what you want to do—and you think you're ready for it—of course you are. *But* . . . that didn't answer my question."

Sophie sighed.

She'd been hoping Edaline wouldn't notice that.

"Honestly?" she said, hugging Ella tighter. "I have no idea."

They were four tiny words.

But they felt *enormous*.

Fitz had been all she wanted for so long that part of her couldn't believe she wasn't twirling around her room, humming her favorite human love songs and replaying every sweet thing he'd said during the Inquisition.

But another part of her was very aware of the giant chasms that were still separating them.

And then, another tiny, extra-confusing part of her brain kept whispering, *What about Keefe?*

"Ugh," Sophie groaned, pulling the blankets up over her head. "I can't believe I'm acting like one of those annoying characters."

"What annoying characters?" Edaline asked, gently easing the blankets back down.

"The ones in the movies my human mom loves. They were always like, *Oh no—how will I ever decide between these amazingly perfect guys? Let me obsess about it endlessly and change my mind a billion times*—and meanwhile their world was on fire and they weren't doing anything about it because they were too busy thinking about their love life, and it made me want to throw stuff at the screen."

"Okay, first of all, I would like a little credit for the fact that I'm *not* going to ask any questions about this mysterious other guy it sounds like you're thinking about," Edaline told her. "I'm *dying* to. But I won't. So I deserve all the mom points ever! More importantly, though . . . none of that makes you an annoying character. You're a teenager, Sophie. You're trying to figure out who you are and what you want. And that means you're absolutely allowed to spend time obsessing about crushes if that's what's on your mind. These feelings are new and complicated and huge and intense—and you're supposed to ask questions, and try different things, and change your mind if something doesn't seem right."

Sophie shook her head. "Yeah, but I'm not *just* a teenager. I'm the moonlark. And a Regent. And the leader of Team Valiant. And a Cognate. And—"

"Hey," Edaline said, reaching for Sophie's hands again. "You're right. You are all of those things. *But.* None of them changes the fact that you're also a real person with real emotions that need to be acknowledged. Sometimes I worry that you put so much pressure on yourself to be this great hero—"

"But that's literally what I was *made* for!" Sophie reminded her. "Everyone's counting on me to stop the Neverseen—and every second I waste could lead to mistakes. And mistakes could get someone killed!"

"Whoa," Edaline said, pulling Sophie out of her fluff cocoon and into a tight hug. "That's a heavy burden you're carrying, sweetheart—and it's not fair. Our world has been broken for thousands of years. It's *not* your responsibility to fix everything.

The Black Swan didn't make a robot. They made a brilliant, beautiful, kind, caring, wonderful person. So give yourself a chance to just be you. The funny thing is, I bet you'll find that having more freedom makes you a better moonlark. And a better leader. And a better Regent. And a better Cognate. And—"

"Okay, I get it," Sophie jumped in.

"Do you, though?" Edaline asked, leaning back to study her. "I know you *think* you do. But it doesn't really sound like it." She reached up and smoothed the worry crinkle between Sophie's eyebrows. "In fact, let's try something. I want you to repeat after me." She cleared her throat. *"I am a person."*

"You're serious?" Sophie asked.

"I definitely am."

Sophie stared Edaline down, waiting for her to blink. When Edaline didn't, Sophie said, "Fine. *I am a person.*"

"Good. Now say: *I'm allowed to take time for myself.*"

Sophie sighed louder. "This is pointless."

"Humor me," Edaline insisted. "Say it: *I'm allowed to take time for myself.*"

"Ugh, *I'm allowed to take time for myself.*"

"Excellent. And now I want to hear you say: *It's okay if I don't know what I want or don't have everything figured out.*"

That one felt much scarier for some reason.

But Edaline was waiting, so Sophie cleared her throat and said, *"It's okay if I don't know what I want or don't have everything figured out."*

Edaline smiled. "Last one—I promise. And this one's really important. I want to hear you say: *I am special and amazing, and I deserve to be with people who see that and want me to be happy.*"

The creatures in Sophie's stomach started squirming a whole lot faster. "What are you trying to say?"

"No agenda, I promise," Edaline assured her. "I just know that sometimes you don't see how incredible you are—and I would never want that to influence your decisions. So please, Sophie, say it—and try to mean it."

She tightened her grip on Sophie's shoulders and gave her a gentle shake until Sophie mumbled, *"I am special and amazing, and I deserve to be with people who see that and want me to be happy."*

"Thank you," Edaline whispered, pulling her into another hug. "Now promise me you'll work on believing it."

"I promise."

"Good. And I know I'm pushing my luck, but I want you to promise me one other thing too." She pressed Sophie's hand against Sophie's own heart. "Listen to this, okay? And be really honest with yourself—without worrying about hurting feelings or losing friendships or what anyone else is going to think. And that includes me and Grady. We love you and support you no matter what."

"We do," Grady agreed from the doorway.

Sophie sat up taller, wondering how long he'd been standing there.

She hadn't heard anyone open the door.

Thankfully, it must not have been very long, since his next question was "So, uh, what exactly are we supporting?"

"Nothing specific," Edaline told him. "Sophie's still figuring it all out. And she's allowed to take as little or as much time as she needs and let us know whenever she's ready— isn't that right?"

Grady groaned. "Why does that sound ominous?"

"Don't worry, you'll be fine," Edaline assured him. "And so will you," she told Sophie. "Just remember, let this guide you." She pressed Sophie's hand against her heart again. "And now I'll stop talking your ear off and let you get back to your pillow cocoon."

"Actually . . . I think it might be time to switch to a Wynn-and-Luna snugglefest," Sophie decided, dragging herself out of bed.

She couldn't sit still anymore.

She had too much twitchy energy.

Plus, it was hard to stress about anything when she was being nuzzled by two tiny alicorns.

But as soon as Wynn and Luna galloped over to greet her, she could hear that they were still faithfully transmitting, *KEEFE! KEEFE! KEEFE! KEEFE! KEEFE! KEEFE!*

And Keefe was clearly still ignoring them.

She knew that was smarter and safer for him—and she was *really* glad she had more time to try to make sense of everything.

But . . . her heart still felt like it sank into the pit of her stomach and got tangled up with all the squirmy things.

And Edaline's advice started echoing around her head.

So she pressed her hand to her chest and sent a transmission of her own, even though she knew Keefe wouldn't hear it.

She just . . . needed to say it.

Even if it was just to the endless void.

I miss you. It's better when you're around.

THIRTY

WHAT'S GOING ON?" SOPHIE asked, gasping for breath as she burst through the door to Magnate Leto's office and stumbled into the triangle-shaped room.

She'd sprinted up all the stairs to reach the apex of Foxfire's glass pyramid as fast as her legs could carry her.

Even Sandor looked winded and sweaty from trying to keep up.

"Did the Neverseen attack again?" she asked, squinting through the windowed walls, half expecting to see smoke and rubble where the elite towers usually stood. Thankfully, the twisted gold and silver buildings still gleamed in the afternoon sunlight—and the rest of the campus looked as colorful and shimmery as ever. So either the attack had happened elsewhere, or she'd asked the wrong question. "Did Cadfael make a move against King Dimitar? Or have you heard from the Council? Or—"

"Why don't you rest for a moment?" Magnate Leto interrupted, gesturing to the empty armchair across from him. When she hesitated, he leaned forward, resting his arms on his desk and studying her with his piercing blue eyes—the only feature that didn't drastically change throughout his various disguises. "You can relax, Miss Foster. Nothing has happened."

"Nothing?" Sophie repeated, collapsing onto the stiff cushions. "Then . . . why did you leave me this note?"

She unclenched her fist and uncurled the small square of paper she'd found waiting in her locker after she'd finished her morning session:

> *I'm assuming you would like an update.*
> *So meet me in my office during lunch—*
> *and don't be late.*

Magnate Leto patted the sides of his heavily gelled black hair. "Hmmm. I suppose I can see how my wording may have implied more urgency than I intended. That's always the risk when shaping a message around a rhyme—but I know that rhyming notes are your preference. What I meant was that we've reached the end of the first week of school, so I figured you'd be eager to check in—that way you can decide the best use for your weekend. And I thought it would be better to call the meeting myself, rather than risk finding more demands scrawled across my office door. In fact, I figured we could make this our weekly tradition. That way you'll know you're staying fully up-to-date and can continue with your studies each week, confident that everything is under control. How does that sound?"

"I . . . don't know," Sophie mumbled, still trying to process the fact that he'd called her there for basically no reason—and that a whole week of school had somehow flown by. She'd been so busy trying to pretend that everything was normal around Fitz—while desperately hoping he'd either forget about the third step of the Inquisition or decide they didn't need it—that the days had all squished together. "You really don't have any news?"

"I didn't say that," Magnate Leto corrected. "But it's clearly not the kind of update you came here expecting. We're still in a holding pattern on most fronts—"

"Which fronts?" Sophie cut in, determined to drag as much information out of him as she could. "Have you heard from Tinker? Has she figured out what happened in Brumevale yet? And have you found the person who leaked Brumevale's location? What about the Council? Are they close to a decision on the meeting with Trix? Did you talk to them about opening their caches to help us find Elysian? And have you heard anything from King Dimitar? Or—"

"Okay," Magnate Leto said, reaching up to massage his temples. "Clearly I should've anticipated your exuberance. And since I'd like you to still have time to eat lunch before your next session, how about I take over? To answer your *many* questions, yes, I'm in regular contact with Tinker. She found several unique shards of crystal mixed within the rubble of Brumevale, and she suspects they were part of the power source for whatever explosive device was triggered. But she's still in the process of analyzing them to determine precisely what they are and how they worked—and she appreciates Mr. Dizznee's offers of assistance, but at the moment, there's little he can do. If that changes, she'll let him know. As far as the leak, as I said before, that's a situation that requires subtlety and patience. I *am* working on it. But I can't reveal anything beyond that without creating unnecessary complications. And the Council haven't given me any indication that they're ready to make a decision. For the record, I'm still hoping they'll deny the meeting, but it's not up to me. I also haven't requested access to their caches, because I know what they'll say."

"Not if you make a strong enough case," Sophie argued.

"I assure you, Miss Foster, there is no case strong enough to convince the Councillors to provide access to several millennia's worth of highly classified secrets to a somewhat impulsive teenager. Nor do I think they should. The mental toll alone would be—"

"I can handle it," Sophie insisted.

"I highly doubt that. And even if you could, you're not familiar enough with the intricate history of our world for most of the information to make any sense. Perhaps with more study—"

"Is *that* what this is about?" Sophie interrupted. "You want me to be a good little prodigy and focus on my sessions? Because I've already had elvin history this week, and the whole lecture sounded like a story the Council came up with to make themselves the heroes. We're studying Atlantis, and my Mentor didn't even acknowledge the role Vespera's experiments played in the human uprising—"

"That information is still not common knowledge," Magnate Leto reminded her. "Nor should it be, given the fragile state of our society. We need to foster confidence in our leaders."

"By pretending like all the bad stuff they did never happened?" Sophie shook her head. "That's just as pointless as burying secrets in caches! We need to start digging this stuff up and calling it out so we can deal with it—before the Neverseen use it against us."

"Then it may comfort you to know that Councillor Oralie has raised several issues with the cache system," Magnate Leto informed her. "I'm not sure what alternatives she suggested, but she told me the Council is giving it serious consideration. And she's also been working to locate Elysian—or whatever place Kenric brought her to in that memory. Right now, her primary focus seems to be searching for the crystal Kenric used, in case he didn't destroy it. She actually thought she'd found it among Kenric's remaining belongings—but that turned out to be a crystal leading to Hushwood. The good news is, Kenric must've planned to bring her there someday, because he programmed the door to respond to her DNA."

"Or he assumed she'd find Hushwood if anything happened to him," Sophie mumbled.

"Also possible—though I'm sure Oralie prefers my explanation. Either way, she's now searching Hushwood in the hope that Kenric hid the crystal there—or left more details about the map. And it's a *lot* to sort through, so she let me know that she would be grateful for some help if you or your friends felt so inclined."

"What about *our* search?" Sophie asked, definitely not in the mood to spend a bunch of time with Councillor Oralie. "What are *we* doing to find Elysian?"

"Nothing," he admitted. "I realize you disagree with that decision—and you're welcome to make your own plans with your friends. But I've lost far too many years searching for rivers that do not exist. I'm not willing to lose any more—particularly when there are other projects that need my attention."

"Like what?" Sophie demanded. "Reviewing detention reports? Arranging parent-Mentor conferences? Writing more speeches to give during morning orientation?"

"You say that with such disdain," he noted. "And yet, the morale in our world has drastically improved since Foxfire reopened. The longer sessions are also allowing for much deeper insight into each subject."

"Maybe they are—but I'm pretty sure everyone hates the longer sessions," Sophie warned him. "Even most of the Mentors. If you don't believe me, I have linguistics next. You're welcome to join me for three hours of listening to Lady Cadence grumble about how she'd rather be back in Ravagog working on her research instead of mentoring a Polyglot in languages I'm already fluent in."

"That does sound far from ideal," Magnate Leto admitted. "Thankfully, I've asked *Master* Cadence—remember, her title changed when she took over my old position as Beacon in the Silver Tower—to prepare some vital lessons for you on the language of interspeciesial politics. There are many nuances to political discourse that even a Polyglot cannot instinctively understand. And given the Neverseen's focus on disrupting interspeciesial relations, it seems prudent for you to improve your ability to translate the deeper meaning behind these conversations."

"Greeeeeeeaaaaaaaaat," Sophie grumbled. "Sounds even worse than the three hours I just spent learning to identify different rare seeds."

Though she honestly felt a little bad for complaining about her agriculture session. Her gnomish Mentor had been

488 STELLARLUNE

adorably enthusiastic about the topic, sharing stories about the seeds as if they were his children—and he got so excited when Sophie responded with questions. He didn't even mind when she strayed off topic and asked about Noxflares—and he actually knew what they were.

Apparently, Noxflares were an "elvin plant," hybridized long ago by the Ancient Councillors.

For a moment Sophie thought that proved the blossoms actually *were* important—but when she voiced that theory, her Mentor . . . laughed.

When he finally stopped chuckling, he explained that the Ancient Councillors believed they should be "masters of all in order to rule all"—so they spent a great deal of time trying to do things that were far better suited for other intelligent species. They created their own microbiology experiments like the ogres, tried building tunnels like the dwarves, smelted gold like the goblins, shifted the tides like the trolls, and designed plants like the gnomes. But most of their efforts were such obvious failures that they finally admitted that certain skills were better left to other species. Noxflares were a part of that, and her Mentor assured her that every gnome who's ever tended to the blossoms would agree that they're unnecessarily temperamental and predictably grumpy—whatever that meant.

And Sophie definitely wasn't surprised that the Noxflares were nothing more than weird flowers.

But she still felt like screaming into a pillow.

Now she had even more proof that they truly didn't have any valuable leads at the moment.

"I understand your frustration, Miss Foster," Magnate Leto said, watching her tug out an itchy eyelash. "It's so hard to see the purpose of each individual piece when the larger picture remains obscured. But rest assured that everything you're doing—including your education and training—will come together in a significant way. In the meantime, I hope meeting like this at least helps assure you that we *are* making progress."

"Are we?" Sophie asked. "Name one thing that's actually been accomplished—besides Tinker finding a few shards of crystal at Brumevale and some people being happy we're back at Foxfire."

"All right." He propped his feet up on his desk. "I've gotten several reports that security has vastly increased in Ravagog. So clearly King Dimitar took Ro's warning far more seriously than Ro expected him to. Have you heard from her at all?"

Sophie shook her head, fighting the urge to fidget with the hidden straps of her holster. She still wasn't carrying Hope to Foxfire. But she'd tucked the packet of Linquillosa inside, and there was something soothing about knowing it was with her—as if being prepared somehow increased the chance that Keefe might turn up and give her a reason to use it.

"Is that all?" she asked, forcing herself to stay focused. "Crystal shards, increased morale, Oralie searching a dusty library, and reports of extra guards in Ravagog—is that really everything we have to show for an entire *week*?"

"That's actually a lot," Magnate Leto insisted. "Especially when you add in your Cognate Inquisition."

Sophie slouched in her chair. "Tiergan told you about that?"

"Of course he did. I've been wondering if an Inquisition would be necessary for quite some time. And I hope you realize how truly valuable the process is. I've known one other pair of Cognates who saved their connection that way— Councillor Emery and his former partner—"

"Former?" Sophie interrupted. "Kinda sounds like it didn't help."

"It absolutely did. Councillors simply aren't able to have Cognates. They must keep too many secrets. Plus, the Cognate connection creates a bond that is similar in many ways to a marriage. So Emery had to end the partnership after he was elected to ensure he would have no biases. But before that, I remember vividly how the Inquisition transformed his power. Emery still laments the feats he can no longer accomplish. And I have no doubt that you and young Mr. Vacker will be virtually unstoppable once you finish working your way through the Inquisition. So I'm proud of you for giving it a chance. I know it isn't easy."

"It's not," Sophie agreed, wishing her brain hadn't grabbed on to the word "marriage."

She'd never thought of Cognates that way, but . . .

It did kind of fit.

And now she *really* wasn't sure how she was going to talk to Fitz about any of the awkward subjects they still needed to discuss.

Especially Keefe . . .

"I don't have to use my telepathy to know there's a great deal of turbulence going on in your head right now," Magnate Leto told her. "And I don't need to know the specifics. But I hope you'll try to put the worries aside and focus on our most important victories this week: No one was hurt, and we're restoring a bit of peace and normalcy to our world."

"Yeah, but none of that will last if we don't stop the Neverseen," Sophie reminded him.

"It won't," he agreed. "But small steps add up to something significant. Hopefully you'll be able to see that throughout the course of these lunch meetings. And speaking of lunch, you should probably head to the cafeteria. There's just enough time for you to grab something quick to eat on the way to your session—and you're going to need the sustenance to give Master Cadence your full attention. I'm looking forward to hearing what you think of her lecture during our check-in next week. I'll leave another note in your locker when it's time."

Sophie's legs shook as she stood, and she wasn't sure if it was leftover fatigue from her sprint to Magnate Leto's office, or pent-up frustration over how little was getting done.

Either way, she had no choice except to keep walking.

She swung by the cafeteria and grabbed a container of popcorn-shaped snacks—which tasted like tiny bites of peach cobbler—to help keep her awake for the boring lecture ahead.

But Magnate Leto was right that the tone was notably different from how her linguistics session usually went. Master Cadence had chosen to focus on the shifts rippling through each of the intelligent species now that King Enki had fallen and Queen Nubiti had taken over, pointing out subtle ways that the change in leadership stretched far beyond the dwarven world. According to the "language of politics"—as Master Cadence called it—the overthrow sent a clear message to all the other species that *allying with the Neverseen will cost you your kingdom.* She even seemed somewhat hopeful that the loss would motivate the other leaders to solidify their alliances with both the Council and the Black Swan.

And yet, a few days later, Sophie found a much hastier note waiting for her in her locker:

Meet me in my office immediately.

Magnate Leto wasn't alone when she burst through the door, sweaty and out of breath from sprinting even faster.

Lord Cassius stood by the farthest wall of windows, watching the tiny prodigies far below as they made their way to the cafeteria.

"Welcome back, Miss Foster," Magnate Leto murmured.

He looked far less put-together than usual, with weird creases in his hair, as if he'd been trying to drag his fingers through the crispy gelled strands.

"What happened?" Sophie asked, barely able to choke out the words with the way her heart was wedged deep in her throat. "Is Keefe . . . ?"

"Young Mr. Sencen is fine," Magnate Leto assured her. "Or, I assume he is. Technically none of us have heard from him, but it's likely a no-news-is-good-news scenario. And that's not why I summoned you. I realize our next check-in wasn't supposed to be until the end of this week. But I've just learned of a significant development and wanted to keep you informed." He glanced at Lord Cassius before he told her, "Empress Pernille announced this morning that she's canceling all future treaty negotiations and has no interest in meeting with the Council— or anyone else in the Lost Cities—from this point forward."

Sandor breathed a word that Sophie had never heard him say before.

"Why would she do that?" Sophie asked.

"It could be a power play," Lord Cassius said as he slowly turned away from the windows. "Empress Pernille knows we want to get the treaty settled and could be hoping that such bold, public defiance will force us to relinquish certain demands in order to reestablish negotiations."

"*Or* it could mean she's found a different ally," Sandor argued.

Sophie felt all the blood drain from her face. "The Neverseen?"

"It's possible," Magnate Leto admitted.

Sandor gripped his sword so hard, his knuckles turned pale. "I'll have to inform my queen."

Magnate Leto nodded. "I suspect she's already heard. But . . . that's why I wanted you to know as soon as possible. And you as well, Miss Foster. Obviously we'll do everything in our power to manage the situation—and there's a good chance Lord Cassius is right and this is simply a negotiating ploy. But if it's not . . . then we all need to prepare ourselves. This could be the first step toward war."

THIRTY-ONE

THAT'S IT? THAT'S ALL MAGNATE LETO said?" Biana asked, glancing over her shoulder at the crowded cafeteria. She leaned in, lowering her voice to barely a whisper before she added, "Just 'FYI, we might be heading to war with the trolls—now go have a good lunch'?"

"Pretty much." Sophie stared at the pastries she'd grabbed before joining her friends at their table—big chocolate-covered puffs that had seemed like the perfect comfort food to stress-eat when she'd grabbed them.

But she couldn't even think about eating.

Not when her mind kept picturing an army of trolls surrounding each of the Lost Cities.

Weapons shining.

Muscles flexing.

Feet stomping as they waited for the order to attack.

"Okay," Marella said, leaning in even closer. "But . . . can there even *be* a war? It's not like we have an army."

"You don't," Sandor agreed. He'd stayed right by Sophie's side—but his voice sounded distant when he added, "My people would have to defend you."

Sophie shivered.

So did the rest of her friends.

"Don't look so scared," Grizel assured them, tossing her long ponytail. "We'd win. Our training and weapons are far beyond anything the trolls could muster. Everyone knows that."

"Yeah, but . . . there would still be casualties," Sophie mumbled, trying not to picture all the gilded, aurified bodies that would be added to Gildingham's Hall of Heroes.

"The trolls would lose far more," Lovise promised.

Dex sighed. "And that's why none of this makes any sense. Why would the trolls want to lose a ton of soldiers in battle when they could just sign a scroll and keep everyone safe?"

"Because signing that scroll means giving up power," Tam reminded him.

"Or their soldiers are expendable." Biana glanced over her shoulder again before she whispered, "What if their army's a bunch of those mutant trolls like we found in the hive?"

Sophie had been wondering the same thing.

She shoved her lunch away—not even able to *smell* food anymore.

"But wouldn't they need another total lunar eclipse to hatch any more of those beasts?" Marella asked.

"Who knows?" Tam muttered. "Maybe they already hatched a bunch in a different hive that we didn't know about."

"The Council has been worried about that," Sophie mumbled. "So has Lord Cassius."

Linh reached across the table and took her brother's hand.

Apparently the threat of a deadly troll attack was what she'd needed to finally make peace.

"Ugh, you're all so dramatic," Stina said, not bothering to lower her voice. "I'm sure this is all just a bargaining tactic. It's like when I threatened to leave the unicorn pens open if my mom tried to make me clean them. We both knew I'd never actually do it. I just hated scooping unicorn poop and wanted the gnomes to do it instead—and I thought if I made a big enough threat, she'd cave."

"Did it work?" Maruca asked.

"Nope. She grounded me for a week—*and* made me clean the stalls every night for the next month. I bet it'll be the same thing with the trolls. They're just . . . throwing a tantrum. It'll backfire. It has to. Otherwise we wouldn't have had *thousands of years* of peace."

"Is this peace?" Woltzer asked, crossing his arms. "Or forced submission?"

"Either way," Sandor jumped in, glaring at Woltzer until he shrank back a step, "the threat should not be taken lightly."

"And it won't be," Fitz assured everyone. "I'm sure the Council is already on it—and yeah, I know, they're not always the greatest at handling things. But treaty negotiation is something the Councillors are actually pretty good at."

Tam tightened his grip on Linh's hand. "That won't matter if the Neverseen already made the trolls a better offer."

Fitz shook his head. "If that's really what happened, then all the Council will have to do is remind Empress Pernille that the Neverseen made that same offer to King Dimitar, and he ended up with half of Ravagog destroyed."

"And King Enki is no longer king because of his bargain with the Neverseen," Sophie added.

"Exactly." Fitz flashed one of his perfect smiles, and for a moment it looked like he might even reach for her hand—but he stopped himself at the last second. "The most important thing to remember is that we don't know if any of this is true. It could be a big misunderstanding. So let's try not to overreact, okay?"

"We cannot ignore this!" Sandor argued. "You elves have grown far too complacent and do not understand the realities of war—probably because you won't have to fight it. My people *will*, and we need time to prepare."

"How do you prepare for something like this?" Sophie wondered, hoping it wouldn't involve trenches and barbed wire and stockpiles of weapons like in human wars.

"Lots of ways—but the most vital step will be creating a solid battle plan," Sandor told her. "Which means we need concrete information. A clear sense of the enemy's plans, goals, and motivations."

"Great. So . . . the same things we've been trying to figure out for how many years now?" Stina asked, glancing at Sophie. "I don't suppose our fearless moonlark has any brilliant ideas for how we're going to start getting some actual answers."

"Not yet," Sophie admitted.

No one else had any suggestions either.

And the fear and frustration felt like a thick, itchy blanket depriving her of air.

Sophie knew she needed to break the miserable silence. But she had no idea how—until Jensi saved her.

"Uh . . . is this a bad time to ask if I can sit here?" he said as he came up behind her.

"Of course not! Take a seat!" Sophie scooted over to make room.

But Jensi hesitated, studying everyone's expressions. "You sure? I feel like I interrupted some sort of 'How are we going to save the world *this* time?' conversation."

"You did," Dex confessed. "But we're not really getting any-where."

"Yeah—our fearless leader just admitted she doesn't have any plans," Stina added. "Inspiring, isn't it?"

"Actually, it *is*," Jensi said, setting down his tray. "I'm sure it wasn't easy to admit that—but it's way better than pretending she knows everything like *some* people."

Stina rolled her eyes. "Great. Another member of the Foster Fan Club."

"Uh, not sure what *that's* supposed to mean," Jensi snapped as he plopped down next to Sophie, "but if you're jealous because people like her more than they like you, you should try being nicer."

Dex cracked up. "I'm so glad Jensi's sitting with us again."

"Me too!" Biana agreed.

Jensi's cheeks turned red. "Really?"

"Of course," Dex and Biana both told him—and everyone else nodded like they agreed.

Except Stina. "Aren't we talking about classified things?"

"No one told me it was," Sophie argued. But she turned to Jensi just in case. "Maybe don't mention anything you hear, to be extra safe?"

"Of course." Jensi placed his hand over his heart. "I know I talk a lot—and that makes people think I must be a huge blabbermouth. But I swear, I'm actually supergood at keeping secrets. It's one of those things that's hard to prove because you can't be like, 'Of course I can keep secrets—I never told anyone about *this*!' without totally ruining your point—but I mean it. I won't tell anybody. And I promise I won't interrupt with a ton of annoying questions either—or expect you to waste all kinds of time catching me up on stuff. I'm okay with being confused. I can usually figure it out on my own later if I need to."

"What if I mention Pyrokinetic stuff?" Marella asked. "Will that weird you out? Because I was planning to tell everyone about something that happened during my last training session, but I've found that even though everyone loves to gossip about my ability behind my back, some people get bothered when they actually hear me talk about it. It's like they want me to pretend it's this shameful thing."

"Ugh, people can be the worst," Jensi grumbled.

"They can be." Marella tossed her gilded hair. "So does that mean it won't make you twitchy if I talk about fire?"

"Nope! I think your ability is awesome. Seriously! I'm super jealous—and not just because I still haven't manifested."

He paused for a second, like he was waiting to see if anyone would freak out.

No one blinked—not even Stina.

Jensi blew out a relieved breath. "I had no idea the Council was letting you train in pyrokinesis," he told Marella. "Is it cool? I bet it's cool."

Marella grinned. "It can be a little intense—mostly because I'm stuck training with Fintan at his freezing prison. But there aren't a lot of Mentor options, you know?"

"Yeah, that does make it tough," Jensi agreed. "So how does that work—do they let Fintan out of his cell?"

Marella snorted. "Uh, no. He'd totally try to murder

everybody. The guy is still super unstable. But he thinks I have a chance to prove that Pyrokinetics shouldn't have to hide who they are, so we've worked out a system. Usually he tells me about some cool fire trick he misses being able to do and gives me a few instructions for how to pull it off. And then I go somewhere safe and give it a try. Linh sometimes comes with me for that part, since it's kinda important to have a handy water supply in case I lose control. And occasionally Maruca helps too, since she can either shield us or contain the fire in a force field. And then I go back and tell Fintan how it went, and he gives me some pointers on what I did right or wrong. *Aaaaaaaaaaaand* . . . then I go home, and the Council has one of their Emissaries stop by to make sure I'm not suddenly running around screaming, 'I need to burn down the world!'"

"Is it wrong that I kinda hope you do that sometimes?" Jensi asked. "Just to freak them out?"

"Oh, I'm tempted, trust me," Marella assured him. "But . . . I have to be careful about how much I mess with them. I don't think I'd last very long if the Council decided to forbid me from training and I had to try to ignore the flames calling to me." Goose bumps streaked across her arms and she shuddered. "*Anyway*, I just realized I still haven't shared my news! I was waiting for Sophie to get here so I wouldn't have to repeat it—but then she dropped the troll bomb and totally killed the mood. *But* . . ." She pounded on the table for a drumroll, waiting until she had everyone's attention before she told them, "I got Fintan to agree to show me one of the memories in his cache!"

"Seriously?" Sophie realized she should lower her voice, since a lot of people were suddenly staring at her. "Does that mean the Noxflares worked?"

Marella nodded. "You were right, he's totally obsessed with those ugly flowers. At first he tried to pretend he was all confused when I brought them up, like, *What are Noxflares and why would I care about them?* But then I told him I went to his old house and picked a few, and he was like, *You must let me see them.* So I was like, *I will—but you have to open your cache,* and then he got really quiet and I thought maybe I'd pushed too hard, but after a couple of minutes he told me I had a deal— but only for *one* memory because I was only giving him one thing he wanted. I tried to talk him into trading nine Noxflares for all nine of the memories—but he wasn't impressed. And then he told me the offer expired in ten seconds and started counting down, so I figured you'd want me to jump on that."

"Good call," Sophie told her.

"Did he already give you the memory?" Fitz asked.

"Yep. It took a little while because he was like, *Give me the cache,* and I was like, *Uh, how do I know you're not going to destroy it or try to hold it for ransom or something?* And he kept saying, *You'll just have to trust me,* and I realized there wasn't a whole lot I could do about that, so . . . I handed over the cache. Then he did some weird stuff to it and—"

"Do you remember what it was?" Dex asked.

"Not really. But it was all about his DNA—and these little codes he tapped in. So I doubt we'd ever be able to open the cache without him. But . . . I don't know if that matters because I gotta say, the memory he showed me? *Not* impressive. It was just this tiny projection of him standing in a huge, empty field, burning Noxflares. He started with white flames, and then added purple. Then yellow. And then he started mumbling about how something was missing."

Sophie and Dex shared a look.

"What?" Fitz asked.

"Fintan said that same thing in the memory we saw in Kenric's cache," Dex told him. "He set the Noxflares on fire, and then he kept mumbling 'something's missing' over and over and over."

"Was that the whole memory?" Sophie asked Marella. "Fintan didn't do anything else?"

"He added some pink flames to the Noxflares—and that made them spray sparks for a few seconds, which did look pretty cool. It reminded me of the way the sky looks during the Celestial Festival—and I thought for sure the whole field was going to burst into flames. But only the Noxflares burned. And I wondered if maybe the sparks meant he'd figured out what was missing. But then he stared up at the stars and said 'something's missing' again. And then the memory faded out."

"Did Fintan say anything after the memory ended?" Biana asked.

"Nope. He just stood there staring at the cache with the same glazed look he always gets whenever he thinks about fire. And when I asked him if he ever figured out what was missing, he told me, *Noxflares are full of possibility. But they need to burn.* Which, you know, not super helpful, since the whole memory was about burning Noxflares. And when I started to ask another question, he told me, *Context was not part of our bargain.* So I have no idea why a memory like that would need to be erased from his mind and stored as a Forgotten Secret."

"Me neither," Sophie admitted. "But . . . maybe it's like the stuff in Kenric's cache, and it seems pointless because we haven't connected it to anything yet—like one of the other memories in the cache."

"*Or,*" Stina jumped in, "the memory wasn't even a Forgotten Secret at all. Fintan still had his cache with him after he left the Council, right?"

Sophie nodded. "Why?"

"Because he could've added that memory later," Stina reminded her. "And maybe he erased it because pyrokinesis had been banned and he didn't want anyone to know he was still setting things on fire—and now he's showing it to us just to waste our time."

"Could be," Marella said. "He did smirk when he gave the cache back to me."

"Huh," Jensi mumbled before taking a huge bite of his lunch—which looked like bright blue celery.

"What?" Stina asked.

Jensi struggled to chew faster, crunching super loud. "Sorry. I think I'm just not used to this stuff like all of you are. It sounds like you think the memory means nothing—but it seems kinda important to me. I've never seen different colors of flames get layered like that before, or shoot sparks like a light show—especially without catching anything else on fire. Have you?"

"Not that exact combination," Marella told him. "But fire can do way more than people realize. The Council just hasn't let anyone control it for so long that everyone's forgotten how versatile it is."

"I guess that's true," Jensi said. "Like I said—you're all way better at this stuff than I am. I just thought it was weird that Fintan was so excited to see a flower, and then it seemed like he had this whole fancy method for burning them—so I wondered if he's planning to do something with it, you know?"

Maruca sucked in a breath. "Could he use the Noxflare to escape?"

Marella shook her head. "I had Mr. Forkle *and* the guards check everything before I gave it to Fintan, to make sure the Noxflare didn't have any stored-up heat—or anything else he could use against us. Everyone said it was safe, but the guards wanted to be extra careful, so they froze the Noxflare into a big cube of ice, and *that's* what I gave him—and then he wasn't allowed to have the cube in his cell. It had to be just outside the walls. And Fintan was fine with all of that. He just wanted to stare at it—and you'd think if he were planning to use it for something, he would've fought that."

"True," Jensi told her. "Makes sense—I figured I was probably wrong."

"You might not be," Sophie said quietly. "That's why this is so hard—we get these teeny slivers of information that could be interpreted a zillion different ways. Like this—it could be like Stina said, and Fintan just didn't want anyone to know he was burning Noxflares after pyrokinesis was banned. That's kinda what happened in the memory Dex and I saw too—he set them on fire mostly to show Kenric that he wasn't going to follow the rules when he was alone. *But* it could be that the reason he said 'something's missing' in both memories is because Noxflares are important and we just don't know *why* yet. *Or* it could be that Fintan was the Councillor who created Noxflares in the first place, and that's what these memories are about. My agriculture Mentor told me the Ancient Council wanted to prove that they could do everything the other species could do, so they took on all these projects—and the Noxflares were one of them. But my Mentor said all the projects were kind of a fail. So maybe that's what's 'missing'—whatever would've made the Noxflares better—and the memory is a Forgotten Secret because the Council's embarrassed about how badly they messed the projects up. *Or* there could be a whole other reason we haven't thought of yet."

"So how do you figure out what's true?" Jensi wondered.

"Right now? Mostly trial and error," Sophie admitted. "Or the Neverseen make another move and suddenly everything makes sense, and we realize, *Yep, they beat us again!*"

"You know what I think is weird?" Dex jumped in. "The fact that Fintan gave Marella a memory about Noxflares after she gave him one of the flowers. Like . . . what are the odds that he'd randomly pick that jewel in the cache?"

"Oh, it wasn't random," Marella told him. "Fintan said he'd show me what Noxflares could do, since I brought one back into his life."

"Why are you and Dex staring at each other like that?" Fitz asked Sophie.

"That's just . . . not how caches are supposed to work," Sophie explained. "No one knows what's in them until you play the actual memories."

"So Fintan must've opened his cache already," Dex added. "He probably figured he might need to know what's in there if he was going to try to take over the world."

Sophie nodded. "But that means we *really* need to know what's in there too. I'm betting he shared what he learned with the rest of the Neverseen—and I find it hard to believe that out of *nine* memories, there's nothing important. Is there anything else we can trade with him?"

Marella sighed. "Just his freedom. I've seriously offered him everything else. The *only* thing he was remotely interested in was the Noxflare, and now we've used that up."

"So why don't you trick him into telling you?" Jensi asked, blushing again when everyone turned to look at him. "Sorry—wasn't trying to tell you what to do."

"You're fine," Marella told him. "But what do you mean?"

"Well . . ." He fidgeted with his piece of blue celery. "You're Marella Redek. You're better at getting people to tell you stuff than anyone I've ever met—that's why you always know all the good gossip. So if Fintan knows what's in the cache, why don't you do whatever you do when you want to know any other huge secret?"

Marella twisted a braid around her finger. "I mean . . . I could try. Fintan does love to talk about himself, which helps. But this is way different than getting someone to admit they have a crush, or repeat something they've heard. Plus, usually I have *some* idea of what I'm trying to find out—I've heard a rumor and I'm just trying to get it confirmed or whatever."

"We could help you try to brainstorm some questions," Dex offered, "based on the stuff we saw in Kenric's cache."

"True—but if I start getting too specific, he might catch on," Marella warned.

"Yeah, but so what?" Maruca told her. "The worst he could do is refuse to answer your questions—or tell you to leave him alone."

"Not true," Fitz argued. "He could also make up a bunch of lies to throw us off. And we can't afford to lose that kind of time."

"So I'll start going with Marella to her lessons," Stina jumped in. "I'm an Empath, remember? I'll be able to tell if he's lying."

"Will you, though?" Sophie asked. "Fintan's mind has been shattered and healed and then broken again every time he's killed someone. His thoughts are all over the place, so I'm sure his emotions are just as confusing."

"That just means his emotions will be more intense," Stina insisted. "Which makes them easier to read. And if they shift a bunch, I know how to keep up. Unicorns are seriously the moodiest creatures on the planet—and I've had tons of practice staying on top of their mood swings."

"Seems like it's worth trying," Biana said quietly. "Especially since we don't have a lot of other options."

"Will Fintan get suspicious if Stina starts going to your lessons?" Sophie asked Marella.

"I doubt it. I can just tell him the Council wants to monitor *my* emotions, to make sure I'm not turning evil. That'll get him all riled up about the unjust treatment of Pyrokinetics. Might even be a good way to get him to start talking—make him so mad at the Council that he wants to share some of their dirty little secrets to get back at them."

Jensi grinned. "And that, right there, is why she's the Gossip Master."

Marella smirked.

And that seemed to settle it.

It wasn't a perfect plan.

But at least it was *something* they could try.

And Sandor said he needed information.

"You should start by asking him about the trolls," Sophie realized. "If there's anything in his cache that could help us get the treaty talks going again, we need to know."

"It might be something the Ancient Council did to the trolls to make them hate us," Tam warned. "Like the drakostomes with the gnomes."

"Then we *definitely* need to know that," Sophie told him—and for once, no one argued.

"When's your next lesson?" Fitz asked Marella.

"Not until this weekend."

Which sounded like an eternity—and felt like one as the days crawled by.

Sandor did a lot of whispering about war strategy with the other goblins at Havenfield. And Sophie did a lot of racing to her locker, hoping to find another summons from Magnate Leto.

Finally, at the end of the week, there was a new note.

> *It's time to catch up—try not to worry.*
> *But I'm sure you'll have questions,*
> *so you might want to hurry.*

Sophie probably set a new land-speed record as she raced up the stairs.

And once again, Mr. Forkle wasn't alone.

But this time it was Councillor Bronte scowling at her as she struggled to catch her breath.

"Did the trolls . . . ?" she gasped.

"The trolls have done nothing—yet," Magnate Leto assured her.

"But they've refused to open any lines of communication," Bronte added, turning to pace. "And since we need to know what we're truly dealing with, we've decided to pursue answers another way. It wasn't a unanimous decision—"

"I should think not," Magnate Leto interrupted.

Bronte ignored him. "All of us definitely have our reservations. But extreme challenges call for extreme measures. So we're officially giving you and your friends permission to set up a meeting with Trix—and you need to make it happen as soon as possible."

THIRTY-TWO

THIS IS A TERRIBLE IDEA," SANDOR muttered.

It had to be the ten billionth time he'd repeated those words.

He'd also marched around the perimeter of their force field enough to wear a groove in the frigid soil.

"I told you we should've given the goblin some sort of silencing elixir," Glimmer said, catching the edge of her black hood before a gust of wind could knock it back and uncover her face. "Though I suppose it would've worn off by now."

"It would have," Wylie agreed. "We've been here *a while*."

"Yeah, I'll need to refresh the force field again pretty soon," Maruca added.

"Already?" Wylie studied his cousin. "That seems faster than the last time—and you're looking a little shaky. Is it draining too much energy?"

"I'm fine. Seriously. I've got this." Maruca traced her fingers over the glowing white dome, making the force field crackle and hum before it flared so bright that everyone had to squint. "See?"

She'd started out with a blue force field, but it had fizzled away after a few minutes—and when the second one did the same thing, Sandor *insisted* she switch to something more stable.

But even the white force field would start flickering after a while.

It also couldn't keep out the wind.

Maruca had tried everything she could think of to create at least a partial barricade, but the wind was just like Linh's water.

Clearly the elements were much too strong.

"How many times can you refresh that thing before you wear yourself out?" Wylie asked.

"As many as we need," Maruca assured him. "Seriously. My Mentor said my endurance is *very* impressive, and that I'm already holding out way longer than most Psionipaths at my level. Plus, I brought snacks to keep my energy up."

"Smart," Tam told her. "Wish I'd thought of that."

Sophie was pretty sure she could hear his stomach growl over the howling flurries.

"Happy to share," Maruca offered. "Sounds like you need them more than I do."

Tam shook his head. "I'm used to being hungry. I got lots of practice when Linh was banished—and while I was trapped with the Neverseen. Their food really is the worst."

"It is," Glimmer agreed. "That's why I brought these for Trix." She reached into her cloak and pulled out several blue-striped bags labeled CRUNCHTASTICS. "Thought they might be a good way to show this is a friendly visit. But he doesn't need all of them—want one, Tam?"

Tam's stomach growled even louder.

Glimmer tossed him a bag.

"Thanks," he mumbled, pouring a few Crunchtastics into his mouth. "Huh. Very . . . crunchy."

"WHAT IS HAPPENING RIGHT NOW?" Sandor yelled. "We're standing on a cliff, waiting to be attacked—and you're *snacking*?"

Tam shrugged and shook his bangs out of his eyes. "I'm hungry."

"And we're not *waiting* to be attacked," Glimmer argued. "Trix would never do that."

"But I have us covered if he does," Maruca added.

Sandor gritted his teeth and went back to muttering about terrible ideas.

Tam pointed to their shadows, which had stretched long and thin as the afternoon dragged on. "Anyone know how long we've been here?"

"I lost track after the first five hours," Sophie admitted.

She'd started out counting the seconds, trying to keep her mind focused as she stood in the center of the force field, refusing to let herself pace or fidget.

She wanted to look strong when Trix arrived.

Confident.

Like a leader.

But her feet had gone numb as the hours dragged by, and she'd finally plopped down on the cold ground and curled her knees into her chest, wishing they'd chosen a spot with something she could lean against—and that she'd been smart enough to wear her hair tied back in a ponytail.

She'd known they were headed somewhere windy—Glimmer had been adamant about that, claiming that Trix would never show himself unless they were out on an open bluff where he could approach from any direction he wanted. But Sophie had foolishly assumed the force field would provide at least some shelter. She also hadn't considered how annoying it would be to have her hair whipping against her cheeks and getting tangled in her eyelashes for so many hours.

Then again, she hadn't expected Trix to take so long to get . . . wherever they were.

Glimmer refused to share any specifics about their location, so all Sophie knew was that they were on top of a wide bluff that was part of a series of steep cliffs. But the view was *amazing*. The jagged, white-capped mountains in the distance were the perfect backdrop for the enormous glacier below, which flowed into a lake that was a stunning shade of blue.

Apparently, this was one of Trix's favorite places to go when he wanted to "recharge"—probably because the wind was so wild. Gusts battered them from all sides, and Sophie had to strain to hear anything over the relentless roar.

She pulled her cape tighter as a particularly strong blast tried to tear it off her shoulders. "Is anyone else starting to think that Trix isn't going to show?"

Glimmer groaned when everyone nodded. "Considering you all had no problem wasting an entire week fighting with me about every tiny detail of this meeting, I thought you'd be a little more patient now that we're here."

"Yeah, but you told Trix what time to meet us, right?" Wylie asked.

"Of course I did. But we got here early—and there's usually a delay with these kinds of meetups."

"Five hours is more than a *delay*," Sandor argued.

"Plus, you made us pick a date that was a whole week *after* you dropped off the note because you wanted to give Trix time to find your message and prepare," Sophie reminded her.

"Yeah, but that was still just a guess. I don't actually know how regularly he checks our drop-off spot anymore—or if he'll need to wait before he can sneak away."

"So what are we supposed to do?" Wylie asked. "Camp out here for days, hoping he'll turn up?"

"Of course not. We'll wait until it's dark, and if he still hasn't shown, we'll head home and see if he left me a note with new instructions. If not, we'll leave a note of our own and try again in a few days."

"We can't lose that much time!" Sophie argued, finally letting herself stand and pace. "We've already wasted two weeks! Plus, I doubt the Council will agree to let us do this again and—"

"Stressing isn't going to make him suddenly appear," Glimmer interrupted. "So how about you sit back down and give this a chance? I have a feeling he'll be here really soon."

"A *feeling*," Sandor muttered.

"Hey, you don't get to spend hours grumbling about how you think meeting with Trix is a terrible idea and then get mad that I can't guarantee it'll happen!" Glimmer told him. "Pick one complaint and stick with it."

Sandor gripped his sword and resumed circling the force field.

Sophie sank back to the ground, hugging herself a little tighter. "What makes you think he's going to show?"

Glimmer turned to stare at the mountains. "Maybe it's hope. Maybe it's a hunch. Or maybe it's because I planned this so perfectly, he won't be able to resist."

She'd made that same claim every time someone tried to push back on one of her demands for the meeting. And the fact that everyone eventually backed down spoke volumes about how desperate they were to make this happen.

The Council had left Glimmer in charge of pretty much everything.

She chose the day.

The time.

The place.

They even let her pick the group, and she decided on: Tam—because he was the only person she really trusted. Maruca—because she could protect them with a force field. Wylie—because the Council was counting on him to give a complete report. Sophie—because Trix would want to speak with the moonlark. And Sandor—because she knew there was no way Sophie would be allowed to go without him.

And that was it.

No Councillors.

No members of the Collective.

None of Sophie's other friends.

No exceptions.

Glimmer also insisted that none of them—except Sandor—should bring any weapons.

They had a bodyguard, a force field, and their abilities if they really needed them. Anything beyond that could make the situation escalate.

And Sophie definitely understood Glimmer's concern.

But . . . she'd still slipped Hope into her secret holster before they left.

She'd been faithfully practicing with Hope every night like Ro had shown her—and maybe the process really was forming a bond, because the added weight against her shoulders felt oddly soothing, and her fingers kept itching to reach back and grab it.

Or maybe all the waiting just made her want to stab something.

"So we'll leave after the sun sets?" Wylie said, pointing to the sky, where the sun was slowly sinking toward the mountains, painting the clouds with gold and orange. "You realize that's probably only an hour away, right?"

Glimmer nodded. "A lot can change in an hour."

It could.

And yet, several more minutes dragged by with a whole lot of nothing.

"You're sure Trix would've been able to understand your message?" Sophie had to ask.

Glimmer had refused to explain her secret code, so Sophie had no idea what the note *really* said. When she'd checked it, all she found was some weird story about two birds that flew into a storm, got separated, and were trying to find their way back to each other. But Glimmer assured her that Trix would know exactly what it meant.

She claimed she'd spelled out every detail of who would be there and what protections they'd have in place, so he'd know there was no trap waiting for him when he arrived—which made sense. But Sophie didn't see how that was possible when the message had no names or numbers in it.

"I actually wouldn't be surprised if he's already here," Glimmer said, catching her hood again before the wind could knock it back. "He's probably hiding on one of these ridges, watching to make sure there's no trick."

"THEN SHOW YOURSELF!" Sandor shouted. "STOP BEING SUCH A COWARD!"

"Super helpful," Glimmer muttered as the taunt echoed off the mountains. "You realize that treating him like the enemy is only going to make him act like one, right? We need to stick to the plan."

"What plan?" Sandor snarled. "You haven't explained anything to us."

"Uh, yes I have. You're assuming there's more to it—and there's not. Complicating things only leads to confusion or problems. So once Trix shows up, we're just going to talk. I'll tell him why I left the Neverseen—"

"Which will probably sound really weird since you're still wearing their cloak," Wylie noted.

"That's because *this*"—she gestured to the long black fabric—"is how Trix knows me. He won't recognize Rayni Aria—and he won't trust her either. He trusts Glimmer. So that's who I have to be today."

"And maybe you also don't want him knowing who you really are?" Maruca suggested.

"Why would I care? My life's already been ruined—and it's not like I have any family to protect. I just want Trix to see that I'm still the person he remembers. Still his friend, despite the group I'm now standing with. And once I explain *why* I've switched sides, and we've munched on some Crunchtastics, I'll ask him about Empress Pernille, since I know you're all super freaked out about that. Plus, if the Neverseen are teaming up with the trolls, Trix will be even more willing to help us. There's no way he'll want to work with the same creatures who crushed the life out of Umber."

"And yet, he's working with the people who ordered her to open the hive in the first place," Wylie reminded her. "And left her broken body in the rubble."

Glimmer sighed. "We've already had this fight, remember? I'm not doing it again—especially here, when we need to stay focused. Whether you like my plan or not, it's time to trust me."

"Why?" Sandor countered. "You've yet to deliver on any of your promises!"

"BECAUSE YOU HAVEN'T GIVEN ME A CHANCE!" Glimmer's shout drowned out the roaring wind. "I swear, it's like no one gets that my freedom is riding on this!"

"It is?" Tam asked.

Glimmer nodded, wrapping her arms around herself. "This is my one chance to prove to the Council that they don't need to keep me locked away in Solreef anymore—or worse. So, yeah, I'm basically risking everything right now—and all anyone wants to do is fight me and doubt me and insult me. It's like you *want* me to fail, even though you also *need* me to succeed, and I'm getting *really* sick of that impossible pressure."

"I don't blame you," Tam said, moving to stand beside her. "And . . . we're with you."

She laughed. "No, you're not. Even you, Tam. I bet your dwarven bodyguards are hiding beneath us right now, despite the fact that you were supposed to tell them to stay away."

"I *did* tell them to stay away," Tam insisted. "But . . . they can be pretty stubborn, so it's possible they're down there. I can't control that. Just like I know you can't control Trix, or make him appear because we need to talk to him."

"I can't," Glimmer agreed. "I really think he will, though. I know everyone's cold, and tired, and restless, but let's give it a little more time."

"We will," Sophie promised. She angled her head toward the sky, watching the winds scatter the darkening clouds. "Do you think . . . ?"

Her voice trailed off, and she jumped to her feet again.

"What?" Sandor asked, rushing to her side.

"Did you hear that?" She closed her eyes. "It almost sounded like . . . the wind was whispering."

Glimmer sucked in a breath. "What did it say?"

"Nothing. It was just gibberish—unless I imagined it." She shook her head and squeezed her eyes tighter, trying to concentrate as the wind swirled around her.

It felt different from the other drafts.

More restrained.

Or maybe a better word was *"controlled."*

"He's here," Glimmer breathed.

Maruca sent another blast of energy into the force field as they all rushed closer to the center—except for Sandor.

"SHOW YOURSELF!" he demanded, raising his sword and marching to the edge of the glowing barrier.

Wind slammed against him so hard, it sent him stumbling backward.

"BAD IDEA, TRIX!" Glimmer shouted as Sandor dropped into a crouch and dug his claws into the ground. "DON'T PICK A FIGHT WITH THE ANGRY BODYGUARD!"

The wind swirled faster, and this time Sophie could definitely hear a distinct voice laced through the shifting air.

Why should I trust you?

"Because it's me," Glimmer said. "And you need to hear what I have to say."

I don't need anything from someone siding with the enemy, the wind whispered again.

"They're not the enemy," Glimmer promised. "We agree more than we disagree."

Do we? the wind asked. *Then why do they work to stop our plans? Why do they ally with the Council?*

"Better than teaming up with murderers!" Wylie shouted.

Is it? You have no idea what the Council is capable of.

"So why don't you tell us?" Sophie asked.

It's not my job to educate you. Do your own work if you want to find the truth.

"We're trying," Sophie assured him.

Your lack of success isn't my problem.

"Yes, it is!" Glimmer argued. "Because one of these days they're going to figure it all out and pull off some victories—and I don't want you getting caught on the wrong side."

So that's what this is? You're here to SAVE me?

"No, I'm here to tell you the truth. You know me, Trix. You know how loyal I was to Lady Gisela. But I saw who she really is when I was in Loamnore. I saw her break her promise without the slightest hesitation. I saw her treat us like we're nothing more than tools to toss aside once she is done using us. She only cares about herself—and her projects. Everything else is expendable."

Maybe so, Trix told her. *But Gisela isn't with us anymore.*

"She's not?" Sophie asked, her brain exploding with questions. She didn't know where to start.

But Glimmer did. "Who's with you, then? Vespera and Ruy—who both stood there cowering behind a force field while Umber died?"

The air turned colder.

Interesting words, considering where you're standing, the wind told her. *And your group isn't any better. Your Shade is conflicted. Your Psionipath is untrained. Your Flasher hides truths from himself. And your goblin only protects the moonlark—who doesn't have what it takes to be a true leader. None of them care about you. None of them trust you. None of them will save you.*

"I don't need saving," Glimmer told him. "I can handle myself."

Can you? The wind sharpened into claws, raking against everyone's skin, and laughter filled the air when Sophie and her friends tried to swat the drafts away.

But Glimmer stood calm and steady. "You're not going to hurt me. You're not going to hurt any of us."

If you really believe that, prove it.

"How?" Sophie demanded.

The wind spun faster. *Drop your force field.*

"DON'T YOU DARE!" Sandor shouted.

It's the only way I'll talk, the wind pressed. *Otherwise I'm leaving.*

"WHY?" Glimmer yelled as the wind grew even louder.

Talking is a waste of time if you don't trust me. I'll give you ten seconds. Then I'm gone.

He started counting down.

"What do you think?" Sophie asked Glimmer.

Glimmer wrapped her arms around her waist. "I think . . . if he wanted to hurt us, we'd already be bleeding."

Definitely *not* reassuring—and when Sophie glanced at Tam, Wylie, and Maruca, they looked just as torn as she felt.

"Time to prove Trix wrong," Glimmer told her. "Step up like a leader."

"DO NOT!" Sandor warned.

But . . .

They *really* needed answers.

And they'd come all this way—and wasted so much time . . .

Sophie squared her shoulders and told Maruca, "Lower the shield."

Interesting, the wind hissed as the white dome of energy flickered and vanished.

"Now it's your turn!" Glimmer told him. "Time to show yourself."

"I suppose it is," he said as the wind whipped into a storm, pelting them with dust and pebbles.

Sandor tried to drag Sophie behind him, but she wrenched her arm free and stumbled forward.

"This was my decision," she shouted. "If I'm wrong, I should face the consequences."

"How very noble of you," a deep voice said.

A familiar voice.

Straight from Sophie's kidnapping nightmares.

She'd known Trix had been a part of that, of course. But the flashback made her knees wobble as the wind whisked away, revealing a black-cloaked figure at the edge of the bluff, silhouetted against the mountains.

"We just want to talk," Glimmer said, even though Sandor looked ready to start stabbing.

"You've said that," Trix told her. "And someday I'd love to

hear all about why you decided to betray us, but—"

"I *didn't*," Glimmer insisted.

Trix laughed. "You can keep telling yourself that if it makes you feel better. But we both know you did. And that's not why I'm here."

"Are you here about the trolls?" Sophie asked.

Trix angled his head. "Why would I be? You're the one who called this meeting. We just decided to take advantage."

"Take advantage how?" Wylie demanded.

But Tam had a much better question. "Who's *we*?"

"I always knew you were the smart one," a different voice said—one that felt like icicles piercing Sophie's skull.

She stumbled back while Glimmer asked Trix, "What have you done?"

"Exactly what I told him to," the voice said as Trix waved his arms, sending the last of the winds rushing far away.

As the dust settled, Sophie remembered her elementalism Mentor warning her that she could never trust a Guster—and he'd been right.

Standing next to Trix was another figure.

She wore a loose-fitting silver gown instead of a black cloak, which only made her look much more terrifying.

Vespera smiled one of her eerie, emotionless smiles as her azure eyes focused on Sophie and she asked, "Are you really surprised to see me?"

THIRTY-THREE

YOU SHOULD'VE MADE ME DROP my weapons before you showed yourself!" Sandor snarled, his body a blur as he lunged for Vespera.

He raised his sword, and Sophie braced for the horrible sound of a weapon hitting its mark—but all she heard was a soft *hiss* as Vespera's form seemed to dissolve, followed by creepy laughter and the painful thud of Sandor slamming against the ground much harder than he intended.

"Goblins are so predictable," Trix said as he blasted Sandor with intense winds, sending him toppling toward Sophie like a battered tumbleweed.

"They always fall for the illusion," Vespera agreed, still

laughing as she reappeared in front of them. She tucked a loose tendril of her raven-black hair behind one of her Ancient, pointy ears. "Then again, the rest of you were fooled just as easily. You simply lacked the capacity to take any violent action. Not surprising, but . . . disappointing all the same."

It was.

Sophie hadn't even *thought* to reach for her dagger when Vespera appeared—despite all her hard work trying to bond with Hope.

"At the same time, did you honestly think I would stand before you without any defenses?" Vespera asked, adjusting the ability-blocking headpiece she always wore, which reminded Sophie of a French Tudor hood, with jeweled silver chains wrapping her hair in a shimmering net.

"Why not?" Wylie asked. "You demanded that we lower our force field."

"I did. And your group remains completely unharmed, does it not?" Vespera countered. "But I knew you would not do me the same courtesy."

"You call *this* unharmed?" Sophie snapped, crouching to make sure Sandor was still breathing.

He was.

And he looked mostly conscious.

Just dazed—and a little banged up and bruised.

"Actually, I call that *getting what he deserved*," Vespera corrected, "given that he attacked me when I posed no actual threat."

"You're always a threat," Sophie argued, straightening up again.

She glanced at Maruca, who nodded—palms glowing white—ready to form another force field the second Sophie asked for it.

Vespera shook her head. "Such dramatics. This is why I knew I would have to rely on illusions once again—and turning them portable proved to be quite tricky. But it works rather well, actually. It is nearly impossible to differentiate this from reality—though there is one small issue that I have yet to correct."

She pointed toward the ground, and it took Sophie a second to realize that Vespera's shadow was missing.

"A projection cannot block the light the same way a body does," she explained. "But you would be surprised how rarely people notice those kinds of details. Even Shades."

Tam looked away, cheeks flushing.

"No need to be embarrassed," Vespera told him. "You still show far more potential than the rest of your group—though some of them seem to finally be realizing that they must change their ways. At least that is my hope." Her gaze shifted back to Sophie. "I did not expect the wide-eyed moonlark to start burning down buildings. And while I am certain you had some *encouragement*"—she raised an eyebrow at Glimmer—"it still shows more fight than I ever thought you would be capable of. Perhaps I underestimated you. Only time will tell.

Though you should know that your little fire did not deal the blow you intended. You simply destroyed the remnants of ill-conceived plans that had all been abandoned."

"If that's true," Sophie countered, "I wonder why you bothered retaliating."

Vespera frowned. "I do not know what you mean."

"Riiiiiiiight." Sophie crossed her arms. "Someone *else* destroyed Brumevale."

Vespera's frown deepened, and a tiny pucker formed between her arched eyebrows. "I have never heard of such a place."

"Maybe you didn't know its name," Sophie insisted. "But you left your symbol in the rubble, so . . ."

"*This* symbol?" Vespera pointed to the swirling lines in her necklace—a careful arrangement of runes that spelled out her signature.

"No." Sophie pointed to the creepy white eye stitched onto Glimmer's sleeve. "Your usual."

"Interesting," Vespera murmured. "I realize you will not want to believe this. But whatever happened to your 'Brumevale' had nothing to do with me—or my organization. It must have been Gisela, trying to frame us, though why she would bother, I do not know."

"So Gisela *really* isn't with the Neverseen anymore?" Wylie asked, beating Sophie to the question.

Vespera's dull smile returned. "She is not. The Neverseen

are *mine* now. They have been for quite some time, actually—long before Gisela realized what was happening. But she should have seen it coming. I warned her from the beginning that our philosophies were opposites and could not be combined, and she insisted on forcing an alliance anyway. So I let her make her foolish plays. Let her focus on the wrong goals. Let her *fail*. Then I seized my chance to take over—though I did not expect anyone to save her from capture. A very unfortunate oversight." She turned toward Glimmer. "You have chosen the wrong loyalties."

"No, I haven't," Glimmer snapped. "I kept my word. But I never signed on for war, or murder, or any of the other creepy things your *organization* has been doing—"

"Of course you did," Vespera interrupted. "You signed on for change. How else do you think that happens in our stubborn, foolish world? And before you claim that those currently standing beside you will bring about any sort of ultimate victory, consider how little their weak-willed efforts have actually accomplished all these years. I assure you, they will do nothing of any consequence—unless they change tactics. And perhaps they are ready to—which would be quite another thing. That is why I decided to let Trix accept your invitation."

"I didn't invite *you*." Glimmer turned to face Trix. "And I can't believe you went to her for permission."

"Why?" he demanded. "You're with the Black Swan now, Glimmer—did you really think we were going to hang out and eat snacks like old times while you're standing there with people who'd rather let their goblin kill me?"

"Uh: First? I'm not *with* anyone. I'm done having an organization define who I am or control my decisions. Second: You don't deserve the snacks I brought for you. And third: At least I told you that Sophie and her friends would be here—and they just want to talk. They're also willing to stand openly for what they believe in and put their lives on the line, instead of hiding behind cloaks and code names and portable illusions. In fact . . ." Glimmer tossed back her hood, letting her long shiny hair catch the wind as she faced Trix and Vespera for the first time. "You can call me Rayni from now on. I have nothing to hide. But I bet you're not willing to do the same."

Trix left his hood in place.

But Vespera pointed to her own exposed face. "For the record, I agree with you. And I fully intend to make sure my followers are far more open in the future."

Rayni laughed. "Congratulations, Trix! You're a *follower* of the person who got Umber killed."

"Watch it," Trix warned as the wind kicked up around them.

"Why?" Rayni asked. "What are you going to do?"

"There is no need for this hostility," Vespera intervened. "This meeting is not what you clearly think it is."

"Then what is it?" Sophie demanded.

"Patience, little moonlark. I will get there in a moment."

Vespera focused on smoothing the front of her dress, which made the loose fabric droop even worse, Her body still looked starved from her years in prison. "I realize your instincts will tell you not to listen to anything I have to say. But that would be a grave mistake. You seek answers. Progress. Success. Possibly a bit of revenge. I can help you achieve all of that—and more. So I implore you to hear me out. And to remember that while I stand here as an illusion—and some may judge that decision—I could just as easily have sent soldiers."

"You mean the trolls?" Sophie clarified.

Vespera frowned again. "That is the second time you have mentioned that species. I do not understand your sudden obsession with them."

Sandor barked a squeaky laugh as he dragged himself to his feet, swiping blood off his lips. "You expect us to believe that?"

"You should. It is always wise to believe the truth."

"So you *haven't* formed an alliance with the trolls and made them shut down all communication with the Council?" Wylie asked.

Vespera raised her arched eyebrows. "I have not."

"I'd be long gone if she had," Trix added.

Sophie refused to believe it. "Then why did Empress Pernille tell the Council she wasn't going to negotiate with them anymore?"

"How should I know?" Vespera asked. "This is the first I

have heard of such things. I suppose the tactic could be some sort of dramatic bluff on Empress Pernille's part—or Gisela could be behind this as well. Perhaps she is hoping to keep us distracted so we do not interfere with her other efforts. I am sure she's also scrambling for a new set of allies—though I do not see how she would entice the trolls into committing such open defiance against the Council. She has a gift for inspiring foolish choices—but risking war seems like it would require something more tangible than one of her pretty speeches. I shall have to give the matter longer consideration. In the meantime, it only makes my offer far more prudent."

"Your *offer?*" Tam repeated.

"Let me guess," Rayni added. "You're going to suggest we team up to take down Gisela?"

"Why do you say that with such disdain?" Vespera asked. "Stopping Gisela *should* be the top priority for us all. She still has many things planned—particularly for her son. Surely you know that?" Vespera's eyes flicked back to Sophie. "He is your friend, is he not?"

"Of course he is," Sophie told her, wishing her heart hadn't picked that moment to insist on shifting to confusing flutters.

It made it even harder to breathe when Vespera told her, "Then you are going to want to accept my offer. I can help you protect him from what comes next."

"What comes next?" Wylie, Tam, Maruca, and Rayni all asked at once.

But Sophie stayed silent.

She was pretty sure she knew the answer.

And yet her heart still caught in her throat, choking out all her air, when Vespera said, "Stellarlune is far from over."

THIRTY-FOUR

HEY," TAM SAID, GENTLY SHAKING Sophie's shoulder. "Don't let Vespera get in your head. She's just trying to scare you into giving her what she wants."

"Am I?" Vespera asked with a particularly sharp smile still aimed at Sophie. "Clearly your disorganized investigations have uncovered facts that agree with what I'm saying. Otherwise you would not be trembling like a withered leaf at the mere mention of stellarlune. But you must not have shared your discoveries with your friends, given their obvious confusion. And I doubt you have a clear picture of the stakes as well. If you did, you would be begging to work with me."

Sophie closed her eyes, wishing she could hold out her hands and scream, *STOP!*

Or better yet, grab her friends and leap away.

She didn't want to know any more.

Her brain had already reached maximum worrying capacity.

But fleeing wasn't going to get the answers they needed.

Fleeing wasn't going to help Keefe.

Sandor grabbed her wrist, turning her to face him. "Hear me now, Sophie—and please believe me. Working with the enemy is *never* a successful option."

"It can be," Vespera argued, "when both sides go into the arrangement with a proper mindset. I never said we would be working together permanently. But for now, we have a common enemy, and a shared problem that neither of us will be able to resolve on our own—especially in the little time we have left. So we can fail individually. Or conquer the threat together—and share the rewards—with no delusions of forming any lasting friendship. Once Gisela is no longer a problem, you will be welcome to make some ill-conceived move against me—and I will make my own moves as well—and we will see who proves to be stronger. But none of that prevents us from teaming up now."

"Uh, pretty sure that's *exactly* what it means," Rayni told her.

"A cease-fire is pointless if both sides are planning to attack each other the second it's over," Tam added.

"Not if they accomplish something vital together during their truce," Vespera insisted. "And getting ahead of Gisela *is* vital. She has stumbled across the most dangerous secret our world has ever buried—but she is still missing several key pieces at the moment. Which gives us a rare opportunity. We both have unique advantages that will allow us to work much faster. But only if we work *together*. So you can hate me. Mistrust me. Plot and scheme to destroy me. But for the next ten days you must also find a way to cooperate with me—because the power we will gain is far beyond anything you can imagine. And there is still a chance Gisela will find the means to get her hands on it. The only way we can ensure she doesn't is to get there first."

Sophie had no idea how to process most of that information—so she tried to focus on the fact that seemed to be key: "What happens in ten days?"

"It doesn't matter!" Sandor shouted.

"Yes, it does!" Sophie insisted, keeping her eyes focused on Vespera as she repeated her question.

"I honestly thought you knew, given the timing of your note," Vespera told her. "Interesting that you do not, and yet are already feeling so very desperate. That is good news for our alliance—so I am happy to fill you in. But it will go much smoother if you resist your tendency for interruption. Will you agree to hold your questions until I've finished?"

Sophie shook her head. "Not a chance."

Tam and Rayni both snort-laughed.

Vespera reached up to trace her fingers along the beaded chain near her temples. "Fine. If you would like to waste some of the precious little time we have, so be it. How much do you know about stellarlune?"

"How much do *you* know about stellarlune?" Sophie countered.

Vespera's jaw tightened. "All right. Have it your way—for the moment." She smoothed her dress again before she added, "Gisela has long believed that the Ancient Council—in an effort to maintain control over our growing population—chose to hold back our species by blocking access to certain vital sources of power. And she is convinced that the only way for us to reach our full potential is to expose ourselves to those natural forces. She created stellarlune to prove her theory and has been working to acquire those power sources and test their effects on her son—and regardless of whether her experiments turn out to be effective, no one can deny that the Ancient Council buried a significant amount of knowledge, even from our current rulers. They've hidden the true power of magsidian and left most of the supply with the dwarves so that no elf would have access to it. Same with ethertine. And they removed five crucial stars from any maps—and hid all trace of Elysian."

Sophie couldn't stop herself from sucking in a breath.

"So you have learned that much at least," Vespera noted. "Good. Hopefully you have also determined that Elysian is a place, kept off any records to prevent it from being discovered. It is a small piece of land, framed by five rivers, with little there worth mentioning, aside from a quarry filled with a rare kind of stone that was never given a name—and up until two days ago, that stone was nothing more than an unimpressive piece of dark rock. But for the next ten days, it is so much more. Just as ethertine absorbs the power of quintessence, and magsidian absorbs the power of shadowflux, this stone has the capacity to contain the power of a seventh element."

"*Seventh*," Maruca, Wylie, and Rayni all repeated.

Tam counted them off on his fingers. "Earth, wind, fire, water, quintessence, shadowflux, and . . . what?"

"The element also does not have a name, because the Ancient Council did not want there to be *any* record of it. But it is believed to be a manifestation of the three Prime Sources: sunlight, moonlight, and starlight—and not just any starlight. The light from a sixth unmapped star—a star that can only appear when the other five unmapped stars align during something the Ancient Council called Nightfall."

Sophie felt her knees wobble.

The star only rises at Nightfall.

Lady Gisela had carved those words in runes around the door to her Nightfall facility, which she'd built in the side of a lonely mountain and sealed with Keefe's blood. And Sophie had assumed the phrase was a reference to the Lodestar Initiative and Vespera's old human experiments.

But none of the clues she'd found had really fit into the kind of huge revelation that Sophie had been hoping for—and she'd assumed the reason was because the Neverseen kept changing their leaders and their plans.

What if she'd been wrong about everything?

"Does that mean either of the Nightfall facilities are in Elysian?" she asked.

Vespera shook her head. "No. I chose the name from the legend of the sixth unmapped star, because I used to wonder if its light could be the key to unlocking our inner ruthlessness, and could finally enable us to defend ourselves properly. But Gisela discovered that Nightfall is a specific window of time that only comes around every few millennia."

"Ten days," Rayni mumbled.

"Twelve," Vespera corrected. "As I said, two have already passed. Which means we only have ten more to make our way to Elysian, where each night, the light from the sixth unmapped star is touching the sunbaked rocks in Elysian under a veil of moonlight, allowing the stones to absorb the power of all three Prime Sources. The stones must be severed from the earth before Nightfall ends; otherwise all that power will simply flow back into the ground. But if they are gathered properly, they will contain the strongest, most vital energy of all—and the missing piece to Gisela's plans for stellarlune."

The power source Keefe probably needed.

"Are you seriously buying all this?" Wylie asked, studying Sophie. "Doesn't it sound—"

"Ridiculous?" Tam finished for him.

"See, I was going to say 'far-fetched,'" Wylie corrected.

"I don't know," Rayni said quietly. "It does match some of the things Lady Gisela used to talk about—especially when she thought no one could hear her."

"That doesn't make it true, though," Maruca reminded her before turning to Vespera and asking, "Do you have any proof?"

"Yes and no," Vespera admitted. "Gisela has been very careful with her notes on the subject—she did not even include any mention of this in her Archetype. But you can see hints of it in her stellarlune symbol. The star in the center has twelve points, surrounded by a sun and a moon that have aligned."

"Huh, I don't think I've seen that symbol," Maruca said. "Have any of you?"

Sophie nodded.

The same mark had been on the seal of a letter that a much younger Keefe had been tricked into delivering to Ethan Benedict Wright II in London—not long before Lady Gisela murdered him and his daughter.

She closed her eyes, letting her photographic memory pull up the symbol, and sure enough, the star had twelve points. And now that Vespera mentioned it, the two curves wrapping around it did look like a moon and sun in perfect alignment.

She used the heel of her shoe to scratch the same markings

in the rocky soil, and everyone gathered around to study the rough rendering.

"Okay, but . . . all this symbol proves is that Gisela believes these stories," Tam reminded her. "That doesn't mean any of them are true."

"Perhaps not," Vespera said. "But Elysian *does* exist. I have been there. I am the one who created the illusions to hide the quarry—though I had no idea where I was or what I was doing at the time. The Ancient Council gave me no explanations. They simply ordered me to use every trick in my arsenal to ensure that no one could ever discover what had been hidden. And I must have done my job well, because Gisela could not find anything when she went there."

"Wait—*Gisela's* been to Elysian?" Sophie asked.

Vespera nodded. "I do not know when, or how she found it—but she told me she once had a starstone that remembered the location. She could never see past my illusions—but she did find three tiny shards of a strange kind of crystallized stone, which she believed were remnants from the last time Nightfall was upon us. And when she tested one, it set off an incredible kind of explosion, where the rubble somehow took on the shape of the blast."

Sophie covered her mouth, trying to stop herself from gasping.

But everyone noticed.

"That's exactly what happened in Brumevale," Sophie decided to explain. "There was some sort of explosion, and part of the tower was obliterated, and the rest took on the force of the blast—and the Black Swan found remnants of a strange crystal that probably caused the explosion, but they're still trying to figure out what it is and how it worked."

Vespera's pale skin turned even paler. "Sounds like Gisela is trying to tell us to stay away from Elysian."

"There is no *us*," Sandor snarled.

"Not yet—but there must be. Especially if Gisela fears it. She knows she'll never break through those illusions without me. And her starstone was damaged somehow, *and* she has been unable to acquire a replacement. Apparently she commissioned one, but—"

"My mom never gave it to her," Wylie jumped in. "And then Fintan had my mom killed before Gisela could find out where the starstone was hidden."

"And Elysian has been lost ever since," Vespera added. "Gisela has tried every possible means to make her way back there. But all her efforts have failed. Which gives us this unique chance to get ahead of her. If you can bring us to Elysian, I can guide us through my illusions—"

"I can't get us there," Sophie interrupted, seeing no point in lying. "I've already tried teleporting, and there was some sort of barrier that kept me back."

"That is unfortunate," Vespera admitted. "But not the only option. If you find the missing starstone—"

Wylie groaned. "Ugh, how many times do I have to tell

you? *I don't know where it is!* You've already kidnapped me, and tortured me, and had Gethen search my memories—and *I've* tried searching my mind and—"

"This is why I did not reach out to you," Vespera interrupted. "I reached out to the moonlark, who has shown time and again that she possesses a specific kind of relentless resourcefulness when she's properly motivated—and I highly suspect that with stakes this high, she will find a solution to ensure that this power will never fall into Gisela's hands—"

"Okay, so I have a question," Maruca interrupted. "If Gisela can't get there, and this fancy Nightfall star-alignment thing only happens every few millennia, can't we just sit back for the next ten days and make sure we *all* miss our chance?"

"And risk that Gisela goes there and gets the power without us?" Vespera countered. "That would be far too dangerous."

"I doubt it's more dangerous than basically handing you a super-important power source and hoping you don't use it against us," Tam argued.

Vespera shrugged. "You could just as easily use it against me. As I said, at some point, our alliance *will* end, and we will each make our own plays. But that should not stop us from allying on this mission."

"YES, IT SHOULD!" Sandor shouted, spinning Sophie around to face him. "I have tried to stay quiet and let you make your own decision. But I cannot stand by any longer. If you do this, it *will* become your greatest regret."

It definitely could be.

But if they didn't get that power—and Gisela *did*—Vespera was right about how terrifying that would be.

And if Gisela *didn't* get it—then Keefe . . .

Sophie didn't know what horrible possibilities best finished that sentence—but she never wanted to find out.

Plus, wasn't this what she'd been looking for?

A way to take control of stellarlune so that Keefe could have whatever he needed without having to deal with his mother?

Vespera cleared her throat. "Well, I have a feeling we have reached the tedious, exhausting part of this conversation, where there will be a great deal of arguing—and I definitely do not need to be present for that. So I will leave you to your bickering. But remember that time is of the essence, and you do not have the luxury of indecision. When you have hopefully come to your senses and found the starstone, reach out to Trix—I will let him tell you where and how to best make that work. Oh, and in the hope that an additional bit of trust might speed your decision along—and sway you the correct direction—I will offer you one final piece of information to prove that I am truly trying to help at the moment." Her cold gaze focused on Sophie. "I hear that Gisela's son has left the Lost Cities, to prevent her from continuing her experiments— and likely to keep whatever new abilities he's developed a secret. But there is nowhere he can hide. Gisela has a very specific way of tracking his exact location. She can find him whenever she wants. She's just waiting for the opportune moment."

THIRTY-FIVE

S HE'S TELLING THE TRUTH," TRIX SAID
as Vespera's illusion blinked away with one last
chilling peal of laughter. "But I'm sure you're still
going to freak out and argue and ask ten thousand
questions—so how about I tell you everything I know before
you start into all that?"

Sophie could only nod.

All this time, she'd thought she was keeping Keefe safe by
not going after him.

But . . . what if his mom had already dragged him away
somewhere?

Was *that* why Keefe hadn't responded to any of her—or the
alicorns'—transmissions?

And even if Gisela hadn't made her move yet . . .

She can find him whenever she wants.

"Okay, this is going to sound weird," Trix warned, fidgeting with the sleeves of his cloak. "And I'm not a Shade, so I don't fully understand it myself. But the way Umber explained it to me is that the tracking is all done with a tiny bit of carefully placed shadowflux—and the trickiest part was getting it into Keefe's system without him realizing what was happening. So while Keefe was pretending to be a part of our order—and not fooling anyone, by the way—Umber slipped minuscule amounts of shadowflux into his meals. He didn't notice because our food is already disgusting. And then Umber guided that shadowflux from his stomach to his heart."

"His *heart*?" Sophie pressed her hand against her chest as the ghost of her old shadow monster seemed to stir under her skin. "He has an echo in—"

"Not an echo," Trix corrected. "Keefe would've been able to feel that. So Umber only gave him enough shadowflux to create a *ripple*."

"What's a *ripple*?" Maruca asked, glancing at Tam.

"I've never heard of it," he admitted.

"Pretty sure most Shades haven't," Trix told him. "They're too afraid to explore the possibilities of shadowflux."

"Uh, it's more like most of us don't want to do creepy stuff like track people without their knowledge," Tam argued.

"Whatever," Trix said, and Sophie could practically hear his eyes roll. "A ripple is pretty much what it sounds like—a tiny shock wave. I guess the rhythm of Keefe's heartbeat makes the shadowflux slowly pile on top of itself until it eventually topples over—and that sudden shift causes a ripple. It takes a while to build up again, so Keefe only gets two ripples a day, always at the eleventh hour—just enough to track him down if anyone needs to find him."

"Okay . . . but . . . *how*?" Rayni asked.

"It's nothing that any of us can see or feel," Trix told her. "It's kind of like dropping a stone into water, only in this case, the ripple radiates across the shadowplane—"

"There's a *shadowplane*?" Maruca interrupted, glancing at Tam again. "Shades are seriously the coolest."

Tam's cheeks took on a slight flush, and he tugged his bangs lower over his eyes. "I've never heard it called that—but my Shade Mentor has talked about how the natural state of everything is pure, endless darkness. And even though light tries to drown it out, the darkness never goes away. That's why we have shadows. They're glimpses of the darkness hidden underneath everything."

"I guess that syncs with what I was taught in my flashing sessions," Wylie told him. "Though my Mentors would go on and on about how we need light to keep the darkness at bay."

"My Mentors talked about that too," Rayni added. "But I still don't get how any of this works like a tracker."

"That's because you're not a Shade," Trix told her. "Umber

could feel the ripples whenever she was in the same room with Keefe at the right time."

"But Lady Gisela isn't a Shade," Sophie reminded him. "And she isn't in the same room as Keefe."

"She doesn't need to be. She stole the modified Spyball our Technopath made for Fintan. I guess it's been rewired to access the shadowplane—which basically means it focuses only on darkness. And then it was programmed to search for anomalies. So all Gisela has to do is turn the Spyball on and wait for the eleventh hour, and it'll pick up Keefe's ripple and track it back to the source."

"Okaaaaaaaaaay," Sophie said, trying to squish all this new weirdness into her brain.

It shouldn't have sounded so impossible, given that she lived in a world of light leaping and teleporting and levitating.

But something felt . . . wrong.

And then she realized why.

"Wait—none of this times out right!" she argued. "Gisela was trapped in an ogre prison while Keefe was living with the Neverseen—and Fintan changed the timeline and wasn't following her plans. So why would he have Umber set up a tracker on Keefe?"

"Because he knew Keefe was trying to take us down from the inside, and he figured it would be smart to have a way to find him in case he ran off with something important," Trix explained. "Plus, Fintan knew there was a chance that Gisela might escape, and then he could grab Keefe and use him as leverage."

Leverage.

The word felt like a spark crashing into the dark pool of rage that Sophie kept buried away—and she was tempted to channel that burning anger and blast Trix with one of her red-lightning Inflictor beams.

He must've noticed her mounting fury because he raised his hands like a stop sign—or maybe to reach for the wind in case she attacked. "Fintan was the one who called Keefe that—not me. Honestly . . . I like Keefe. He was always telling hilarious stories about tormenting Dame Alina or hiding gulons at Foxfire. And he definitely doesn't deserve the things his mom has done to him. But it's only going to get worse. Gisela told Umber that the last step of stellarlune was designed to break him. She said she couldn't simply make Keefe powerful—she had to make sure he's also *obedient*." He paused to let that sink in before he added, "Gisela might have tried to make people think otherwise to keep them guessing, but Keefe and his abilities are crucial to her plan—she told Umber as much. So I know you hate the idea of working with us—and I'm not a fan of it either. But if Gisela finds Elysian and gets ahold of the power source there, it'll be game over for your friend. Game over for all of us, honestly—why do you think we're giving you so much proof? Check the sky and you'll see how the unmapped stars are all aligned right now. And I'm sure your

Technopath can tweak a Spyball to access the shadowplane and prove I'm not lying about the tracker—and if you want to keep Keefe safe, you can have Tam pull the shadowflux out of his heart."

"He can do that?" Sophie asked, glancing at Tam, who definitely did not look convinced he possessed that skill.

"Umber could," Trix told him.

Tam scowled. "Yeah, but she's also the one who put it in there—I love how you keep dancing around that, by the way. It's like, 'Look how cooperative we're being, telling you about all the evil, manipulative stuff we've done and giving you a chance to fix it before it gets so much worse—doesn't that totally prove we can be best friends now?'"

"We're not looking for friends," Trix corrected. "This is a temporary alliance—one we'll both equally benefit from. And you'll regret it if you don't take this chance. But I'm not getting sucked into this argument. I've said my part. Now it's up to you. If you decide to be smart, let me know." He turned to Rayni. "I'll be checking our usual drop-off point at least three times a day, so it shouldn't take me long to find any notes you leave there—but just to be safe, I'll also stash some vials of wind near the tree. Break all of them at the same time, and the drafts will race straight to me to let me know you're ready, okay?"

Rayni nodded.

"And remember—we don't just need you on board with

the plan," he added. "We need the starstone. There's no point reaching out until you have it. And you only have ten days—maybe less if Gisela figures out how to get there on her own."

He turned his back on them with that bombshell, and Sophie expected him to hold a crystal up to the moonlight and glitter away.

Instead, he walked to the edge of the cliff and jumped, letting the winds whisk him into the night.

"I know what you're thinking," Sandor said as Sophie craned her neck to study the sky. "But you cannot be fooled by—"

"I'm *not*," she interrupted, focusing on Elementine—the first unmapped star she'd ever located.

She'd barely been able to see Elementine that night with Dex—even with the help of a stellarscope.

But now it was a bright, silvery star flickering through the darkness.

And it was right by the twinkling, rosy star of Marquiseire.

And the pale, glimmering star of Candesia.

And the cool, icy star of Lucilliant.

And the vibrant, opalescent star of Phosforien.

Sophie wasn't supposed to be able to find any of them, but the Black Swan had planted their locations in her memory—and the unmapped stars had always been much more scattered.

Now they formed a perfectly straight line.

And in the middle of their row was a dim, flickering speck, glowing with the faintest hint of green.

"*That*," she said, pointing to the brand-new star she'd never seen before, "is the power source Gisela's looking for. Vespera wasn't lying."

"She wasn't," Sandor agreed. "She was also *very* clear that she plans to turn on us once she has what she wants—and if you think you'll be able to arrange some clever trap—"

"I don't," Sophie cut in.

Sandor heaved the hugest sigh of relief she'd ever heard him breathe.

So did Wylie and Maruca.

Even Rayni.

"But . . . what about Keefe?" Tam asked, squinting at the new greenish star. "Didn't you say he needs that power?"

"He does," Sophie agreed. "So here's what we're going to do. We're heading back to Havenfield to grab my Spyball, and we're bringing it straight to Dex so he can figure out how to make it access the shadowplane. Then we're finding Keefe— and you're going to get that shadowflux out of his heart so his mom can't track him anymore. I know you said you don't know how to do that—but you didn't know how to help with my echoes either, and you figured that out, right?"

Tam hesitated a beat before he nodded.

"What about Elysian?" Wylie asked.

"I was just about to get to that," Sophie told him. "I know Vespera wants us to think we'll never find the quarry without her. But she always underestimates us. Plus, she already taught us one of the tricks to see through her illusions. We look for things that don't cast shadows. And we let our two Flashers search the light, since that's what she uses to hide things. Maybe Dex can even make a gadget to help—who knows? The point is, Vespera needs us—but we *don't* need her. We're going to get to Elysian, grab that power, and make sure no one else can ever get their hands on it."

"Okay," Wylie said slowly. "That's . . . not a terrible plan—if it weren't for the fact that I seriously *don't* know how to find that starstone. I swear I've tried everything. So has Tiergan. I've even worked with my dad, and—"

"Did you ever have them work together?" Sophie asked, remembering what Tiergan had told her about how he and Prentice could've been Cognates. When Wylie shook his head, she said, "I think you should give that a try. You trust both of them—and they trust each other—and that level of confidence may be exactly what your mind has been waiting for."

"I guess," he mumbled, definitely not sounding convinced. "But you might want to come up with a backup plan."

"I already have one. Councillor Oralie is trying to track down a crystal Kenric made, which might lead to Elysian, and she told Mr. Forkle she'd love some help."

"Which brings up an interesting question," Rayni added. "What are you going to tell the Council? And keep in mind that we're now trying to find something they went to tremendous lengths to keep hidden for several thousand years."

"They're counting on me to give them a full report," Wylie reminded her.

"Oh, I know," Rayni said. "My freedom depends on them being extremely happy with what you tell them—and I'm pretty sure they won't love hearing that the Neverseen tried to recruit us into helping them steal a secret power source. Or that we're planning to go rogue and find it on our own instead. And if they tell us to stay away from Elysian and we go anyway, that *won't* go over well—especially for me."

"It won't," Sophie agreed. "So I think this is a time when we should only tell them what they *need* to know. Like . . . they *need* to know that Trix did show up for our meeting—and that Vespera was sort of with him. And they *need* to know that Lady Gisela is no longer a part of the Neverseen—and that she might be the one causing the problems with the trolls in an attempt to gather new allies. They also *need* to know that Gisela's probably the one who blew up Brumevale, using a special kind of crystal she's trying to find more of—but they *don't* need to know that we're aware of what that crystal is. And I guess we might as well tell them that Vespera asked about the missing starstone, and that we're working hard to locate it—but it's totally fine if they think we just want to understand why the Neverseen are so obsessed with finding it. And we can tell them that Keefe might be in danger, so we're going to try to find him. And since Oralie is already searching for Elysian anyway, it won't be weird if we tell them we'd like to help. All of that is true and vital and should make the Council very satisfied with Wylie's report—and get you the credit you need to finally be given some freedom—without giving away too much. We can always give them another update if we find the starstone, or if things start feeling scarier. But in the meantime . . . less is more."

Rayni grinned. "Huh."

"What?" Sophie asked.

"You know what you sound like right now?" Rayni said.

"Not really," Sophie admitted, hoping it wasn't something bad.

But Rayni's smile widened—and Wylie, Tam, and Maruca grinned too when Rayni told her, "You sound like a real leader."

THIRTY-SIX

HOW DO WE KNOW IF THE SPYBALL'S working?" Sophie asked, fighting the urge to get up from her squishy beanbag chair and pace—though exploring Dex's bedroom would've provided a much-needed distraction.

The huge cluttered room was definitely as chaotic as she'd imagined, with every available surface covered in gadgets and tools and gears and wire and springs—plus beakers and vials and ingredients for all of Dex's alchemy projects.

"Honestly?" Dex said as he moved from his worktable to one of the beanbags between Sophie and Tam. "I have no idea." He spun the Spyball around his palm. "All the parts are communicating the way I told them to, but now that I'm having it search for anomalies in the shadowplane, there's nothing for it to project until it finds something."

"And the eleventh hour is . . . the hour before midnight?" Tam asked.

"That's what I'm assuming," Dex said. "Or the hour before noon. But we're way closer to the late one."

They were.

It was 10:47.

Thankfully, it had only taken Dex a couple of hours to rewire the Spyball after Sophie and Tam showed up at Rimeshire and explained what they needed.

"But wait," Sophie said, realizing their mistake. "Won't the ripple go by *Keefe's* time zone? Not ours?"

Dex frowned. "What do you mean?"

"You know, like how the east coast of the U.S. is three hours ahead of the west coast, and Hawaii's three hours behind them and . . ." Her voice trailed off when she noticed the way Tam and Dex were staring at her. "What?"

"The Lost Cities are all on the same time," Dex said—which Sophie had definitely noticed, even though she had no idea how it worked, since the houses and cities were scattered all over the planet.

Maybe the elves had created some sort of illusion to keep everything synced up.

Either way, that didn't answer her question.

"But Keefe isn't *in* the Lost Cities right now," she argued.

"Yeah, but Umber created Keefe's ripple loop—or whatever we want to call it—when he *was* here," Dex reminded her. "So that's what Keefe's body is still going by."

"Oh. Well. I guess that makes sense," Sophie said—and it was good news, since it was now 10:49.

Only eleven more minutes until they found Keefe—which had half of her brain screaming, *WOO, HURRY UP!* and the other half shouting, *AHHH, I'M NOT READY!*

There was also a tiny, anxious voice in the back of her mind that kept telling her this was too sudden—too easy.

Finally she had to ask, "Do you think this could be a trap?"

"Yes," Sandor and Lovise both told her.

"I don't know," Tam jumped in. "This seems like an awful lot of trouble to go through just to lure us somewhere—especially since Trix could've just grabbed us after we lowered our force field."

Somehow that wasn't very reassuring.

Neither was the fact that Bex kept trying to phase through the walls, and Lex kept launching ice cubes at them through the crack under the door and freezing parts of the floor.

Little constant reminders of why Keefe ran away in the first place.

And why he might not want to come home.

We're just finding him so we can remove the shadowflux, Sophie kept telling herself. *We're not bringing him back with us.*

That was safer.

And smarter.

And so much less confusing.

And also very . . .

. . . disappointing.

She wanted to strangle the part of her brain that kept wishing for a happy homecoming—especially since it was the same voice that kept asking her what she was going to do when she saw Keefe.

What would she say?

Better yet: What would she *feel*? Since Keefe was going to feel it too—and if her sweaty, shaky palms were any indication, it was going to be awkward on top of embarrassing mixed with a whole lot of terrifying.

Or . . . it could also be really, really great.

Keefe would flash his famous smirk.

Maybe wrap her up in a hug.

And . . .

FOCUS, she screamed at herself. *IT'S ALMOST TIME.*

Now it was 10:53.

10:54.

10:55.

Each minute felt like an eternity.

By 10:57, Sophie had actually started to wonder if time had slowed to some sort of half speed.

And at 10:58, Sandor cleared his throat and told them, "I hope you realize that I *will* be going wherever that thing"—

he pointed to the Spyball—"tells you to search."

"Not if it's in the Forbidden Cities," Sophie warned.

"I'll wear whatever disguise you want," Sandor insisted. "But I go where you go."

Sophie didn't have time to argue.

It was 10:59.

11:00.

"Nothing happened," she mumbled when they got to 11:01.

Dex closed his eyes and tapped the Spyball. "It still feels like it's working. Maybe the whole 'eleventh hour' thing isn't super exact?"

Or maybe the Neverseen were just wasting their time.

Breaking their focus.

But . . . why would they do that when they *needed* Sophie to find the starstone?

And why—

"Wait," Dex said, holding up the Spyball as it started to glow. "I think this is it!"

Sophie held her breath when a blinking red dot appeared in the middle of the orb.

"That's him," Dex whispered. "It has to be."

"Okay . . . so . . . where *is* that?" Tam asked.

"Working on it," Dex said, scanning the Spyball with some sort of modified Imparter.

He tapped the flat screen a few times.

Then a few more.

Sophie tugged out a couple of itchy eyelashes when he kept on tapping.

"Got it!" he finally announced, holding out the Imparter screen to show them the word that had appeared.

London.

Sophie jumped to her feet and made a sound that was much more squealy than she intended.

She cleared her throat before she said, "That *has* to be Keefe!"

He'd probably made his way to London to try to find out more about what happened to Ethan Benedict Wright II and his daughter—which was smart, but also *really* risky, since Lady Gisela had her own special paths to the city.

"Do you know *where* he is in London?" she asked. "It's a big place."

"No—but I have the Spyball feeding into the Imparter like it's a homing signal, so it'll tell us if we're getting closer as we walk through the streets."

"Perfect!" Sophie grabbed his hand and Tam's hand and pulled them to their feet.

Sandor and Lovise blocked the door. "We're going with you."

"Seriously," Sophie said, "you'll be way too conspicuous—even in a disguise. And we don't have time to argue—"

"We don't," Sandor agreed. "So let's just accept that you're not leaving this room without me."

"Or me," Lovise added.

"As you said, this could be a trap," Sandor reminded her. "And—"

Lex chose that moment to launch a whole lot more ice cubes under the door. He also froze the bit of floor right under their giant goblin feet—and the combination left Sandor and Lovise slipping and sliding as they fought to keep their balance.

Sophie knew an opportunity when she saw one.

"Thanks, Lex!" she shouted as she whipped around and dragged Tam and Dex toward the nearest window—which was thankfully already open.

"Uh, I don't think my room is high enough for us to teleport," Dex warned as Sophie launched them out into the night.

It wasn't.

But Sophie scraped enough concentration together to levitate them higher and higher and higher—until they were surrounded by nothing but stars.

Then she closed her eyes and let them drop.

Her stomach wanted to turn inside out as they plummeted, and she definitely missed using her new run-to-teleport method.

But they still crashed into the void, which was all that mattered.

"Any idea where we should start looking in London?" Sophie asked, mentally sorting through all the different landmarks.

"Not really," Dex admitted. "Maybe just head where we went last time so I'll be somewhere familiar?"

"Works for me."

The void cracked open, and they skidded to an ungraceful stop in front of Buckingham Palace.

"Oh good, it's raining," Tam grumbled, flailing to cover his head with his cape. "Really wish Linh were here."

"Me too," Dex said, swiping water off the screen of his Imparter as he led them toward a nearby park.

Sophie wasn't thrilled that she was going to look like some sort of tangled sea monster for her big reunion with Keefe. But there was nothing she could do about it except try to run faster and avoid puddles as Dex led them out of the park and onto a busy street.

Several taxis splashed by, and Sophie was tempted to hail one. But they didn't have any human money—and maybe they weren't going to need it, because Dex pointed to a gray building up ahead and told them, "He's in there!"

"You're sure?" Sophie asked as they sprinted over and ducked under the stone arches.

"Why? What is this place?" Dex asked, peering through the foggy windows.

Sophie tried to wring some of the water out of her hair. "It's a super-fancy hotel."

So fancy that Sophie asked Tam to cover them with as many shadows as he could before they tiptoed into the lobby, which was decorated with the kind of rugs and chandeliers that looked like they belonged to human royalty.

She was pretty sure the top-hat-wearing bellhops would call security if they spotted three drenched teenagers sneaking through late at night. So she held her breath until they made it to the elevators.

"I don't understand," she mumbled as Dex told the elevator to take them to one of the highest floors. "This place costs thousands of dollars. Well, actually, it costs thousands of *pounds* since we're in London—but whatever. My point is . . . how could Keefe afford to stay here? He doesn't have any money."

And yet the Spyball led them to a door that clearly belonged to one of the biggest suites in the entire hotel.

"You're *sure*?" Sophie asked Dex.

He pointed to the Imparter's screen, where the dot had stopped flashing. "Looks like it."

"All right," Sophie said, combing her fingers quickly through her tangled hair and wishing she'd changed into something a little cuter than her boring gray tunic and black leggings. Her hands were shaking, but that was probably from the cold. "Let's hope this isn't a mistake."

Especially since they'd already be heading home to some *very* angry bodyguards.

She raised her fist to knock, and they all flinched as the sound echoed down the hall.

Please let it be Keefe, she begged. *Please don't let it be some grumpy rich human who will be very angry about being woken up.*

She had to knock a second time before footsteps slowly

started plodding toward them, and the door opened just enough to let a familiar blond boy peek out.

His ice blue eyes were droopy with sleep, but they widened when they focused on Sophie, and for a moment he just stared at her.

Then his lips curled into a smirk, and he whispered, "Foster?"

That was all Sophie needed.

She leaped forward and tackle-hugged Keefe.

THIRTY-SEVEN

U M . . . NOT THAT I'M NOT GLAD TO see you, Foster," Keefe said, "but . . . *how did you find me?* Is everything okay? Also: At some point, I'm going to need to breathe."

"Sorry!" Sophie said, realizing how tight she'd been squeezing. She dropped her arms and stumbled back, trying not to think about how red her cheeks had probably turned.

"No need to apologize," he told her. But he coughed a little as he flicked on the lights and stepped aside to let her farther into his room—which was much bigger than she'd imagined. It seemed like it even had multiple bedrooms. "I had a feeling you were going to strangle me if I ever saw you again."

The "if" in the joke totally snuffed out any giddiness Sophie had been feeling.

She looked away, fidgeting with her soaked cape. "You really weren't planning on coming back, were you?"

Keefe fussed with his blue flannel pajamas—which looked so distinctly human. "I thought I explained that. I don't *want* to stay away—it's just not safe for me to be in the Lost Cities, between my mom and . . . everything else."

"But it seems like you're able to talk without giving commands now—so that's some major progress," Dex said behind them.

Sophie jumped.

She'd forgotten that Dex and Tam were with her.

"It's not as much progress as you think," Keefe mumbled, kicking the carpet with his cushioned hotel slipper. "Plus, there's still all the other stuff, you know?"

"I *do* know," Sophie told him, waiting for him to meet her eyes before she added, "about everything."

Keefe swallowed hard. "Dex told you?"

"She guessed a lot of it," Dex clarified. "And I didn't tell anyone else."

All eyes shifted to Tam.

He shrugged. "I'm super good with not knowing. Feel free to keep all your secrets to yourself."

"Deal!" Keefe told him before turning back to Dex. "Um . . . how is your family, by the way?"

"Kinda the same," Dex admitted, glancing at Tam.

Tam nodded and wandered over to the windows at the far end of the room as Dex lowered his voice and told Keefe, "You know what happened isn't your fault, right? I've had a lot of time to think about it, and I realized . . . you didn't *change* anything. Everything is exactly the way it was always going to be."

"Yeah, but—"

"No," Dex interrupted. "There's no 'but.' I'm not saying you don't still need to learn how to control that ability—and the fewer people who know about it, the better. But I don't think you need to hide, either."

"Especially since you've already made a ton of progress controlling your voice ability," Sophie added. "If you can do that, I'm *sure* you can control the others."

Keefe dragged a hand through his hair, which was already extra messy from sleeping—but somehow it only made him look more adorable. "It's just . . . It's hard to tell if I'm really controlling the whole command thing or if I only think I am because . . ."

"Because what?" Sophie pressed when he didn't finish.

"I don't know. Maybe my brain instinctively realizes that controlling humans would be a nightmare. I swear, the longer I'm here, the less their world makes any sense. Do you know they have a food called bubble and squeak—and it has zero bubbles, and definitely no squeaks? And don't even get me started on the way they decorate." He waved his arms around the suite. "What's with all the flowers? Vases of them. Paintings of them. Carvings of them. Even pillows and curtains and comforters printed with them. I think humans might be more obsessed with flowers than elves are with sparkles."

Sophie could tell he was changing the subject to avoid answering her question, but she let it go—for the moment.

"Most places aren't decorated like this," she told him. "Which reminds me—uh . . . how can you afford to stay here?"

Keefe smirked. "Technically, Mommy Dearest is paying for it. I raided her jewelry box at Candleshade before I left, and the stuff I took turned out to be worth a *lot* of human money."

That was actually a *brilliant* plan—and something Sophie never would've thought of. She obviously needed to give Keefe's human survival skills more credit.

But . . .

"How did you know where to sell everything?" she asked, imagining Keefe trying to negotiate with the owner of a dingy pawnshop—and then leaving with a huge stack of cash in his pocket, practically begging to be robbed. "And don't hotels require some sort of ID before they'll check you into a room—especially a room like this?"

"It's been a lot of trial and error," Keefe admitted. "Took me a few days of pretty much nonstop light leaping to find the facet on the pathfinder that got me to London. And then I just kinda wandered around, trying to figure out how everything worked—and I realized it's all about who you know. Ask the right questions, make the right friends—"

"Friends?" Sophie interrupted. "You have friends here?"

She wasn't surprised, given how smart and funny Keefe was—and part of her was glad he hadn't had to spend all these weeks alone.

But the idea of him settling in and finding a group of humans to hang out with definitely stung.

"Let's just say I've had a little help and leave it at that, okay?" Keefe asked, and there was something almost pleading in his expression. "I promise, someday I'll tell you all about my adventures in Humanland, including a particularly awesome anecdote involving a giant spider and a horrible paste called Vegemite. But right now, I think I've been very patient, waiting for you to tell me why you're all here—soaking wet, in the middle of the night—and how you found me when I've done a *really* good job of staying hidden. I'd also love to know how you managed to ditch Gigantor for this little adventure, since I'm guessing that was a pretty epic struggle."

"That's a really long story," Sophie told him.

"Well then, I guess it's a good thing my room has all these chairs!" He pointed toward the sitting area, which looked like somewhere a group of princesses would gather for high tea. "Warning: They're not as comfortable as they should be. Nothing is, honestly. What I wouldn't give for a gnomish-made bed. And maybe a slice of mallowmelt. Oh, and some bottles of Youth! Human water is *terrible*. I can't decide if it tastes like feet or dirty rocks. Should we do a taste test at some point and take a vote? I have a bunch of bottles."

"Actually, what we *should* be doing is getting rid of your tracker," Tam said as he made his way closer.

Keefe stumbled back like he'd been punched. "Um . . . I have *a tracker? How? And more importantly, from who? Also: Please tell me getting rid of it isn't going to require melting off my skin!*"

"No skin-melting," Sophie promised. "But Tam's right—we should've started working on that immediately. Any idea what you're going to need, Tam? Should he lie down or sit or—"

"Whoa—Bangs Boy is doing what, now?" Keefe cut in. "Because the last time he used one of his little Shade tricks on me, I kinda ended up almost dead and woke up with a bunch of freaky new abilities—and I'm not blaming you for that," he told Tam. "I told you to do it, remember? But that doesn't mean I'm ready to repeat the process."

"I get it," Tam said. "But this will be different. I'm not sending any shadowflux into you—I'm just drawing some out."

"Yeeeeeeaaaaaaaaah, see . . . that doesn't actually sound any better," Keefe noted.

Explaining the whole "ripple" thing didn't help a whole lot either. Even when Dex showed Keefe the special Spyball-Imparter contraption he'd made—and then went off on a tangent about how next time he needed to make sure it would warn them about the weather so they wouldn't get drenched.

"So . . . you're telling me that Fintan had Umber lace my food with creepy shadows and move them to my heart—and then my mom stole his special Spyball, so now she can find me anytime she wants and show up at my door just like you all did?" Keefe verified when they'd finished.

"Well, she'd have to wait for the eleventh hour, but . . . yeah," Dex admitted.

Keefe's laugh had very sharp edges.

"You know, sometimes I think, '*Surely* I've found all the messed-up ways my mom and her creepy little minions have been manipulating my life.' But NOPE! There's always another fun surprise just waiting to be discovered! Anyone want to guess what it'll be next time? Maybe there are light beams hidden in my eyeballs that let her see everything I'm seeing! Or maybe the Neverseen's Technopath made some sort of tiny listening device that's hidden in one of my teeth! Think they can hear us talking right now?"

"I doubt it," Dex said. "The teeth would be a *terrible* place to hide a listening device—you'd have to hear every time someone chews or . . ." His voice trailed off. "Sorry, you meant that hypothetically, didn't you?"

"The sad thing," Keefe said, "is that we probably *should* treat those ideas like possibilities. I mean, *there's a shadow-ripple-tracker thing hidden in my heart!*"

"Not for much longer," Sophie promised, trying to think of something she could add that might somehow soften the blow.

But there wasn't a good way to say, *Sorry your mom and her evil organization keep using and abusing you over and over.*

Keefe sighed and tore his hand through his hair again. "Well . . . I guess the sooner we get rid of it, the better."

"Uh, what are you doing?" Tam asked when Keefe started unbuttoning his pajama shirt.

"You said it's in my chest, right?" Keefe reminded him.

"Yeah, but if I'm already drawing the shadowflux through skin, bone, and muscle, I can also pull it through a little bit of fabric," Tam argued.

Keefe dropped his arms to his sides. "I suppose that's a valid point. So . . . should I sit? Lie down? Do a little dance?"

"Sitting might be wise," Tam decided.

"It's okay to be nervous," Sophie told Keefe, wondering if she should reach for his hand—or sit on the couch next to him.

She wasn't sure how he'd interpret those gestures—or how she *wanted* him to interpret them.

Being around him was so much more awkward now that she was feeling all the things.

It didn't help that Keefe hadn't made a single reference to her emotional turmoil. Not a joke or a raised eyebrow—and there was *no way* he couldn't feel what she was feeling. She was pretty sure everyone in the room could hear how loud her pulse was pounding—maybe everyone in the entire hotel.

So why was Keefe ignoring it?

She knew she was overthinking everything—but how could

she not? Her brain was *very* aware that only a few weeks earlier, Keefe had written her a note telling her he liked her and then disappeared, planning to never see her again. And now they were face-to-face, and neither of them had acknowledged all the changes between them, and it was weird and confusing and—

"You with us, Foster?" Keefe said, tilting his head to study her. "Tam just asked if you wanted to enhance him for this."

"Oh! Sorry." She tried to hide behind her soggy hair as she told Tam, "Whatever you think would be best."

"Might be a good idea," Tam said. "Since I'm not really sure what I'm doing."

"Just so you know, that's *not* making me more excited for this," Keefe informed him.

"It'll be quick," Tam promised. "I think."

"One second," Sophie said when Tam reached for her hand.

She closed her eyes and took a slow breath, feeling for the nerve buried deep in her chest and letting her will slide down it.

Click.

"You've gotten pretty good at that," Keefe noted as her enhancing switched on. "Maybe you can teach me some of your ability-controlling tricks."

"Sure—but only if you want," she added, trying not to sound too eager. She even threw in a shrug—then rolled her eyes at herself.

"Ready?" she asked Tam, trying to focus.

He nodded, and she took his hand, letting sparks of her energy flow through her fingertips into his skin.

"Wow," Tam breathed. "I forgot how intense that is."

"Foster has that effect on people," Keefe said with a smirk that made Sophie want to shout, *Seriously—what does that mean?*

Instead she watched Tam close his eyes and stretch out his other arm.

His lips moved, whispering words too softly for any of them to understand, and his dark brows scrunched together as he curled his fingers, like he was grabbing an invisible rope.

"Okay. I think I know how to call the darkness free. You might feel a little pull," Tam warned as he flicked his hand in a strange pattern—then yanked his arm back like he was playing tug-of-war.

Keefe jerked forward and let out a startled grunt as a tiny whiff of darkness blasted out of his chest and hovered a few feet in front of him.

"It's kinda sad that this isn't even in my top five weirdest experiences," he mumbled, squinting at the shadowy cloud.

"Does it hurt?" Sophie asked when he reached up to rub his chest.

Keefe shook his head. "Not anymore. But that tug was like getting kicked in the ribs."

"Sorry," Tam told him. "I was worried if I went slow, it'd drag out the pain."

"It probably would have," Keefe admitted. "It's all good—

thank you for, uh . . . Huh. I can't think of a non-weird way of saying, 'Thanks for dragging the freaky ripple-tracker thing out of my heart.'"

Tam grinned. "You're welcome."

"You're sure you got it all?" Sophie had to ask as she mentally switched off her enhancing.

Tam nodded and called the shadowflux closer, letting it hover over his palms.

"What are you going to do with that?" Dex asked.

"No idea," Tam admitted. "It'll probably evaporate if I release my hold, but there's a chance Umber did something to it that'll make it unwieldy."

"Oooh—I know!" Keefe jumped up and raced for the trash can, returning with an empty water bottle. "Trap it in there. Then it'll go out with the recycling, and if the tracker is somehow still working, it can lead my mom to a big pile of trash."

"Works for me," Tam said, taking the bottle from him and filling it with the puff of darkness before sealing the lid.

Keefe called the front desk and buried the bottle in the bottom of the bin before leaving it out in the hall for housekeeping.

"Sooooo," he said, plopping back onto the couch once that had all been taken care of. "Does this mean you're ready to tell me the rest? And don't give me the confused eyebrow crinkle, Foster. You told me about the tracker, but you've conveniently *not* told me how you came across a bunch of very specific information about ripples and eleventh hours and altered Spyballs. So hit me with it—what's going on? What is my darling mommy up to now?"

"Honestly, we're not sure," Sophie told him—and she considered leaving it there.

But after everything he'd been through, Keefe deserved a *real* answer.

So she sank into the armchair across from him and told him about the memories they'd found in Kenric's cache. And Elysian. And all the dead ends they'd been hitting. And even though she knew it would be brutal for him, she told him about the memory his dad had recovered, and the possibility of a third step to stellarlune. She figured he might need that context when she told him about their meeting with Trix and Vespera, and the alliance the Neverseen wanted to form now that Gisela was no longer a part of their order.

Keefe was very quiet when she finished.

Also very pale.

And under normal conditions, Sophie would've wrapped him up in a huge hug.

But nothing about the situation was normal.

So she stayed right where she was.

Keefe was the one who stood and crossed the room, stopping in front of her chair.

Her mouth went dry as he leaned closer, and for a second it looked like he was going to take her hands. But he pivoted at the last moment, placing his palms on her shoulders—which would've felt more intimate if his fingers hadn't made a squishy sound when they touched her soaked cape.

"Please tell me you didn't agree to this horrible plan," he murmured. "I know you're the queen of huge risks, but—"

"I didn't agree," Sophie said, trying not to think about the fact that he was close enough for her to see the tiny flecks of darker blue in his ice blue irises. "We're going to find Elysian on our own."

Keefe nodded and stepped back to pace, making it much easier for Sophie to breathe as she explained what Wylie was doing to try to find the starstone, and how she was convinced they'd be able to see through the illusions. And Dex chimed in, saying he had plans for a gadget to separate beams of light.

When they finished, there was a much thicker, heavier silence as Keefe watched the rain streak down one of the windows.

"We'll be careful," Sophie assured him. "And once we get that power source—"

Keefe spun back to face her, his expression angled into serious lines. "You have to destroy it, Sophie! I mean it. I need you to listen to me on this. If you actually do find Elysian and track down these special glowing rocks—or whatever they are—you *have* to destroy them. Otherwise *everyone* is going to come after you. The Council. The Neverseen. My mom. Who knows—maybe the other species will even get in on the action. Sounds like the trolls definitely will. And there's no way you're going to be able to protect it through all of that. So you *have* to destroy it. Otherwise you'll put yourself—and everyone you care about—in worse danger than they've ever been in before. And the power will probably still end up in the wrong hands."

"No, it won't," Sophie argued. "I'll hide it—"

"And they'll start hurting people you love until you tell them where it is," he insisted, moving closer and taking her by the shoulders again. "You know I'm right."

Sophie shook her head.

She forced herself to stare into his much-too-pretty eyes, wondering if he could feel how fast her heart was racing when she told him, "The thing is . . . you might need it."

She didn't care that the last step to stellarlune might be designed to break Keefe.

There had to be a way to use the power to fix anything he was struggling with.

Keefe's smile was the perfect mix of beautiful and devastating when he told her, "I had a feeling you were going to say that. And I appreciate it—you have no idea how much. I've never had anyone try to take care of me the way you do, and . . ." He started to say something else, then changed his mind, taking a deep breath before he added, "But this is bigger than me, Sophie. And it's bigger than you. It's bigger than *everyone*. So I need you to promise me that if you get anywhere near that power source, you'll do everything possible to destroy it."

She could tell he wasn't going to let this go.

"Fine," she said, sitting up a little taller. "I promise."

Keefe sighed—but his lips also curled into a determined smile. "Clearly you still haven't learned that you can't lie to an Empath. So I guess that only leaves me one other option."

"Wait—where are you going?" she asked as he marched toward one of the suite's bedrooms.

"To get my stuff," he called over his shoulder. "I'm coming with you."

THIRTY-EIGHT

WELCOME HOME!" EDALINE shouted from somewhere up ahead as Havenfield's moonlit pastures slowly glittered into shadowy focus. "Thought I'd wait outside so I could keep an eye on our new family of gremlins, who seem determined to dismantle their enclosure. Plus, I figured I should warn you that Sandor and Grady are up in your room, debating some *very* creative ways to punish you for running off without a bodyguard. I got a message from my sister explaining that Kesler was about to bring our furious goblin home, and there's been a lot of grumbling and stomping around here ever since. You *might* want to consider apologizing. And Dex: You should probably

head to Rimeshire to face the wrath of Lovise and . . . wait—
is that Dex?"

"No, Dex already went home," Sophie called back.

She couldn't tell where Edaline was—her eyes were still
adjusting to the darkness after so much time in the bright
London suite.

But Edaline must've been able to see them much more
clearly because her next guess wasn't Tam—even though she'd
known that Tam had also been with Sophie.

"Keefe? Is that you?"

"Uh . . . yeah," Keefe mumbled, fidgeting with the strap of
the large duffel bag he'd packed before leaving his hotel. He'd
also changed out of his pajamas—but for some reason he'd
put on human jeans and a blue zip-up hoodie. "Surprise?"

Sophie honestly had no idea how her parents were going to
react to her showing up in the middle of the night with a runaway boy after breaking a ton of rules to go find him.

But Edaline obviously didn't care about any of that.

She raced over and pulled Keefe into a huge hug. "I'm so
glad you're back—we've missed you around here!"

Keefe's voice sounded a little choked when he asked, "You
have?"

"Of course!" Edaline leaned back to study him with the
same look that always made Sophie feel like Edaline was trying to peer into her soul. "How are you doing? And before
you answer, I want you to know that you don't have to tell me

anything you don't want to, or feel any pressure. In fact, you don't have to talk at all if that's still a struggle for you. I just want you to know that I'm here if you need *anything*, okay? And I'm always happy to listen if there's something on your mind."

"Huh." Keefe cleared his throat a couple of times—but his voice was still thick when he added, "So that's what a mom is supposed to sound like. Good to know."

Edaline hugged him even tighter until Keefe finally teased her about not letting him breathe.

"You and Foster should have a strangle-hugging contest," he said as Edaline released her hold. "It's hard to tell who would win—though Foster almost knocked me over."

"Did she, now?"

Sophie refused to look at her adoptive mother.

Her heart and her stomach were already in the middle of some sort of backflipping competition, and she knew seeing Edaline's goofy grin would only make it worse.

But she did steal a glance at Keefe and . . .

Nothing.

No smirk.

No glint in his eye.

No fanning the air like he was trying to keep her emotional storm away.

If anything, he looked . . . confused.

It seriously didn't make any sense.

Unless . . .

Was he trying to spare her feelings by pretending to be oblivious?

Had something changed since he left her that note?

"Can I get you something to eat?" Edaline asked as Sophie fought the urge to dig a hole and bury herself. "I baked some mallowmelt this morning and—"

"YES, PLEASE!" Keefe interrupted. "I'll take all the mallowmelt I can get!"

"And some bottles of Youth, right?" Sophie said, forcing a smile.

Keefe jumped up and down. "THAT WOULD BE AMAZING!"

He actually looked a little teary when Edaline snapped her fingers and made a tray full of glass bottles appear at his feet, along with the entire pan of mallowmelt. And he let out a long, happy sigh as he grabbed one of the Youth bottles and chugged the whole thing.

"Wow—this is even better than I remembered. That's it, I'm never leaving again."

"Oh really?" Sophie asked, trying to keep her tone teasing and casual.

But she was dying to know what Keefe was planning.

He hadn't made it clear before they left London whether this trip was his way of coming home for good, or if he was just back until the Elysian-Nightfall-star-alignment stuff was no longer looming over them.

And he didn't give her an answer then, either.

He just shrugged and took a huge bite of mallowmelt, letting out some sort of unintelligible moan.

Edaline laughed, but her smile faded when her gaze shifted to Sophie. "You okay?"

"Yeah," Sophie promised. "It's just been . . . a really long day."

"It *has*," Edaline agreed, and the hint of weariness in her tone made Sophie realize how stressed her parents must've been.

After all, she'd left that morning to go meet with the Neverseen—and then *many* hours later, she'd shown up with Tam, grabbed her Spyball, and rattled off some excuse about needing Dex to help them test something before leaping away again. The next thing Grady and Edaline knew, she'd run off to a Forbidden City without her bodyguard. And they'd been waiting for her to come home ever since.

"I'm sorry if I worried you," Sophie said quietly. "And I'm sorry for ditching Sandor. I just—"

"It's okay," Edaline interrupted, tucking Sophie's hair behind her ear. "I'm sure Grady and Sandor would do a lot more grumbling if they heard me say this, but . . . I think you've been through enough at this point that if you decide to leave your bodyguard behind because it feels like the safer move—I trust you. I'll still worry, of course, but . . . that's just part of mom life. And I would also *love* an update, since clearly a lot has happened."

Sophie frowned. "Sandor didn't tell you about our meeting with Trix?"

"No, he did. But I want *all* the details." She raised her eyebrows with the last words and tilted her head quickly toward Keefe.

Sophie choked back her groan.

"Not tonight," Edaline added, temporarily letting her off the hook. "I'm sure you're ready to collapse into bed."

"I am," Sophie admitted—and it suddenly occurred to her that she had no idea where Keefe was planning to sleep.

"Are you . . . going back to Elwin's?" she asked.

Keefe paused midbite. "Huh. I hadn't thought about that. I definitely can't handle Daddy Dearest at the Shores of Sadness right now—but it'd probably be weird to show up at Elwin's place this late. Plus, Ro's probably been setting up some sort of elaborate torture chamber there."

"Actually, Ro left the Lost Cities a few weeks ago," Edaline told him.

Keefe stood up taller. "Was that because of me?"

"No—she was pretty determined to stick around so she could figure out the best way to punish you," Sophie assured him. "She even stayed with me for a while."

He snorted. "Bet *that* was an interesting little slumber party."

"It definitely was. But then Mr. Forkle asked Ro to warn King Dimitar because he'd heard rumors that Cadfael and the other rebel ogres are planning some sort of uprising. And at first Ro didn't want to go because she doesn't think it's a real threat. But Mr. Forkle talked her into it—and she decided that if she was leaving, she was going to try to track down Cadfael so she could interrogate him about the Neverseen. She's been gone for a couple of weeks now. Not sure how much longer it'll take."

"Did she go by herself?" Keefe asked. "Or are Ro and Bo off on a romantic adventure that needs to be added to their epic ballad?"

Sophie laughed. "Bo's still here—for now. We'll see how long that lasts. He's been guarding Glimmer, but the Council's probably going to give her a little more freedom now that she set up the meeting with Trix. Oh, and her real name's Rayni, by the way."

Keefe blinked. "Sounds like there's a *lot* you still need to fill me in on."

"There is. A *lot* has changed while you've been gone."

"Yeah . . . I'm noticing that."

"What does *that* mean?" Sophie asked before she could stop herself.

It kinda seemed like he might finally be acknowledging the new feelings he had to be picking up from her.

But maybe she was just imagining it, because he sounded pretty sincere when he told her, "Nothing. It just hit me that I'm officially bodyguard-free!"

"Not for long," Sophie warned as he did an adorable little happy dance. "Ro gave me a packet of bacteria and made me promise to smear it on my skin as soon as you showed up so she'd know to hurry back."

"Aw, but . . . we both know you don't want to do that, right, Foster? I mean . . . it's ogre bacteria!"

"It is. But if I don't do it, I'll have to deal with an angry ogre princess when she finds out I broke my promise—and I already have a fuming goblin warrior up in my bedroom."

"Ugh. I suppose that's a fair point." Keefe sighed. "Oooh, how about we ditch them both and head back to London! I've still got plenty of cash—and I keep hearing I need to try something called banoffee pie. No idea what a banoffee is, but I'm always down for desserts! And we can take the rest of these Youths so we don't have to drink their gross water, and—"

"Fun as that little adventure sounds," Edaline jumped in, "I'm pretty sure Sophie's father will have a meltdown if she disappears again."

"Yeah, and we only have ten days left to find Elysian," Sophie reminded him, even though the London escape plan had sounded pretty awesome—not that she actually thought he was serious about it. "Or is it nine now?"

She glanced at the sky, wondering if she'd be able to tell by the stars.

Keefe followed her gaze. "Fiiiiiiiiiiine. I guess we can try being responsible—and, whoa, I didn't realize you were armed," he said as Sophie removed Hope from her holster to get to the golden packet of Linquillosa tucked underneath.

"Neither did I," Edaline noted.

"Oh. Yeah. Ro thought it might be good for me to start being more prepared, so she gave me one of her daggers. And Flori made me a holster, and . . ."

She stopped herself before she mentioned that she'd given the dagger a name.

Keefe would have *way* too much fun with that knowledge.

Then again, maybe it would help ease some of the awkwardness if they started joking around a little more.

Or would it feel painfully forced?

"So how does that stuff work?" Edaline asked as Sophie used Hope's blade to slice open the packet.

"It's supposed to make the same bacteria on Ro's skin change color to match the color it turns on mine." She sprinkled the Linquillosa on the underside of her left wrist and fought back a giggle. "Sorry. Ro warned me it would tickle."

And even in the moonlight she could see a purple-blue mark forming on her skin.

"That's not a bruise," she promised when she noticed Edaline's frown. "Doesn't hurt at all. But if Ro doesn't show up quick, I might have to wear a bracelet or something to cover it."

"Oh, I'm sure she'll race back as fast as she can, armed with all kinds of fun new microbes to torment me—and I can't even blame her." Keefe chugged another bottle of Youth. "I guess I should try to make the most of my last few hours of freedom—not that I have anywhere to go or anything to do."

"You're welcome to stay here," Edaline offered. "Jolie's room is all cleared out—I could have the gnomes set you up in there."

"A gnomish bed does sound amazing. But . . ." Keefe stole a glance at Sophie. "I'm not sure it's a good idea for me to be locked in a house with Grady and Gigantor when they're both in rage mode."

"Oh, would their emotions be too much on your senses?" Edaline asked. "I could also set you up outside under the Panakes tree. Sophie used to do that all the time."

"I remember." Keefe smiled for a second before he shifted his gaze to his feet. "I don't know. I think I might need to find somewhere with no memories attached to it. I know that probably sounds weird, but . . . everything's so different now. It kinda helps to be somewhere new. Somewhere I'm not thinking about how it used to be, if that makes sense."

"It does," Edaline told him. "And I hope you know that there's no right or wrong way to process what you've been through, Keefe—what you're still going through. If something helps, you should trust that instinct."

"You should," Sophie agreed, even if a small, sad part of her wondered if that meant he wasn't planning to stay in the Lost Cities.

Was *that* why he'd chosen to wear human clothes?

"If you're looking for a new experience," Flori said, stepping out of the shadows, "might I suggest staying in the Grove? There are many empty trees always ready for visitors, and one is particularly known for its vibrant melodies. I believe it will do wonders to clear your head."

"Uh . . . sure. I'm down to try a gnomish sleepover," Keefe told her.

Flori flashed a green-toothed smile. "I'll prepare a bed."

"And I'll let you two say good night," Edaline added, giving them each a huge goofy grin before she turned and fled. "Take your time!"

Sophie was tempted to chase her down and clobber her.

Instead she stood there, shuffling her soggy feet, trying to figure out how to break the uncomfortable silence.

"Gotta say . . . ," Keefe finally said when he'd finished his last bite of mallowmelt. "This definitely wasn't how I thought my day was going to go."

"Me neither." And just in case he was upset about it, she added, "You didn't have to come back with me."

"Yes, I did."

There was something strange about his voice—a pained edge to each word.

Sophie looked away. "No, you didn't. I can handle myself—"

"I know you can, Foster. Why do you think I'm here? I have zero doubt that you're going to find Elysian, break through those illusions, and scoop up a big old bag of those powerful stones, thinking you can use them to save me. But . . . it isn't going to work that way. I know the Black Swan had to reset your abilities—"

"*Twice.*"

"Right. But remember: Project Moonlark was designed by a supersmart team, with Calla and Forkle and Livvy and who knows how many others. Stellarlune is my mom's creation, and . . . all she makes are giant messes."

Sophie's heart ached at the rawness in his voice. "You're not a mess, Keefe."

"Trust me, I am."

"You're *not*. You're already getting a little better—look how easily we're talking right now. A few weeks ago you couldn't have done that!"

He shook his head. "That doesn't mean what you think it means."

"Then what does it mean?"

"It means . . . I don't know."

"I'm pretty sure you do, and you just don't want to tell me."

"Maybe." He turned away, dragging his hands through his hair. "Ugh, this is so not how I thought it would go if I ever saw you again."

There was that *if* again.

But this time it seemed a little less definitive.

Which gave her the courage to ask, "How did you think it would go?"

"Well . . . I figured there would be a whole lot of groveling—by me, of course. And then when that didn't work, I'd switch to bribery."

"Bribery?"

"Yep. I even had my first gift ready to go."

It was hard to tell in the moonlight, but Sophie was pretty sure his cheeks were blushing as he unzipped his duffel and pulled out . . .

. . . a tiny stuffed elf.

If Sophie had been a cartoon, her eyes would've turned into giant hearts.

The elf had pointy ears and a cute little hat and curled shoes with little bells on the toes!

"I know it's silly," Keefe said, totally misreading her burst of giggles, "but I also know you love stuffed animals. And, I mean . . . look at his little elf face!"

He shook the elf's striped legs, making him do a little dance.

Sophie giggled harder. "Seriously, it's perfect! I love it!"

She just couldn't tell if she was supposed to reach out and take it.

Keefe hadn't really offered.

He also didn't seem to notice that her mood was screaming, *WHY DON'T YOU HUG ME RIGHT NOW?*

Or maybe he did, because he mumbled, "Oh good, well . . . it's yours, then," and kinda half handed, half tossed the tiny elf to her. "Glad I brought it with me. I almost didn't, in case . . .

Anyway, I should probably, uh, go find Flori. See you tomorrow, Foster!"

She blinked, and he was gone, basically sprinting away through the pastures.

And she wasn't sure how long she stood there, staring at the tiny elf, wishing it could tell her what just happened, or what she'd done wrong to turn such an incredible moment into something that felt so empty.

Sadly, his tiny smiling mouth didn't have any answers.

So she hugged her new stuffed animal tight and slowly made her way inside, bracing for a goblin inquisition.

But Edaline must've convinced Sandor to save his lecture for the morning. Her room was blissfully empty when she got there—with trays of mallowmelt and lushberry juice waiting on her bed.

Sophie considered barricading the door and hiding in another fluff cocoon for as long as she could. Maybe she'd even reread Keefe's letter a few thousand times trying to decide if she'd misunderstood it—or if it seemed like he regretted what he'd said.

Instead, she set Keefe's gift on her nightstand and focused on getting ready for bed.

Showers always helped clear her head, so she tried to imagine all her biggest worries and insecurities washing away as she stood under the colorful streams of water. And maybe it worked, because her brain was much quieter as she changed into her favorite alicorn pajamas and settled back against her pillows to hug Ella.

The truth was, she didn't need to know what the tiny elf meant, or why Keefe fled after giving it to her. The point was, he'd thought of her—even when he wasn't sure if he was ever coming back.

And he *was* back—at least for the moment.

He was also clearly still dealing with tons of huge things, so he didn't need her adding any more pressure with lots of questions.

He'd sat patiently by while she worked through her feelings with Fitz.

Maybe now she needed to give him some time.

And maybe that was better, since she had plenty of enormous challenges to keep her busy.

Nine days to find the starstone.

Nine days to convince Keefe to let her keep a little of the power.

Nine days to *finally* get ahead of their enemies.

THIRTY-NINE

KEEFE HOME! KEEFE HOME! KEEFE
HOME!

Silveny's chant woke Sophie up much
earlier than she'd wanted. And there was absolutely no way to ignore it—especially once Wynn's and Luna's
tiny voices chimed in.

*KEEFE HOME! KEEFE HOME! KEEFE HOME! KEEFE
HOME! KEEFE HOME! KEEFE HOME!*

I KNOW! she tried transmitting to all of them. *I'M THE
ONE WHO BROUGHT HIM BACK!*

*KEEFE HOME! KEEFE HOME! KEEFE HOME! KEEFE
HOME! KEEFE HOME! KEEFE HOME!*

Sophie finally threw back her covers, knowing the only way

to quiet the chaos was to head down to the pastures for whatever reunion the alicorns were demanding.

But she might've spent a little extra time getting ready first.

She even asked Vertina to walk her through pulling the front part of her hair back into a couple of loose twists and applying the tiniest bit of eyeliner.

Maybe it was silly, but she'd felt way too much like a soggy sasquatch the night before and wanted to feel a little more confident that morning.

And she had to admit . . . she looked pretty awesome.

"Going somewhere?" Sandor asked, blocking her path when she opened her bedroom door. "I see you're in your school uniform—but that could be a ruse."

"It's not," Sophie assured him. "I'm heading down to the pastures because Silveny and the twins are calling for me, and then . . . I'm going to Foxfire."

She'd gone round and round on whether it was a bad idea to sit through tedious school sessions when they were on such a tight timeline. But it was the easiest way to check in with her friends—and Magnate Leto—and make sure she knew what they were working on.

Plus . . . she had a feeling that Keefe might need a little space—and going to Foxfire gave her a way to make that happen without seeming like she was avoiding him.

"Is there anything you'd like to say to me?" Sandor asked, still standing in her way.

Sophie nodded, and her mouth turned sour as she noticed all the scratches and bruises on his arms and chest—probably from when Trix had slammed him with winds. "I'm sorry for leaving you at Dex's house yesterday."

"Are you?" he pressed. "Or would you do it again?"

"Can't it be both?" She sighed when he glared at her. "Come on, Sandor—you *have* to know that as this all gets bigger and scarier, there are going to be times when I have to do things on my own. You won't always be able to protect me."

"It's my *job* to protect you!"

"I know. And you're amazing at it! Seriously! I wouldn't be alive without you. And I know you make huge sacrifices for me every day." She pointed to a particularly big scab running along his chin.

"*But?*" he prompted.

"But . . . I can't be a leader if I'm having to follow my bodyguard's orders all the time. Sometimes I have to be able to decide for myself."

She expected him to argue.

Instead he hung his burly goblin head. "I suppose you may have a point—but only a *small* one that affects a *limited* amount of decisions. Great leaders surround themselves with those wiser and stronger and more experienced than them—and rely on their judgment as much as possible!"

"And I *do* rely on you," Sophie promised. "I'll even take whatever punishment you and Grady have been planning for me. Just . . . maybe also *try* to trust me? At least some-times?"

He stood up taller. "I'll do my best."

"Thank you. And I'll try not to abandon you around the trip-lets again," she said, fighting back a smile as she remembered the look in his eyes when the floor had first turned slippery.

"Funny you should mention that, since your father decided that Lovise and I deserve a day off—and so do your fami-lies," Sandor told her. "So he's signed you and Dex up for a day of triplet babysitting—just the two of you. Though Tam is welcome to join in. And I realize you're on a timeline at the moment, so this won't happen immediately. But it's *definitely* happening. Think of it as a chance for you to prove how well you handle things without my protection."

His grin was so gleeful that Sophie had to laugh.

"Well played," she said as he finally stepped aside to let her pass. But she couldn't resist adding, "Maybe you can use your day off to finally wear those silver pants I've heard so much about and take Grizel dancing."

Sandor muttered something about foolish bets as he fol-lowed her down the stairs.

Sophie's head was still filled with a whole lot of chanting, so she went straight outside to the pastures to track down the demanding alicorns.

"You're up early," Edaline called from the gremlin enclo-sure, which was now mostly torn apart—just a few wobbly bars with several tiny furry creatures climbing all over them. "Eager to see someone, perhaps?"

Sophie rolled her eyes. "Yeah, Silveny, Wynn, and Luna won't stop calling for me. I was going to offer to help you before I head over to their pasture—but not after that comment!"

Edaline laughed. "Guess it's a good thing Grady will be back any minute with more building supplies—and maybe some sort of sedative for these fluffy terrors." She scooped up two gremlins and plopped them back in what remained of their enclosure. "In case you were wondering: Gremlins are some of my least favorite creatures to rehabilitate."

"I bet," Sophie said. "Well . . . if you need me, you know where to find me."

"I definitely do! Have fun! And remember, I still want details!"

Sophie threw her arms out in the most dramatic way possible. "You're ridiculous!"

"I love you!" was all Edaline said.

Sophie spent the rest of her walk trying to calm her buzzing nerves and reminding herself that she was giving Keefe time and space. But her heartbeat still felt like galloping alicorn hooves when she found Wynn and Luna rolling around on the grass in the middle of some sort of baby-alicorn wrestling session—with Keefe tangled up in the middle.

Deep breaths, she told herself. *Act normal.*

"Awww, this is so much cuteness!" she said, laughing when

Keefe bolted upright, conking his head on an alicorn wing. "I was talking about Wynn and Luna."

Keefe smirked. "Of *course* you were."

This was good.

She could do this.

She just needed to tease him a little.

Keep it lighthearted.

And she needed to try very hard to not think about how good Keefe still managed to look despite the fact that his pants and tunic were covered in mud and bits of grass.

It was also *very* nice to see him back in elvin clothes.

Made her wonder if he was thinking about staying after all.

She almost asked him about it, but . . . he was staring at her with an unreadable expression.

"Everything okay?" she said, tugging on her vest to make sure it wasn't buttoned crooked or something.

He cleared his throat. "Yeah. I just . . . didn't realize Foxfire was open again."

"Oh. Yeah." She fussed with her cape. "The Council's trying to boost morale by pretending everything's normal. You'd hate it. They extended the sessions to three hours to make up for all the lost time."

"Ugh, yeah, definitely *not* sorry to be missing that."

But . . . it kinda sounded like he was.

"Did you sleep okay?" she asked, changing to a safer subject. "Glad to be back in a gnomish bed?"

"*So* glad," he agreed. "Though I think the tree's songs gave me really weird dreams. I was a wildflower swaying in the breeze, letting the wind dance through my petals—"

"Your *petals*?" Sophie had to interrupt.

"Yeah, like I said—*weird* dreams. And then these little monsters woke me up," he said, trying to untangle himself from all the flailing legs. "Don't be fooled by their big sparkly eyes. They keep tackling me and headbutting me—and don't ask me how, but they've found a way to fill my mind with transmissions. It's brutal. Is this what it's like in your head when you're around them? How do you not have a constant headache? And they keep telling me—*very loudly*—that I need to apologize for something."

On cue Wynn and Luna unleashed a round of *SAY SORRY! SAY SORRY! SAY SORRY!*

"See?" Keefe said, ducking before he got clonked in the face by one of Luna's wings. "It's *so* loud! And they won't tell me why they're mad—I don't suppose you know?"

Silveny chose that moment to drop out of the sky, landing right in front of them.

Keefe stumbled to his feet, shaking grass out of his hair. "Hey, Glitter Butt! Did you miss me?"

KEEFE! KEEFE! KEEFE!

"Whoa—I can hear you now too!" He glanced at Sophie. "Think that has something to do with the whole stellarlune thing?"

"It could—but it might also be that they figured out the trick to transmitting to non-Telepaths. You have to send your thoughts with a lot more force—and a *lot* more volume."

KEEFE! KEEFE! KEEFE!

Keefe rubbed his head. "That might be it."

He took a step closer, reaching out to pet Silveny's nose—but she opened her mouth and chomped.

Keefe jerked his arm back *just* in time. "Whoa—what was that for?"

SAY SORRY! SAY SORRY! SAY SORRY!

Keefe rubbed his temples harder. "You too, huh?"

Wynn and Luna joined in, trotting circles around him.

SAY SORRY! SAY SORRY! SAY SORRY! SAY SORRY! SAY SORRY! SAY SORRY!

"Okay . . . ," Keefe said, turning to Sophie. "I seriously have no idea what I did."

Silveny jumped in before Sophie could answer.

WHY IGNORE? WHY IGNORE? WHY IGNORE?

"After you left, I asked them to try transmitting to you," Sophie explained, "even though I knew it was a long shot since you're not a Telepath. It just . . . seemed like they'd be more likely to get your attention if they could figure out how to reach you. So they've been calling you every day—for weeks—wanting to make sure you were okay."

"Oh." Keefe looked away. "I . . . didn't realize it was every day."

Which meant, of course, that he must've heard at least some of the alicorns' calls—and probably Sophie's transmissions as well.

Suddenly Sophie felt like joining Silveny when she repeated, *WHY IGNORE? WHY IGNORE? WHY IGNORE?*

"Well . . . it seems like they want an apology," she told him. "And it might help if you answer their question."

Keefe sighed. "Yeah, probably."

He kept his eyes on the ground, making it impossible to tell who he was talking to when he said, "I really *am* sorry. I didn't *want* to ignore anyone. I just . . . didn't know what else to do. Leaving the Lost Cities was seriously the hardest thing I've ever done—and every time I let myself think about what I'd left behind, I wanted to grab my stuff and leap back home. So I tried to block everything out and pretend it didn't exist. I knew I was being a jerk, but . . . I didn't know how else to get over it."

JERK! JERK! JERK! Wynn and Luna transmitted, charging toward Keefe and knocking him over again.

Sophie's brain, meanwhile, was much more focused on the whole "get over it" part of that explanation.

Was *that* why he hadn't brought up the note he'd left in her room?

Had he spent the last few weeks getting over whatever he'd been feeling and now he didn't know how to tell her?

"You okay, Foster?" Keefe asked, frowning as he studied her.

Silveny saved her from having to answer by chasing Wynn

and Luna away so they couldn't taunt Keefe anymore. Then she made her way over to where Keefe sat in the trampled grass and nuzzled his cheek.

"Well . . . at least Glitter Butt forgives me," Keefe mumbled.

"I'm sure Wynn and Luna forgive you too," Sophie promised.

She could still hear some faint *JERK! JERK! JERK!* chants in the distance—but she was pretty sure the bratty alicorns just liked the word.

"That's . . . not who I'm worried about," Keefe said quietly.

"Oh." Sophie crossed her arms, trying to think of something she could say that wouldn't drag them into too messy of a conversation. She wasn't sure her heart was ready for that. "I'm not mad at you, Keefe. It's just . . . a lot to process. You were gone. Now you're back. And . . ."

He nodded, like he knew where she was going with the rest of that sentence—even though she honestly had no idea.

"Sorry," he said, tearing out blades of grass and tossing them away. "I used to be better at this stuff. But I don't know how to talk to people anymore."

"That's right." Sophie hated herself for not realizing how thoughtless she was being. "I'm sorry. Is that because of the whole voice-command thing?"

He shredded more grass. "That's part of it."

"What's the other part?" When he stayed quiet, she tried guessing. "Does it have something to do with what happened with Rex?"

He closed his eyes. "Unfortunately, that's a whole other nightmare. I keep feeling like I shouldn't touch anyone's skin—or let them touch mine—now that I'm here, in case it triggers something in them, or tells me they'll be Talentless. I don't even know if that's how the ability works—I was so overwhelmed when Rex, Bex, and Lex were grabbing at me during those experiments that I don't know if they touched my clothes or what. But . . . your enhancing is connected to touch, so it seems pretty logical. That's why I grabbed your elbow when we leaped here, and I keep wearing long sleeves and thick fabric— and I know I should probably also wear gloves, but . . . gloves are so itchy. I seriously don't know how you wore them for so long. Plus, wearing them makes me picture my mom pointing at them and shouting, 'I won! I changed him!'"

"Okay, wow, that's a lot of words," Sophie said, sitting on the grass beside him. "I can tell your mind is racing—and I understand why. But . . . deep breaths." She waited for him to breathe in and out a couple of times before she told him, "She *didn't* win, Keefe. I get why it might feel like that—but you have to fight that fear, because you're still you. I mean it. She's made you more powerful—but that doesn't change who you are. You're a *good* person who would never try to hurt anyone—"

"I might not have a choice anymore."

"I think you have more control than you realize. Want to find out?"

"Uh . . . how?"

"Just go with me on this. Do you *want* to be able to trigger abilities?"

"Yeah, no—hard pass."

"Okay," Sophie said. "Focus on that as I try something."

She scooted closer, holding his stare as she reached out and slowly placed her hand over his, making sure her fingers pressed against his skin.

Keefe didn't move.

She wasn't sure if he was breathing.

"Feel anything?" she asked—then realized how that sounded. "Any sign that I'm about to develop a new ability?" she clarified. "It's okay if you are. I have five already—what's one more?"

Keefe snorted a laugh and closed his eyes. "Well . . . I hate to break it to you, Foster, but I don't feel anything—any new abilities," he corrected, turning bright red. "But . . . that might just mean you're done manifesting."

"It might. But . . . I don't know. Forkle's said some things that kinda make it seem like there's some other stuff that hasn't switched on yet. So it *could* be that the reason you're not feeling any of that is because you're choosing not to. Or it could be that we don't know how your ability works. Or maybe what happened with Rex, Bex, and Lex was all a coincidence and had nothing to do with you. Your powers are too new for us to know. And you'll never figure it out if you're too afraid to test them. You just have to convince yourself that you're in control when you try them out."

"But I'm *not* in control. You just think I am because I'm not giving you any creepy commands."

"That's a huge victory! You went from barely being able to say a few words to being able to have whole conversations."

"Yeah, but it's not the same. I barely know how to talk to people anymore. It's so much harder without being able to read them."

"What do you mean?"

He covered his face with his free hand—and Sophie resisted the urge to press him.

She decided to try Edaline's taming-a-dinosaur method instead and just sat there quietly, waiting him out.

Sure enough, after a few agonizing minutes, he told her, "The reason I'm not giving commands right now is because . . . I feel kinda . . . numb."

Numb.

The word exploded in Sophie's brain—shaking loose a whole new avalanche of worries.

"You mean like . . . what you told me can happen to Empaths?" she whispered.

"Not *that* bad. At least not yet—but I don't know if that's where I'm heading. I was getting so bombarded by emotions that I tried to find a way to switch my empathy off, like you do with your enhancing. But nothing worked. And it got so over-whelming that I had to just tune everything out, and . . . now I mostly feel this, like, flat, dull ache. I mean, obviously I have moments where my emotions still take over, or I pick up something a little stronger from someone"—he stole a quick glance at where her hand still rested on his—"but most of the time it's like my brain doesn't know what to do with anything I'm feeling. And I keep saying the wrong thing or making everything awkward because I don't know how to read people anymore, and it's the most annoying thing ever, and . . . like I said . . . I'm a mess."

"You're *not* a mess," Sophie told him, hoping he couldn't pick up any of her relief.

She knew he was scared and struggling—and she didn't want to minimize that.

But she also couldn't stop her brain from shouting, *MAYBE HE HASN'T GOTTEN OVER ME.*

"You just need more time," she told him. "And more training."

"Sophie's right," Grady said behind them, making them both yank their hands back and scramble to their feet.

Even Silveny whinnied and launched into the sky.

Grady cleared his throat. "Sorry. I didn't mean to startle you. And I didn't mean to eavesdrop, either. In fact, I was turning to walk away, but I caught just enough—without trying to listen, of course—and . . . the thing is, Keefe, what you're experiencing actually sounds pretty normal. Strong abilities have a way of taking over if you don't manage them properly. Sophie and I have talked about this before as she's struggled with her inflicting—and I ran into the same thing with my mesmerizing. I got to a point where I didn't even have to decide to give the command—the words would just pour out of me like second nature. But that didn't mean I was broken and never able to speak again. It meant I needed to get a better handle on my power."

"But I've been trying—"

"I'm sure you have," Grady interrupted. "But you also woke up with how many new abilities all at once? And it's been how many weeks since that happened? Give yourself time. And give yourself permission to struggle. And give yourself some help. We all need lots of training to manage these powers."

"Yeah, but . . . no one has abilities like mine," Keefe reminded him.

"Doesn't have to be an exact match," Grady told him. "Just someone who understands the push and pull that comes with an intense power. I'd be happy to work with you, if you want."

"Really?" Keefe asked, swallowing hard before he added, "You would do that?"

"Of course, Keefe. You're not in this alone."

"Wait—what's happening?" Sophie asked, trying to process the sudden shift. "You two are going to . . . train together?"

Keefe raised an eyebrow. "What? You think I can't handle a little one-on-one time with the Gradynator?"

"I think the fact that you're calling him the Gradynator kinda makes my point for me," Sophie countered.

Grady laughed. "I'll admit, it's not my favorite nickname. But it's fine. If I can tame mastodons and velociraptors, I'm pretty sure I can work with Keefe for a few hours every day while you're away at Foxfire. And if I could rein in my mesmerizing, I can certainly help him gain better control of his empathy—and any other abilities he's struggling with."

"Not sure how I feel about some of those comparisons," Keefe noted, "but . . . I've tried everything else I can think of at this point. So I'm willing to give it a go if you are."

"Sounds like a plan," Grady told him. "Just let me help Edaline with the gremlin situation, and then I'll come find you—and shouldn't you be heading to orientation?" he asked Sophie.

"I . . . guess."

Grady laughed again. "Relax, kiddo. What's the worst that could happen?"

Sophie could think of *many* things that could go *very* wrong with this plan.

Especially when Keefe asked, "Should we call ourselves Team Gradeefe or Team Keefrady? Or maybe Team Krady?"

"We'll be fine," Grady told her. "Go to school. Learn things."

"Don't do anything I wouldn't do!" Keefe added as Sophie reluctantly turned to head to the Leapmaster.

Maybe she imagined it, but she almost swore he added under his breath, "I'll miss you."

FORTY

WELL . . . YOU'RE NOT
barricaded inside any of the animal
enclosures," Sophie said when she
leaped back from Foxfire and found
Keefe sitting in the shade of Calla's Panakes tree. "So maybe
training with Grady didn't go *as* bad as I feared?"

Keefe snorted. "Very funny."

"What? I'm serious! I half expected to come home and find
that Grady had mesmerized you to do an embarrassing wiggle
dance over and over because you kept trying to convince him
to call you Sir Smirks-a-Lot—and honestly, I wouldn't have
minded seeing that."

"Wow, someone's full of jokes today," Keefe noted.

"Is that bad?" Sophie asked.

"Not at all. You just seem . . . I don't know." He tilted his head as he studied her. "You're different somehow. . . ."

"I keep hearing that," Sophie told him—which was true.

But.

There was a chance that Keefe's empathy was finally starting to pick up on something way more complicated and potentially embarrassing than her recent mastery of the snarky comeback.

Especially since he was sitting there with Panakes blossoms scattered through his perfectly mussed hair and a stack of journals and colored pencils in his lap, as if he were playing the role of the artsy heartthrob in a human teen rom-com—and her heart was definitely a fan.

She just wasn't sure what to do about it.

She didn't want to bombard him with her newfound *feelings*.

But she couldn't just switch them off, either.

So what were the options?

Hide and avoid him?

That didn't seem right.

There had to be a way to be his friend *and* want to kiss him—though thinking about kissing him definitely wasn't helping the situation.

"You okay there, Foster?" Keefe asked. "You kinda look like you want to tug out all your eyelashes."

"Do I?" She forced herself to sit next to him—but kept a pocket of "friend" space to hopefully make it less weird. "I was just . . . wondering how training went. Do you think it'll help?"

Keefe leaned his head back against the wide trunk of the Panakes. "I don't know. Everything Grady had me try is stuff I've already been doing—and getting nowhere. But . . . it was only the first lesson. Hopefully he was just laying the groundwork and tomorrow we'll build on it."

"Does he know about *all* the things you can do—or might be able to do?" she asked. "Because that could change his approach—though I definitely understand if you don't want to tell him."

"I gave him a couple of hints, just in case it helps the process. But . . . Grady's an Emissary. I don't want to force him to hide stuff from the Council."

"He'd do it, though—and I'm not saying that to pressure you. I just want to make sure you know he *will* keep your secrets if you decide to trust him."

"I know he will," Keefe said quietly, turning to stare out into the pastures. "But I'm tired of complicating everyone's lives."

"You're not! No—don't shake your head. I'm right about this. Life is complicated, but that's because we're caught in the middle of a huge rebellion. You have to stop blaming yourself for things that are completely out of your control, okay?"

"Yeah. I guess."

"Wow, could you sound any *less* inspired by my brilliant pep talk?" she asked.

"I mean . . . I can try." He slumped his shoulders and let

his head loll to the side as he heaved a whiny-sounding groan. "How's that?"

She gave him a playful shove, and when he smiled, it felt like an enormous victory.

"Anyway," he said, sitting back up. "How was Foxfire? Learn anything important?"

Sophie sighed. "Not really. My sessions were a huge waste of time—which wasn't surprising. But I hoped I'd at least get some news when Magnate Leto called me to his office. Sadly, all he wanted to do was give me a lecture on how I better not be planning anything dangerous without telling him—"

"So you lied to the Leto-Forklenator," Keefe interrupted.

"I didn't lie. He's well aware that I'm looking for Elysian— and we're not planning anything *dangerous*. We're planning . . . a quick visit."

"Uh-huh. Keeeeeeeeeeeep telling yourself that."

"I will! And no one had any other updates at lunch. Maruca confirmed that Wylie's having Prentice and Tiergan search his memories together—but so far they haven't found anything. And Marella said she's going to try mentioning the sixth unmapped star to Fintan to see if that'll trick any information out of him—but she won't see him again until her next training session. Dex is working on an illusion-shattering gadget, but I guess right now it mostly just makes everyone dizzy. And Biana, Fitz, Tam, Linh, and Stina all volunteered to help Oralie search Kenric's library for that other crystal I told you about—but I'm not really expecting them to find anything since it's never that easy, you know? Jensi tried to tell me, 'Don't worry, it'll all work out—it always does,' but clearly I need to come up with a better plan—"

"You mean *we* need to come up with a better plan," Keefe cut in. "This isn't all on you."

Normally she would've argued that he was dealing with enough already, but . . .

She liked hearing him say the word "we" a little too much.

In fact, she couldn't believe how quickly her mind could curl up with the idea and let it snuggle in.

It was still scary.

Still complicated.

And it might not even be a real possibility.

But if it was . . . she was really starting to like the thought of Team Foster-Keefe.

Keefe cleared his throat, and the awkward tension in his posture had her bracing for some sort of horrifying "Okay, we need to talk about what's going on with your emotions" conversation.

But all he said was "So . . . does everyone know I'm back?"

"Yep! Dex was the one who told them, since I was late to lunch thanks to Magnate Leto. But they still had a million questions about where you'd been hiding and what you'd been doing for all these weeks. Don't worry, I didn't tell them much," she added when his shoulders drooped further, "mostly because you haven't really told *me* anything. I mean, I can obviously guess why you chose to go back to London—even though that probably wasn't the safest decision if you were trying to stay hidden."

"I know." Keefe tightened his grip on his journals. "I told myself I was only going back for a day—just to walk around a little more and see if I remembered anything."

"About Ethan Benedict Wright II?"

Keefe winced at the name. "Yeah. And you can save your speech. I know I was just a kid when that happened. I know I was following my mom's instructions. I know all I did was deliver a sealed envelope—or that's all I can *remember* doing anyway. But that doesn't change the fact that I brought a letter from my mom to a guy she was trying to recruit for something, and not long after that, he—and his ten-year-old daughter—ended up dead. I even found their graves, so there's no way it's a misunderstanding."

He picked up his silver journal and flipped to a beautifully detailed drawing he'd done of two small gravestones resting side by side in a cluttered cemetery.

Their epigraphs were short and simple:

Ethan Benedict Wright II	Eleanor Olivia Wright
Beloved Father	Cherished Daughter

"I brought them flowers," he mumbled, pointing to the bouquets of bright blue forget-me-nots he'd drawn beneath the names. "I guess that's what some humans do when they visit graves. Doesn't make a whole lot of sense, since then the flowers are going to wither and die too, so that seems extra depressing. But . . ."

"There's probably some weird symbolism behind it, but I think most people do it because it makes the graves look a little less gloomy," Sophie explained. "And I'm sure any other visitors will really appreciate seeing them."

"Except they're not going to have any other visitors. The groundskeeper told me I was the first one in all these years. Which I guess makes sense. My mom wouldn't have targeted anyone with a lot of friends or family. She'd want someone who could disappear and no one would notice."

"Well . . . *we* noticed," Sophie assured him. "And someday we'll make sure she pays for what she did."

"Will we? I walked literally every single street in all of London, trying to find the green door I brought that letter to. But someone must've painted it a different color. And nothing triggered any memories. Even when I went to the spot where they died."

He flipped the page, revealing a drawing of the somewhat plain redbrick building that housed the British Library—and he'd drawn one of the red double-decker buses on the street outside, right where Ethan and Eleanor had been struck and killed in what human authorities had ruled "an accident."

"Isn't that at least a little bit of a relief?" Sophie had to ask. "I know your mom was really good at messing with your memories, but . . . it seems like you would've felt *something* at the crash site if you were there when it happened or had anything to do with it."

Mr. Forkle had found evidence that Keefe's mom had been in London that night, and she'd definitely had enough time to murder them. But Keefe kept worrying that she might've involved him in that too.

"I guess. I don't know." He snapped the journal shut. "I just wish I knew what my mom wanted from this guy that made it worth killing him—and his daughter. But I couldn't find even *one* clue."

"Well . . . I don't know if telling you this is going to make it better or worse," Sophie said quietly, "but . . . do you have a drawing of the symbol that was on your mom's letter?"

"Of course." He flipped back several pages to a perfect rendering of the envelope's golden seal, with a twelve-pointed star surrounded by two different-size crescents pressed into the wax.

Sophie pointed to each mark and explained what Vespera had told her about the connection to stellarlune.

Keefe closed his eyes. "So . . . it really is my fault."

"How? You didn't ask to be a part of any of this!"

"Yeah—but that doesn't change the fact that I am!"

It did, actually.

But she could tell he wasn't ready to accept that.

"Should I not have told you?" she asked when the journal slipped out of his hands.

He shoved it off his lap—along with the other journals, sending them tumbling across the flower-strewn grass.

He flung a few of his colored pencils as well.

"No, this is good," he told her. "I need these kinds of reminders—especially since I was sitting here feeling sorry for myself because none of my friends wanted to stop by and see me. Like anyone would want to—"

"Hold on," Sophie interrupted, grabbing both of his hands before he could throw any more art supplies. "No one stopped by because of *me*, Keefe. They wanted to. But I wasn't sure if you'd still be training with Grady, or if you'd be wiped out from that, or if you were ready to be around that many people. So I told them to let me check with you first, to see how much you could handle, and then we'd figure out who could visit tomorrow. I'm sorry if that was the wrong call. Want me to hail them all and tell them to head over?"

He shook his head. "No, you were probably right. It's better for me to be alone."

"You're *not* alone."

She almost added, *I'm here*—but that seemed really obvious.

And maybe it also wasn't what he wanted.

"I'm sorry," she said instead as she crawled over to gather up his notebooks. "I'm probably handling this all wrong. Want me to hail Fitz? I know he'd rush right over."

"Yeah, to see you," he muttered.

"No, to see *you*. You're his best friend, and . . ." Her voice trailed off as she noticed her face staring back at her from the page of a notebook that had fallen open—and it took her a second to recognize the memory.

It was the day she'd started Cognate training, and she sat with Fitz in one of Alluveterre's tree houses. They each had their black Cognate notebooks in their laps as they worked through a trust exercise—and *now* she understood why Keefe loved to tease them about "staring into each other's eyes."

Their expressions were *intense*.

But she was much more interested in the way Keefe had drawn her.

Her hair was slightly messy, and her tunic was a little crooked, and she was slouching the way her human mom used to tell her would turn her spine into a twisty pretzel if she didn't work on better posture.

But mostly, she looked like *her*.

A little awkward.

A whole lot nervous.

Definitely not perfect.

And . . . she kinda loved that about it.

"Oh, um, thanks," Keefe said, taking the journal from her. "Guess I shouldn't throw stuff."

He snapped the journal shut, and Sophie noticed it had a green cover—which wasn't just a random color.

He'd told her one time that he drew all his important memories in his silver journal, and all his happy memories in his brown journal. There was also a gold journal he didn't explain. But his green journal was for . . .

The exact phrase he'd used was "hard stuff."

So why was her first Cognate lesson in there?

She was about to ask when her brain reminded her that Ro had made it sound like Keefe had liked her for a *while*.

And Fitz was Keefe's *best friend*.

And her crush on Fitz had been pretty painfully obvious.

And their Cognate training had brought them *much* closer together.

"You okay, Foster?" Keefe asked. "That was just, um . . ."

"Fitzphie," she said.

He was the one who'd first started calling them that.

She'd thought he was just giving them a hard time because the Cognate training made them have to share all their secrets. But maybe that was how he was trying to train himself to think of them, to keep his own feelings in check.

Or maybe she was reading *way* too much into that.

Either way, she couldn't seem to stop herself from blurting out, "You know we broke up, right?"

Keefe blinked. "Uh. Yeah. I remember something about that. . . ."

He seemed to be waiting for her to add to her little out-of-the-blue subject change.

But sadly, all she had was "Yeah . . . well . . . we did."

He cleared his throat. "I'm sorry. I'm sure that's been

rough—but don't worry, Foster. Once you don't have so many people trying to kill you all the time, you'll feel more ready for the dating thing, and then you two will be back to all the blushing, and hand-holding, and—"

"No, I don't think we will," she jumped in, very aware that she was making the conversation worse by the second. "I mean, he told me he still wants us to, but . . . it's weird. I always thought . . . if there are feelings there, it'll work. I never realized you could want something and still not have it be *right*. Like . . . I knew it wouldn't be easy—especially with the whole horrible matchmaking thing. But I never thought it would be so hard, either, you know?"

"I guess? Hard to say, since I haven't really tried the whole relationship thing yet."

"Yeah, why is that?" Sophie asked, hoping he'd realize she'd just kicked the door wide open for him.

It was the perfect moment to tell her, *I was waiting for you.*

She even would've taken an *I was waiting for the right moment.*

Instead he looked away, hugging his notebook tighter as he said, "I don't know."

"Are you . . . waiting for something?" she prompted, giving him another chance.

His cheeks turned pink and he licked his lips, and she thought, *THIS IS IT.*

But he shook his head. "I guess . . . sometimes it feels like I should wait until this whole horrifying game my mom keeps playing is over. Otherwise it would just give her one more way to hurt me, or try to control me. One more thing she could possibly take away."

"Oh," Sophie mumbled. "Yeah . . . that . . . makes a lot of sense."

It really did.

But somehow it also felt like a herd of woolly mammoths had just stampeded through her chest.

Maybe because he still wouldn't look at her.

Plus . . .

He could've asked her to wait for him.

But he didn't.

She even stood there for a few more breaths, just in case he was working up the courage.

"Right," she finally said, "sorry. I don't know how we got on this subject—but I should let you get back to drawing your memories. And I need to, um . . . go practice with Hope—I mean my dagger. It's . . . yeah . . ."

"You named your dagger Hope?"

"Kind of? It's a long story. And I should probably also add another layer of Linquillosa to my wrist since it seems a little weird that Ro's still not here yet, and it might be that I did something wrong when I put it on—"

"Hey," Keefe interrupted, stepping closer. "Are you okay? Your voice has gotten really squeaky."

"Yep. All good."

He could've called her out on the lie.

But he didn't.

"Okay," she said, clapping her hands. The sharp noise felt like an *end*. "Happy drawing. If you need me, I'll be . . . stabbing things."

She turned and fled before he could respond.

FORTY-ONE

SOPHIE?" EDALINE ASKED, PEEKING her head into Sophie's bedroom. "Shouldn't you be getting ready for school?"

"Probably," Sophie admitted.

But she stayed right where she was—which at the moment meant lying flat on her back in the middle of her bed, staring up at the dangling crystal stars and generally questioning her place in the universe.

She'd already spent most of the previous night curled up in a fluff cocoon with Ella.

She'd also skipped dinner—and then raided the kitchen for pastries and candy in the middle of the night.

She even dug out her old iPod and blasted a mix of angry

and sad songs and sang along with the angsty lyrics.

So she'd hit pretty much every possible cliché for relationship turmoil.

All that was left was sulking.

But she couldn't sulk for very long.

Not when they were down to only eight days left on the stellarlune countdown.

Plus, she was very aware that skipping school would mean spending the day at Havenfield. And the odds of running into Keefe and having to acknowledge any part of their last humiliating conversation were strong enough to make her want to race for the Leapmaster and try to convince Magnate Leto that he should extend their sessions to cover all waking hours.

Then again . . . it was ability-training day, and going to school would mean three hours of one-on-one time with Fitz in that dark little telepathy room, trying to avoid having to share any of her recent memories. And with her luck, he'd probably decide that today was the day they needed to move forward with the third step of their Cognate Inquisition.

So maybe the best option would be to grab Iggy and teleport to some sort of tiny deserted island and build herself a cute little grass hut to hide away in. She'd always enjoyed eating fresh coconut.

Edaline crawled up on her bed and snuggled in next to her.

"If you're trying to dinosaur-tame me into talking," Sophie warned, "it's not going to work this time."

"Fair enough," Edaline told her. "But I was actually trying to decide if you seem too distracted at the moment for what I really came here to discuss. I had a thought about Gisela's conjuring last night and—"

"You figured out how she's planning to use the ability against us?" Sophie asked, sitting up so fast, she gave herself a major head rush.

"Sadly, my realization isn't as exciting as you're thinking. But it still seemed worth sharing. Are you up for it?"

"Absolutely!"

It was a relief to be thinking about an actual life-or-death problem instead of drama that just *felt* like it was going to bring about the end of the world.

Edaline reached for her hand and laced their fingers together. "Okay. Remember when Mr. Forkle brought me to Alluveterre to help you hide Kenric's cache somewhere no one would be able to reach it?"

"You mean before Keefe figured out my fail-safe phrase and mimicked my voice to steal it?" Sophie asked.

"That was definitely unexpected," Edaline admitted. "And not one of my favorite decisions he's made. But yes—and don't let that make you doubt the security of the void. Being able to tuck vital items away in that space is an invaluable asset for any Conjurer."

Sophie sucked in a breath. "So you think Lady Gisela is hiding stuff in there?"

"I don't see why she wouldn't be. It's far safer than any physical storehouse—particularly given your recent inferno and Vespera's takeover of the Neverseen. The only limit is how many items our minds can keep track of. Given Gisela's lack of formal training, I'd wager she could only store a small handful."

"Can you find them and steal them?"

"I had a feeling you were going to ask that. And sadly, no. For me, the void is a boundless web of invisible threads of energy. I can pull on those threads to bring things back and forth as needed. Or I can tangle something up in them and leave it hidden in the darkness. But I can't feel anything beyond those threads."

"Could you tell if you pulled on one and something was caught in it?" Sophie asked.

"Possibly . . . though in all my years I've never experienced anything like that. But that's probably because there are an infinite number of threads."

"Okay . . . well . . . what about me?" Sophie asked. "My teleporting lets me physically enter the void. So couldn't I dig around when I'm in there?"

"I have no idea. But . . . have you ever felt anything tangible when you were in there? Or even noticed the threads?"

"No," Sophie admitted. "It's just an endless sea of empty black. But I've also never really tried to feel around much either. I'm always focused on where I'm going and trying to make sure the void cracks open again to let me out. So if I *did* look around, I might find something."

"I suppose it's possible. But . . . as you said—the void is endless. So your chances of locating whatever tiny items Gisela hid would be far less likely than randomly scouring the entire ocean hoping to find a specific shell."

"Yeah, I guess." Sophie slumped back against her pillows. "So . . . this doesn't really do us a whole lot of good, then."

"I wouldn't say *that*. The void has certain limitations as far as what can and can't be stored there, so if we put some thought into what Gisela might choose to hide within those parameters, it could help us uncover new insights into her plan."

"Maybe," Sophie said, trying not to sound whiny.

She knew Edaline was trying her hardest to help figure everything out.

And it *did* seem significant to know Gisela might be hiding stuff in the void.

She just wished they actually had a way to find it.

"Wait—what about Gisela's fail-safe phrases?" she asked, sitting up taller again. "If we could guess what those are, and someone mimicked her voice when they said them, wouldn't they just have to snap their fingers and ta-da? Just like how Keefe stole Kenric's cache from me?"

"It depends on whether Gisela's a skilled enough Conjurer to know how to tie fail-safe phrases to her items," Edaline warned. "But if she does . . . that *could* work. You should talk to

Keefe—see if he has any thoughts on what her phrases might be. And he's good at mimicking his mother, isn't he?"

"He is . . . ," Sophie said slowly, tracing her finger along one of the ruffles on her comforter. "But, uh . . . do you think you could tell him about this for me? It's just that I haven't had a chance to tell him his mom's a Conjurer yet—there were so many other things to go over, and I didn't want to derail the conversation. So I'm sure he's going to have fifty thousand questions about that—and then he's going to want to start testing all the phrases right away, and . . . I need to get ready for Foxfire."

"You'd rather go to school than work on this?" Edaline asked, reaching out to check Sophie's forehead like she suspected she might have a fever.

Sophie leaned away, rolling her eyes. "Hey, I never know when Magnate Leto might call me into his office with an update!"

"True." Edaline tucked Sophie's hair behind her ear. "But this could also wait until you're back home this afternoon. I'm sure Keefe will be training all morning with Grady anyway."

"I guess—but . . . you'll explain it way better than I can. I'm not a Conjurer, you know? So it's probably still better if you're the one to talk to him."

Edaline nodded slowly. "If that's what you'd prefer."

"It is." Sophie ducked her chin and scooted past her, needing to get away from Edaline's searching stare. "I should probably get dressed, or I'm going to be late."

"Of course." Edaline stood to leave. But halfway to the door, she turned back and told Sophie, "Okay, I have to ask one thing before I go, and then I promise I'll stay out of it—and I also promise the question isn't *that* embarrassing."

Sophie couldn't imagine how that would be true.

But Edaline wasn't really giving her a choice, so she crossed her arms and said, "Fine."

Edaline stepped closer, placing her hands on Sophie's shoulders, like she wanted to hold her in place in case she was going to bolt. "Whatever happened between you and Keefe yesterday—and I *know* something happened, so there's no point trying to deny it—are you going to talk to him about it? And I mean *really* talk to him and tell him how you feel?"

Sophie twisted free. "I don't—"

"Yes, you do," Edaline insisted.

"You don't even know what I was going to say!"

Edaline smiled. "Pretty sure I can guess. And I understand the instinct to hide these kinds of feelings—sometimes even from ourselves. But . . . I know they're there. And not just for you."

She pointed to Sophie's new stuffed elf as evidence—and Sophie could've sworn its little smile turned a bit smug.

"I'm definitely *not* trying to tell you what to do or who to choose or put *any* pressure on you in *any* way," Edaline assured her. "I also know that what I'm asking you to do isn't easy. Having an open conversation about feelings with someone can be really scary. Especially when they're also your friend. It's natural to be afraid of getting hurt—or of ruining all the good things you already have. And I can't guarantee that won't happen. *But*"—she reached for Sophie's arms again—"it's still super important to have that conversation. Because it's *way* too easy to jump to the wrong conclusion. So just . . . talk to him, okay? I'm not saying *right this moment*. But don't let it go too long, either. And I know you're going to tell me you have all these huge things going on and you need to focus on them, but . . . this is important. I can tell Keefe is important to you. So just . . . do what you always do when you're getting ready to face some epic showdown with the Neverseen."

"You're comparing this to a *battle*?" Sophie had to ask.

"Why not? Sometimes relationships feel like that. So put your shields up if you need to. But don't let that stop you from charging headfirst into the unknown. Be bold. Be brave. Be honest. And be *you*. You're Sophie Foster. I know you can do this!"

FORTY-TWO

I CAN DO THIS," SOPHIE TOLD HERSELF, ordering her legs to carry her forward.

If she didn't start moving, she was going to look like a creepy stalker, hiding behind the pterodactyl enclosure to spy on Keefe.

He'd still been training with Grady when she got home from Foxfire, so she'd headed upstairs and paced around her room, trying to figure out what she was going to say.

But now she had her speech prepared. And Keefe was sitting all alone next to Verdi's pasture, drawing more of his memories. And Sandor was off checking in with the patrols, giving her a little goblin-free privacy.

She was out of excuses.

I can do this. I can do this. I can do this.

And she *had* to do this—because Edaline was right.

If she didn't talk to Keefe, all those unspoken words were going to morph into a giant, ugly truth monster that would eventually gobble up their friendship and spit it back out in lonely, broken pieces.

Keefe meant too much for her to let that happen.

Even if she was pretty sure she was about to get rejected.

And after that less-than-peppy pep talk, her legs refused to get moving.

This is ridiculous, she told herself, adding a mental countdown.

Three.

Two.

One.

She'd barely taken a step before Silveny swooped out of the sky and landed next to Keefe, flapping her wings and stamping her hooves and letting out an exuberant whinny and . . .

There was *no way* Sophie could get through the conversation with a steady chorus of *KEEFE! KEEFE! KEEFE!* flooding her brain.

She'd have to find another time.

The next morning seemed promising. Sophie had barely slept anyway, so she got up early and grabbed a platter of sweetberry swirls, figuring she could pretend she'd stopped by the Grove to bring him breakfast and then slowly ease into the scarier subjects.

But Keefe was already awake, pacing under the swaying branches of the Panakes tree. And as Sophie started to head over, she heard him snapping his fingers and saying evil-sounding things in his mom's eerie voice:

"The star only rises at Nightfall!"

"Stellarlune is my legacy!"

"You would have a queen!"

Nothing appeared from the void—but Keefe seemed determined to figure it out.

And when he tried a particularly bitter *"I will destroy my son!"* Sophie knew it definitely wasn't the right time for a nice long chat about her feelings.

Keefe looked a little less gloomy when she checked on him after school that afternoon—but he also asked her if she thought it was weird that Ro hadn't shown up yet. And Sophie had actually been getting a little worried about that—even though she knew it could easily be that Ro was so close to ambushing Cadfael that she was choosing not to leave. It felt like they should at least *try* to check on her—and by the time they'd added a fresh layer of Linquillosa to Sophie's wrist and asked Grady to see if he could get an update from King Dimitar, it seemed smarter to wait another day for all the intense emotional stuff.

But Sophie overslept the next morning.

And Keefe trained late with Grady that night—long past when Sophie went to bed.

So he was still asleep when she left for Foxfire the following day.

All of which made Sophie wonder if the universe was trying to thwart them.

Maybe it was, because her friends picked that afternoon to finally pay Keefe a visit.

Keefe went quiet when the group first arrived. And he stayed on the fringes, mostly keeping his head down—until Dex asked him about human foods.

Then Keefe had everyone cracking up with stories about the horror of beans on toast, and the cheesy wonder of Welsh rarebit. And how he'd searched high and low for the elusive Ding Dongs he'd heard about—and when he finally got to take a glorious bite, he . . . wasn't sure the creamy center actually counted as edible.

It reminded Sophie of her early days in the Lost Cities—before there were legacies and scars and way too many enemies. And she wished she could pause time and let them all really soak up the moment, because some tiny, twitchy part of her brain kept worrying that this would be the last time they'd all get to hang out together like this.

She hoped she was wrong.

But they only had five days left in Vespera's timeline.

And she couldn't shake the feeling that Elysian was going to change everything.

Assuming they managed to get there in time.

The one damper on the night was their quick update session, which once again added up to a whole lot of nothing.

Sophie knew how hard everyone was trying. But unless something changed, it wasn't going to be enough.

And she hated how little she was actually contributing.

It seemed like all she did was check on other people's projects—and waste days stressing about her silly feelings.

And yet, even as she mentally beat herself up and vowed to do better, she also found her mind clinging to some of the words that Edaline had once made her repeat:

I am a person.

I'm allowed to take time for myself.

She really did believe that.

She just needed to get this conversation over with and keep it from taking up so much space in her head.

So she made herself promise that the next day would be *the day*—no matter what.

If she had to drag Keefe out of whatever tree he was sleeping in, or chase her friends and family away with goblin throwing stars—or barricade the two of them in a room.

It.

Was.

Happening.

She even put on her favorite red tunic when she got dressed that morning—with lace sleeves and supersoft fabric—and spritzed on a little of the Panakes perfume Dex had made for her as a midterms gift. And she practiced her speech until she could pretty much give it backward if she wanted to.

But when she marched down to the pastures, Keefe was nowhere to be found.

The only clue came from Wynn and Luna, who kept chanting, *KEEFE FLY! KEEFE FLY! KEEFE FLY!* followed by *JERK! JERK! JERK!*

Sophie had to smile at the combination. But she also wished she'd never helped Silveny figure out how to communicate without her, because Wynn's and Luna's memories showed the mama alicorn letting Keefe hop on her back—and then they were off! Soaring higher and higher, Keefe laughing with wind whipping his hair—until Silveny tucked her wings and plummeted into the void.

All Sophie could do was take a seat under the Panakes and wait.

And wait.

And *wait*.

She must've dozed off at some point, because it was dark when the sound of flapping wings had her stumbling to her feet.

SOPHIE! SOPHIE! SOPHIE! FRIEND! FRIEND! FRIEND!

"Is everything okay?" Keefe asked as he hopped off Silveny's back and made his way over.

Sophie nodded, reminding herself to stick with honesty. "Yeah, I was just . . . waiting for you—and I was starting to think you weren't coming back."

Keefe fidgeted with his cape. "Sorry. I wanted to see what would happen if I had Silveny fly me around in the void while I talked in my mom's voice. I thought maybe if I managed to say at least a couple of the right words while I was in there, whatever she hid would come crashing toward me."

"Did it work?"

"Not particularly. And in case you were wondering, the void never gets any more exciting. It's just darkness and more darkness—and oh, hey, even more darkness! I'm sure Tammy Boy would love it, but man, I'm glad to see color again."

His eyes shifted to the vibrant red of her tunic—then quickly away.

Sophie felt her cheeks warm. "You could've taken me with you, you know. Or at least left me another note telling me where you went."

They both froze.

She hadn't meant to mention his note yet.

That was supposed to come at the *end* of her speech.

But apparently she was going off script.

And maybe that was better, because now that he was in front of her, dragging a hand through his windblown hair and chewing his lower lip, she didn't feel like saying most of the things she'd planned.

She didn't want to talk about Fitz.

Or the Great Foster Oblivion.

She wanted to just . . . stay in the moment.

So she asked, "Do you want to go for a walk?" and breathed a sigh of relief when Keefe agreed.

"Are we heading anywhere in particular?" he asked as she led him into the pastures.

"Not really. I just need to move. I've been stuck in one place for way too long."

"I know the feeling. And if you don't have a specific spot in mind, then follow me—I found the coolest place the other night after training with Grady."

He led her into the Grove and pointed out which of the strange, bulbous trees he'd tried sleeping in. His favorite had all these tiny glowworms inside, covering the walls with flecks of blue light.

"Sounds amazing," Sophie told him, even if the idea of sleeping that close to worms also made her skin *very* itchy. And she was debating about asking how much longer he'd be staying there when her toe clipped the edge of a root and she toppled forward.

"Sorry," she mumbled as she crashed into his back and clung to his shoulders like a Sophie-koala.

And she couldn't help noticing how good he smelled—like wind and salt air and something a little citrusy.

"You okay?" he asked when she didn't let go. "Did you hurt your ankle?"

"No. Just . . . uh . . . getting my bearings."

"Will this help?" Keefe asked, taking one of her hands and

shifting their positions so they were now walking side by side—and she couldn't answer because *KEEFE WAS HOLDING HER HAND!!!!*

She didn't care that he was just trying to keep her from falling on her face.

She'd take it.

"It's so weird," she said, mostly to herself. "I'm so used to having you feeling everything I'm feeling. It's strange not having you call me out on it all the time."

"Tell me about it," he grumbled.

"Sorry—I didn't mean—"

"It's okay, Foster. I know what you meant. And just so you know, I can still pick up on certain things—especially from you. Pretty sure your emotions will always be stronger than everyone else's."

"Really?"

She couldn't help smiling when he nodded.

It was nice to know she made a little more of an impact.

"I just . . . wish I could get back to how it used to be," Keefe said quietly. "It's hard not getting the whole picture. Makes me not want to trust anything I'm feeling—if that makes sense."

It did, actually.

And a few tiny sparks of hope flared to life.

But she was still dancing around the subject.

Skirting the edges.

And that wasn't going to get them anywhere.

She needed to jump in headfirst.

"Here we go," Keefe said, pulling back a curtain of vines and guiding her into a small clearing.

"Oh wow," Sophie breathed, craning her neck to take it all in.

Hundreds of delicate vines covered with sheer, twinkling flowers wove back and forth through the trees, creating a canopy that looked like shimmering gossamer lace. And the ground was dotted with wide, flat toadstools glowing green, purple, and blue, making it feel like they'd stepped into some sort of fairyland.

"Did you know this place existed?" Keefe asked.

"Flori mentioned it—but I haven't had a chance to go looking for it. She was trying to convince Sandor to bring Grizel here for a date, since it's so romantic."

She realized how that sounded the moment the words left her mouth—and the way Keefe froze told her he'd caught the slip as well.

But . . .

Wasn't that exactly what she needed to talk to him about?

She tightened her grip on his hand, telling herself, *I can do this*, as she closed her eyes and said, "I'm glad I got to come here with you. Even if it was kind of an accident."

Keefe sucked in a breath—but she needed to say the rest before she let him talk; otherwise she was never going to get through it.

"I know you said you got over a bunch of things after you

left the Lost Cities, and I'm sure that probably includes the stuff you told me in your note. And I know you said you're not looking for a relationship right now—and I get it. But . . . it makes me a little sad. Mostly because it means I missed my chance to be with this really incredible guy who makes me laugh and always finds ways to be there for me when I need him. And that's fine. It's my fault—and I'm not trying to, like . . . guilt you into liking me again. I just felt like you should know why I might get a little awkward around you right now. I'm trying to figure out how to go back to only seeing you as a friend, and it's not easy, because I'd just started realizing how much I care about you."

She kept her eyes squeezed shut when she finished, giving herself a couple of seconds to process the fact that she did it!

She told the truth!

And it was *absolutely terrifying*.

But also such a relief.

Her brain felt a thousand pounds lighter—even if her stomach kinda wanted to crawl into her throat and—

"Sophie?"

Keefe's voice was barely a whisper—and it sounded so much closer.

He said her name again before she scraped together the courage to open her eyes and found him standing right in front of her, staring at her like . . .

There weren't words for his expression.

But her heart seemed to understand—stretching a little more with every beat, like it wanted to fill every part of her.

"You realize," Keefe breathed, and his ice blue eyes seemed to shimmer as they reflected the twinkly light, "that if we do this . . . it could get *very* messy."

Sophie looked away, kicking her toe against one of the glowing toadstools. "Because I'm unmatchable?"

"No—the Council can feed their match lists to the gorgodon for all I care. But . . . I wasn't lying when I said my mom will try to use anyone I care about to hurt me."

"Yeah, but I'm pretty sure I'm already at the top of your mom's list of targets," Sophie reminded him. "And I'm ready for her."

She patted the holster of her dagger.

Keefe caught her hand before it returned to her side, cradling her palm in his. "That might not be enough to stop her."

"It might not," Sophie agreed. "But I'm not afraid of her. And I'm not going to let her control my life. So if she's the only reason—"

"I think we both know she's not," Keefe said. But he still stepped a little bit closer—close enough that she could feel his breath on her cheeks when he asked, "Would you like me to list off all the complications?"

Sophie shook her head.

She was pretty sure she could guess most of them.

And she didn't care.

"All I care about is how you feel," she whispered. "If you're only doing this"—she held up their clasped hands—"because you don't want to hurt my feelings—"

He twined their fingers together and shook his head. "Trust me—this is what I've wanted from the moment I first saw you, wandering through the halls in the middle of session covered in alchemy goo. I knew right away that I'd just met someone incredibly special—and every minute I've spent with you since then has proven how true that is. But is this really what *you* want?" He squeezed her hand, and she could feel him shaking a little when he admitted, "I can't tell what you're feeling—and it's seriously terrifying."

Sophie's mind flooded with words.

Promises.

Confessions.

But somehow they felt like too much and not enough all at the same time.

So she tilted up on her toes and leaned forward, meeting his eyes as she lined her lips up with his—careful to leave a tiny wisp of space.

A chance for him to change his mind.

Keefe closed the distance between them.

And then . . . everything was new.

The soft press of his lips against hers.

The way their breath seemed to fall perfectly into sync while her heart and her brain screamed, *FINALLY!*

Some tiny part of her had always wondered if kissing could really be as great as everyone claimed.

But kissing Keefe was So. Much. Better.

He was the one to finally pull away, leaning back to study her in the shimmering light. "You're okay, right? No regrets?"

She grinned. "Absolutely none."

His relieved smile was the sweetest thing she'd ever seen—but it faded a little as he leaned his forehead against hers. "I don't want to mess this up," he whispered. "Please don't let me mess this up."

"I won't," she promised, tilting her chin up to steal another quick kiss.

But someone cleared their throat, and Sophie and Keefe practically flung themselves as far apart as they could get.

Please don't be Grady, Sophie begged as she stumbled toward the sound.

Thankfully it wasn't.

Flori stood there, flashing a huge smile as she said, "I'm *very* sorry to interrupt. But you have a visitor, Miss Foster. And I thought you might want a moment to collect yourself."

"Is everything okay?" Sophie asked as she tugged at her hair and wiped her mouth, wondering how badly her face screamed, *I'VE BEEN KISSING KEEFE.*

"I believe so, yes," Flori said. "But they wanted to come find you, and since I knew where you were, I thought it would be best if I came to get you myself."

"Yeah. Um. Thanks," Sophie said, stealing a glance at Keefe, wondering if he was as flushed as she felt.

He definitely looked stunned.

But his smirk returned pretty quick.

He even blew her a kiss, and she couldn't decide if she wanted to laugh or roll her eyes.

"Are you ready?" Flori asked, and Sophie took one last look around the twinkly clearing, suddenly worried that everything wouldn't feel so magical once they stepped back into reality.

But her eyes landed on Keefe again, and he whispered, "I'm ready for anything."

Sophie was too.

"Good," Flori said, motioning for Sophie to follow her, "because I'm not sure how much longer we should keep them waiting."

"Them?" Sophie asked, fanning her cheeks and smoothing her hair as she scrambled to keep up with her. "Who's them?"

"You'll see."

Sophie could hear Keefe trailing a few feet behind her—and she was *so glad* he kept that safe distance when Flori led her into Havenfield's living room and she saw her "visitor" sitting on the sofa with Grady and Edaline, studying her with striking teal eyes.

"Fitz?" Sophie asked, suddenly finding it very hard to keep breathing. "What are you doing here?"

FORTY-THREE

SORRY TO SHOW UP OUT OF THE BLUE,"
Fitz said as he made his way over to where Sophie
had basically frozen into a statue near the doorway. "I tried to hail you, but you didn't answer."

She blinked, realizing she needed to breathe as she patted
her tunic.

It didn't have any pockets—which would've been a huge
strike against it if it weren't so soft and cute. "I . . . guess I left
my Imparter in my room," she mumbled.

She stopped herself from asking why Fitz hadn't tried reaching out telepathically and just celebrated the fact that he hadn't.

She didn't want to imagine how awkward it would've been
to hear his voice in her head while she and Keefe were . . .

Nope.

She couldn't think that word right now.

And she definitely couldn't look in Keefe's direction.

For the moment he didn't exist.

And nothing had happened.

And everything was one hundred percent *super* normal.

Otherwise her brain was going to melt out of her eyeballs.

She'd stopped Keefe from mentioning any of the "complications" they'd have to deal with if they changed their relationship, because nothing was going to prevent her from taking that next step.

But that didn't mean she was ready to be face-to-face with the King of All Complications—in front of her parents—when her heart was still racing and her knees were all wobbly and her lips were still tingling and—

"You okay?" Fitz asked, tilting his head to study her. "You look a little . . . overwhelmed."

"You know how Foster is," Keefe jumped in. "She's always worrying about five hundred things at once. And she's probably stressing about the fact that I've spent pretty much the whole day searching the void, trying to find whatever my mom hid in there—and getting nowhere."

Fitz frowned. "I didn't realize your mom had hidden anything."

"It's still just a theory," Edaline told him. "We're trying to figure out what advantages she might have as a Conjurer, since

SHANNON MESSENGER   655

she worked so hard to keep the ability secret. And Conjurers can tuck things away in the void."

"That's right—I forgot about that. But it may not matter," Fitz said, turning back to Sophie. "Prentice and Tiergan had a huge breakthrough tonight!"

Sophie stumbled closer. "Did they find Wylie's memories of the starstone?"

"Not yet. But they're pretty sure they've found where the memories are hidden. They uncovered a path deep in Wylie's subconscious—but they couldn't follow it. As soon as they tried, some sort of defense mechanism kicked in, and they barely managed to pull their minds back before they got dragged under—and Wylie couldn't figure out how to shut it down, since his conscious mind isn't even aware of it. I guess he tried hailing you, but you didn't answer, so he hailed me— but I couldn't follow the path either. The pull was *way* too strong. It's going to take both of us to push through—and even then, I don't know if we're ready yet."

Sophie closed her eyes, guessing what he was about to say and wishing she could plug her ears and shout, *LA LA LA LA LA LA*, so she wouldn't have to acknowledge it.

But she heard Fitz loud and clear when he said, "I think we're going to need to finish the Inquisition first."

"Uh, what's the Inquisition?" Keefe asked. "And why did Foster just turn, like, six different shades of green?"

"It's not going to be as bad as you think," Fitz said, keeping his focus on Sophie. "We already did the hard part."

Sophie snorted. "No, we didn't! The third step is the worst!"

"Seriously, what's the Inquisition?" Keefe pressed.

"It's a Cognate thing," Fitz told him. "Don't worry about it."

"Um, I kinda think we all should be worried, since Foster looks like she's about to hurl all over the place."

"You do look a little pale, Sophie," Edaline noted. "Why don't you come sit down?"

Fitz sighed as Sophie wobbled over to the couch—and Sophie couldn't blame him for getting a little frustrated.

They'd both known this was coming.

And she'd had weeks to mentally prepare.

But.

She couldn't do an exercise with him that required total honesty five minutes after kissing his best friend!

A slightly hysterical laugh bubbled up her throat as the reality of her situation fully sank in.

This was probably the end of their Cognate connection.

Probably the end of their friendship, too. At least for a while.

She hadn't done anything *wrong*—but that didn't mean that Fitz wasn't going to feel hurt and betrayed once he found out.

And she'd probably feel the same way if she'd told him she wanted to get back together and he'd run off and kissed Linh or Marella or someone a few weeks later.

So how would their minds ever trust each other again?

"I think we're fine without the Inquisition," she told Fitz, realizing they needed to follow the path in Wylie's head *before* there was an abundance of drama—not after. "Why waste time? If we could dig through King Dimitar's mind—and you could guide me through Fintan's broken consciousness—I'm sure we can handle a simple defense mechanism from someone who's not even a Telepath."

"Tiergan said you would say that," Fitz told her, reaching into his cape pocket. "He also said to remind you that you and I were in a much more solid place when we pulled off those other things. And since he knows you'll go barreling into Wylie's subconscious whether it's safe or not, he gave me this"—he held out the fluffy silver gadget Tiergan had used to measure their mental strength—"and said we should test to see where we're at before we decide anything. I guess Tiergan and Prentice tested themselves after they almost got dragged under, and they were at 428. So he said we need to be at least at six or seven hundred."

"Perfect! We already tested at 634."

"Yeah, but readings change all the time," Fitz reminded her. "So let's see where we're at right now—and Tiergan said we need to get three consistent readings if we're on the low end of the range, just to make sure the mental strength is really there."

"Fine," Sophie said, closing her eyes and scraping together every single drop of mental strength she could spare as she opened her mind to Fitz's. "On three?"

Fitz counted them down, and they slammed their consciousnesses against the gadget.

407.

"Wow, that's even worse than our first test," Fitz mumbled.

"Well . . . it's a little late," Edaline reminded him. "And I'm sure Sophie's tired. Maybe if you try again tomorrow, it'll be better."

"I doubt it," Fitz said quietly. "This is why Tiergan had us do the Inquisition." His gaze shifted to Sophie. "I swear, it won't be as bad as you're thinking. I spent super long on the second step because I've *really* tried to understand how much you need privacy. So I've been able to let almost everything go. There are just a couple of things that I think we should probably talk out—but neither of them should be a big deal."

Sophie wanted to believe him.

But she had a horrible feeling that Keefe was one of those subjects.

And even if he wasn't, Keefe *had* to be why their level was already lower.

It was too huge of a secret to keep hidden.

"You can always tell me that you don't want to talk about something," Fitz reminded her. "Then it would just be on me to accept that—and I would."

"So . . . can't she just tell you right now that she doesn't want to talk about anything and *boom*—Inquisition handled?" Keefe asked.

"Nope. That won't create the same level of understanding," Fitz argued. "I know it sounds weird—even I don't totally understand it. But Tiergan said we have to trust the process."

Sophie slumped back against the couch cushions.

She didn't see how the process would save them.

But . . . wasn't it worth trying?

Especially since it might be the only way to find what was hidden in Wylie's mind?

"Okay," she said, barely able to choke out the word. "Where . . . do you want to do this?"

Fitz's smile practically beamed. "Wherever you want. We can do it right here, if that's easier. I'm sure everyone will leave us alone if you want a little privacy."

"I dunno," Keefe jumped in. "It's been a while since I've had a chance to tease you two about staring into each other's eyes."

He smirked at Sophie as he said it—but she knew he was really trying to stay close in case she needed him.

And she appreciated it.

But this was definitely something she needed to work through with Fitz alone.

I'll be fine, she told him, opening her mind to Keefe's thoughts. *But . . . I'm probably going to have to tell him about us—and he might not want to talk to you for a while once he knows. Are you okay with that? He's your best friend.*

It'll definitely be a bummer, Keefe admitted. *But . . . I've always known that was the risk. So don't worry about me. I just want to make sure YOU'RE okay with this, since you still look kinda vomit-y.*

It's not going to be fun, she mumbled. *But . . . I'm trying to believe that honesty is better. Even if it's scary.*

Look at you, being all brave and mature! Remind me to give you a supportive hug later.

Yes, please, Sophie told him, feeling her heart swell like a giant balloon.

She wanted to say more, but she was pretty sure Fitz could tell that she and Keefe were talking to each other, so she shut down the mental connection and focused on Grady and Edaline. "Would you mind going in the other room to give us a little privacy?"

"Of course," Edaline told her, dragging Grady to his feet. "We'll be upstairs."

"But if this works, will you tell us before you run off to test it on Wylie?" Grady asked.

"I'll make sure of it," Sandor said, practically melting out of the shadows along with Grizel.

He was always much sneakier when they were together— probably because stealth was Grizel's specialty.

"You won't need to," Sophie told him. "I promise I'll keep everyone updated—so you don't have to stay here either," she told Sandor. "We both know you don't need to stay so close by my side when I'm at Havenfield."

Otherwise she would've had a seven-foot-tall awkward chaperone ruining the romance of her big kiss.

Thank goodness he had to check in with his patrols.

"Come on, Gigantor," Keefe said, motioning for Sandor to follow him. "There's an awesome clearing I need to show you two—and, Grizel, you can thank me later."

Somehow Keefe convinced Sandor to agree.

And suddenly they were gone, and Sophie and Fitz were very, very alone.

I can do this, she reminded herself. *I can do this. I can do this.*

Honesty had made things *so* much easier with Keefe.

Maybe it would also help with Fitz.

And if it didn't . . . it still had to be better than lying or sneaking around.

"Is it okay if I open my mind to yours?" Fitz asked as he sat beside her on the couch. "I think we should probably talk telepathically."

Sophie took a second to lock all her recent memories away in a mental box before she agreed. That way she could control when she hit Fitz with the Keefe bombshell.

Do you want to start? he asked as his crisp-accented voice filled her mind. *I figured that might help ease you in a little—but if you'd rather have me go first, I can.*

No, your plan is probably smart.

She was just struggling to remember what she was supposed to ask him.

The first part of the Inquisition felt like a lifetime ago.

Okay . . . She dragged out the thought, wondering how much courage she was capable of scraping together in a single day. *For me, there were really only two things.*

She went with the easier one first: *It seemed like it bothered you that I'm trying to step up as a leader.*

And the second thing? Fitz asked.

Shouldn't we talk about the first?

Fitz reached up to drag a hand down his face. *Yeah, we probably should. And . . . I guess it is a little hard watching you take over—not because I don't think you're doing a good job. It's just . . . I'm a Vacker. I grew up with everyone expecting me to do all kinds of great things. And sometimes I still want to be that guy that everyone looks to—even though I know it's silly. Clearly I just need to remind myself that I already did the most important thing I'll probably ever do. I found the moonlark.*

Sophie smiled. *You did.*

So . . . are we good on that topic, then? Should we move on to the second thing you wanted to talk about?

Sophie would've preferred to stall a bit longer—but she took a deep breath and forged ahead. *Okay. The other thing is . . . I can tell it REALLY bothers you that I'm unmatchable. And . . . that bothers ME.*

Fitz sank back into the pillows. *I had a feeling you were going to bring that up. And . . . I wish I could be one of those people who doesn't care about matchmaking—especially since I do see how* unfair it can be. I just don't know if I'm brave enough to be a bad match. But . . . I'm trying to work on it.

Sophie wasn't sure what to say to that.

She wanted to point out that it made all his confessions about liking her and wanting to kiss her pretty irrelevant—but none of that mattered anymore anyway.

It's okay if you don't want to deal with a bunch of drama, she told him. *I'd rather not deal with it either. But I can't change what I am—and I know you think I can, but I swear, if there were any way I could reveal my genetic parents, I would. So can you at least believe me on that and stop pressuring me about it?*

Of course. And . . . I'm really sorry for making you feel pressured.

Thanks, Sophie's mind mumbled as Fitz tore his hands through his hair.

My turn? he asked.

Sophie curled her knees into her chest. *Yeah, I guess.*

Don't look so scared. I actually only have two things to talk about too. And the first one's really easy. I just want to make sure you've fully forgiven me for all the awful things I've said over the years, because I really, truly am sorry.

I . . . think I have. I was a little surprised when it seemed like I had any lingering resentment, because I wasn't aware that I did.

Do you think maybe that's because you try to tell yourself what you SHOULD feel? Fitz asked.

Maybe? she admitted. *But I don't know how to stop that.*

I don't either. But just . . . know you have every right to let me know when you're angry at me. I'm sure if you are, I deserve it. And I can handle the Foster Rage.

Can you? Sophie asked. *Let's not forget I'm an Inflictor.*

I suppose that's a good point. So how about you promise to try to stick with simple yelling?

Sounds like a plan.

Awesome. Then we just have one more thing.

She held her breath, sending a silent plea into the universe for his last topic to be anything other than Keefe.

But of course she wasn't that lucky.

I don't really know what I'm asking with this, he told her. *It just . . . seemed like you had a strong reaction when I mentioned Keefe, so I'm kinda wondering what that was all about.*

Why DID you mention Keefe? she countered.

I'm not sure, Fitz admitted. *It just . . . felt like maybe I needed to.*

Unfortunately, he was right.

And she knew she could still tell him, *I'm not comfortable talking about this,* and see if that was enough.

But . . . that would just put a Band-Aid on the problem.

So she hugged herself as tight as she could, reminding herself that it was better to be honest, before she told him, *The truth is . . . I like Keefe. And not just as a friend. I don't really know when it happened—it kinda crept up on me.*

She gave him a couple of beats to let that sink in before she added, *And . . . I think Keefe likes me back. Actually, I know he does.*

And since she was going all in, she went ahead and told him, *He kissed me tonight. And I kissed him back.*

Fitz jumped to his feet, and Sophie braced for lots of angry shouting.

But when his eyes met hers, he looked . . .

Shocked.

Confused.

Devastated.

I . . . don't know what to say, he admitted. *That really hurts, Sophie. Like, really, REALLY hurts. I mean . . . you kissed him? You didn't even kiss me!*

Sophie couldn't look at him when she said, *I know—though it wasn't like I planned on that. You and I were interrupted, if you remember. And then we were just . . . never on the same page.*

And you and Keefe are? Fitz countered. *Even though he ran away and abandoned everybody?*

He had good reasons for that—and you know it.

Fitz sank back on the couch, burying his face in his hands. *Clearly I don't know anything. All this time, I thought you liked me.*

I did.

The past tense on that wasn't one hundred percent accurate.

But it was easier to leave it that way than remind him how complicated crushes could be.

I . . . don't even know where we go from here, Fitz confessed. *I mean . . . how are we supposed to work together? I don't think I can handle trust exercises if I have to hear about how great it is kissing Keefe.*

Sophie shuddered. *Yeah, I definitely don't want to talk about that with you. But . . . we're supposed to trust the process, right? We've been SUPER open and honest—so maybe that's enough. Think we should at least test it?*

Fitz let out the world's longest sigh before he held up the silver fluffy gadget and told her, *Let's go on three.*

Sophie nodded.

He counted down, and she pushed with all of her strength as Fitz did the same, and . . .

1,012.

They both just stared at the reading.

"Think we should test it again, just to make sure it's not a fluke?" Fitz asked.

"Definitely," Sophie told him.

And this time . . . 1,016.

"Wow," Fitz breathed, tearing his hands through his hair again. "I . . . still don't know what to do with anything you told me. But I guess only one thing really matters right now."

"Right," Sophie agreed, daring to meet his eyes.

And together they said in total perfect unison, "We need to go see Wylie."

FORTY-FOUR

WILL I BE ABLE TO SEE WHAT you see?" Wylie asked, sitting up, then leaning back and shifting his weight to the other side of his gilded chair.

"I'm not sure," Sophie admitted. "Probably not, since it sounds like we'll be in your subconscious, and I don't think you can see anything in there—but I promise I'll replay anything we uncover as many times as you want. I can even implant it in your mind so it'll be part of your permanent memories."

"Maybe." Wylie crossed and uncrossed his arms. "I guess it depends on what you find."

"True." Sophie hadn't really thought about the fact that this would likely be a very unhappy memory for him.

Now she understood why he seemed so fidgety.

It had to be pretty unsettling knowing he might be about to witness the reason his mother was murdered—as well as the memory that caused the Neverseen to kidnap and torture him.

It probably also didn't help that they had *quite* the audience.

Fitz had made the mistake of hailing Biana to ask her to tell his parents he'd be home late. And Biana had demanded to know why. Then she'd hailed everyone else, telling them to meet up at Solreef—that way they'd all be together if there was a big discovery. So now they had Biana, Dex, Keefe, Tam, Linh, Marella, Maruca, Stina, and Rayni all crammed into Solreef's sitting room.

And their bodyguards.

And Tiergan and Prentice.

At this point, Sophie was wondering if they should start selling tickets.

"You realize there's a chance we're not going to find anything, right?" She felt the need to remind everyone.

"Nah, I believe in the power of Fitzphie," Marella told her, making Sophie and Fitz both cringe.

It took a *lot* of willpower not to glance at Keefe.

Fitz cleared his throat. "You ready?"

Sophie nodded—then realized they'd forgotten something. "Wait—am I enhancing you? Or will that be overkill?"

"Given the strength of these defense mechanisms," Tiergan told them, "I would recommend taking any help you can get."

"There's more than one?" Sophie asked.

"Yes. Prentice and I fought through two in order to reach the path," Tiergan explained, "and then the pull proved to be too much for us. Should you and Fitz be able to conquer it, there's a chance there may be additional pitfalls. That's why I wanted your minds to be as strong as possible. I'm glad the Inquisition was so successful."

"Yeah, it was *great*," Fitz muttered under his breath.

Fortunately, no one seemed to hear him.

"I still don't understand how I can have all these defenses without knowing about them, or being able to control them," Wylie said, smoothing his hand over his cropped hair.

"That's easy," Prentice said quietly. "I'm sure I trained your mind extensively while you were a baby. I don't remember doing it, of course, but . . . it sounds like me. Information is power in our world, and those who cannot guard it are far too vulnerable. I would've done all I could to ensure my son was protected." He frowned, toying absently with one of his dreadlocks. "So strange that I can remember the abstract problems, but not my own specific actions."

"The mind is a mystery," Tiergan said as Sophie switched on her enhancing and reached for Fitz's hand.

Fitz shivered when their fingers touched, and Sophie wondered if Keefe was ready to explode from all the little comments he had to be holding back.

Or . . . was he bothered?

She couldn't imagine Keefe would be, since he knew better

than anyone how her abilities worked—but it was still a strange thought as she reached her free hand toward Wylie's temple.

"Do you need a minute?" she asked as Wylie leaned away.

He set his jaw and shook his head. "No. Let's do it."

"We might not be able to hear you once we're in your subconscious," Fitz warned him. "So if you need a break, squeeze my shoulder as hard as you can."

"I'm not going to need a break," Wylie assured him. He locked eyes with Sophie. "Just . . . find it, okay?"

Sophie nodded, remembering the much younger version of Wylie she'd met the first time she'd entered his mind—the brave boy who begged her not to let anyone erase the memories of his kidnapping because he might need them to find out what happened to his mother.

That boy was still waiting for answers.

She owed him—for so many reasons.

And suddenly this was about so much more than Elysian.

Sophie rallied her concentration, letting her mental strength swell like a wave as she pressed her finger against his temple and let her concentration flood his mind.

Wow—it's REALLY bright in here, she told Fitz, wishing she could shield her brain the way she could shield her eyes when she first stepped into the sun.

And even when her mind adjusted, Wylie's memories looked washed out and blurred, like overexposed photographs swirling around her.

Don't worry, it gets darker as we go, Fitz promised, his voice cutting through the garbled hum that echoed all around them.

Do you need me to guide you to the path? Tiergan transmitted over the din.

No, I remember the way, Fitz assured him.

His consciousness swirled around Sophie's, and she clung to him, letting him drag her deeper into Wylie's mind as he told her, *We need to follow the silence. You'll know it when you feel it.*

Sophie hoped so, since silence was the absence of sound, so she didn't see how they could follow an absence.

But as they sank through the murky mental layers, Wylie's memories turned into a gradient. Light slowly graying to dark. Sound slowly fading to a hush that grew thicker and heavier— pressing in around them, making Sophie hyperaware.

Her pulse pounded in her ears and her breath rattled around her head and—

You have to tune everything out, Fitz warned. *That's how the silence protects him. It makes us too aware of our bodies to fully be in our minds—or that's what Tiergan told me earlier.*

How much farther do we have to go? Sophie asked, struggling to shift her focus.

Pretty far—and I guess it's better to drift with his thoughts and let his mind forget we're here as much as we can, even though it takes longer.

They stretched their consciousnesses, floating like a feather on a breeze—sinking and sliding and dipping and diving.

Lower.

And lower.

And lower.

The air turned cold.

The last wisps of light blinked away.

And their minds caught in a loop, swooping around and around and around.

Second defense mechanism, Fitz explained. *Way more disorienting than the silence. Tiergan called this one "the confusion." It's supposed to make us think there's nowhere else to go. But if we push up . . .*

He slammed their consciousnesses against the dark ceiling, making a web of cracks scatter all around them—tiny slivers of glowing warmth that slowly widened until there was a jagged gateway just wide enough for them to crawl through.

Chaos waited on the other side.

Welcome to Wylie's subconscious, Fitz told her. *It's super confusing here.*

He wasn't wrong.

Whispers were shouts.

Scents were sounds.

And streaks of color twisted and tangled, trying to pull them in every direction at the same time.

But they clung to the edge of the darkness, slowly creeping to the opposite side, where everything inverted and toppled into a jumbled path of light and shadow.

This is as far as I got, Fitz told Sophie, *so you should probably take the lead from here. The pull kicks in as soon as we move ahead—and I'm pretty sure we need to surrender to it. I just don't know how we'll find our way back.*

Neither do I, Sophie admitted. *But there's always a way.*

She'd been in enough minds to know she just had to rely on her instincts, keep her senses open, and trust her own strength.

Are you ready?

I think so. Fitz pressed even closer as Sophie dragged them forward, letting her guards fall away as an invisible force wrapped around them and yanked them down, down, down, into a bizarre mental storm.

Thunder flashed and lightning boomed and the rain washed up, pooling around them as the wind squeaked and slithered against their senses. Sophie wanted to blast them out of the fray—but she told herself not to fight it, remembering that she was strong, even if she did not use her strength.

The storm whipped them this way and that way, forward and back, up and down, until Sophie no longer had any bearings.

But she trusted Wylie.

She trusted Fitz.

And she trusted herself.

She couldn't worry about the path back.

She needed to believe that they could still move forward.

And with that thought, the storm evaporated, dropping them into a bubble of swirling blue.

Quiet—but not too quiet.

Warm—but not too warm.

Sophie let them fade into the soft color, and the blue swirls parted like a curtain, revealing a redheaded figure in a long violet gown hovering before them.

Cyrah.

She didn't smile.

Didn't acknowledge them at all.

And there was something flickery about her image.

I think this is a memory, Sophie told Fitz. *It reminds me of the holograms I saw in the caches.*

I wonder who helped her hide it here, Fitz said.

No idea.

But it didn't matter at the moment.

They needed to hear Cyrah's message.

"I don't know who's watching this," she said, her violet eyes gazing into the middle distance. "But hopefully it's someone on our side. Otherwise I'll hate myself for leaving it behind. I wasn't going to. I don't want my son involved. But . . . there's a chance I might've miscalculated. Hidden everything too well. Or maybe no one will believe I resisted as much as I could. Or perhaps I'm dead right now, and my son is alone, needing help, grappling to understand how I could've left him when I'm all he has. So if any of that has happened—or if these enemies have grown too strong—someone should know that I didn't destroy their starstone. I have no idea where it leads, but it feels significant. A place they shouldn't be allowed to go—but that we may need to find someday. So I hid the stone in one of my designs and sent it somewhere safe."

She reached into her pocket and pulled out a folded slip of paper—a detailed sketch of a small hair comb with swirls of metal weaving around five round jewels in an intricate pattern. "This design is one of a kind. You'll know it if you have it. And if you do, hopefully you'll know what to do with it. Maybe you can end this, since I clearly couldn't." Her gaze shifted then, seeming to focus when she added, "And, Wylie, if you're watching, I'm so sorry for not finding a better way out of this mess. I hope you're happy and thriving. I love you. And wherever I am, I'm sure I'm missing you every moment. Be strong—and resist!"

Is that it? Fitz asked when Cyrah fell still and silent.

I think so, Sophie told him. But they waited several minutes just to be sure.

Your photographic memory got all that, right? Fitz asked. *You'll be able to show it to Wylie?*

I will, Sophie promised—though she had a feeling he was going to be disappointed.

She definitely was.

A drawing of a random hair comb and some vague comment about someone knowing if they have it wasn't the kind of clear answer they needed with so little time left.

But it was all Cyrah had given them, so they had to hope it meant something to Wylie as they tangled their consciousnesses together and launched up and around, over and through, until they were back in their own bodies, gasping for breath.

"Well?" Biana demanded. "What did you find?"

"Wylie deserves to see it first," Sophie told her, switching off her enhancing so she could take Wylie's hands and project the memory into his mind.

Tears streamed down his face as he watched, and everyone shoved closer to hug him.

I definitely want that memory, he told her when he'd finished, his mind wobbly and weary. But his grip was steady in Sophie's grasp as she wrapped the memory in warmth and pushed it into his head.

She shared the projection with Prentice next, and he clung to his son and wept.

Tiergan held them both when it was his turn.

And Sophie wished she could give them more time.

They deserved to hold Cyrah's message just between the three of them.

But everyone else was waiting—and they needed that information, even if it wasn't much.

With each replay, Sophie kept hoping she'd spot something they could actually use.

But it was just the same vague clues.

And everyone looked equally confused at the end.

Except Biana.

Biana looked very, very pale.

"You okay?" Dex asked.

She shook her head. "I need to check something. Meet me at Everglen."

She held up her home crystal and leaped away, leaving everyone no choice except to follow her back to the glittering Vacker mansion—though Prentice said he felt too emotionally exhausted to join them, and Tiergan chose to stay with him, knowing no one would listen to his advice anyway.

The house was dark when they arrived, the only light coming from a single lamp in a small sitting room toward the back of the estate, where Biana was already seated at a small table, digging through a jewel-encrusted box filled with hairpins.

"My dad bought me some combs from Cyrah one of the times he brought me to Mysterium," she mumbled, "but they weren't the ones I wanted. Cyrah had a set with big pink tourmaline flowers, and I wanted to get those—but she kept insisting that the other pair was special. I think I even remember her telling my dad she made them specifically for a Vacker. So that's what my dad bought me, and I never wore them because I thought the white stones were super boring."

She kept digging, pulling out comb after comb, until she sucked in a breath and her hands started shaking.

Biana lifted two silver combs from the box and set them on the table, tracing her fingers over the swirls of metal before she stepped back and flicked on the room's massive chandelier.

And when the light hit one of the smooth white stones, it flashed vivid blue.

FORTY-FIVE

"CAN I SAY SOMETHING?" SOPHIE called out, grabbing the starstone comb and climbing up on one of the chairs to make sure she had everyone's attention.

Her knees wobbled a little as she fought to find her balance on the cushion.

Or maybe the shaking came from finally holding the vital piece she'd started to worry they would never find.

"I know this is when we usually get into a huge fight about what we should do and who should go and how to be safe," she said, "and we definitely still need to be smart. *But* . . . we're running out of time. And all of us are here. And we have four bodyguards. And right now, we're the only people who know we've found the starstone. So I say we use it before any of that changes." She held up the comb, letting the stone flash blue again. "If you think that's a bad idea—no problem! You can stay here or go home. And if you want to come—great! Just know that it might be dangerous."

"Oh, it definitely *will* be dangerous," Sandor assured her.

"Maybe not," Sophie argued. "We're going somewhere no one else can find."

"But there might be traps," Fitz warned. "Or other defenses that Vespera didn't tell us about in case we decided to go there without her."

"So what are you saying?" Sophie asked. "You'd rather go *with* Vespera?"

"Of course not! But that doesn't mean I think we should go rushing right over either!" Fitz snapped.

"Okay, but . . . what will be different if we wait?" Sophie countered.

"I don't know—we'd at least have put more than five seconds' worth of thought into it," Fitz said. "And I'm sure we'd have a lot more weapons."

"We have *four* goblins with weapons," Sophie reminded him. "And we have a Pyrokinetic. And a Psionipath. And a Hydrokinetic—who's going to be near five rivers she can draw on for power. And a Shade. And two Flashers. And—"

"You're assuming they'll all choose to go with you," Stina pointed out rather smugly.

Sophie wanted to scream, but she settled for a heavy sigh, knowing she needed to keep her voice low.

If Alden or Della woke up and joined them, this conversation would get a whole lot more complicated.

"Fine," she told Stina. "Let's take a quick poll. Raise your hand if you're planning on coming with me tonight—and there's no pressure either way. It's absolutely okay if you'd rather stay behind."

Everyone except Fitz and Stina raised their hand—though some of the group definitely looked a little torn.

Linh pointed to Rayni. "She shouldn't be allowed to come! She could be part of whatever the Neverseen are planning. In fact, this whole thing could be one huge setup—and she could be the inside person to make sure it happens."

"Ugh, for the billionth time, I'm on your side!" Rayni shouted. "But you know what? If you don't want me there— fine! Keeps me out of trouble with the Council."

"She agreed to that awfully quickly," Stina noted. "I bet that's exactly what she wants, so she's nice and safe while we walk into her trap."

"So . . . if I go, I'm part of the trap—and if I stay, *that's* the trap?" Rayni clarified. "Do you hear yourself?"

"Rayni's right," Tam said. "You can't keep accusing her of *everything*."

"And we can't keep arguing," Sophie added. "We're *never* going to agree on a perfect plan. Everything has risks. So I say we do what gets us answers the fastest. Think about it—for all we know, this isn't even the starstone that goes to Elysian. And if that's true, then we've lost precious time that could've been spent trying to figure out where it is."

"But . . . it has to be the right starstone," Biana insisted. "What else would it be?"

"I don't know," Sophie admitted. "That's why we need to check. So who's with me?"

"I am!" Dex said, holding up a small crystal cube that flashed different colors in the dim light. "I even brought my Illusion Breaker tonight, just in case. I got it working—you just don't want to stare directly at the beams because they'll make your head a little spinny."

"I'm in too," Biana said, staring at the comb in Sophie's hand. "I can't believe I've had it sitting in my jewelry box all this time and never realized."

"You weren't supposed to realize," Wylie told her. "I'm sure that's why my mom chose you—knowing you'd have a million other fancier combs you'd like better and it'd be safe in your jewelry box at Everglen, with the full protection of the Vacker family if it was ever discovered."

"Maybe," Biana mumbled, picking up the matching comb from the table. "But I think you should keep this. Your mom made it. And . . . it really is beautiful."

She placed the comb gently in his palm, and Wylie's fingers curled around it.

"I guess this one should technically be yours too," Sophie realized—but she couldn't quite bring herself to hand over the comb.

Thankfully Wylie didn't expect her to.

"My mom lost her life trying to keep that stone away from me," he said. "You are welcome to keep it. And I'm definitely in for whatever comes next. I want to see what my mom protected—and I'm going to use it to tear the Neverseen apart."

"I'm down for that," Marella said.

"Me too." Maruca hooked her arm around Wylie and added, "I'll keep everyone shielded."

"And I'll test the shadows, looking for illusions," Tam said.

Linh's silver-blue eyes focused on Rayni as she told everyone, "I'll drown any threat."

Rayni crossed her arms, not looking the least bit intimidated. But she still said, "Then I'm staying here. Otherwise I'll get blamed if anything goes wrong."

"I'm staying too," Stina informed them. "Because anyone who knows anything about battle strategy—"

"And you're an expert on that?" Sophie had to cut in.

Stina tossed her hair. "I've been reading up. And clearly you haven't been or you'd know that you can't send all of your top soldiers into the first battle. You need to keep some on reserve in case anything goes wrong."

"And *you're* our reserve?" Sophie clarified, heaping a whole lot of skepticism into her tone.

Stina raised an eyebrow. "Uh, someone needs to be able to take over if you get yourself injured again—or worse."

The words seemed to ripple around the room, and Sophie was tempted to point out that everything Stina was saying could just as easily be an excuse to keep herself safe.

But . . . Stina did have a small point.

So Sophie let it go, turning back to the group and asking, "Is that everyone?"

That's when she realized she hadn't heard from Fitz or Keefe yet.

"I'm in," Fitz said *very* begrudgingly, and Sophie wasn't sure if his hesitation was with the plan or with her.

All eyes turned to Keefe.

"It's okay if you think it'll be too overwhelming," Sophie told him.

"Oh, I'm definitely going," he said. "I just wanted to make sure I had everyone's attention because there's something super important we need to talk about first. I know Foster doesn't want me to say this—"

"Then *don't*," she jumped in, hoping he wasn't about to announce to everyone that they'd been kissing.

"But we need to be clear on something," Keefe continued without pausing. "This power source we're about to go find? We *have* to destroy it. I don't care if Foster's told you I'm going to need it to help fix all my malfunctioning new abilities. And I don't care if you think it'll give us some huge advantage. We *can't* let my mom—or Vespera—get her hands on it. And the only way to guarantee that is to get rid of it."

"We don't even know if we *can* destroy it without setting it off," Sophie jumped to remind everyone.

"That's actually a good point," Fitz admitted. He still didn't seem happy about backing Sophie up—but maybe he was willing to since it shut down Keefe. "If it's as powerful as Vespera made it sound, it might be extremely volatile."

"Which means we don't know if there's a safe way to gather any of it either," Keefe argued.

"Exactly!" Sophie told him. "Add that to the list of reasons I want to go *now*, so we can get there and see what we're actually dealing with. *Then* we can start making these kinds of decisions and coming up with a real plan. Otherwise we're just standing around, debating what-ifs."

No one could argue with that.

Even Keefe.

"Are we ready, then?" she asked—ignoring the abundance of grumbling from Sandor as she stepped down off the chair and instructed everyone to form a big circle for the leap.

She also made sure everyone had a home crystal easily within reach in case they needed to make a quick escape.

"Remember," Sophie said as everyone held hands. "There are going to be layers and layers of illusions there. Watch the shadows. Try to rely on other senses beyond your eyes. And don't believe anything you see."

"And you wonder why I'm not going," Stina muttered from the corner.

Maybe Stina was smart.

But Sophie was done playing it safe.

So she held the starstone up, casting a blue beam in the center of the circle.

And she let the cold, sharp light drag her away to Elysian.

FORTY-SIX

"**W**HERE SHOULD WE START?"
Dex asked, holding up his Illusion
Breaker and taking a cautious step
forward. Moonlight hit the crystal
and sent several thin beams shooting in every direction—but
they vanished without finding a mark. "This place is way bigger than I expected."

It definitely was.

The field of rolling hills sprawled on and on and on, fading into the murky darkness.

But Sophie could hear the gurgle of a river in the distance.

Actually, it must've been multiple rivers, because she couldn't tell which direction the sound was coming from.

Hopefully that meant there were *five* rivers.

But even if she were right, and they were now standing in the middle of Elysian, there was . . .

Basically nothing to see.

A few twisted trees.

Some scraggly shrubs.

Lots of long, windswept grass.

But Vespera was a master of illusions.

There had to be so much more hidden beneath the surface.

"I think we should split up," Sophie said. "That way we can cover more ground—but let's stick to teams. No one should go alone. And let's also make sure each team has a bodyguard with them."

"I CALL TEAM FOSTER-KEEFE!" Keefe announced, wrapping an arm around Sophie's shoulders. But his huge grin faded when he glanced at Fitz. "I mean . . . if that's not going to cause any problems. Did you, uh . . . need to do your Cognate thing here? Because if you do—"

"It's fine," Fitz told him—but his tone wasn't very convincing.

Everyone stared at them.

"Okaaaaaay," Biana eventually said. "Well . . . I think I'll work with Dex. He has all the cool gadgets."

"Sure do!" Dex tossed her the Illusion Breaker and started showing her how to use it.

"I'm with Wylie," Maruca said, letting her palms glow white—ready to form a force field if they needed it.

And Wylie snapped his fingers, making a golden bubble of light flare over their heads to illuminate their path.

"Yep—definitely want to be on *that* team!" Fitz said, making his way over to join them, along with Grizel.

"You're missing out!" Marella called after him as she sparked a flickering orange ball of flame over her palm. "Linh and I are going to take everyone down!"

"How is this a contest?" Tam asked as he joined Biana and Dex's group.

Marella formed a second ball of fire. "What's the matter? Is our moody Shade afraid he might actually have a little bit of fun?"

"No, I just thought we were all trying to find—and maybe destroy—a super-important power source before Lady Gisela or the Neverseen get their hands on it!"

"Tam's right," Sophie jumped in. "We need to focus."

"THAT DOESN'T MEAN WE CAN'T MAKE IT A BET!" Grizel shouted. "First one to find something gets to punish the other teams!"

"Oh, it's ON!" Marella hooked her arm around Linh as Woltzer ran over to them—not looking at all sad to leave Lovise in charge of Dex, Tam, and Biana. "Let's go see if we can find anything weird with these rivers!"

Sandor muttered something that sounded a lot like "not again" as he followed Keefe and Sophie while the rest of the groups branched off in different directions.

"Let's do regular check-ins," Sophie called after them. "Just quick shout-outs so we know everyone's safe and whether anyone's found anything. And remember, we all have different strengths, so just because one of us checked a spot doesn't mean someone else shouldn't."

"You're so cute when you get all serious and leader-y," Keefe leaned in and whispered.

Sophie sighed.

"What? I mean it! You're really good at it. And it's fun watching you take charge and order us all around."

"Really? It . . . doesn't bother you?"

"Why would it bother me?"

She shrugged, deciding not to dredge up any of her Fitz issues. "I just hope this works. If we don't find what's hidden here, I don't know what we're going to do."

"I do! We'll find a better way to stop my mom—one that definitely *doesn't* involve making any deals with Vespera, right?"

Sophie ignored the question.

"Uh-uh." Keefe jumped in front of her. "I'd like a guarantee that there will be no working with the enemy."

"Find me the power source, and I'll give you one," she countered.

He sighed. "Yeah . . . okay . . . time to get serious."

Sophie nodded, and they headed for one of the trees— which looked ancient and gnarled and tangled in dark vines, but otherwise normal. The bark felt scratchy under her fingers. Everything cast a shadow. And the leaves . . .

"Wait. I think this is one of the trees from Kenric's memory," Sophie said as she reached up and squeezed one of the crumpled-looking leaves, showing Keefe how it didn't make any crunching sound—though now that she could feel the leaf's texture, she understood why. It was thick and soft, like crushed velvet. And Kenric had told Oralie the tree wasn't significant.

Still, it sent chills coursing through her to know she really had pieced all the clues together.

Kenric had found Elysian, and now she had as well.

She just needed to find what the Council was hiding.

She closed her eyes and concentrated, listening to the tree's soft melody.

It was a sad song.

A lonely one.

But that made sense, since they were standing somewhere that gnomes had probably never been allowed to visit.

"Find something?" Keefe asked as Sophie stretched out her consciousness.

She shook her head. "Just . . . checking."

Kenric had mentioned feeling an "awareness" in his memory, and she wondered if she could pick up the same sensation.

And there was *something*.

A strange sort of tension.

Like Elysian was holding its breath, waiting to see what they'd do next.

"Can you feel that?" she whispered. "I know your empathy's not cooperating, but—"

"If you mean your overwhelming urge to grab me and kiss me again, I'm *definitely* picking up on that," Keefe told her.

Sophie groaned. "I thought you were being serious!"

"Sorry—it's just so much more fun to watch you blush!" He looked away when she glared at him. "Okay, fine. Maybe . . . it's also easier to make a joke than admit I'm *not* feeling anything right now—and it's super unsettling."

"Just right now?" Sophie asked. "Or the whole time we've been here?"

He kicked the grass. "The whole time we've been here. Guess I'm a pretty useless teammate, huh?"

"Not at all. Seriously, Keefe—I mean it. In fact, that could be your body's reaction to being closer to the power source."

"Uh, wouldn't my abilities get *stronger* if the power source is what I need?"

"Not necessarily. It could be like when you're really hungry and end up surrounded by food you can't have. That always makes me feel weak and sick, like my body is screaming at me, *Please give me some of that.*"

"Maybe." Keefe didn't sound convinced.

And the slump in his shoulders made her call out, "FIRST CHECK-IN!" hoping the others were having better luck. "ANY-ONE FIND ANYTHING?"

Everyone shouted back various versions of "Not yet!"

Same thing happened the next time she checked in.

And the time after that.

And Sophie could tell how hard everyone was trying. She kept seeing flashes of light and color. Flickers of flames and hisses of water. Streaky lines from Dex's gadget and shifting shadows.

But every check-in still led to nothing, nothing, nothing.

Until even Grizel had lost her enthusiasm for the bet.

And at the next check-in, someone finally called out what they all had to be thinking: "There's nothing here."

Sophie glanced at the sky, where the unmapped stars were still perfectly aligned, shining brighter than ever.

"There *has* to be something," she murmured.

They'd fought too long and too hard to get there.

Followed too many clues.

And it all fit.

The starstone. The rivers. Even Vespera's confidence in her illusions.

If they gave up, they were basically admitting that Vespera was better than them. And Sophie refused to accept that.

So she turned in a slow circle, searching for anything she could be missing.

"It's okay, Foster," Keefe told her. "We don't need this."

"Yes, we do."

He might not want to take control of stellarlune.

But she *had* to—and not just for him.

He was only the beginning of Gisela's plans.

So she kept going, even when dawn began to break.

She'd actually hoped a little sunlight might show something they missed.

But when she took Dex's Illusion Breaker and made a final lap around the main grassy area, there was still nothing.

"I know what you're thinking," Keefe said as she watched the sixth unmapped star fade with the sunrise. "And I'm going to need that guarantee now."

Sophie shook her head.

She wasn't going to pretend that Vespera's offer wasn't an option.

She didn't care if every single person disagreed with her decision.

This was too important.

Keefe sighed. "Okay, how about this? At least promise me you'll go home, get a little sleep, and meet up with everyone before you make any new decisions?"

It was a reasonable enough request.

"Fine," Sophie told him, taking his hand when he offered it.

But as she held the starstone up to the light, she knew she'd be back.

She'd do whatever it took to uncover the power in Elysian.

FORTY-SEVEN

ARE YOU READY TO TRUST ME?" asked a voice straight out of Sophie's nightmares. So it took her a second to realize the voice was really there in the room with her.

She ripped open her eyes and bolted upright, gasping for breath as she squinted at a pale, dark-haired figure in a loose-fitting royal-blue gown, looming at the foot of her bed.

"I would not have expected you to be able to sleep after such a colossal failure," Vespera said, her lips curling into a chilling smile. "But perhaps you are used to such disasters."

"HOW DID YOU GET IN HERE?" Sophie scrambled for the dagger under her pillow—trying not to picture some horrible path of carnage through the rest of the house.

But how else could Vespera have gotten past all the goblin patrols?

And Flori?

And Sandor?

And her parents?

And . . .

Vespera sighed. "There is no need for such hysterics. I would have thought you would at least be able to recognize *this* illusion. But you are welcome to throw that dagger if you need further convincing."

There was no way Sophie was giving up her only weapon. But she leaned slowly forward—just enough to get a glimpse of the floor where Vespera stood, and . . .

Vespera had no shadow.

"Feel better?" Vespera asked.

"Not really. I'm sure you still had to get past Sandor's security to pull this off."

"Indeed I did. And it was gloriously easy. I just had to cause a bit of turmoil in one of the pastures and sneak past while everyone rushed to deal with it. No one has been hurt, if that is what you are worrying about—though they could have been, if that was what I had wanted. And I do not say that as a threat, but rather as further proof that I mean you no harm at the moment. I thought I had made that clear, and yet you still foolishly ran off to Elysian without me—did you think I would not be watching?"

Sophie pulled her covers around her, feeling suddenly exposed. "What do you want?"

"The same thing you do. But you have surrounded yourself with too many fearful people who keep trying to change your mind. And I do not have time for you to waver with indecision any longer. So I thought I would make things much easier for you. Forget leaving me a note, or sending wind, or gathering all of the others. I am close. I am ready. And I have created an opportunity for you to sneak away. Bring me the starstone, and I will take you to Elysian so we can claim the power we both need. You have my word that you will make it home safe."

"Your *word*," Sophie repeated.

"Yes. Have I not been truthful with you thus far? Did you not find the tracker, exactly as I said you would? And can you not see the stars aligning? Even your failure yesterday proves I do not lie. I said you would be fooled by my illusions, and you were. So when I say you will make it home safe, you have no reason to doubt me."

"Except that you're trying to lure me there alone, and you're wearing *that*." Sophie pointed to Vespera's ability-blocking headpiece. "You realize I can inflict through that, right?"

Vespera trailed her fingers over the chain. "I am aware and prepared. But I prefer to keep my thoughts private. If that makes you so uncomfortable, as a compromise, I will allow you to bring two of your friends."

"Three," Sophie countered—not sure why that number

sounded so much better. Mostly she just didn't want to let Vespera dictate everything. "And a bodyguard."

Vespera sighed. "Fine. But you must gather them quickly. I will not wait around while you argue and scheme."

Sophie was pretty sure Vespera would, given how much trouble she'd gone through in order to arrange this little conversation.

She also couldn't believe she was actually considering going along with this plan.

This was heading way past "risky" and straight into "reckless" territory.

But . . . she was almost out of time.

This might be her last chance to find the truth—and the power—she needed.

She *might* end up regretting this decision.

But she definitely *would* regret it if she didn't try.

So she asked Vespera, "Where do I meet you?"

Vespera's smile was pure ice when she told Sophie, "I believe you are well acquainted with the caves beneath the cliffs of your home."

Bile soured Sophie's tongue.

She'd been drugged and dragged out of those caves once.

But she'd been caught off guard.

Now she was prepared.

"What time?" she asked.

"Fifteen minutes."

She shook her head. "I'll need at least thirty."

Vespera's jaw tightened, but she nodded. "I would not recommend being late," she added before her illusion blinked away.

For a second, Sophie wondered if she'd dreamed the whole encounter.

But when she stumbled to her window, she could see chaos in the pastures.

The gorgodon had escaped from its cage—and it couldn't be a coincidence that Vespera had chosen to free the beast that Gisela created.

So she raced to her closet and threw on a dark tunic with a wide belt for holding weapons and filled it with the starstone, as many goblin throwing stars as she could fit, and Dex's Illusion Breaker—which she still had from the night before. She had a feeling if she shone its light in Vespera's eyes, it would give her a chance to get away if she really needed it. And she strapped on Hope, making sure the dagger was in easy reach before covering it with her cape.

Then she grabbed her Imparter, trying to decide which of her friends to hail, knowing she could be dragging them into a trap—which automatically ruled out Keefe.

He was much too close to all of this.

Plus, she needed to be *very* strategic.

Maruca was the most obvious choice, in case they needed a force field.

And with all that dry grass for kindling, Marella's fire could be a vital weapon.

The third was the hardest to pick.

Tam and Linh were so enormously powerful, and Dex was so clever and loyal, and Biana was so fearless and confident, and Wylie was so brave and commanding.

But even though their relationship was on the verge of unraveling, the person Sophie wanted with her was Fitz.

They were so much stronger together.

And she trusted him completely.

She just hoped he still trusted her.

She didn't have time for big speeches or long drawn-out explanations. So when she hailed each of her friends, she simply said, "Please." Then she told them where and when, asked them to come alone, and begged them not to tell anyone.

She had no idea if they'd listen.

But she had a bigger problem ahead.

Even luring Sandor away from the gorgodon proved quite a challenge—until he noticed her expression. Then he quietly followed her to the Cliffside gate.

She could tell that was as far as he'd go without some sort of explanation, so she told him, "I could've snuck off without you"—which might not have been the smartest way to start the conversation. But it at least got a reaction. And there was nothing else to say except "But I need you."

Sandor sighed and took Sophie's hand. "I go where you go."

"So do I!" Keefe shouted, jumping out of the bushes and grabbing Sandor's arm. "I don't know what's going on, but I can feel how huge it is, even with my messed-up empathy. So you're not going anywhere without me."

Sophie opened her mouth to tell him it wasn't his decision.

But when they locked eyes, she could see more than determination in his stare.

There was desperation.

And honestly, maybe it would be better if he were there.

Maybe he would finally understand why she had to do this, once all the illusions were gone and the new source of power was right there in front of him.

So she nodded and told him, "Follow me."

And down they went, no one speaking as they followed the narrow stairs to the small sandy shore lined with caves.

They stayed out in the open until Fitz, Maruca, and Marella joined them, and Sophie had to fight the urge to throw her arms around all of them and thank them for showing up.

"I said *three*," Vespera called from somewhere in the dark recesses. "But I suppose in his condition, the fourth barely counts."

Sophie could see the exact moment when each of her friends recognized the voice.

"What have you done?" Keefe asked.

"What she should have done the moment she found the starstone," Vespera said, stepping out of the shadows. "I am showing her the *real* Elysian."

FORTY-EIGHT

I T'S NOT TOO LATE TO CHANGE YOUR MIND,"
Sandor murmured as the rolling hills of Elysian shimmered into focus once again. He pointed to Vespera with the edge of his sword. "She's actually here this time. I can end her."

"Or I can trap her under a force field," Maruca suggested.

"Or I could cage her in a ring of fire," Marella added.

"For the record, I'm a big fan of all these plans," Keefe jumped in.

"So am I," Fitz said.

Sophie shook her head. "This is a truce. We won't be attacking—unless Vespera gives us a reason."

"And if you think I cannot defend myself from anything

you just mentioned, you are foolishly mistaken," Vespera called over her shoulder. "You also might want to keep in mind that I already got what I wanted from this bargain. I'm *here*." She stretched out her arms toward the grassy fields. "From this point on, *you* need *me*—but I am done with all of you. And the only reason you are still breathing is because I made a deal with your leader."

"Do you think she's bluffing?" Marella asked Sophie. "She has to be bluffing, right? No one's *that* good. Plus, she got herself arrested once—"

"And I will *never* let that happen again!" Vespera spun around to face Marella. "Prison made me crave freedom in a way you cannot possibly understand. I will fight for it—far more ruthlessly than anyone."

Marella swallowed loudly.

"Look," Sophie said as she stepped between Vespera and Marella. "I know some of you probably think this is a bad idea—and maybe it is. But . . . I *have* to know what's hidden here. I think it's going to be super important. And she's the only one who can show me. So I really appreciate all of you trusting me enough to come this far—but I don't want to force you either. If you'd rather go home . . ."

Fitz shook his head, sharing a quick look with Marella, Maruca, and Keefe before he told her, "We're with you, Sophie. We just *really* hope you know what you're doing."

"So do I," Sophie mumbled.

"Are we ready, then?" Vespera asked, her blue gown billowing in the breeze as she motioned for them to follow her up one of the grassy hills.

Elysian looked much more vibrant in the afternoon sunlight than it had the night before. The hills were now a deep green, and the trees were red, orange, and gold—with dark blue vines crawling up their trunks. And every so often, tiny yellow butterflies with red faces would flutter by, proving once again that Sophie was now standing in the same place she'd seen in Kenric's cache.

But Kenric never found what Vespera was about to show them.

Or if he did, he went to tremendous lengths to bury it.

Which felt equal parts exhilarating and terrifying.

"It's strange how little has changed," Vespera said as she headed for the same gnarled tree that Sophie had checked the night before. She trailed her pale fingers over one of the dark blue vines coiled around the trunk.

"That's a lot of Noxflares," Marella murmured.

Sophie sucked in a breath. "Is that what these are? I only saw them at night in Fintan's memory, and they looked a little different. Do they have something to do with the illusion?" she asked Vespera.

Vespera frowned. "Illusions are not made of *flowers*. They're made of light and shadow and very subtle sounds that slowly guide us forward or steer us away. Can you hear them?"

Sophie tried to concentrate, but all she could hear was the tree's lonely song.

She could still sense that strange tension, though—was that what Vespera meant?

Was the illusion trying to make her uneasy so she'd stay away from it?

"This truly was some of my best work," Vespera said as she squinted at something Sophie couldn't see. "It is such a shame I wasted so much of my talent serving such cowardly leaders. But now I can finally claim what they tricked me into hiding."

She rolled up her gown's long blue sleeves and raised her hands toward the sun. "You may want to shield your eyes for this part."

Sandor stepped in front of Sophie to block her—but she scooted back to his side.

There was no way she was going to miss this.

"Want me to put up a force field?" Maruca offered.

Vespera clicked her tongue. "There is no need. I am merely toying with the light. Creating a very precise pattern."

She tilted her hand one way—then the other—then back again—and again—making Sophie notice a delicate ring on Vespera's slender finger. The clear stone was prism-shaped and seemed to flash whenever the sun hit it, causing tiny specks of light to fall to the grass. The glints must've landed on something reflective because they bounced back and split, forming new sparks that collided and flared much brighter before splitting into more glints, and more and more—all of them bouncing and splitting and ricocheting over and over until there were thousands of tiny sparks everywhere, spinning into a funnel and soaring higher and higher before crashing back down like a sparkly curtain, washing away the illusion.

"It's just as I remember," Vespera breathed, her eyes wide and almost watery as she stared at the new reality.

"That's the power source?" Sophie asked, frowning at the cluster of jagged brown rocks.

She'd known they were looking for a quarry, but after everything she'd heard about the Prime Sources and the sixth unmapped star, she'd been picturing something . . .

. . . shiny, or glowing, or sparkly.

"Uh, I'm not feeling any power," Keefe announced—which Sophie had also been wondering about.

"Yeah, shouldn't it be pulsing or buzzing or vibrating or something?" Fitz asked.

"They are warm, though," Marella noted. "I can feel the heat from here."

"But they can't be *that* warm if they're covered in those Noxflare things," Maruca reminded her, pointing to the blue vine tangled around one of the larger boulders.

"Actually, Noxflares are fire-resistant," Sophie said quietly.

But it did seem odd that they were growing across the

quarry. Especially since the vine wrapped around only one rock over and over and over.

"I know a *really* easy way to settle whether this is the power source," Keefe said, stalking closer.

"DON'T!" Sophie shouted, grabbing his arm and trying to drag him back before he could touch anything—but he still managed to scoop up one small piece, and . . .

Nothing happened.

"See?" he said, holding the stone out to show everyone. "It's not burning me or shooting out sparks—and it's definitely not changing me or boosting my powers. It's just . . . a rock."

"But . . . how can that be?" Sophie asked, feeling her insides start to shrivel when she saw the confusion in Vespera's expression.

"I do not know," Vespera admitted.

Keefe snorted. "I do. Sounds like the big secret power source my mom supposedly planned her whole experiment around— which we took all these huge risks to find—is . . . fake."

He almost sounded like he wanted to laugh—but maybe he was just trying to cover his panic.

Sophie couldn't hide hers.

She needed that power source.

Keefe needed that power source.

How could it not be there???

Vespera crouched to study the rocks, murmuring mostly to herself. "It has to be real. Something must be missing."

Marella sucked in a breath. "Maybe it is! In the memory Fintan showed me, he was burning the Noxflares—and he kept saying 'something's missing.'"

"He said that in the memory I saw too—and he also burned Noxflares!" Sophie said, clinging hard to the tiny new shred of hope. "And look at the way the vine wraps around the boulder, almost like someone trained it to do that."

"So what are you saying?" Maruca asked. "You want to burn them?"

"Yes!" Sophie and Vespera both said immediately.

"But didn't you say that Fintan burned them a specific way?" Sophie asked Marella.

"Yeah, he used different layers of colored flames. I remember the order he sparked them in, so that won't be a problem—but it'd be way easier if I had somewhere to test the flames." She scanned the clearing and pointed to a fallen branch. "That should work."

Sophie ran to grab it for her, handing it over as Marella snapped her fingers and turned the branch into a torch with flickering white flames.

She brought the fire toward the Noxflares—but Maruca grabbed Marella's arm. "Are you sure this is safe?"

"Not really," Marella admitted. "It's fire—it's never *safe*. But . . . maybe you should put a force field around me and the boulder. That way if anything happens, I'm the only one who has to deal with it."

"Yeah, but . . . you'd be trapped with it," Sophie argued.

Marella shrugged, and the gold highlights in her hair reflected the fire as she said, "I can handle a few flames."

Sophie was pretty sure it would be more than a *few*.

But before she could argue, Marella told her, "Trust me, I'm not planning on joining the 'almost dying' club anytime soon. I'm a big fan of living. But . . . I really want to try this. I know it probably sounds weird, but it feels like Fintan showed me that memory for a reason. And maybe this is why."

Sophie tugged out an itchy eyelash before she nodded. "Just be careful—and if there's anything I can do . . ."

"I'll let you know," Marella promised.

She waited until Maruca had formed a flickering force field around her and the boulder—then lowered her torch toward the Noxflares.

Sophie held her breath as the vine erupted with white flames.

But nothing changed.

"That's only the first layer," Marella reminded everyone as she added purple flames to the torch, letting them burn for a second before she added them to the Noxflares.

She did the same with the yellow fire.

Then added the pink—jumping back when the Noxflares sparked and shimmered like fireworks.

But no illusions melted away.

And the rocks didn't suddenly glow with power.

"Are we ready to give up yet?" Keefe asked.

"Nope," Marella told him. "Fintan kept saying that something was missing, even after he added the pink. So I think there's still one more step. I just don't know what kind of flame it would be. Green? Red? *Or . . .*"

"Or?" Sophie prompted when Marella squatted and grabbed one of the smaller pieces of rock.

"There's a *lot* of heat in this thing," Marella murmured, squeezing the rock in her fist. "Maybe it absorbed some of that special light from the sixth unmapped star or something. I could find out. Spark it into a flame and see what happens."

"What do you think the odds are that it'll explode on you?" Fitz asked.

"I don't know," Marella admitted. "But . . . my instincts are telling me it'll be okay. I think I need to trust them."

She closed her eyes and squeezed the rock tighter, gritting her teeth as her whole body shook.

Five seconds passed.

Ten.

Then a strangled grunt slipped through Marella's lips as pale blue flames curled out of the rock like smoke.

"Here goes nothing," she whispered before sending the blue fire straight to the Noxflares.

They flared brighter than the sun, whiting out everything as Sophie screamed at Maruca to lower the force field so they could get Marella out of there.

"No, it's okay," Marella called from somewhere in the glaring white. "I'm okay. And I think it worked, but . . . it's weird. You'll see once the flames burn themselves out."

Sophie circled the force field, desperate for a glimpse of her friend—and whatever was in there with her.

And on her third time around, the light faded.

"What is that?" Sophie whispered, rubbing her eyes to make sure they'd adjusted properly.

She'd never seen anything like it—even in the Lost Cities.

The rocks had vanished, replaced with what looked like some sort of small, round . . . gateway.

The burning Noxflares hovered in the air—a perfect circle of flickering blue, yellow, white, purple, and pink. And everything around them was the same normal Elysian scenery.

But *inside* . . .

Sophie couldn't tell.

It looked very, very bright and very, very colorful.

"Can you lower the force field?" Sophie asked Maruca.

"What are you going to do?" Keefe asked as Sophie stumbled closer.

She had no idea.

She just *had* to get a better look, because her gut was telling her, *This is it.*

This is what you've been looking for.

The power for stellarlune is in there.

Sophie picked up a rock as she approached, warning

everyone to duck before she tossed it into the center of the burning circle as soon as the force field blinked away and—

The rock disappeared.

Or maybe she just couldn't *see* it anymore, because she could still hear it crashing and clanging as it landed somewhere just beyond them.

"Is this an illusion?" Sophie asked Vespera, who was staring at the fiery circle with a mix of awe and confusion.

"If it is, then it is remarkable," Vespera breathed. "And if it is not, then it is impossible."

Sophie turned to her friends. "I need to check."

"What are you going to do—climb through?" Keefe asked.

"Maybe," Sophie admitted. "It can't be that much weirder than teleporting, right?"

No one could necessarily argue with that—though Sandor certainly tried. But Sophie didn't see any other option.

"If you go, I should be in front of you," Maruca told her. "Just in case the situation needs a force field."

"And I'd better go too, to make sure the fire doesn't close in on you two," Marella added.

There wasn't space for anyone else, but Keefe and Fitz moved closer, promising to drag them back if anything tried to trap them—and Sandor paced around them with his weapon drawn.

"What are we doing?" Sophie whispered, sharing a look with Marella and Maruca that seemed to confirm they were all seriously questioning their life choices.

But they still stepped closer and closer, slowly leaning past the circle of flames to see . . .

Stained glass.

Lots of it.

Thousands of panes in thousands of colors. Forming curved walls that seemed to vanish beyond the Noxflares.

"I think it *is* another illusion," Sophie mumbled. "Or where we are right now is—I don't know. But I wonder . . ."

She reached into her belt and pulled out Dex's Illusion Breaker.

"I'm going to hold this in the light of the flames on three," she warned her friends.

Maruca's palms glowed white and Marella held her torch up higher, all of them holding their breath as Sophie said, "Three . . . two . . . one . . . ," and raised the crystal cube near the flickering fire.

Beams of light exploded everywhere, and Sophie forgot to close her eyes, too distracted by the world dissolving around her.

She could hear screams and crashes, but her head was spinning, spinning, spinning—and then she was falling back and back and back, into . . .

. . . a pair of strong arms.

"Easy there, Foster," Keefe said. "I guess that's why Dex warned us that the Illusion Breaker could cause dizziness."

"Is that what happened?" Sophie asked, blinking hard, trying to get her eyes to focus. "Was it just an illusion?"

"Honestly? I have no idea what's going on. See for yourself."

Keefe helped her stand back up, and she realized the burning Noxflares were gone—and they were definitely still in Elysian, surrounded by rolling hills and fall-colored trees.

But beyond that was a massive dome of intricate stained glass, closing everything in.

"What *is* this place?" Sophie asked, wondering if the dome was the reason she hadn't been able to teleport to Elysian the first time.

Though if it were, how had the starstone let them slip through?

"I have no idea," Vespera murmured, reminding Sophie she was still with them. "So many illusions on top of illusions on top of illusions."

"So . . . do you think this dome was built to keep something out?" Keefe asked. "Or keep someone in?"

"I was just asking myself the same thing," a new voice said—one that made Sophie want to scream loud enough to shatter all the glass.

"Whatever it is," Lady Gisela said as she stepped out of the shadows and smiled her much-too-tight smile, "it makes for a very convenient trap, don't you think?"

FORTY-NINE

*I*F YOU WANTED TO TRAP US, YOU SHOULDN'T *have come here alone!"* Sandor snarled, raising his sword and charging toward Gisela like a gorgodon on a rampage.

Gisela's smile stretched wider. "But I'm *not* alone."

She clapped her hands, and two enormous beasts tore out of the ground—growling blurs of fangs, claws, and muscle that slammed into Sandor, knocking his weapon from his hands and grabbing him by his throat as they dragged him back into the earth.

NO!

Sophie barely had time to scream—barely had time to register the glowing white force field that flared to life around her.

Too late. Too late. Too late.

"Before you do anything you'll regret," Gisela warned as Sophie's vision rimmed with red and she dove into her boiling rage, letting it sear through her veins, "you should know that the only reason your bodyguard is simply a captive at the moment—instead of getting shredded into tiny pieces by two very hungry trolls—is *me*. Without my regular commands, your bodyguard becomes dinner."

She grinned and tapped her ear, highlighting the silver earpiece running along the outer edge. "My Technopath has been *very* busy since we teamed up properly, making sure I have a means to control these unruly beasts. After all, what good is having an army of trolls in my arsenal if they're going to run wild during battle and forget who their enemy is? Empress Pernille has been quite impressed with the result. She was all but ready to abandon her enhanced newborn project before I reached out."

"So that's how you got the trolls to cancel their treaty negotiations and turn against the Council?" Sophie asked, trying to keep Gisela talking so she wouldn't call any more trolls—while her brain kept screaming, *SANDOR, SANDOR, SANDOR.*

She *would* get him back.

Even if she had to claw her way into the earth.

"That definitely helped," Gisela said, patting her sleek blond updo, which was draped in a net of ability-blocking metal chain. "But the real turning point was when I offered them more land. It's amazing how much loyalty a few human islands can buy."

Sophie stumbled back—the words cutting through her like a throwing star—and she was grateful someone was there to catch her and keep her steady.

She'd forgotten about the disappearing islands her sister had asked her to look into.

How many other vital clues had she ignored?

"Being a leader isn't easy, is it?" Gisela asked, her voice dripping with mock sympathy. "There's so much more to it than setting a fire and carving a symbol into the dirt, isn't there?"

"You're one to talk!" Fitz snapped, making Sophie realize he was the one keeping her steady.

So where was Keefe?

She craned her neck, spotting him crouched near the far edge of their force field, resting his head in his hands.

He's okay, Fitz transmitted. *I already checked to make sure he wasn't having a breakdown. But he's just trying to find a command to control his mom. I guess his ability isn't cooperating.*

Of course it isn't, Sophie grumbled. *The one time we actually need it.*

Exactly—but I'm sure he'll get there. So I'm just trying to keep his mom talking in the meantime.

That's what I was doing too, she admitted, *mostly so I can figure out how to get to Sandor.*

Fitz tightened his grip on her shoulders. *We'll figure it out,* he promised before he asked Gisela, "How many times have you been overthrown now?"

"Too many," she said, trailing her fingers along her cheeks, as if she could still feel the scars she'd gotten when Fintan took over. Removing them had left her skin stretched unnaturally tight. "But now I get to gather a far superior group. And it was very kind of you to bring me a Psionipath and a Pyrokinetic."

"I would *never*—" Maruca started, but Gisela raised a hand.

"I'm sure you're going to tell me you'll never join my cause—just like I'm sure your little friend holding the fireballs"—she gestured to Marella—"is planning to launch them in some sort of dramatic escape. But that's because you haven't grasped the gravity of this situation. I didn't go to all this trouble to track you down just to talk—and no, I'm not going to tell you how I found you. I'm also not looking for volunteers. If you fight me, your bodyguard will die. Your only choice is to cooperate."

"You say that as if it is some drastic change," Vespera called from the shadow of one of the trees, stepping forward and smoothing the skirt of her blue gown.

For a second Sophie wondered if Vespera was going to try to talk her way back onto Gisela's side. But then she said, "I warned you from the beginning that our philosophies are opposite and could not be combined. But you thought you could convince me. Then you thought you could force me. Just like you thought you could force your son. And the Shade. But you are too weak to exercise the control you crave. Why do you think I was able to take over your entire organization?"

"Not my *entire* organization," Gisela corrected, tapping her earpiece again. "And it's funny that you stand there with such bravado, despite being completely alone. This alliance you formed in your effort to team up against me"—she pointed to Sophie and the rest of the group—"how interesting that you're not shielded under their force field."

"I do not need to be," Vespera told her. "We both know I can defend myself. Just like we both know that you are all talk and no follow-through. You have kept your hands mostly clean of all the darker responsibilities that come with this rebellion, relying instead on empty threats. You focus far too much on your son. And you lack the necessary ruthlessness—"

"Yes, the *ruthlessness*," Gisela cut in. "You love to throw that word around. And I can see why you believe it doesn't apply to me. I've been very careful with what I've shown you, since it's far easier to be underestimated. It causes people to make fatal mistakes. Like you—you knew I believed I'd find more of my power stones in Elysian. You even went so far as to team up with my son and his friends in an attempt to beat me. And clearly we've *all* misunderstood whatever this place is." She frowned at the stained-glass dome. "But that doesn't change the fact that you never asked me where I keep the stones I have left—or what I plan to do with them."

She smiled with the last words and snapped her fingers, making a shard of flashing crystal appear in her palm.

Alarms erupted in Sophie's head.

If that crystal was what she thought it was, this was about to get *very* bad.

"I let you underestimate me for too long," Gisela said. "And now it's time for you to see that I can be plenty ruthless."

"Get down!" Sophie screamed as Gisela flung the shard at Vespera. "And reinforce—"

The crystal exploded, shaking the universe as Sophie dove to the ground and covered her head, with Fitz right beside her.

Maruca's force field held back most of the debris, but the dust seeped through, leaving them hacking and choking as they stumbled to their feet to see that . . .

. . . very little had actually changed.

The stained-glass dome hadn't fractured.

The trees stood unscathed.

But one patch of grass now displayed a jagged, twisted shape—the same patch of grass where Vespera had been standing.

And the world turned sideways.

Especially when Sophie noticed the colors streaking through the tangled form.

Blue like Vespera's gown.

Black like her hair.

And lots of red.

Her brain didn't know how to process it.

But the proof was right there.

So she made herself think the words.

Vespera is dead.

FIFTY

S O . . . WHO'S NEXT?" GISELA ASKED, reaching up to smooth her hair with an unnervingly steady hand, considering she'd just murdered someone. Her ice blue eyes even seemed to twinkle.

And her lips stretched into a *very* unsettling smile when Keefe slowly stepped forward.

"Okay," he mumbled, shaking dust off his tunic. "We all know you're here for me. So you win, okay? Just . . . let Sandor—and everyone else—go, and I promise I'll cooperate."

"NO!" Sophie shouted, trying to run over to him, but Fitz held her back.

Keefe told me he has a plan, he transmitted.

Maybe he did.

But it probably wasn't a very good one, given how pale he looked.

Gisela tilted her head and studied Keefe the way a scientist might examine their lab rat. "You don't seem well," she said without a drop of concern. "And the fact that you're not commanding me to slam my head into the ground tells me you've been fighting who you are. That's why I told you to embrace the change, Keefe. Why must you always be so stubborn? If you keep fighting it, stellarlune *will* destroy you. This was never a onetime thing. It's every day, every hour, accepting who and what you're becoming."

Sophie's ears rang with the words, and she had to remind herself to breathe.

Was *that* why Keefe's abilities were fading?

It . . . kinda made sense.

But Keefe seemed way less convinced. "Nice try! We all know you're just scrambling to cover for the fact that you designed stellarlune to have *three* steps. And the third one needs this mysterious new power source that was supposed to be here—but doesn't actually exist."

"It *does* exist," Gisela insisted. "You have your proof right there."

She pointed to the mangled thing that used to be Vespera.

Sophie shuddered.

Vespera is dead.

"I may have been wrong about where to find the quantities I need," Gisela added, "but the stones *are* real. And when I find more of them—"

"You'll what?" Keefe asked. "Blow me up? Thanks, I'll pass. I'm done being your experiment—"

"And here I thought you were surrendering. Weren't you trying to sacrifice yourself to save your friends?" Gisela reminded him.

"That's usually my play," Keefe admitted, glancing at Sophie like he wanted to make sure she was listening before he added, "but the thing is . . . my friends are amazing. They don't need me to get them out of this mess. And they certainly don't need to make deals with you or join your new order. They can fight their way out of this."

Fight their way out of this.

Was that Keefe's plan?

It would explain why he looked so pale.

And yet, as Sophie let those words claw around her brain, she didn't feel the fear or dread she would've expected.

She felt . . . ready.

She wasn't going to stand by like Vespera had and let Gisela destroy everything.

She was going to fight back.

But when she reached behind her to grab Hope, the holster was empty.

A quick glance at Keefe's expression made it clear that he

had it—and confirmed that she was right about what he was planning.

Sophie had no idea when he'd taken it, but she could yell at him about it later.

First they needed to survive this.

"It's strange that you seem so unconcerned about condemning your goblin to death," Gisela noted, reminding Sophie of the additional complication she needed to prepare for. "Is that what happened to your bodyguard? Or did she just decide to give up on you?"

"Actually, Ro's busy trying to snuff out more traitors," Keefe said. "Maybe we'll send her to the trolls next, see how long it takes before they realize they need to abandon you—like everyone else who's ever made the mistake of joining your side."

Keefe's going to attack his mom, Sophie transmitted to Fitz, Marella, and Maruca, connecting all their minds together so they'd be able to communicate. *I'm going to stay and help—but you need to get out of here while Gisela's distracted.*

What about Sandor? Fitz asked.

*Gisela won't hurt him—yet. Not when she needs to use him as leverage. And hopefully we can take her down pretty quickly and grab that earpiece—order her trolls to stand down or . . . I don't know. I'm still figuring it all out. But you need to get somewhere safe. Take this—*she pressed the starstone into Fitz's hand—*and send back some help if you can. But we'll be fine either way. I can hold my own against any trolls Gisela brings in. And Keefe can handle his mom.*

She was pretty impressed with how confident she sounded.

But her friends looked less convinced.

Uh, you're going to need my force fields for that, Maruca argued.

And you're going to need my flames, Marella added.

And I'm going straight for Sandor's sword, Fitz told her. *I know you're trying to protect us right now—but you asked us to come today because you knew you were going to need us. So let us help.*

Sophie chewed her lip. *If you get hurt—*

That's our choice, Maruca jumped in. *And none of us would be offering to stay if we weren't prepared for that.*

And we probably shouldn't waste any more time arguing, Marella reminded them.

She was right about that.

Okay . . . fine—but I need you to promise me: If Gisela snaps her fingers or you see any trace of one of those crystal shards, you'll get out of here as fast as you can. And if something happens to me, you leave me behind. And—

Wow, this is such a great pep talk! Marella cut in. *I feel so inspired!*

Sophie couldn't help but smile.

So . . . we're doing this, right? Maruca asked. *When should I drop the force field?*

Sophie glanced back at Keefe, noting the way he kept slowly inching toward his mother. *I have a feeling Keefe will let us know.*

He moved a little closer.

Then a little more.

And a little more after that.

But Gisela frowned when he took another step. "What are you doing?"

"Can't a son just want to be close to his mother?" Keefe asked.

Her posture turned rigid. "Enough!"

"You know—I was just thinking the same thing," Keefe told her. "I've definitely had enough."

And with that, he lunged with all his strength.

Gisela dodged him easily, warning, "You'll pay for that," as four trolls burst out of the ground.

"Wanna bet?" Sophie shouted as Maruca dropped their force field.

Fitz grabbed Sandor's sword and charged as Marella unleashed a flurry of fireballs and Sophie closed her eyes, trying to tune everything out.

She couldn't think about the roars and screams and grunts.

She dove deep into the darkest parts of herself, letting the rage and fury fester.

Picturing Sandor's face as the trolls dragged him under.

Keefe's expression every time he had to admit he'd been changed.

Gisela's easy calm after committing murder.

And as the emotions seethed and swelled, she found her mind focusing on the same word Gisela had shouted.

Enough.

She poured her fury into that word, letting it burn and burn and burn until the heat became unbearable.

Then she raised her arms and aimed for the troll charging toward her and screamed, "ENOUGH!" as searing bolts of red lightning blasted out of her palms and forehead.

She gave herself over to the frenzy, striking again and again and again.

This wasn't just a battle.

This was the end.

She'd had enough.

It was time to finish this.

She charged forward, barely seeing—barely breathing—as she blasted everything in her path, again and again and again, until . . .

It almost felt like someone reached into her head and flicked off a switch.

Shutting everything down.

Her rage cooled.

Her power ebbed.

Her vision cleared.

And she watched in a daze as Maruca's force field blinked away.

And Marella's flames were snuffed out.

And Fitz's sword slipped from his hand as he reached up to cradle his head.

"What's happening?" Keefe asked, stumbling back and staring at his hands. "I . . . I can't feel anything."

Even Lady Gisela couldn't conjure anything with a snap.

"I don't understand," Sophie mumbled.

"You're not supposed to," an unfamiliar voice said—in a tone that was dark and raw and somehow melodic.

"Who's there?" Keefe shouted as everyone scrambled to their feet. "Who are you?"

At first there was no answer.

Then a figure in a gray cloak stepped out of thin air. "My name is Elysian," she said. "And *I* am the power source you're all here looking for."

ACKNOWLEDGMENTS

Here we are again—another Keeper book, another cliff-hanger! Do I at least get credit for being consistent with my evil endings? (Probably not . . .) And since I do realize that some of you are likely glaring at this page thinking, *WHY ISN'T THERE ANOTHER CHAPTER?* I thought I should maybe try to explain.

See . . . the moment I just left you with? (You know, the one that has you wondering, *What does it mean???*) That's a moment I've been building toward for this entire series. It's the game changer of all game changers! The biggest secret in the Lost Cities! And even though it comes about rather suddenly, I *had* to pause there so we can all reset, regroup (possibly even recover?), and get ready for all the twists and turns ahead!

(And, hey, you can always go back and reread chapter 42 if you need to fill the days between now and book 10!)

Also: I know everyone had to wait an extra-long time for

me to write this part of Sophie's story—thank you *so* much for bearing with me. I wrote *Stellarlune* with a brand-new baby, in a house under constant construction, while life threw every possible curveball it could at me. So it is one hundred percent true that I *never* would've been able to finish if it weren't for the support, guidance, and wisdom of a multitude of people.

First up: Kara Sargent and Jessi Smith—I don't know what I would've done without our weekly brainstorming Zooms. (And I hope you're not sick of them, because "Hello, book 10!") Thank you for helping me find my way whenever I hit a wall or fell into a plot hole. And I am so sorry for putting you through the World's Most Miserable Deadline Schedule!

And speaking of deadlines . . . my team at Simon & Schuster deserves a truckload of cupcakes and puppies for all the hoops they jumped through in order to give me the time I needed to finish writing. I truly feel like Keeper has its own army at this point. Thank you, Valerie Garfield, Anna Jarzab, Jon Anderson, Mike Rosamilia, Chel Morgan, Rebecca Vitkus, Elizabeth Mims, Olivia Ritchie, Adam Smith, Jen Strada, Julie Doebler, Sara Berko, Alissa Nigro, Caitlin Sweeny, Mitch Thorpe, Michelle Leo, Nadia Almahdi, Nicole Russo, Ian Reilly, Jenn Rothkin, and the entire sales team. I also have to thank Karin Paprocki for designing the absolutely amazing cover and Jason Chan for creating a piece of art that actually had my jaw dropping when I first saw it.

I also would be lost in this complicated publishing business if it weren't for my brilliant agent, Laura Rennert (and the rest of the Andrea Brown Literary team), as well as the Taryn Fagerness Agency, who have worked so hard to bring the Keeper series to so many countries. In fact, I've now reached a point where I'm running out of space to thank all of my incredible foreign publishers and translators—so if you're a part of any of those teams, please know how much I appreciate you! And to my assistant, Katie Laird: You are officially my hero for keeping me organized during these mom-brain times! Also: I *have* to give a quick shout-out to Liesa Abrams Mignogna for all her advice over the years—and for taking a chance on this series in the first place.

On a personal front, I have to thank Ashley and Amanda for keeping my son alive, happy, and as clean as he's capable of being every time I had to duck away to do this Working-Mom Thing. (And I'm sorry he poops so much!) And thank you, Betsy (aka Grandma) and Melinda (aka Nana), for filling in when the deadline got tighter and work hours crashed into personal time. And thank you, Paul (Grandpa) and John (Pa), for always coaxing out a few more baby giggles whenever you stop by. Thank you, Brett and Chris, for helping us put our house back together with the least amount of construction chaos. And thank you, Deb, Amy, Kasie, Jared, Kelly, Eddie, Elyse, Ronnie, Roshani, Abby, Natalie, Faith, Brandi, Eric, Mike, and Katie, for checking on me, sending hilarious texts, or helping me sneak away for nonwork things (occasionally!).

And to the two guys in my life—my Papa Bear and Baby Bear—I could go on and on and *on* about the joy and adventure and wonder you bring to every single moment. But I've had to be away from you both so much as I've fought through this deadline that I'm going to stick with a simple "I love you." You two truly are the best surprises that life has ever given me. And now: Mama Bear is coming home from hotel purgatory for ALL THE SNUGGLES.

Finally, since I am one hundred percent positive that my tired brain has forgotten all kinds of super-important people, here is a space for you to fill in your name(s):

————————————————————.

Thank you, whoever you are! This totally counts as including you, right? ☺

Hello, wonderful Keeper readers! Some of you might already know that I love to sneak a little something extra into the paperback versions of my books whenever I can (since I don't think hardcover readers should get to be the only ones who sometimes find fun bonuses). For those who didn't know that: surprise! ☺

I knew I wanted to include a story from Marella's POV this time. Not only is she on the cover (looking fierce and fabulous!) and a fan-favorite character, but she also had some key scenes in *Stellarlune* that we only got to "hear" about. The Keeper books are limited to Sophie's POV, so I can only include moments where Sophie is present—and since Sophie didn't go with Marella to her meetings with Fintan, we only learn what Marella tells Sophie later. But what if there was something Marella didn't share?

Over the next few pages, you can watch one of Marella's conversations with Fintan play out in real time and hear all Marella's thoughts and reactions to what's happening. I've called this story "The Trade"—and I've worked in lots of fun little extra details (some of which might even turn out to be important later . . . *wink*).

For those wondering, this story is based a scene in chapter 31 of *Stellarlune*—and if you haven't read *Stellarlune* yet: **SPOILER ALERT! SPOILER ALERT!** Reading this first will probably be confusing and will also give away a few tidbits too early. You'll be much happier if you start by reading *Stellarlune* and then come back here for all the Marella fun once you're done.

Happy reading!

THE TRADE
Marella

"UGH, I HATE THIS PLACE," MARELLA muttered, shaking the freshly fallen snow-flakes out of her gilded blond hair much harder than necessary and yanking her thick velvet cape tighter around her narrow shoulders.

She said the same thing every time she had to trudge through the knee-high snowdrifts and found herself staring at the icicle-crusted entrance to the now familiar cave.

Didn't matter how many times she'd gone there—or how important her visits were.

She was never *not* going to dread making the long, slippery trek down to Fintan's frozen cell.

The cave looked like some sort of open-mouthed snow beast waiting to devour everything in its path—which was probably intentional, since the prison was designed to be as miserable as possible.

Especially for someone like *her*.

The goblin guards even gave her pitying stares as they moved aside to reveal the endless icy path that wound down and down—and down a whole lot more—to a place where the tiniest glimmer of heat had long since been swallowed up by the suffocating cold.

No amount of clothing could keep Marella warm in the heart of the prison. She'd actually tried wearing so many layers that she'd looked like an overstuffed gulon—and she *still* couldn't stop shivering. And the whole "body temperature regulation" thing wasn't exactly possible when she had to use so much concentration to make sense of Fintan's ranting.

It wasn't fair.

Everyone else got to train their special abilities in fancy rooms at Foxfire, with Mentors who weren't creepy, unstable murderers.

But *they* weren't Pyrokinetics.

Marella was lucky the Council was letting her use her ability at all.

They could just as easily label her Talentless, kick her out of their snobby academy, and ban her from ever sparking another flame.

Or they could decide she was too dangerous and lock her away.

In fact, Marella wouldn't have been surprised at all if the Council was already building an icy cage just for her—but the thought still made her shiver and wish she could've manifested as . . .

Nope.

She stopped herself from finishing that sentence.

If life had taught her anything, it was that there's no point wanting things that were never going to happen.

Instead, she focused on the thin beams of sunlight streaking through a gap in the gloomy gray clouds. The light was far from warm, but if she really concentrated, she could feel a hint of lingering heat tangled among the brightness.

She called the warmth closer and soaked it in—let it pool under her skin, pounding with her pulse, swelling with every heartbeat. Growing hotter and hotter and hotter until . . .

Snap!

A flick of her fingers sent a small tangle of flames sparking to life above her left palm.

"Feel better?" Linh asked as Marella let out a long, slow sigh.

Marella nodded—though she definitely could've done without the whispers that were now hissing around her head.

The flames had a soft, crackly voice. And they always made the same plea.

Feed me.

Feed me.

Feed me.

Fire craved fuel—constantly wanting *more, more, more*—and it would've been *so* easy for Marella to let the fire swell bigger and bigger and bigger.

But that was the kind of thing that would lead to a lifetime of shivering in an underground ice cube, so she forced her gaze to shift to Linh, who stood in a small, snowless circle surrounded by a halo of hovering snowflakes—none daring to touch her long silver-tipped hair or shimmery purple cape.

Marella knew how hard Linh had fought to achieve that level of control—and how tentative Linh's hold over her ability still was. But the fact that Linh could stand in a sea of frozen water and do nothing except keep the falling snow from settling on her flushed pink cheeks was very . . .

Annoying.

Then again, everyone annoyed Marella a little.

Her dad used to call her "fiery" long before he realized how accurate that description truly was.

But it wasn't Marella's fault!

People tended to be annoying.

Especially a Hydrokinetic who was currently looking all peaceful and pretty and *perfect* while making snowflakes flutter and spin in intricate patterns.

That didn't mean Marella wasn't *also* grateful that Linh was willing to tag along to her Pyrokinetic lessons. It was nice to see a friendly face after hours of Fintan's rambling. Plus, it seemed like a good idea to have someone with water powers around while she practiced setting things on fire.

They were even finding some pretty cool ways to work together. Fire and water might be opposites—but that didn't mean they couldn't be combined. Marella had actually figured out a way to ignite Linh's rain, and she couldn't wait to use that little trick on the Neverseen—assuming those black-cloaked losers ever showed up again.

For a fearsome, unstoppable rebellion, they sure spent a lot of time hiding.

"Are you going to start by asking him about the cache or do the lesson first?" Linh asked, reminding Marella why they were there.

Marella shrugged. "Depends on Fintan's mood."

Sometimes he was already babbling about some fancy new fire trick when she arrived, as if he'd started the lesson without bothering to wait for her. Other times she couldn't get any-where with him until she'd let him go on and on and *on* about how foolish the Council was, or how badly he'd been wronged, or how much he missed the feel of a flickering flame—and she didn't necessarily blame him for the last one.

Part of her wanted to hold on to her fireball forever.

Make it her smoky little pet.

Instead, she curled her fingers into a fist and snuffed it out—but she didn't let all the heat dissipate. She called a single tingling glint deeper, letting it sear through her veins and settle into her heart.

She knew it was a risky move—even with all the defenses she wrapped around it. But she couldn't bear the cold empti-ness of Fintan's prison without at least a tiny fleck of warmth tucked away.

A secret spark whispering, *I'm here. You're not alone.*

"Okay," she said, weaving a few strands of her hair together to calm her twitchy fingers. She'd picked up the nervous habit years ago—after her mom's accident—and the tiny braids were kind of her trademark now. "I guess I should stop stalling and head down to deal with Sir Creepysparks, huh?"

Linh smiled. "Probably. Unless you want to rehearse what you're going to say."

"Nah. I'm just going to offer him an ugly flower—that doesn't exactly need a big speech. Oh, but that reminds me . . ."

She reached into her cape pocket and pulled out the spiky dark blue Noxflare—which looked more like a dying weed than a super-rare flower—and held it up to the guards. "Mr. Forkle already checked this before I brought it here, to make sure it's safe for me to offer to Fintan. But I figured you'd want to check it too."

"We do," they agreed in unison as one of the biggest, deadliest-looking guards took the Noxflare from Marella and brought it over to the other goblins.

A lot of mumbling about potential kindling and fire hazards followed.

Eventually, the guards decided to quick-freeze the Noxflare into a block of ice in case there was any heat stored inside.

"Whoa," Marella said when the scary guard returned with the flower-filled ice cube—which had turned out as big as her head. "How heavy is that thing?"

The guard studied Marella's skinny arms. "I can carry it for you if you'd like."

"That'd probably be smart." Marella was pretty sure she'd drop it, or her fingers would freeze off during the long walk—and using telekinesis would drain her mental energy. "But can you stay out of sight? I was planning to tell Fintan he can only see his weird flower thing if he gives me access to his memories, and that's kinda ruined if there's a giant goblin holding it right next to me."

Not that it made the plan any less pointless.

Fintan was *obviously* going to turn her down.

He'd already made it super clear that the only trade he was interested in was for his freedom—which was never going to happen.

Marella doubted a dying flower frozen in ice was suddenly going to make him be like, *You know what? Who needs out of this horrible prison when I can have that!*

But she was out of other ideas.

And Sophie wanted her to try the Noxflare thing, so . . .

Whatever.

Marella didn't care about Sophie's current power trip the way Stina did.

As long as *she* didn't have to be the one coming up with all the plans—or almost dying all the time—Marella was fine following orders. Especially if she got to say *I told you so* when they turned out to be a huge waste of time.

"Sure you don't want me to come with you?" Linh asked as Marella pulled thick gloves onto her hands. "Fintan likes me."

Marella wasn't sure if "like" was the right word, since Fintan didn't seem to *like* anybody. But he'd definitely been impressed with Linh.

He'd demanded to speak with "the Hydrokinetic" after Marella mentioned she practiced her pyrokinesis with Linh, so Marella had convinced the goblin guards to let Linh down into the prison. And when Fintan asked for a demonstration of Linh's ability to ensure she wouldn't "hinder his training," Linh had stirred up all the ice shards on his floor and made them rain around him like he was trapped inside a snow globe—which actually made him applaud.

Apparently, most Hydrokinetics struggled to manipulate water in its solid form, and were limited to liquid water or water vapor.

But not Linh.

Of course.

Marella was pretty sure that Linh was more powerful than any of her other friends.

"Well, if you need me, you know where to find me," Linh said as Marella forced her feet to carry her into the cave. "I'll just be here, making another snow menagerie." She flicked her wrist and wove the hovering snowflakes into a soaring alenon.

"Ugh, at least make some ugly creatures this time," Marella called over her shoulder. "I want to see a row of snow ghouls when I get back here. Or a giant Princess Purryfins!"

Linh gasped. "Princess Purryfins is *not* ugly! I'm going to tell her you said that!"

Marella laughed. "I'm sure you will."

She would've teased Linh more about her ridiculous obsession with her pet murcat, but the frigid air from the prison hit Marella hard, and she had to lock her jaw to keep her teeth from chattering.

At least she didn't have to make the journey by herself this time.

Marella could hear the scary goblin guard keeping pace several steps behind her as her eyes slowly adjusted to the dim blue light cast by a series of glowing spheres dangling from the ceiling. The downward slope grew steeper with each winding curve, and Marella was always tempted to try sliding down the icy floor instead of walking—but she'd probably end up crashing into one of the weird ice thrones outside Fintan's cell. And she knew better than anyone that injuries couldn't always be healed.

Plus, the trudge gave her a chance to add extra defenses to the heat she'd tucked away in her chest.

She often wondered if Fintan had hidden a few sparks of his own when he was arrested. After all, he had to know the Council would put him on ice for the rest of eternity. Wouldn't he try to preserve what little heat he could?

But Marella had stretched out her senses a zillion different ways and never felt the slightest tingle of warmth when she was around him. So either there was nothing to find or Fintan was *that* good.

She had a horrible feeling it was the latter, and he was waiting for *just* the right moment to reveal his grand plan—but that wasn't the kind of thing she should be thinking about before having to face him.

Still, she spent the next few turns trying to figure out what she'd do if she were right.

Her feet turned numb while she plotted, and her bones were officially aching by the time the path widened—the only warning that they were getting close to Fintan's cell.

A few curves later, his cage came into view: a stark, icy bubble in the center of a circular cavern.

The round wall was reflective on the inside, so even though Marella could see Fintan pacing along the edge of his frozen barricade, he wouldn't be able to see her until she triggered the sensor by sitting in one of the freezing thrones positioned at the only point Fintan could peer through.

He looked extra tired that day—his sky blue eyes sunken by more shadows than usual—and he kept muttering under his breath about incompetence as he tucked his messy blond hair behind his pointy ears with a bit more force than necessary.

Marella glanced back at the scary guard, making sure he'd ducked into the shadows near the back of the cell before she made her big appearance. Then she took a deep breath and pressed her hand against her heart, reaching for her secret spark of warmth one last time before plopping into the closest ice throne.

"Awwwww, looks like you missed me," she said, tossing back her hair and flashing her brightest smile.

She liked to start her visits by showing Fintan she wasn't afraid of him—even if she totally was.

But Fintan didn't glance her way.

"I'm not in the mood for games," he warned as he continued his slow march around his cell.

"Neither am I," Marella assured him, deciding that was her cue to start with the cache. She sat up taller, trying to look extra confident as she added, "But I do have an awesome trade to offer you!"

Fintan sighed. "If this is about my cache, I already told you what I'm willing to accept. Unless you're here to grant me a day of freedom—"

"I'm definitely not. *But!* I found something you should like even better." She paused, hoping the extra bit of anticipation would somehow make her offer sound more exciting when she told him. "Noxflares!"

Fintan scrunched his slender nose. "What are Noxflares, and why would I care about them?"

Marella tilted her head, trying to tell if he was faking.

She hadn't expected him to jump around or applaud or anything—but she *had* expected him to at least know what Noxflares were.

Then again, his mind had been shattered and pieced back together so many times, his memories had to be in shambles—and Ancient minds tended to be a total mess anyway, since they were crammed with thousands of years of information and the past and present blurred together.

"Would it help if I told you I stopped by your old estate on my way here?" she asked. "Your garden could use some gnomish help, by the way. All the plants have turned into a giant dying tangle. But I dug around and managed to find this scraggly vine with dark pointy flowers—and I *hear* that plant is special to you, so I picked a few and—"

"*You picked my Noxflares?*" Fintan snapped, rushing to the wall of his cell and pressing his palms against the ice. "*You must let me see them!*"

Marella's lips curled into a huge smirk. "I thought you didn't know what they were."

Fintan gritted his teeth so hard, it sounded like cracking ice.

"Hey, I'm not saying I won't share. *Buuuuuuuuuuut* it'll cost you—and I'm pretty sure you can already guess what I want." She paused for another beat before she added, "Just so we're clear: I'll show you one of your Noxflares *if* you open your cache and show me what's inside."

Fintan's jaw tightened even more, and his hands curled into fists.

But he didn't say no.

He didn't say anything—which was definitely new.

Marella had already offered him a long list of trade suggestions that she, Linh, Maruca, and Stina had all come up with— some really cool ones! And Fintan had shot each one down before she could even finish the offer.

She couldn't believe he looked so tempted by an ugly flower.

But as the silence dragged on, Marella started to wonder if she'd misread the situation.

Maybe she'd pushed him too hard—taunted him too much—and now Fintan was letting her sit there in the cold, knowing the icy throne was turning her butt and legs numb.

She was trying to decide if she could make standing up look like a power move when Fintan told her, "Fine. You have a deal—but since you're only offering *one* Noxflare, I'll only show you *one* memory."

Marella barely stopped herself from blurting out, *SERIOUSLY?*

"Orrrrrrrrrrrrrr," she said instead, wanting to kick herself for not bringing more Noxflares with her. The whole thing had just seemed so silly—and the first few she'd picked had crumbled to dust. But the vine had lots more flowers, so she could fix the mistake super easily. "How about I go back, grab eight more Noxflares, and then you show me all nine memories?"

Fintan grinned. "Tempting. But one Noxflare is really all I need."

Need?

Marella wasn't a fan of that wording.

But before she could ask him what he needed it for, he added, "My offer expires in ten seconds," and started counting down.

By "six," she decided that one memory was better than nothing.

"Fine," she said, pulling the cache from her pocket and holding the marble-size orb up to the light. "But you go first. How do I open this thing?"

No way was she going to risk letting him back out—especially since he probably wasn't going to be happy when he saw his precious flower was stuck in the middle of a giant ice cube.

Fintan held out his hand. "Give me the cache, and *I'll* open it."

Marella laughed. "Hard pass."

"Ah, but you don't have a choice. I'm the only one who can access the memories. And I need to make physical contact with the cache in order to do so."

Marella squinted at the tiny gadget.

She didn't know much about caches—aside from the fact that only Councillors used them and that each colorful inner crystal held a single Forgotten Secret. But she *did* know that Dex had already tried everything he could think of to open the cache and failed—and he was one of the best Technopaths ever.

"Do I need to start counting down again?" Fintan asked. "I believe we'd gotten to *five*. . . ."

Marella chewed her lip. "Uh, how do I know you're not going to destroy the cache or try to hold it for ransom or something?"

Fintan's smile was colder than his cell. "You'll just have to trust me."

"Yeah, I don't see that happening."

Fintan shrugged. "Then our deal is off."

Marella rolled her eyes. "Come on. Even if I wanted to, it's not like I can open your cell door and hand the cache to you."

She wasn't even sure if his cell *had* a door. The wall looked like one big solid piece of ice.

"You've proven to be very resourceful during our lessons," Fintan reminded her.

"Yeah, but—"

"It's your call," he interrupted. "If you want a memory, you'll have to trust me."

She snort-laughed—but before she could get another word out, he repeated, "You'll just have to trust me." And she could tell that was the only response he was going to give.

She turned to the scary guard, who had started pacing in the shadows. "Is there a way to pass Fintan a small item?"

"Ah, you have a hidden goblin escort—I knew you were resourceful!" Fintan clapped his hands. "And yes, there *is* a way to pass me my cache, otherwise I wouldn't have suggested it. Any guard can open the disgraceful tube they pass my horrid, frozen bits of food through. The cache should fit nicely."

The guard gripped his sword. "I cannot allow any unauthorized item to enter his cell."

Fintan clicked his tongue. "Clearly you're not considering the fact that I've already had plenty of chances to make this trade—and turned them all down. Do you think I would do that if the cache was even remotely useful to me?"

The goblin couldn't argue with that logic.

Neither could Marella.

And when Fintan went back to counting down, she told the guard, "The Black Swan knows I've been trying to make this trade—and they're working with the Council now. No one would let me do this if they thought the cache was dangerous."

Then again, they'd never discussed the possibility of handing the cache over to Fintan—but surely *someone* must've considered that during all their endless talking and obsessive overplanning . . . right?

Besides, if anything went wrong, she could always remind them that this was Sophie's idea.

"I don't like this," the scary guard growled. But Marella gave him her *I-totally-know-what-I'm-doing* glare until he set the frozen Noxflare down with a particularly dramatic *thud*, snatched the cache, and spent an eternity squinting at the tiny crystal, spinning it all different ways. "If anything happens, my priority will be subduing the prisoner—*not* protecting you. Are you certain you want to take that risk?"

Marella absolutely wasn't.

But . . . this might be their only shot at seeing one of Fintan's Forgotten Secrets.

Plus, she had her tiny little spark buddy she could call on if she needed. Surely she could use that to . . .

To *what*?

Take down a superpowerful, much more experienced Pyrokinetic with a history of murdering people?

But . . . did she really want to wimp out?

Sophie wouldn't.

And yeah, Sophie had, like, a permanent bed in the Healing Center. But Marella was pretty sure their whole group would vote "DO IT!"

There were also a dozen other armed goblins who would rush down as backup.

And Linh could attack Fintan with her cutesy snow animals.

It'd almost be worth it to watch Fintan get swallowed up by an ice wave shaped like Princess Purryfins.

"I can handle myself," she decided, using a tone that hopefully sounded intimidating.

Fintan's gleeful laughter echoed off the ice.

The scary guard muttered something about the arrogance of elves as he reached toward the top of Fintan's frozen cell and felt around for a specific spot. A faint clicking sound followed, and a tiny round door slid open—far out of Fintan's reach.

"I can neutralize you within seconds," the guard reminded him as he held the cache up to the opening. "By *numerous* means. Some far more painful than others."

"Yes, I'm well aware of the absurd lengths the Council has taken to keep me contained," Fintan assured him. "But I don't plan on giving you a reason to use any of them. Not today, at least."

The guard bared his supersharp pointy teeth, and Marella wanted to shout, *NEVER MIND, JUST KIDDING!* But she let the guard shove the cache through the tiny opening—and then it was too late to change her mind.

All she could do was watch the glass orb make its slow descent, rolling around and around and around—down some sort of invisible path etched into the wall of the cell.

Her stomach backflipped with each rotation, and she felt more than a little vomit-y when the cache dropped low enough for Fintan to catch it. But he simply held it up and studied it.

Then he coughed on it.

And sneezed on it.

"Ewwwwwww," Marella groaned when he followed that up by drooling on it. "You know, there are better ways to give it your DNA."

"Yes, I'm aware." Fintan cleared his throat and launched a slimy blob of spit at the cache. "I *also* know your little Technopath friend is going to ask you how I accessed the memories, so feel free to give him a detailed list." He wiped the cache dry with his fingers and then ran it through his greasy hair before sneezing and coughing on it again. "Some of these methods are vital. Some are distractions. None can be re-created without me—but it'll be fun if he tries, don't you think?"

He laughed so hard, it brought tears to his eyes, and he smeared them across the cache before sneezing and spitting on it again—making Marella *very* glad she had gloves to keep her hands clean once he returned the cache.

Assuming she actually got it back . . .

She tried to make out what he was saying when he started mumbling a bunch of stuff into the crystal, but the words were all mushed together. He also tapped the cache in so many different places that she doubted even Sophie and Keefe with their fancy photographic memories would be able to re-create the patterns. And he looked so smug as he did it all that Marella decided to look as bored as possible—which was why she was barely paying attention when the cache flared to life, projecting a small hologram of Fintan standing alone in a wide, empty field.

"Huh," Marella mumbled. "Gotta admit, I was expecting

something a little more exciting than a tiny glowing Fintan in the middle of nowhere doing . . . nothing."

"Then you should learn to be more observant." Fintan pointed to the swaying grass around the hologram's feet, and after a few seconds, Marella realized there was a vine of blooming Noxflares. "I figured I'd show you what Noxflares can do, since you're so generously bringing one back into my life."

Marella squinted at the tiny flowers, waiting for something to happen.

And waiting.

And waiting.

"So . . . they . . . blow in the wind?" she asked.

Fintan sighed. "No, they do *this*."

The hologram of Fintan waved his arms, and all the Noxflares erupted with searing white flames.

"Yeeeeeaaaaaaaaaah, still not seeing why this needed to be a super-hush-hush Forgotten Secret," Marella grumbled as the Fintan hologram flicked his wrist and added purple fire to the white.

Sure, the flames were pretty—but all flames were beautiful.

"Try thinking like a Pyrokinetic!" Fintan snapped. "Tell me, are there any other flowers that could remain intact under such an inferno?"

Marella couldn't think of any.

And the Noxflares still didn't burn when the Fintan hologram added yellow flames to the fiery mix.

But other than clearly being fire-resistant, Marella didn't see the Noxflares actually *doing* anything—and the hologram of Fintan must've been equally unimpressed.

He frowned at the flaming petals and dragged a hand down his face, mumbling "something's missing."

"Still not seeing the point of this," Marella noted. "I mean . . ."

Her voice trailed off as the tiny Fintan waved his arms again and blasted the Noxflares with pink flames—which made the flowers spray sparks in every direction.

The effect was breathtaking.

Kind of like the sky during the Celestial Festival.

But that still didn't necessarily scream, *THIS MEMORY IS IMPORTANT.*

"How come the grass isn't catching fire?" she asked, grasping for anything that might be significant. "Do the Noxflares protect it or something?"

"No, *I* was protecting it. A Pyrokinetic should always be in control of their flames."

He sounded so smug, Marella was tempted to remind him that *he* let five Pyrokinetics die when he tried to teach them how to call down Everblaze and they all lost control—but that would probably make him throw one of his tantrums and send her away.

She needed the cache back first—and to hopefully find something useful in this boring memory. But sadly, all Fintan's hologram did was stare blankly at the stars and mumble "something's missing" again before the image flashed away.

"That's *it*?" the scary guard demanded, beating Marella to the complaint.

"Yeah, so . . . you put on a little fire show all by yourself with some spark-shooting flowers," she added, trying to sum up what she'd seen. "You were clearly disappointed by that little show. And then you must've remembered you needed to . . ."

She waved her hands, cuing Fintan to fill in the blank with whatever was "missing."

But he just stood there, staring at the cache with the same glazed look he always got whenever he started rambling about the beauty of fire—and Marella wished Linh had come with her after all.

Linh could pelt him with snowballs or something to snap him out of it.

But then she realized . . .

"You never figured out what was missing—did you?"

Fintan blinked and met her gaze. "Noxflares are full of possibility. But they need to burn."

"That doesn't answer my question," Marella noted.

Fintan shrugged. "Context was not part of our bargain."

"Yeah, because I figured when I saw the memory, it would be obvious why it's this big *Forgotten Secret*. How does you setting some flowers on fire and then realizing you did it wrong matter to anyone?"

"I did *nothing* wrong," Fintan assured her, with a particularly haughty smile—but Marella wasn't buying it.

There was a tightness around his eyes that was way too familiar.

Her dad had that same tightness every time her mom was

having one of her "bad days," and she knew exactly what it meant.

Disappointment.

Frustration.

A hint of helplessness.

So she marched over to the guard and grabbed the frozen Noxflare from the floor—too irritated to even notice how heavy the ice must've been as she hauled it back.

She plopped it in front of Fintan's cell. "Ta-da! One ugly flower, as promised—and I'm sure you're not surprised that I had to freeze it before I brought it down here."

"I'm not." Fintan dropped to his knees and gazed at the Noxflare like he was seeing a long-lost friend.

He pressed his hand against his cell, trying to get as close as he could. "Such power. Such . . . promise."

"Uh-huh," Marella agreed, letting him stare and stare, hoping it would help him let his guard down.

When his eyes turned a little teary, she went in for the kill.

"But there *is* something still missing, isn't there? *That's* why you saved this memory—to remind yourself to keep looking."

A whole lot of painful silence passed before Fintan slowly nodded.

Marella wanted to feel triumphant.

But all she'd done was prove the entire trade had been pointless.

There was no game-changing clue.

No dirty little secret about the past.

Certainly nothing to help them stop their enemies.

And she had a pretty strong hunch the other eight memories in the cache would be just as ridiculous.

"The answer *is* out there," Fintan murmured. "I can feel it. I just can't grasp it. Perhaps . . ."

"Perhaps?" Marella prompted when his eyes locked with hers.

Fintan stepped closer to the ice, keeping his voice low, like he didn't want the guard to hear him. "Perhaps a different Pyrokinetic is meant to find the truth. One who's already convinced the Council to trust her."

Marella laughed. "The Council doesn't trust me."

"The fact that you're here for a pyrokinesis lesson says otherwise—particularly since the lesson is with *me*." He started circling his cell again, mumbling under his breath and nodding. The only words Marella caught were "possible," "improvising," and "best option."

After three more times around the cell, he stopped in front of Marella again, leaning even closer to the icy wall as he whispered, "I believe it's time for me to offer a trade of my own."

"A trade," Marella repeated, not missing the way the scary guard gripped his sword.

Fintan glared at him. "This conversation is between *me* and my *prodigy*. She stands here of her own free will, shielded by who knows how many different kinds of protections—and she can leave anytime she pleases. Your presence is no longer needed."

"You still have her gadget," the guard argued.

"I suppose I do. But that can easily be remedied." Fintan set the cache on whatever invisible ledge it had slid down in the first place and gave it a good shove, sending it spinning up the path toward the top of the cell.

The guard had to scramble to catch it when it launched out of the ice bubble.

"See?" Fintan said, shifting his gaze back to Marella. "I *can* be trusted."

"Pretty sure the only thing I can trust is that you'll do what's best for *you*," Marella countered.

"As long as *you* get what *you* want, why would you care? After all, no matter what, I'm still stuck in here, aren't I?" He waved his arms around his little ice bubble, which suddenly looked way less secure than it had during her other visits. "Oh, relax—all I'm asking for is a little information."

Marella crossed her arms. "Right—and *information* has never gotten anyone hurt or killed."

"It's not that kind of secret. It's . . ." He frowned. "Honestly, I don't know what it is—and for someone my age, with my connections, that says something, doesn't it? I doubt any of the Vackers even know the full truth."

"Then how am I supposed to find it?" Marella demanded.

"As I said, you've proven to be quite resourceful. Particularly when you team up with your little friends." He scowled at the guard again before motioning for her to step closer—until her ear was practically pressed up against the ice.

A voice in the back of her head kept screaming, *WHY ARE YOU LISTENING TO HIM?*

But . . . she was curious.

And there was nothing wrong with *hearing* his offer, was there?

Fintan's breath fogged the ice, obscuring his face as he whispered, "All I ask is that if you ever find out what's missing from the Noxflares, you share it with me."

"Why?" Marella glanced at the frozen flower, wishing she could see something more than just ugly shriveled petals.

"Because I want to know," Fintan said simply. "And because I can give you what you want in return."

"The rest of the memories in your cache," Marella clarified.

Fintan nodded. Then his lips curled into a smile. "And one other—something you've long wondered about, even though you probably don't admit it to yourself."

Marella raised one eyebrow, refusing to show any more interest than that.

Fintan cupped his hands around his mouth and pressed them to the ice before he whispered, "I know what happened to your mother."

Marella sucked in a breath.

"Yes," Fintan added. "I'm talking about her 'accident'—if we can really call it that. I know why she fell. And why her injuries were so incurable."

Marella stumbled back, collapsing into the nearest throne and hugging herself to stop her body from shaking with tremors that had nothing to do with the cold.

A tiny, terrified part of her had always thought the story she'd been told about her mom's fall hadn't totally made sense.

But everyone—*everyone*—was convinced it had been an accident.

Even her father.

And if it wasn't . . .

She leaned toward Fintan. "I don't need your games."

"Oh, this definitely isn't a game. But it's the only way you'll ever know the truth, and before you start overthinking everything, consider this: You have all the power here. Make the trade, don't make the trade—it's totally your call. You also don't have to make a decision right away. I'm trapped in this prison. I'll never find the answer on my own—and I'll never know if *you* find the answer unless you decide to tell me. So there's zero pressure. No one even knows we've had this conversation—and don't worry about the guard. See how frustrated he looks? That's because I made sure he only heard what I wanted him to hear. The rest is our little secret."

Our little secret.

Fintan was probably the last person she should have a secret with.

And yet . . . he had a point.

No one knew he'd made her this offer—and it wasn't like she'd come to any decision.

She didn't even have the information Fintan wanted anyway!

And with the way their investigations always seemed to go, she'd probably only find a whole lot more questions.

So there was really no point telling anyone about this.

She could tell them when she needed to.

If she needed to.

That wouldn't be wrong . . . would it?

It didn't *feel* wrong—or it wouldn't have if Fintan's smile wasn't so creepy.

"I'm not agreeing to anything," she said, wanting to make that *very* clear.

"You're *not*," Fintan assured her. "So how about we put this out of our minds and get started with our lesson? I'm sure your Hydrokinetic friend is wondering why you haven't come up to practice yet."

Linh probably was starting to worry.

She'd probably also built enough snow animals to make a frozen Sanctuary.

"Fine," Marella said, standing up and dusting ice off her cape. "What do you want me to work on today?"

"How about I teach you how to make those colored flames you saw in the memory," Fintan suggested. "You know, in case that ever comes in handy."

He winked, and the guard groaned and held out the cache to Marella. "Sounds like I'm no longer needed."

"You aren't," Fintan agreed.

The guard growled—looking scarier than ever—and turned to march away. But he spun back after a few steps. "He's right that I don't know what he offered you. But I can tell you're tempted. And I hope you're smart enough to reject it. Never make a deal with someone who has nothing to lose."

"I'm not," Marella promised.

And she wasn't.

She hadn't made *any* decisions—except to keep this to herself. But that didn't mean anything.

She was just trying to avoid a ton of drama and arguing and having people give her advice she didn't need.

Plus, everyone has secrets.

Shoot—the great Sophie Foster had more secrets than anyone.

So it was fine.

Everything was fine.

Nothing had changed.

Time to focus on controlling her fire.

And yet, for the rest of the lesson, the tiny spark in her heart burned hotter and hotter and hotter. Whispering a new plea.

Trust me.

Trust me.

Trust me.